Chapter One

The smoked glass door of the Tulsa Fertility Center swooshed closed behind Jake Chastaine, sealing out the rumble of late afternoon traffic on Peoria Avenue. Jake squinted, despite the fluorescent lighting. After the glare of the mid-May sun, the reception area seemed unnaturally dark.

But not nearly as dark as the emotions churning in Jake's belly. He was unprepared for how hard it hit him, the old, familiar pain. Two years had passed, yet here he was, his gut aching as if it all had just happened yesterday, the hurt as raw as freshly ground hamburger.

It was being in this place again, this place on which he and Rachel had pinned their highest hopes. A rush of old memories crowded in and piled on top of each other, threatening to scale the wall of numbness Jake had built to hold them at bay.

He drew a steadying breath and stepped deeper into the waiting room, his eyes adjusting to the light. Funny how silent and colorless the clinic was, considering all the bright, noisy dreams he and Rachel had invested here—dreams of a warm, squalling bundle in a pink or blue blanket, of bright balloons and boisterous birthday parties, of flannel-clad feet scurrying to see what Santa had left under the tree on Christmas morning.

A baby. A family. A long and happy life together. Hard to believe he'd ever been naive enough to think that happily-ever-after endings were possible.

Well, he knew better now. Dreams were nothing but diving boards for disappointment. The higher you climbed, the deeper you plunged. He used to think life had meaning, but now he knew it was just a cosmic crapshoot. There was no meaning, no reason for anything. If there was a God—and Jake wasn't betting on it—He was either a disinterested observer or a celestial tyrant who got his jollies from setting people up just to watch them fall.

What else could account for the senseless car wreck that had cost him his wife and his parents just as it looked as if everyone's dream of a child was about to come true?

Jake's gaze scanned the room. Two years had passed, but everything was just the same—the spotless beige carpet, the pristine white walls, the gray-and-beige chairs standing in military precision across the room. Even the faint, pungent scent of pine cleaner and antiseptic was the same. Rachel had always been impressed with the center's cleanliness, but it struck Jake now as a cruel mockery.

The clinic was sterile. Just like the patients who came here.

Jake resolutely strode toward the reception counter at the front of the room, where a pudgy young woman slouched behind an open sliding glass window. The blotchy pattern on her black-and-white dress reminded

8

RAVE REVIEWS FOR ROBIN WELLS, WINNER OF THE NATIONAL READERS' CHOICE AWARD AND THE GOLDEN HEART AWARD!

"Robin Wells is an author to watch. We will be hearing much more of her. [Her writing] . . . is hilariously funny, tender and sensuous."

—*Rendezvous*

"Robin Wells's . . . touches of humor and passionate fireworks will steal readers' hearts away."

—*Romantic Times*

"Ms. Wells dishes up a rousing good romance with liberally sprinkled flashes of love and laughter."

—*Romantic Times*

PRINCE CHARMING

"Ms. Wells's talent shines on every page of this terrific story. . . . An enchanting read filled with humor, passion and a cast of desirable characters, *Prince Charming* had me laughing out loud with delight. A must read for connoisseurs of laughter and romance."

—*Rendezvous*

"*Prince Charming* is a funny, sexy, and charming Pygmalion tale. Highly enjoyable reading!"

—*Romantic Times*

"*Prince Charming* is an enjoyable and humorous contemporary romance that readers will fully enjoy. . . . Ms. Wells will charm readers with this offbeat novel."

—*Affaire de Coeur*

TALL, DARK AND DADDY

"So," he asked. "What made you want *me?*"

Annie shrugged. "You had a good family health history. And your educational level and profession indicated that you were somewhat intelligent." He grinned, and she continued. ". . . And your physical description fit what I wanted."

He glanced over at her. "And what, exactly, was that?"

Annie looked down at her hands. "Someone tall, with dark hair and eyes."

"Why was that part of your criteria?"

Annie continued to stare at her manicure, her cheeks heating a little. She lifted one shoulder. "I don't know. I guess I just find it attractive."

"You wanted a dark-haired child?"

"Oh, that wasn't really the issue," she admitted.

He glanced at her curiously. "So what was?"

Annie lifted her shoulders and glanced away. "Fantasy, I suppose."

"Fantasy?"

She nodded, and he pressed further. "You mean the sexual kind?"

She blushed fiercely. "You're getting into a pretty personal topic here."

"The fact that we've had a child together is already pretty personal, if you ask me."

The man was right. The thought that they'd made a child, and without him ever having kissed her . . . it was enough to make Annie break into a sweat. There was something intensely primal about him anyway, despite his outward polish. Why did he have to be so good looking? It was impossible to look at him and not think about sex.

Other *Love Spell* books by Robin Wells:
PRINCE CHARMING

Robin Wells

Baby, Oh Baby!

LOVE SPELL ⬧ NEW YORK CITY

To Ken—Baby, oh Baby!
This one's for you.

A LOVE SPELL BOOK®

February 2001

Published by

Dorchester Publishing Co., Inc.
276 Fifth Avenue
New York, NY 10001

ISBN 0-505-52427-9

The name "Love Spell" and its logo are trademarks of Dorchester Publishing Co., Inc.

Printed in the United States of America.

Jake of a dairy cow. So did the flat expression in her large brown eyes when she reluctantly pulled them away from the tabloid magazine spread in front of her.

The woman's demeanor changed the moment she set eyes on Jake. Straightening in her chair, she thrust out her chest and flashed a flirtatious grin.

Jake shot her a tight, I'm-strictly-here-on-business smile. Females had been fawning over him ever since his junior year in high school, when he'd shot to six-foot-two, developed a cleft in his chin and lettered in football, baseball and basketball. He was used to receiving undue attention from the fairer sex, but he was still somewhat baffled by it.

Rachel used to say it was because he had the face of a movie star and the body of a professional athlete. "You're to women like catnip is to cats," she used to say. Instead of being threatened by his appeal, though, Rachel had encouraged him to use it to his advantage. "Pack the jury box with women and flash them that killer smile," she'd told him. "You'll win every case."

When he'd gone into practice with Rachel's father, he'd done just that. Once again, Rachel had proven right. Rachel was almost always right. Nothing in Jake's life had felt right since she'd been gone, and nothing was likely to ever be right again.

The receptionist tossed her stringy brown hair as if it were Cindy Crawford's mane. "May I help you?"

Jake shifted his stance uneasily. "I phoned earlier. Whoever I talked to said I needed to come in and sign some papers."

"What kind of papers?"

Jake shoved a hand into the pocket of his navy trousers and angled a glance over his shoulder at the patients in the waiting room. A worried-looking woman in her early forties sat at the back of the room. A thirty-

9

something couple huddled together near the front. A young man in jeans slumped in a chair against the wall, four seats away from a freckled, heavyset blonde with a magazine on her lap. All of them abruptly looked away as Jake caught them staring.

Damn. He hated stating his personal business in a roomful of strangers—especially a room as quiet as this one, where every sound was amplified by the sheer force of everyone's boredom. Rachel had always managed things so that he'd never had to engage in a public conversation here.

Efficient, well-organized, far-thinking Rachel. Good God, how he missed her! She was the only woman he'd ever known who was as rational and logical as he was. They'd been peas in a pod, a perfect match. The pain in Jake's chest pulsed harder, deep and unrelenting, like a scarred-over shotgun wound with the buckshot still inside.

"My, uh, wife . . ." To his dismay, his voice cracked on the last word. Damn it all. Two years had passed, but he still couldn't talk about her without his throat clenching up. He gritted his teeth, cleared his throat, and tried again. "My wife and I were patients of Dr. Borden."

The receptionist's face fell when he said "wife." Her eyes turned doleful and cowlike again. "I'm sorry, but Dr. Borden is no longer with us."

"No longer. . . . You mean he died?"

"Oh, my. I hope not." The receptionist chortled, revealing large, flat teeth that reinforced her bovine appearance. "He retired and moved to Florida."

It was a sad commentary on his state of mind that he'd immediately assumed the man was dead, Jake thought grimly. Well, it was no wonder. His whole world seemed to have died around him. His wife. His parents. Even the fish in his office aquarium. Sometimes it seemed as if he'd died, too, and the news was just late in getting to him.

The receptionist smacked a gray wad of gum. "Would you like to make an appointment with someone else?"

"No. I'd like to clear up a mistake." He pulled a folded white paper out of the inside pocket of his tailored suit jacket. "I got this in the mail." Jake thrust the form letter through the window. He could recite its contents from memory:

> Dear Mr. Chastaine:
> Sperm donors like yourself provide an invaluable service to infertile couples. We appreciate your past support of our center, and encourage you to come in soon to make another donation. As before, we will be happy to pay you $350. Please call our office today to schedule an appointment.

The receptionist scanned the note and glanced up. "So you're here to make a donation?"

Jesus—she made it sound like he'd stopped by the Salvation Army with a bag of old clothes. Did he look like the kind of jerk who'd jack off in a jar for money?

With a dark scowl, he opened his mouth to ask her as much, then abruptly recalled the conversation he'd had with his father-in-law and legal partner, Tom Morrison, just that morning.

The distinguished, silver-haired man had strolled into Jake's oak-paneled office, looking uncharacteristically ill-at-ease. Tom had stood behind one of the two chairs that faced Jake's desk, drumming his fingers on the cordovan leather wingback. After an unusual amount of small talk, he'd finally gotten to the point.

"Some of the staff have been complaining about you, Jake."

11

Jake had looked back down at the complicated corporate merger he'd been studying when Tom had walked in. "Sharon again, huh? Well, if she's not happy, she can shove off."

"She's the fifth secretary you've had in six months," Tom had said mildly. "But it isn't just Sharon. Dottie says the entire staff is upset."

A note of concern in Tom's voice grabbed Jake's attention. Dottie had been Tom's office manager for more than twenty years, and the older man put a lot of stock in anything she had to say. "What's the problem?"

Tom had rubbed his clean-shaven cheek as he eased himself into a chair. "Well, everyone seems to think you're a little—ah—harsh."

Jake had scowled. "What the hell is that supposed to mean?"

Tom had lifted his shoulders, his tanned face creasing into a placating smile. "Guess they want to be addressed in a kinder, gentler manner."

"Fine. I'll start calling everyone 'Sugar' and 'Honey Pie.' "

Tom had raised both hands. "Look, Jake, I have no complaints. You're doing a great job, and you're making money for the firm hand over fist. I support you one hundred percent. It's just that . . . well, some of the folks in the office have thin skins." Tom's face had been a study of discomfort. He'd leaned forward and picked up a brass paperweight from Jake's desk. It was shaped like a golf ball, and it had been a gift from Rachel. Jake watched Tom roll it between his palms. "I found Nancy in accounting in tears the other day, and two of the gals in the file room complained that you chewed them out for no reason. We've been through three law clerks in the last year, and then there's your secretary situation. . . ."

Jake's fingers had tightened on the arm of his high-backed leather chair, a pang shooting through his gut. He'd always been close to Rachel's parents, had always considered himself lucky to have drawn Tom and Susanna out of the great cosmic in-law card deck. He'd known them for most of his life. His family had moved next door to the Morrisons when Jake was thirteen, and he'd spent more time at their house during his high-school years than he'd spent at his own. In a lot of ways, they'd been more like family to him than his own parents had been. It hurt to see Tom squirming like a lawn grub under the weight of whatever news he had to break.

Jake tried to make it easier on the older man. "You want me to leave the firm, Tom?"

Tom's head had jerked up, his gray eyes startled. "Hell, no! You know better than that. I'd fire and hire a whole new staff every week before I'd let you go. We're family. Partners." Tom leaned forward and replaced the paperweight on Jake's desk. "It's just. . . ." He pulled back his hand, but his torso still tilted forward. His gaze locked with Jake's. "Look. I know you've been through a hard time. Hell—no one knows that better than me, right? But for the sake of harmony and the staff's morale, would you . . . could you . . . ? Ah, hell. Could you try to lighten up a little?"

"Sure." Jake had accompanied the word with a curt, single nod.

"Good." Tom had thumped his knuckles on the desk as he rose, his expression relieved. "I knew I could count on you." The older man had walked around the desk and clapped Jake on the shoulder before he'd headed out the door.

Jake had stared at the door as Tom closed it behind him, then slumped forward, his elbows on the desk, his head in his hands. Hell. He knew he'd turned into a real son of a bitch since Rachel's death. He knew it, but he

13

seemed powerless to stop it. Anger was his only defense against the black, empty vacuum in his soul, and the truth was, he welcomed its heat. It was the only emotion that hadn't deserted him. Besides, he liked the distance it made people keep. If he couldn't be dead, he could at least be left alone.

All the same, he'd promised Tom he'd make an effort. And as much as it chafed him, he knew Tom was right. Lately he'd been snarling at people like a wounded pit bull just because they were alive and Rachel wasn't. Instead of getting better with the passage of time, he seemed to be getting worse.

Jake blew out a harsh breath. He had to get a grip on his behavior. Genuine niceness was probably too lofty a goal to shoot for, but he could at least aim at civility. Behavior was nothing more than habit, and habits could be changed. All it took was practice. He'd vowed to himself then and there that he'd turn over a kinder, more courteous leaf in all of his interactions.

Jake turned his gaze back to the receptionist, who was chomping her chewing gum like a wad of cud. As much as it pained him, he knew this was the perfect occasion to practice his new persona. He forced a pleasantness he didn't feel into his voice. "Let me explain. My wife and I were infertility patients, and—"

"Oh," she interrupted. "So you want to make an appointment to see another doctor?"

"No. I—"

"Give me your name and social security number, and I'll pull up your records."

Crimony. Couldn't Old Bossy here let him finish a freakin' sentence? Biting back his irritation, Jake gave her the information. She typed it into the computer with plodding slowness, then glanced up. "It says here you're a sperm donor."

14

"And I say I'm not."

She gazed at him blankly, as if the discrepancy was beyond her comprehension.

"It's the sort of thing I'd be likely to remember, don't you think?" Jake snapped.

The freckled blonde against the wall tittered like one of Alvin's chipmunks. Jake heaved a sigh, remembering too late that he was trying to turn over a new leaf. "I think you'd better let me talk to your supervisor."

The receptionist nodded agreeably, oblivious to his agitation. Lifting the phone, she punched in two digits. "There's someone here who wants to speak with you." A slight pause. "No, he didn't say what it was about." She lowered the receiver and looked up at Jake. "Mrs. Holden will be right out."

Jake reached through the window and snatched back his letter. "No need for her to come all the way out here. I'll just head on back." He started for the door beside the reception counter.

"But—but you can't go. . . ."

Ignoring the receptionist's protests, Jake strode through the door into a large room lined with color-coded files. Two women in floral medical-assistant jackets sat at separate computer stations. A gray-haired woman dressed in a navy blazer and tan slacks stood by one of the desks, pointing out something on the screen.

She turned to Jake as the door closed behind him. "May I help you?"

"I'm looking for Mrs. Holden."

"That's me."

Jake was relieved to note that the blue eyes behind her wire-rimmed glasses seemed alert and intelligent. He hauled a smile out of cold storage. "Is there some place we can talk privately?"

"Of course." She led him across the room into a beige

cubicle. Jake glanced around, noting the touches of color. Photos of children—grandchildren, no doubt—sat in blue and red plastic frames on her desk. A mountain landscape photo calendar was thumbtacked to the nubby-textured wall, and a yellow Happy Face sticker smiled from the back of the computer.

Mrs. Holden settled herself into the swivel chair behind the modular desk. Jake lowered himself into one of the two wooden-armed chairs opposite her.

"Now, what can I do for you, Mr. . . ."

"Chastaine. Jake Chastaine."

The woman nodded pleasantly.

Jake tossed the folded paper on her desk. "I've been receiving this letter every month for the past six months."

Mrs. Holden quickly perused it, then looked up, her eyes questioning.

"My wife . . ." *Dammit!* His voice did that weird cracking thing again. He cleared his throat and started over. "My wife and I were fertility patients here a couple of years ago. We were getting ready to do an in vitro procedure when she. . . ." Jake's short, blunt fingernails dug into his palm, giving the pain in his chest a physical outlet. ". . . My wife died in an accident."

"Oh, I'm so sorry," Mrs. Holden murmured.

The only thing worse than dealing with Rachel's death was dealing with sympathy over it. "Yeah. Well, under the circumstances, getting this notice is pretty disconcerting. Especially since I left a—a *sample* here to use in the in-vitro procedure."

Mrs. Holden smiled. "You must mean the back-up specimen."

"Yes." The doctor had explained to Jake and Rachel that while the clinic preferred to use fresh sperm, all in-vitro patients were asked to provide a back-up specimen in advance. The back-up, the physician had said with a smile, would be frozen and used in case the pressure to perform the day of the procedure made it difficult for the husband to "ante up."

Jake placed his left ankle over his right knee. "I've never been a donor, and I don't like the idea that my name has somehow ended up on your donor list. And since I'm no longer a patient here, I want to make sure that my, uh, *back-up* was disposed of. I called and spoke to someone about it, and I was told I had to sign a written permission form."

Mrs. Holden nodded. "We can take care of that easily enough. I've got a form right here." She opened a file drawer in the bottom of her desk, pulled out a pink slip of paper and handed it to Jake.

Jake read it carefully. It was a standard release form—the same kind of thing he would have insisted upon if he'd been the clinic's attorney. Pulling a gold pen from his jacket pocket, he signed his name in tight letters. "Well, that settles one issue," he said, shoving the paper across the desk.

The woman's eyebrows rose over the rim of her glasses. "There's something else we can do for you?"

"Yes. I want to know why your computer says I'm a donor instead of a patient."

The woman waved her hand. "Oh, I'm sure someone just pulled up the wrong list when we did our monthly mailing."

"The receptionist looked me up and said I'm listed as a donor."

Mrs. Holden's eyebrows shot back up. "Really? Well, let me check." Referring to the letter he'd handed her, she typed in his information. A frown formed, twisting her brows as she gazed at the screen. She hit some other keys, then studied the screen again. The twin furrows between her eyebrows deepened.

17

Jake leaned forward. "Is something the matter?"

"No, no, I'm sure everything's fine." She tapped more keys, then gnawed her lower lip. She didn't sound like everything was fine. She sure as hell didn't look it, either. "What's wrong?"

"Nothing." She clicked back to the screen saver, then abruptly rose from her chair. "Excuse me for a moment. I need to go check on something."

All of Jake's instincts immediately went on red alert. In his old job as an assistant district attorney of Tulsa County, he'd read people's expressions on a daily basis. He knew when someone was scared or worried or hiding something, and Mrs. Holden appeared to be doing all three.

Jake waited until she'd left the cubicle, then circled the desk, seated himself in front of the computer and typed in his name. He hit the ENTER button, then watched the screen flicker. There was his name, all right, wedged between "Chambers" and "Cousins" in a vertical list. The blue header at the top of the page read "Sperm Donors." He reached for the mouse, highlighted his name, and clicked. The screen changed. Suddenly he was reading about himself on a page entitled "Sperm Donor Profile."

Name: Jacob James Chastaine. Sperm Donor Number: 13013.

How appropriate, he thought dryly. Just his luck to have a number with two thirteens in it. He read further: *Age: 33. Race: Caucasian. Height: 6'2". Weight: 197. Hair: Dark brown. Eyes: Brown.*

A detailed family health history followed—his great-grandfather's heart attack, his grandmother's bout with cancer. He recognized the information as the facts he'd provided when he and Rachel had filled out forms the first time they'd visited the clinic. Everything seemed to be in order—everything, that was, except a line at the very bottom.

Status: One insemination.

Icy needles prickled up Jake's spine. Rachel had never been inseminated.

Dear God. Had someone else?

His joints moved like rusty machinery as he highlighted the "status" line and clicked the computer mouse. The screen flickered and changed, this time to the profile of someone named Annie Rose Hollister. *Age: 31. Race: Caucasian. Height: 5'6". Weight:112. Eyes: Blue. Hair: Red. Address: 1118 Rural Route 3, Lucky, Oklahoma.*

He skimmed through a bunch of statistics about blood pressure and menstrual history. His gaze shot to the lower half of the screen.

Insemination date: 6-2-98.

His stomach clenched like a knot in a wet rope. Nearly two years ago—shortly after the accident. He rapidly read further.

Sperm Donor Number: 13013.

He scanned the last line on the screen, and the words he read there jumped out and socked him in the gut.

Status: Pregnant.

The air seemed to freeze in his lungs. His hand shook as he pointed the cursor at the "print" icon and clicked the mouse. The printer whirred to life and spat out a page. He'd just retrieved it and stuffed it into his jacket pocket when Mrs. Holden returned, flanked by a tall, thin man in a white jacket.

They stopped in the cubicle entrance, obviously disconcerted to see him seated behind the computer. "Wh— what are you doing?" Mrs. Holden asked, her eyes wide, her skin pale.

Never let them know how much you know. Jake had gotten the advice about interrogating suspects from a

19

mentor at the D.A.'s office years ago, but he'd found it a good rule to follow in life in general. He instinctively hit the escape key on the computer, sending the screen back to an innocuous menu, then rose from the chair. "Just looking at my records."

The white-jacketed man rubbed his long jaw, his forehead creased with a frown. Mrs. Holden's eyes grew as round as blue moons behind her wire-rimmed glasses.

Jake decided to press for answers while they were still off-guard. "Just what the hell is going on here?"

The man pasted on a conciliatory smile as he stepped forward. "Hello, Mr. Chastaine. I'm Dr. Hendrick Warner." All of the doctor's features were long and sharp and pointed, and his smile made his nose curve like the beak of a hawk. Well, Jake would be damned if he'd act like a timid little rabbit. He'd start practicing his new Mr. Nice Guy routine later.

Folding his arms across his chest, Jake deliberately ignored the man's extended hand. "I asked a question, and I'd like an answer. What's going on?"

The doctor withdrew his outstretched hand and awkwardly shoved it into the pocket of his white lab coat. "There, uh, seems to be a small problem with the records."

Small problem? You call knocking up some broad with my sperm a small problem? Jake's jaw ached with the effort of biting back the retort.

"It's simply a data input error," the doctor said soothingly. "We recently changed computer programs, and a few small glitches are bound to occur."

Years in the D.A.'s office had taught Jake to smell something fishy. This guy's spiel reeked like week-old cat food.

"I see. Well, if that's all there is to it, hand over my jar of jizz and I'll be on my way."

Mrs. Holden gasped.

"I'll handle this," the doctor told her. The woman turned and scurried from the cubicle like a rat fleeing a sinking ship.

The doctor folded his arms across his chest and smiled in an amused, between-you-and-me kind of way. Jake was sure it was the sort of smile that usually inspired confidence in nervous patients, but right now it inspired nothing but further suspicion.

"I'm afraid we have a no-return policy on deposits, Mr. Chastaine." The doctor chuckled. "I'm sure you can understand that. If you signed the form, however, you can be certain we'll dispose of your specimen."

Yeah, except you've already disposed of it—in Ms. Annie Hollister of Lucky, Oklahoma. A nerve flexed in Jake's jaw. "I want to take it with me. Now."

The doctor gave another tight smile. "I'm afraid we can't do that. There are all sorts of laws governing the disposal of medical waste."

Jake's chin rose stubbornly. "Well, then, take me to the freezer where you keep the vials or test tubes or whatever, and show me mine."

"I'm afraid that's impossible. It would violate our temperature-control procedures."

Jake's fingers curled at his sides. "It would violate your ass-covering procedures, is what it would violate. It's not here, is it?"

"Of—of course it's here." The doctor's Adam's apple jerked as he swallowed. His eyes were lying. "I'll tell you what. Since this is an unusual situation and you're so concerned, I'm willing to bend the rules just this one time." His lips twitched up in a nervous smile. "After all, we're planning to dispose of your specimen anyway. Just wait here, and I'll go and get your vial."

21

Jake stepped sideways, blocking the door. "I'll come with you."

The doctor's eyebrows rose. "I thought I'd explained. We have a strict temperature-control policy."

"And I have a strict no-bullshit policy."

Dr. Warner's chin inched up. "You're upset, Mr. Chastaine. Why don't you come back tomorrow after you've had a chance to calm down?"

"You mean after you've had a chance to change labels and computer records and get your story straight, don't you?"

The tip of the doctor's long nose grew red. A flash of anxiety shadowed his eyes, just before he drew himself up to his full stature and assumed an air of dismissive authority. "I don't have time to stand here and argue with you, Mr. Chastaine. I have patients waiting. If you care to come back tomorrow, I'll be happy to answer all your questions."

"I don't want your answers. I want the truth." Jake pulled a cell phone out of his pocket and flipped it open. "Maybe the D.A.'s office will have better luck at getting it out of you than I'm having."

The doctor froze. The redness on his nose spread across his face, ruddying the hollows under his cheekbones. "Who—who are you calling?"

Jake jabbed at the phone buttons. "A friend at the D.A.'s office. He'll probably send a squad car to take you in for questioning while he gets a search warrant. That way you won't have a chance to tamper with any evidence." Jake put the phone to his ear.

The doctor stared at him, the veins in his neck standing out like blue cords. He finally hissed out a long, defeated sigh. "Wait. Let's—let's go in my office and talk."

Jake stared at him stubbornly. "Whatever you've got to say can be said right here."

Dr. Warner reluctantly nodded. The threat of a ride in a police car had punctured his arrogant attitude like a nail in a balloon. "All right."

Jake folded the phone, but kept it in his hand. The doctor lowered himself into one of the two chairs in front of Mrs. Holden's desk. Jake warily sat down beside him and watched him run a hand from his receding hairline to his long chin. "Well?" Jake demanded.

Dr. Warner heaved a sigh. "I assume you're aware that Dr. Borden is no longer here."

"The receptionist said he retired."

Dr. Warner nodded. "It wasn't a voluntary retirement. We discovered that he'd made some, er, serious errors in judgment."

"What kind of errors?"

Dr. Warner folded, then unfolded his bony fingers in his lap. "He, um, 'borrowed' sperm from a fertility treatment patient when the sperm bank donor pool was low. From what we could ascertain, he evidently couldn't find a match that met the requirements of an insemination patient. The husband of one of his infertility patients met the requirements exactly, so he used the man's semen."

"Without telling either patient?"

Dr. Warner nodded. "When it came to light last year, Dr. Borden surrendered his medical license and retired to Florida. The insemination patient failed to become pregnant, so we thought there was no harm done." The doctor looked at Jake, his eyes worried. "We thought it was best to keep the whole thing quiet. If it got out, it could ruin the entire clinic. Until now, we thought it had only happened in the one case."

"So you're telling me. . . ." Jake stared at the doctor. The man's story had the ugly ring of truth. "You're saying Dr. Borden inseminated a woman I've never met with my sperm?"

Dr. Warner's thin lips pressed together so tightly they seemed to disappear. His long fingers formed a prayerful steeple in his lap. "That's what the records seem to indicate."

That's what they indicated, all right, but it still hit like a Mack truck, hearing it confirmed aloud. His upper lip beaded with sweat. "The records also indicate that the woman became pregnant."

Dr. Warner reluctantly nodded.

"So I have a child out there somewhere?"

"Well, now, we don't know that a live birth resulted." Dr. Warner squirmed uneasily. "There are no follow-up records."

"But I *might* have a child," Jake persisted.

Dr. Warner fiddled with the bottom of his blue-and-gray tie, deliberately avoiding Jake's gaze. "Look—I suggest that you just go home and forget about this. If you pursue this matter, you'll disrupt a lot of people's lives."

Jake stared at the man incredulously. "You want me to just go home and forget that I have a *child?*"

"Well, now, it's not really yours." The doctor tapped his fingertips together. "I mean, it's not your responsibility. It was a mistake—a mistake made by one bad apple of a doctor, a doctor who's no longer practicing medicine." His eyes were pleading. "Look—you're borrowing trouble. For yourself, for the insemination patient, for her family. And then there's the clinic to think about. This place helps hundreds of infertile couples every year. If word of this gets out, it'll ruin the place."

"To hell with the clinic. You just told me I might have a *child!*"

"Please, Mr. Chastaine—could you keep your voice

24

down?" The doctor leaned forward, his knuckles pale against the wooden arms of the chair. His throat jerked as he swallowed. "Look—dozens of things could have gone wrong during the pregnancy. Why, twenty percent of all pregnancies end in miscarriage in the first six weeks alone." Dr. Warner folded, then unfolded his hands. His voice took on a beseeching tone. "You know, Mr. Chastaine, sometimes a person's better off without all the facts. There's a good chance a live birth never occurred. Why don't you just leave it at that? Everyone will be better off if you just leave well enough alone."

"You sorry son of a bitch," Jake muttered. He rose to his feet, and without another word, strode out of the cubicle, through the file room, across the waiting room, and out the smoked glass entrance.

A wave of dry heat snaked up from the asphalt parking lot as he stalked toward his white Volvo. An even hotter blast of air assaulted him as he yanked open the door, climbed in, and punched the metal button on the glove box. Sweat rolled down his brow as he snatched out a state map of Oklahoma and unfolded it on the passenger seat beside him.

The car felt like a black leather sauna, but it wasn't nearly as hot as the questions that burned inside him. Jake leaned over the map, determined to answer the one question that would lead to all the other answers.

Where the hell was Lucky, Oklahoma?

Chapter Two

Annie Hollister carefully worked the wide-toothed metal comb through the dense white fur on the alpaca's flank. The animal turned and nudged the front pocket of Annie's jeans, pressing her against the split-rail fence of the corral.

Annie grinned and scratched the animal's velvety ears. "I'm almost done, Snowball. Hold still for one more moment, then you'll get that sugar cube you're after."

A warm blast of moist air tickled the back of Annie's neck. Startled, she turned to find another alpaca, this one larger and smoke-colored, straining his long neck over the fence to nibble the end of her shoulder-length auburn hair. Laughing, Annie gently extracted the strand from the beast's mouth.

"Whoa, there, Smoky Joe. My hair is *not* on the menu!" As if in response, the animal nudged the comb in her hand. Annie shot him a reproachful look. "I know you like getting groomed, but you've got to wait your turn. Hold your horses and I'll comb you next."

"Don't know as I've got enough hair left to comb," sounded a deep, familiar drawl from the other side of the fence.

Annie looked up to see the burly form of her ranch foreman, Ben Akins, come around the barn, rubbing his sparse gray hair. Her mouth curved in a smile. "I was talking to Smoky Joe, not you."

"Ohhh." Ben's mischievous grin belied his innocent tone. "Well, as much as those critters seem to like gettin' groomed, maybe I oughta give it a try."

"Maybe you should. But it's not just grooming, you know. It's fur harvesting."

Ben's smile widened to reveal a gap between his two front teeth. He shifted his worn brown Stetson to his other hand and ran weathered fingers over his balding pate. "In that case, I reckon I'm a couple of decades too late."

Annie laughed. Ben had been the foreman of her grandparents' ranch for as long as she could remember, and she'd always loved his good-natured teasing. The big-bellied cowboy and his petite wife, Helen, were two of her favorite people in the whole world. When they'd agreed to stay on and help run the Smiling H after Annie inherited it two years ago, they'd made it possible for Annie to follow her fondest dream.

She'd always longed to live on the sprawling ranch. She'd visited the spread in northeastern Oklahoma every summer during her childhood, and it was her idea of paradise. She loved working with animals, loved the outdoors, loved the concept of setting her own hours and being her own boss, but she'd never learned anything about the actual business of cattle ranching.

The business she'd learned inside and out was adver-

27

tising, and she'd grown sick to death of it. She was tired of trying to please impossible clients, tired of coddling temperamental photographers and prima donna models, tired of living in an impersonal crowd of strangers. Most of all, she was tired of using all her waking hours to help some huge, faceless conglomerate sell more kitty litter and underarm deodorant.

She'd wanted to live in a place where she could see the open sky and smell the scent of rain on the wind an hour before it arrived. She'd wanted a job that filled her heart as well as her Day-Timer and her bank account. She'd wanted to do something meaningful, something with lasting merit, something she would look back on with pride and affection when she was old and gray.

She'd wanted, with all her heart and soul, to have a baby.

Unfortunately, no candidates for fatherhood had loomed on the horizon. Her short-lived attempt at marriage had ended nine years earlier. At thirty-one, her biological clock was ticking like a time bomb, but her job as an account executive with a New York ad agency required too many hours and too much travel to make single motherhood a viable option.

Then her grandparents had died and left her the ranch, and Annie had decided to change her entire life.

Snowball again nosed at Annie's jeans. Annie pulled the comb through the white alpaca's coat one last time, then dug into the front pocket of her faded Levis. "Okay, girl. Here's your treat." The beast eagerly lapped up the sugar cube, tickling the flat of Annie's palm with soft, wet lips.

Ben shook his head. "Those critters are gonna be as spoiled as that old hound dog your grandpa used to keep."

"No, they won't. I don't let them sleep on my bed."

"Not yet. The way you're pamperin' them, though, it's just a matter of time."

Annie smiled and glanced at her watch. "Speaking of time, aren't you and Helen supposed to be on your way to Tulsa?"

Ben placed a booted foot on the bottom rung of the fence rail. "Yep. I came by to tell you we're 'bout to head out. Helen's supposed to be at the hospital for a pre-surgery checkup at four. Elaine's gonna to meet us there." Elaine was Helen and Ben's grown daughter, who lived in Tulsa with her husband and school-aged children. Ben's potbelly heaved as he sighed. "I'll sure be glad when we get this knee replacement thing behind us."

"Helen will be, too. We talked about it when I dropped by your place this morning to pick up Hot Dog." Annie had agreed to take care of Ben and Helen's friendly miniature dachshund while the couple was gone. "Helen said she can't wait to throw away her cane. She's looking forward to racing you to the fishing hole again."

"I better start trainin', then, so she won't put me to shame." Ben smiled, but it failed to chase the worry from his eyes. He turned his worn hat in his hand. "I sure hate her havin' to go through the surgery and physical therapy an' all, though. If there was any way I could do it for her, I would."

"I know you would," Annie said softly, her heart flooding with emotion. "Helen knows it, too."

Helen was Ben's whole world, and he was just as dear to Helen. The couple had the kind of marriage Annie had always wanted for herself—close, supportive, tender and warm.

As a girl, Annie used to wish her parents' marriage had been more like Ben and Helen's. Annie's mom and dad had been too busy climbing corporate ropes and social ladders to pay much attention to each other or to her. When they did spend time together, they invariably ended up criticizing and belittling each other.

Annie had always been glad to escape her parents' bickering for the peacefulness of her grandparents' ranch. The Smiling H was her idea of heaven on earth. As a child, she'd spent her days fishing and swimming in the tree-lined pond with Ben and Helen's children, trailing after Grandpa and Ben as they tended the white-faced cattle, and shucking fresh corn for dinner on the front porch with Gran. She loved waking up to the sound of birds twittering in the tree outside the bedroom window, loved the smell of hay and clover, loved the cool, deep shade of the pine forest that edged the acres of pastureland.

Most of all, she loved the sense of peace and harmony the ranch always offered. No one here cursed or yelled or muttered hateful words under their breath. Grownups looked at each other with kind, warm eyes, and they looked at her the same way. Here on the ranch, everyone worked long and hard, but they still found time to laugh. Most importantly, they all found time for a sad-eyed little girl who'd always felt that her parents' unhappiness was somehow her fault.

Ben shifted his hat again. "Sure you can manage things here alone?"

"I'll be fine," Annie replied. "Besides, I'm not alone. I've got Madeline."

"A fourteen-month-old baby is not exactly a big help." Ben's weathered face creased into a wry grin. "Where is the little rascal, anyway?"

"Napping." The thought of Madeline made her smile. Annie had never known she could love anyone or anything as fiercely as she loved her child. She glanced toward the sprawling rock-and-cedar ranch house, her eyes reflexively stopping at the window of the baby's bedroom. Madeline had fallen asleep on the thick rug in the center of her room after Annie had curled up with her on it to read story books and sing lullabies.

Annie patted the blue-and-white baby monitor clipped to her belt. "I'm listening to her every move."

"Well, I'll be callin' to check up on you two."

"Don't worry about us. You just take good care of Helen."

Ben nodded. "You do the same for that baby. An' for yourself, for a change. Don't stay holed up out here all alone for the whole three weeks we're gone."

Annie never felt as alone on the ranch as she used to feel in the crowds of New York, but Ben was constantly pestering her to get out and socialize. "I won't. I'll have to go into town for groceries, and I promised Pearl I'd bring Madeline for a visit next week."

Pearl was an old friend of Annie's grandmother. The garrulous elderly woman lived at a nursing home in Lucky, and Annie made a point of visiting her every week. "As a matter of fact," Annie continued, "Pearl's grandson is coming out for a tea leaf reading this afternoon."

Ben rolled his eyes. "You're as bad as your grandma."

"I hope I'm as good. She taught me all I know about doing readings."

"Yeah, well, I never put much stock in that hocus-pocus stuff."

"I didn't used to, either. I let Gran give me lessons just to humor her." Annie could still remember the first time her grandmother had mentioned it. It had been the summer she'd turned sixteen. She'd walked into the kitchen late one afternoon and found Gran doing a reading for Pearl.

31

"Oh, I'm sorry. I didn't mean to interrupt," Annie had said, backing out the screen door.

Gran had motioned her back in. "Come sit down. It's high-time I taught you to read leaves."

"Oh, Gran," Annie had protested. "I don't even know that I believe in it."

"That's all right," Gran had said. "It believes in you." Gran had fixed her with an intent gaze across the blue-checked tablecloth on the kitchen table. "You've got the gift, girl."

"How do you know?" Annie had flashed her grandmother a teasing smile. "Did you read the bottom of my iced tea glass at lunch?"

"No. I just know." Conviction had shone in Gran's gray eyes. "Some things, a body just knows. The leaves are for the things you don't."

Ben's voice broke into Annie's memories. "I take it you started believin' somewhere along the line."

Annie nodded. "When the leaves helped me make a big decision." She carefully pulled alpaca fleece from the teeth of her comb, then stuffed the wad of hair into a burlap bag hanging on the fence post. "I was worried about quitting my job and moving back here, even though I knew in my heart it was what I wanted to do, so I decided to go to a leaf reader in New York. I made an appointment with a woman I'd never met before—I'd gotten her name off a bulletin board at a coffee shop. I didn't tell her anything about myself or my circumstances. And you know what she told me?" Annie would never forget it as long as she lived. If she closed her eyes, she could still see the big-boned woman leaning over the dainty, stained teacup, still smell the scent of cooked cabbage clinging to the peeling floral wallpaper in the woman's apartment, still hear the next-door neighbors arguing through the paper-thin walls. And when she remembered the woman's words, goose bumps still crawled up her arm.

Ben shook his head. "What?"

"She said I belonged on a ranch. And she said I would soon have a child."

Ben's eyes rested on her, his gaze fond and warm. "Well, I'm awful glad you made the decisions you made, regardless of how you made 'em."

A lump formed in Annie's throat. Ben and Helen were just like family, but she hadn't consulted them about her decision to become a single mother. Like most of the people in this part of rural Oklahoma, they were very conservative, and she hadn't been sure they'd approve. They'd never discussed the decision, but the couple had been incredibly supportive throughout her pregnancy. They treated Madeline like one of their own grandchildren, and the baby adored them in return.

"The only decision of yours I've ever wondered 'bout has to do with raisin' these here critters." Ben cast a doleful eye at Smoky Joe, who was sniffing Ben's Stetson.

Annie grinned as she led Snowball to the gate. "Diversification is the key to the future."

"Yeah, well, maybe. But I don't see why you didn't just diversify into another breed of cattle."

Annie removed the halter from the white alpaca's nose, opened the gate and watched Snowball prance out. "Now, Ben, you know that beef prices are down. Alpaca fleece sells for fourteen dollars an ounce, and the manure goes for a dollar a pound."

"Hmph. Not much of a market for the stuff, from what I can see."

"I don't need much of a market with just five alpacas. And by the time the herd's bigger, why, the demand for alpaca products will be, too." She shot Ben a mischievious grin. "Besides, that tea leaf reader told me that unusual business ventures would pay off."

Ben rolled his eyes. "There you go with that hocus-pocus stuff again."

"Wait and see. I think the alpacas will turn out to be a good investment."

Ben pulled his boot off the fence rail as Smoky Joe scampered into the corral. "I sure hope you're right." He glanced down at his black rubber watch. "Speakin' of waitin', that's what Helen's doin'. I better get goin' before she leaves without me."

His tone was light, but Annie saw the worry in his eyes. She placed her hand on the big man's arm. "Everything's going to be fine, Ben. Helen's got one of the best surgeons in the country."

The big man nodded, his eyes on the ground.

"Besides, I did a reading for her, and everything looks wonderful. You know what Gran used to say. 'The leaves never lie.' "

"Hmph. Well, this is one time I darn sure hope they don't."

"Look on the bright side," Annie urged. "When this is over, Helen will be able to get around without any pain. She'll be able to work in her garden and go on long walks. Why, she's even talking about dragging you off to square-dancing lessons."

"I hope to high heavens you're right." His mouth slanted into a crooked smile. " 'Bout ever'thing except them square-dance lessons, that is."

Annie laughed. "You don't fool me. If Helen wanted you to take up ballet, you'd be strapping on toe shoes and practicing pliés."

"Prob'bly so." His smile made his cheeks look like stuffed saddlebags. "But I'd draw the line at wearin' a tutu."

The thought of the potbellied cowboy in pink tulle made Annie laugh again. She leaned forward and hugged his neck. Ben awkwardly patted her back.

"Call me tomorrow and let me know how everything went," Annie said softly.

"I will."

Annie watched him amble away, her prayers going with him. As he disappeared around the barn, Smoky Joe grabbed another mouthful of her hair.

"What are you doing, boy? Trying to give me dread-locks?" Tugging the strand away from the alpaca, Annie reached into her back pocket and pulled out the Tweety Bird ponytail holder she'd removed from Madeline's hair when she'd put the child down for her nap. Gathering her curls on top of her head, Annie fashioned a high, loose ponytail and secured it with the cartoon-ornamented elastic band.

"All right, fella." She stroked Smoky Joe's muzzle, then picked up the comb. "It's your turn now."

Half an hour later, Annie had finished grooming Smoky Joe. She'd kicked off her shoes and was washing up in the kitchen sink when she heard the crunch of tires in the circle drive in front of the ranch house.

"That must be Pearl's grandson," she said to the little dachshund at her feet. Hot Dog's long, skinny tail thud-ded on the hardwood floor. "We'd better get the door before he rings the bell and wakes up Madeline." Drying her hands on a blue dish towel, Annie scurried across the room, flipped on the stove burner under the old cop-per teapot, then hurried to the front hallway. The dachs-hund pattered along at her heels.

Annie opened the door, then froze in surprise. Good heavens—*this* was Pearl's grandson? Nothing about the tall, handsome man on her porch looked like it had come

35

from Pearl's gene pool. That woman was tiny and round, with curly white hair, an upturned nose and slightly crossed blue eyes. Annie had always thought the elderly lady looked like a Pomeranian with a perm.

This man was more like a Russian wolfhound—tall, lean and muscular, with a face of intriguing planes and angles. He must take after his father's side of the family, Annie mused. His nose was straight, his hair was dark, and his mouth. . . .

Annie gazed at it in fascination. His mouth was the most sensuous sight she'd ever seen. It was like Elvis's, only better. His lips were like Brad Pitt's and Tom Cruise's and Tom Hanks's, all rolled into one soft, hard, kissable package.

She suddenly realized she was staring. Stepping back, she opened the door wider. "Come on in," she whispered. "I've been expecting you."

The man's dark eyebrows flew up in surprise.

Annie assumed he was startled that she was whispering. "We need to keep our voices down so we don't wake the baby," she explained softly.

The man's Adam's apple bobbed as he swallowed. He gazed at her warily, gave a slow nod, and stepped into the foyer.

The temperature of the room seemed to shoot up twenty or thirty degrees. Annie moved back. She usually wasn't susceptible to good-looking men—in fact, she normally viewed them with suspicion. In her experience, they tended to be spoiled and self-centered. Something about this man, though, cut through all of her normal defenses.

She realized she was once again staring. She hurried to fill the awkward silence. "You, uh, don't look anything like your grandmother."

He looked as if she'd said something odd. "I don't?"

"Not at all." He didn't look like the type of man who'd want his fortune read, either. He was expensively dressed in a dark suit and designer tie, and there was a confident air of authority he wore as well.

Well, Annie thought, it just went to prove you couldn't tell a book by its cover. Pearl had said her grandson was facing some big decisions. In times of trouble, all kinds of people turned to the unexplained. From the tense set of his jaw and the cautious look in his eye, this man was definitely under some stress.

Maybe he was nervous about having his fortune told. Annie stuck out her hand and smiled. "I'm Annie. Pearl didn't tell me your name."

There it was again—that odd hesitation, that strange look. "She didn't?"

"No."

"Oh. Well, I'm Jake." His fingers folded around hers in a strong, tight grip. His hand felt good, like a warm mitten on a cold day. The warmth shot up her arm, through her neck, and across her cheeks.

"Nice to meet you." She looked into his eyes, and another hot current passed through her. His eyes were a clear, light brown, his eyebrows dark and well-shaped. Something about them looked hauntingly familiar. "Have we met before?"

The oddly familiar eyebrows pulled together. "I don't think so."

Annie didn't, either. He wasn't the type of man she'd be likely to forget. "Maybe we met years ago. Did you ever visit your grandmother during the summer?"

His eyes narrowed warily, as if it were a trick question. "Sometimes."

"Maybe we met when we were both kids."

The poor man looked uneasy and bewildered. Remembering her role as hostess, Annie smiled again and gestured down the foyer. "Come on in. I put on the tea when I heard your car, so it should be ready in few minutes."

Annie led Jake into the antique-filled living room, trying to remember exactly what Pearl had told her about him. The elderly woman had a dozen grandchildren and her mind meandered as she talked, so Annie had never been able to keep any of them straight. All she knew for certain was that this grandson was visiting from out of town.

Annie plucked a stuffed purple dinosaur off the blue-and-white ticking-striped sofa, then gestured for him to sit down.

Jake's gaze settled on the toy in her hand. "How old is your child?"

"Fourteen months."

A strange look crossed his face. "A boy or a girl?"

"A girl."

"A girl," the man muttered softly. "A daughter."

He seemed to be talking more to himself than to her. Annie watched him curiously, a curl of attraction uncoiling in her belly. There was an intensity about him that seemed somehow sexual—a sense of suppressed energy and strong emotion. Her gaze locked on his mouth. She would bet he was one terrific kisser.

Annie abruptly shifted the toy dinosaur to her other hand, hoping to shift her thoughts as well. She couldn't remember the last time she'd been so physically drawn to a man.

He turned those familiar-looking brown eyes on her, and she quickly gestured to the sofa. "Please—have a seat," she managed to say.

"After you."

Not just good-looking and sexy, but well-mannered as well. Had Pearl said whether or not he was married?

Annie didn't think she'd said anything about her grandson except that he was facing some big decisions.

Annie perched on one end of the sofa and the man seated himself beside her. Annie self-consciously ran a hand down her orange Oklahoma State University T-shirt, only to discover it felt strangely fuzzy. She glanced down and saw it was covered with alpaca hair.

Jake followed her gaze. She abruptly realized they were both staring at her breasts.

Oh, dear heavens—why hadn't she put on a bra this morning? Her nipples were pointing straight at him like a pair of orange highway cones.

Jake cleared his throat. "You, uh, have cats?"

Annie pulled her shirt away from her breasts and brushed at the loose hairs, her face flaming with heat. "No. I was grooming my alpacas."

"Alpacas." The man's brow knit together. "Is that a breed of dog?"

"No. They're like llamas."

"Llamas," Jake repeated. He looked at her as if he doubted her sanity. "How many do you have?"

"Just five, right now. But I'm hoping to grow the herd."

"I saw cattle as I drove in. You raise them together?"

"Oh, yes. Alpacas are very sociable animals. Very gentle, too."

"And . . . you groom them?"

Annie nodded. "They love to be brushed and combed. They even like to be bathed."

At her words, Jake was tempted to ask if her animals also liked to wear Tweety Bird hair ornaments like the one bobbing around on top of her head. This woman was certainly strange.

And well built.

He realized his gaze had again drifted to her chest. Annoyed at the direction of his thoughts, he forced his eyes away. He was here to learn all he could about her and the child, not to gawk at her breasts.

"So you raise alpacas," he said. "I guess that explains the unusual sign at the entrance to your ranch."

"The one that says, 'Pick a Peck of 'Paca Poop?' "

Jake cleared his throat. "Um, yes. That would be the one."

Annie smiled serenely, as if they were talking about something as commonplace as a serve-yourself salad bar.

Jake decided to explore the topic a little further. "So . . . that's something people come here to do?"

Annie nodded. "Alpaca manure is very rich in nutrients. It's an excellent fertilizer. I sell it to gardeners."

A shrill whistle sounded from the other room. Annie bounded to her feet and set the stuffed dinosaur on an old trunk that served as a coffee table. "There's the tea. I'll be right back." She hurried from the room, the tiny dachshund trailing after her.

Drawing a deep breath, Jake leaned forward and picked up the dinosaur. He rotated it in his hands, his thoughts turning back to the reason for his visit.

A daughter. Unless he was terribly mistaken, he had a daughter.

He did some quick calculations in his head. The age of this woman's child jibed with the insemination date on her medical records. If that was right, it meant the child had been conceived about a month after Rachel's death.

Emotion, hard-hitting and ill-defined, erupted in his chest. How could he have made a child with this woman—a woman about as far removed from Rachel as

40

anyone he could imagine—while the dirt was still fresh on Rachel's grave?

He rose from the sofa, unable to sit still, and strode across the room, past an old curio cabinet filled with what looked like old pharmacy supplies. He glanced at it, but was too agitated to study its contents. Thrusting his hands in his pockets, he drew a deep breath.

It was unfair, damn it—completely, totally unfair! It was beyond unfair. It was a travesty of justice.

He turned as he reached a wood-shuttered window and paced in the other direction. What right did this woman have to bear the child he and Rachel had tried to conceive for seven years? How had this loony-tune woman—this barefooted, Tweety-Bird-haired, alpaca-fleece-covered, poop-scooping woman—ended up the mother of his child?

A hot sense of self-reproach shot through him. Christ. And to think he'd been sitting there, staring at her breasts!

"Well, hell," he muttered, shoving a hand through his hair as he moved to the fireplace, trying to shake off a prickly cloak of guilt. It was impossible *not* to stare, what with all that white fur clinging to her orange shirt, and her shirt clinging to her naked breasts. For that matter, it was hard not stare at any part of her. Everywhere he looked, something about her jumped out and begged to be ogled.

She was the most vivid human being he'd ever met. How could he *not* stare at her, what with that flaming auburn hair piled up on her head with that ridiculous Tweety Bird doo-dad, and those eyes that looked like little pieces of sky, and that mouth that looked like she'd just eaten fresh strawberries? And her clothes!

Well, it wasn't so much *what* she was wearing as it was the *way* she was wearing it. Her Levis were faded at the fly and rump in a way that struck him as inappropriately suggestive, and the way she filled out that fuzz-covered orange T-shirt was nothing short of erotic.

She was obviously unfit to be a mother. Unfit, at least, to be the mother of *his* child. A tide of outrage, bitter and angry, swept through him.

No one but Rachel should be the mother of his child!

His hands clenched, and he realized he was strangling the stuffed dinosaur. He stormed over to the trunk and set it down, then stalked back across the room, his thoughts spinning and gaining fury.

He'd take the child away from her. By God, he would! If it really *was* his baby, he'd figure out a way to get full custody and raise it himself. He was an attorney. He could find a way to do it.

The decision helped him focus his thoughts. *Calm.* He needed to remain calm. Calm, cool, and collected. He needed to apply the same levelheaded, rational, low-key, understated approach he used in the courtroom. People always incriminated themselves if you let them talk long enough. He would need information in order to prove her an unfit parent, and it would be easier to extract it if she didn't feel under any pressure.

He deliberately went into legal counsel mode, willing his mind to scan through the facts with computerlike precision. This woman—this Annie—had evidently mistaken him for someone else. Apparently she was expecting a man she'd never met before—the grandson of someone named Pearl—to come for tea. He wondered what the purpose of the little tea party was. Knowing his luck, he'd probably stumbled into a blind date arranged by some poor slob's meddlesome grandmother.

Well, whatever the situation was, he'd find out soon enough. In the meantime, he'd play along and learn all he could. Information was ammunition, and he intended to gather as much as he could.

Chapter Three

"Here you go."

Jake spun around, startled to find Annie standing behind him, holding out a steaming teacup. He'd been so absorbed in his thoughts that he hadn't heard her return from the kitchen.

"Thank you." Forcing his features out of a scowl and into what he hoped was a neutral expression, he accepted the cup and followed her back to the sofa. He waited until she'd settled back onto it, then sank down beside her and gazed into the white china cup. The distinctive scent of tea wafted up from the blackish-brown brew.

He looked up, noting that her hands were empty. "Aren't you going to have some?"

"Oh, no. I never drink the stuff."

Then why the devil is she forcing it on me? He shifted the cup to his other hand. "To tell you the truth, I don't much care for tea, either. I'm a coffee fan, myself."

"Sorry to hear it, because you've got to drink every drop."

Was she teasing? Her expression was serious, her tone matter-of-fact. Jake gazed at her uncertainly.

"You can let it cool, then gulp it down all at once," she suggested. "It's not so bad that way."

Jake stared at her. She seemed completely serious. Before he could form a response, she cocked her head and smiled, drawing her bare feet under her shapely bottom.

"So what kind of information are you hoping to find out?"

"What?"

"Pearl said you're facing some major decisions."

Thank God. For a moment there, he'd had the disturbing feeling that she'd read his mind. But then, everything about this woman was disturbing on one level or another.

Control, that was the key. He needed to gain control of the conversation. If he didn't, she was sure to discover he wasn't Pearl's grandson.

He set the cup on an old oak side table, then turned toward her and gave his best jury-swaying smile. "I'd much rather talk about you first. How did you end up living way out here?"

"I inherited the ranch when my grandparents died two years ago."

"They left it to you instead of your parents?"

Annie nodded. "My father died of a heart attack eleven years ago. He was an only child, and so am I, so it was willed to me."

Now he was getting somewhere. Information about her family background could prove useful. "What about your mother?"

"She remarried four years ago and moved to Europe.

Now she's living the life to which she always aspired."
Annie gave a wry grin. "She's an Italian countess complete with a villa and a tiara." Her voice held a trace of amusement, but no bitterness. She cocked her head. "I'm surprised your grandmother didn't tell you all about it. My grandmother was her best friend."

Uh-oh. Jake glanced away. "I, uh, think she mentioned it. I guess I just didn't connect the information with you."

He was relieved when Annie grinned. "That's understandable. Pearl's conversations take a lot of detours, don't they?"

"They sure do." Jake ran a finger under his collar, grateful to have slipped out of that one. "So you run the ranch yourself now?"

Annie nodded. "With the help of a foreman and seasonal ranch hands."

There was no mention of a husband. He'd already glanced at her hand and noticed she wasn't wearing a wedding band. The omission reinforced his suspicion that he'd stumbled into a blind date. "What did you do before this?"

"I worked for an ad agency."

"Advertising—that's an interesting line of work. Where was that?"

"New York City."

"This must be quite a change for you."

Annie nodded and folded her legs Indian-style. With a jolt of surprise, Jake noticed that her toenails were each painted a different color. "I spent all my summers here with my grandparents when I was a child, so I was familiar with the ranch, but I didn't know much about actually running it. I'm still learning about that."

Jake found his gaze riveted on her toenails. They were not the toenails of a rancher. Blue, green, yellow, orange, red—the colors were arranged in rainbow order.

What the hell kind of woman painted her toes in rainbow order?

He pulled his gaze back to her eyes, which were even more brilliantly colored than her toes. *Information.* He needed to focus on getting information, on learning about this woman's background and discovering her weak spots. "I'm surprised you didn't just sell the ranch."

The red curls around the large cartoon bird on her head bounced as she nodded. "That was my original plan."

"What changed your mind?"

Unfolding her legs, she pulled her knees to her chin and wrapped her arms around them. "It's kind of an odd story."

"That's my favorite kind."

Annie gave him a measuring look.

"I'd love to hear it," he prompted.

Annie pointed a finger at his cup of tea. "Okay. Start drinking, and I'll tell you."

What was the deal with the tea? Was she trying to drug him? Would he wake up in a ditch with his wallet missing?

Even worse, would he wake up as crazy as she was? Jake picked up the cup and stared into it suspiciously. "What's in here, anyway?"

"Tea. Just tea."

He took a hesitant sip. It tasted like tea, all right— strong, dark and unsweetened, just the way he took his coffee. What the hell. He took a long swig.

His hostess smiled approvingly, then leaned back against the sofa cushion. "It all started in a cab. I was headed to my apartment from LaGuardia after coming here for Grandpa's funeral. I'd listed the ranch for sale with a real estate broker, but I couldn't stop thinking about it. I'd always thought of this place as home. Getting rid of it kind of felt like losing another relative."

The tiny dachshund strolled in from the kitchen. Annie bent and picked him up, settling the creature on her lap. "It was a cold, rainy day, and the traffic was barely moving. I remember that the taxi stank—the driver needed a bath and the back seat smelled like sour milk. Anyway, there I was, stuck in traffic in a stinky cab, and all of sudden, I saw a billboard."

She looked at him as if she'd just made a profound pronouncement. Jake was unsure how to respond. "A billboard?"

Annie nodded. "It was for some kind of home health care service. It said, 'You belong at home.' "

She looked at him as if she expected some kind of reaction. "Hmmm," Jake managed.

"The words weren't what made the sign so amazing."

"No?"

Annie shook her head. "What was amazing was the way the words sounded in my head. I know this sounds strange, but I heard Grandpa's voice. Like he was sitting right beside me, talking in an insistent tone." She scratched the dachshund's ear. The little canine's tail pounded the sofa. "Needless to say, it rattled me. I thought I was really losing it."

No wonder. You were. Jake struggled to keep his expression attentive yet blank as she looked up and continued.

"I closed my eyes, thinking I must be more tired than I realized. When I opened them again, well, there was another billboard."

"You don't say." Jake was tempted to mention that the highways to and from most metropolitan airports were routinely littered with billboards. The fact she'd

47

seen another one was hardly worthy of the wonder or reverence in her expression—the kind of wonder and reverence usually reserved for a sighting of the Holy Virgin in tile grout.

"This one said, 'Follow your dreams.' And once again, I heard Grandpa saying it in a really urgent, insistent tone."

Jake cleared his throat. "So . . . what were your dreams?"

"Well, that was just it. I realized I didn't have any. Not anymore, anyway. My job kept me incredibly busy—so busy that I didn't have time to stop and consider whether or not it was what I really wanted to be doing. That billboard made me stop and think."

"And?"

"And I realized I wanted more out of life than frantic busy-ness. So I started thinking back to what I used to want."

The fat dog on her lap rolled over. Annie absently rubbed his belly. Jake watched her long, slim fingers stroke the animal in slow, sensuous circles and was shocked to feel a surge of envy for the dog. Pulling his eyes away from her hands, he forced his attention back to what she was saying.

"When I was a kid, I used to daydream about living here and raising a family. But my father insisted I get what he called 'a real life.' He said ranching was no life for a woman, that he hadn't raised me with every advantage to have me waste my life out in the sticks." She sighed. "He wanted me to go to an expensive women's college back east, and Dad always managed to have his way. One thing kind of led to another, and my life went along just as he'd planned. I graduated, got a good-paying job, got married—"

"You were married?"

Annie nodded. "For a year. Several years ago." She motioned for him to drink his tea. He took a small sip.

"After the divorce," she continued, "I really threw myself into my career. I focused on deadlines and meetings and all the things listed in my calendar. I never stepped back and thought about what I really wanted. Not until I heard Grandpa read that billboard, that is."

"I see." *I see that you sound seriously disturbed.* What was the mental illness where people thought they heard voices? Schizophrenia?

"You're not drinking your tea," Annie pointed out.

"Sorry." Jake obediently took a large gulp.

"The next thing I knew, there was another billboard. This one was for evening courses at a university, and there was Grandpa's voice again. Just as clear as day, I heard him say, 'It's never too late to start over.' That one really got to me. But not as much as the next billboard."

"Oh?" Jake struggled to keep his expression impassive.

"It was an ad for life insurance, and it featured a picture of an adorable baby. Underneath the picture, it said, 'It's the little things that count.' " Annie leaned back. "I know it sounds crazy, but I heard a click in my head, like everything had just fallen into place."

That wasn't the sound of things falling into place. That was the sound of your mind snapping.

"And all of a sudden, I knew what I was going to do."

Commit yourself to a mental institution? Unfortunately, that apparently had not been her decision. Jake shifted uneasily. "What was that?"

"Follow the dream I'd had as a child." The dog waved his front paws in the air, urging her to resume stroking his belly. Annie complied. "I was sick to death of living in the city—sick of walking on concrete instead of grass, of never seeing anything green that wasn't in a salad or a planter. I was sick of worrying about products instead of people. I wanted to do something fulfilling, something that would make a difference in the world. I wanted . . ."

She hesitated, and her face softened. "I wanted to have a baby. And I wanted to raise it here."

It took all of his resolve to feign ignorance. "So . . . did you remarry?"

She shook her head. "There weren't any candidates. I hadn't even seriously dated anyone in years. I realized I couldn't just keep waiting for Prince Charming to come along. If I wanted my dreams to come true, I'd have to take action myself."

She rubbed the dog's long ears. "I sat there in that taxi, thinking about single parenthood, telling myself how difficult and impractical it would be. And then the next billboard made it all clear." Her lips curved into a Mona Lisa smile. "It was a Nike ad."

Oh, Christ. This was too hokey to be believed. *"Just do it?"*

She leaned back and nodded. "So I did."

Great. The mother of his child was a wacko who thought her dead grandfather talked to her through billboards. Jake drained the cup of tea, only to gag on a mouthful of dregs. He reached for the paper napkin and violently coughed into it.

Instead of asking if he were choking, she simply smiled. "Oh, good. You're done." She reached out and took the cup from his hand. "Now—let's talk about you."

Jake cleared his throat. The woman was nuts. It was time to come clean and get the heck out of here. "Look—I'm not who you think."

"No one is. First impressions are usually deceptive."

She wasn't even looking at him. She was staring intently into the teacup.

Jake shifted uneasily on the sofa. "Yeah, well, there's something I need to tell you."

"No, it's better if you don't give me any clues."

"But I need to . . ."

She held up a hand. "Shh. I need a few moments of silence."

Hadn't she just said it was time to talk about him? Then why the hell wouldn't she let him get a word in edgewise? He stared at her as she swirled the cup three times, then turned it upside down on the saucer. After a few moments, she turned it over and studied the bottom.

"You've experienced a great loss." She spoke in a low, soft voice. "I see lots of pain and suffering. It's clinging to you, close as skin. But you're on the verge of a new life now." She looked up and flashed him a smile so bright he felt momentarily blinded. It was a relief when she turned her attention back to the cup. "A new person is entering your life. No, wait—two new people."

She was reading tea leaves. This crazy woman was reading tea leaves! She didn't think he was a blind date arranged by his grandmother; she thought he was as flaky as she was. She honestly believed he'd come to have his fortune told.

"You're going to have a child." She held the mug closer and peered into its depths. "No, wait—the child is already here."

A chill crawled up his spine. How could she know that? He didn't believe in fortune tellers. He didn't believe in anything but the cold, relentless march of time and the inevitability of pain. Still, there was something about her words that gave him the creeps.

She frowned into the cup. "I see . . . turmoil. Dark,

swirling, inner turmoil—for you, and for the people around you. You'll have to make a decision."

The grandfather clock in the hallway ticked loudly in the silence as she studied the inside of the cup. "It will be a difficult decision. Whatever you decide, everything will change. In fact, the change has already begun." She looked up, her eyes somber. "It'll be the most important decision of your life. You can't decide it with your head. You'll have to follow your heart."

Her eyes bored into his in a way that made the hair rise on the back of his neck. She wasn't looking at him like a casual acquaintance or someone she'd just met. She was looking at him intently, almost intimately, and her expression was worried, as if she cared what happened to him.

Which was ridiculous. She didn't even know him. How the hell could she care?

He squirmed uneasily, his gut tightening. It was time to stop this game. "Look. I tried to tell you this a few minutes ago, but you wouldn't let me."

Her delicate auburn brows drew together. "Tell me what?"

"That I'm not Pearl's grandson."

Her lips parted. His gaze fastened on her mouth, and a totally irrelevant thought flew into his mind. *Would her lips taste as sweet and ripe as they looked?*

"Then who . . . Why . . . ?"

Appalled at his thoughts, Jake ripped his gaze away from her mouth. "I'm surprised the tea leaves didn't tell you." He yanked a business card out of his jacket pocket and thrust it at her.

Annie stared at the heavy vellum card. *Jake E. Chastaine, attorney-at-law,* with the firm of Morrison and Chastaine in Tulsa. She gazed at the emblem of Lady

Justice with the scales on the corner of the card, and felt a kinship to the blindfolded image.

An attorney. Oh, dear—attorneys didn't show up on one's doorstep unless some kind of trouble accompanied them. The last time a representative from an attorney's office had come to her home, she'd been served with divorce papers.

She set the dog on the floor, her stomach clenching with cold dread. "I don't understand."

"I'm here because of the child."

The chill in her belly spread up her spine. "The one I mentioned in the reading?"

"The one you gave birth to."

Annie's heart froze. "Madeline?" she whispered.

"That's her name?"

His eyes were dark and intent and determined. They were the eyes of a man who would not be deterred, who would not be dissuaded.

Fear stabbed her, cold and sharp as icicles. She fought an impulse to rush into her child's room and snatch her up, to protect her from whatever threat this grim-mouthed stranger posed. She wasn't sure why, but she was suddenly certain he posed a threat.

She somehow found her voice. "I—I don't know what you want, Mr. Chastaine, but I think you'd better leave. My child is none of your business." She rose from the sofa on legs that felt too weak to support her weight.

The man rose as well. His height was intimidating. "Oh, yes, she is."

The words were bitten off and curt, but it wasn't his tone that made the blood drain from her face. It was that look in his eyes, that hard, stubborn, unrelenting look. "I have reason to believe that I'm her father."

The floor seemed to lurch and sway beneath her like a runaway rollercoaster. Annie gripped the back of a red-

53

and-beige-checked wing chair for support. "Wh—what are you talking about?"

"I just came from the Tulsa Fertility Center. I saw their records, and it appears you've had my child."

"No." Annie's fingers tightened on the back of the chair, her thoughts thrashing about like wheat in a windstorm. "No. You couldn't have. Those records are sealed."

The moment she said it, she wished she hadn't. Dear God—she'd just confirmed she'd been a client of the clinic! Why did she always babble so when she was upset?

It was too late to try to deny it. "Donors sign a release," she said rapidly. "They surrender all rights, all claims to their . . . their . . . their . . ."

Children. The word reverberated in the air, even though Annie couldn't bring herself to say it aloud. Saying it would make it sound as if the donors were actually parents.

And they weren't. Not really. The nameless, faceless man who'd contributed his chromosomes to create Madeline wasn't really a *father*—not in any meaningful way. He was distant, uninvolved, disembodied, unreal.

Or at least he had been. Until now.

Annie stared at the man before her. She tried to swallow, but her tongue stuck to the roof of her mouth. "Donors have no parental rights."

"I wasn't a donor." His voice was clipped, the words dry. "My wife and I were undergoing fertility treatment. Our lowlife excuse of a doctor decided to help himself to my specimen when the donor bank ran low."

His wife. He was married. He wanted a child. Madeline was his child. The thoughts swirled in her mind, attaching to each other, growing darker and denser, building in force like a thundercloud.

"No." Annie mouthed the word, but no sound came out. Her vocal chords seemed paralyzed. Her entire body seemed incapable of movement.

"Ma-ma-ma-ma."

The familiar call jerked Annie out of her daze. She turned to see Madeline toddle into the room, rubbing her eyes and dragging her favorite yellow blankie. The child's pink-and-white striped romper with the ruffled bottom was wrinkled from her nap, and her dark hair stuck out in short, Shirley Temple ringlets around her ears. Her four teeth gleamed in a predominantly gummy grin as she started toward Annie. Then the child spotted Jake. She stopped in her tracks, stuck a blanket-covered thumb in her mouth, and stared.

Jake stared back. "My God," he whispered.

It seemed as if time had stopped, as if life had been cryogenically suspended. Madeline slowly turned and looked at Annie, her big, brown eyes round and quizzical.

Annie's heart tumbled like a sock in a clothes dryer.

Because she suddenly knew, with horrible certainty, why Jake looked so familiar.

His eyes were the mirror image of her daughter's.

And oh, dear Lord—it was more than just the eyes. Annie's gaze shifted from Jake's face to Madeline's like an oscillating fan. Her daughter had a miniature version of Jake's mouth, Jake's hairline.

Adrenaline flooded her veins in a hot, hard rush. Every protective maternal instinct roared to red alert. Before she had time to think, she'd dashed across the room and snatched up the child as if rescuing her from a charging bull.

Alarmed, Madeline started to cry. Annie held her tightly against her shoulder.

"You're scaring her," Jake said.

He was right, but the idea of this man criticizing the way she handled her own daughter was intolerable. "Get out."

He glared at her, his eyes challenging. "You're not getting rid of me. She's my child, and I have rights."

"No."

"Look at her! She's the spitting image of me."

Annie cradled the child's head against her shoulder. "That doesn't mean anything."

"I've got records from the Tulsa Fertility Center that mean something. But if you still refuse to accept the obvious, I'll be more than happy to pay for blood tests."

"No."

"No?"

"You heard me. Get out."

His chin jutted out at a stubborn angle. "I'm her father, damn it. I'm also an attorney. A damn good one."

Madeline howled louder. Hot Dog barked. The room swirled with the dark energy of a tornado. "Get out," Annie ordered again.

He showed no sign of budging. Fear pumped through Annie's veins. Oh, dear heavens—he was tall and muscular and hard as a wall, and he outweighed her by nearly a hundred pounds. If he tried to take the child by force, she would have no way of stopping him.

A car door slammed in the driveway.

"That must be your voodoo appointment." Jake strode to the door and flung it open. Over his wide shoulder, Annie saw a portly man with Pearl's curly hair heading toward the steps of the porch. Her knees weakened in relief. She'd never been so glad to see another human being in her life.

Jake turned and leveled a steely gaze at Annie, ignoring the man who was trying to wave in greeting. "I'll leave for now, but I'll be back. I'm that child's father, and I have rights. If I have to drag you through every court in the land to exercise them, I'll do it."

He strode past the other man as if he were invisible and stalked to his car.

Clutching her sobbing child, Annie watched him drive off, his tires spewing gravel. Her whole world seemed to swirl away in the stream of dust that rose in the wake of the retreating white car.

He'd be back. He'd said he would, and Annie was sure he meant it. With a sickening certainty, she was equally sure that nothing in her life would ever be the same.

Chapter Four

Annie sat in the darkened corner of the nursery later that evening, rocking her sleeping child by the dim glow of a Cinderella nightlight. It was nine o'clock—an hour past Madeline's bedtime—but the baby had just dozed off.

It had been a long afternoon. Madeline had been cranky ever since she'd awakened from her nap and wandered into the living room. She'd fussed during her bath, thrown most of her dinner on the floor, and balked at bedtime. It had taken four stories and six lullabies to finally lull her to sleep.

No wonder the child was upset, Annie thought, sifting her fingers through the baby's dark, soft hair. Babies picked up on the emotions of the people around them, and Annie had been shaken to the core by Jake Chastaine's visit. Annie had tried not to let her agitation show for the sake of the child, but Maddie's emotional radar hadn't been fooled.

Neither had Pearl's grandson's, Annie thought. The poor man had looked from her to the squawling baby, then suggested it might be better if he came back at another time. Annie had jumped at the suggestion.

"Are you okay?" the man had asked as he turned to leave, his pudgy face creased with concern. His eyes had darted to the cloud of gravel dust still hovering over the driveway from Jake's rapid departure.

Annie was afraid she'd never be completely okay again, but she'd bravely nodded. Whatever she told this man was sure to get back to Pearl. "We, uh, just got some distressing news," she told him.

To put it mildly. Having Jake Chastaine appear on her doorstep and announce he was Madeline's father had turned her world upside down and inside out. She felt as if she'd been hit by a freight train, a steamroller, and a bulldozer, all at once.

Annie gazed down at the child in her arms, her heart filling with a tenderness so strong it hurt. She'd never loved anyone or anything as much as she loved her daughter. She watched the rise and fall of Maddie's chest, listened to the way her breath came out in soft little puffs, felt the sweet weight of the child's head cradled against her breast.

Madeline was so young, so innocent, so trusting. She relied completely on Annie to nurture her, to care for her, to protect her from harm. Annie would rather die than betray the child's faith.

What was it that Jake had said? *"I'm that child's father, and I have rights. If I have to drag you through every court in the land to exercise them, I'll do it."*

Fear, cold and numbing, shot through Annie, leaving her thoughts jumbled and confused. What did he want? Custody?

That had to be it. He said there'd been a mix-up at

the clinic. He'd said he and his wife had been undergoing fertility treatments. Obviously they wanted a child.

They wanted Madeline.

Annie's stomach lurched and knotted, and she fought off a wave of nausea. She tightened her grip on the baby.

"I'm an attorney," Jake had said. "A damn good one."

Annie believed him. The man had a presence, an innate sense of self-assurance about him that spoke of success. It was in his eyes, his voice, his bearing. He was used to winning. He was used to getting what he wanted.

And he wanted Madeline.

Annie stopped rocking and stared at the long shadow Madeline's crib cast against the wall. The slats of the side railing looked eerily like prison bars. Maybe she should make a break for it before the law got involved. Maybe she should just pack up the baby, get in the rusty four-door pickup she'd inherited from her grandfather, and go.

But where? The inside of her lip hurt, and she realized she was biting it. The pain was nothing compared to the cold, gripping ache inside.

Think, she told herself. *Fight back the fear and think.*

She could go to another country, go into hiding. She could leave tonight, before he had a chance to file any papers or have her served or do whatever it was that attorneys did. The thought filled her veins with adrenaline.

But how would she finance such a thing? It would take money—a lot of money, a lot more money than she had—to start a life in another country.

Annie closed her eyes, the man's words reverberating in her head. "I'll leave for now, but I'll be back." His mouth had been hard, his jaw firm as granite, his eyes filled with steely resolve. She'd never seen a more determined look on a human face.

The memory of those eyes, intent and unyielding, sent a shudder racing through her. He was not the kind of man to give up easily. If she ran, he would try to find her. She'd need to change her identity and cover her tracks. She'd need to keep moving until she was sure it was safe.

But would it ever feel safe? Despair surged through Annie like a wave against a rock, pushing her toward the hard, crushing answer.

"No." Annie whispered the word in the darkened room. If she ran now, she would have to keep running until Madeline was grown. She could never be sure that Jake wasn't just about to find her. She'd have to raise her child on the lam, always looking over her shoulder, never putting down any roots.

And the one thing she'd vowed to give her child was roots. She wanted Madeline to know a sense of belonging, a sense of home. Annie had missed having that from her parents, but at least she'd gotten a taste of it from her grandparents. It was why Annie had come back to the ranch to raise her child.

"Oh, Gran, Grandpa—how I wish you were here!" Annie murmured. "How am I supposed to know what to do?"

She no longer felt sure of anything, except her love for Madeline. No one could ever love the child as much as she did, she thought fiercely. And as long as she could draw a breath, she would do everything within her power to keep her child with her.

The baby shifted restlessly, and Annie realized she was clutching her as if someone were trying to yank her from her arms. Madeline's eyelids fluttered open. Her small baby mouth pursed as she let out a mewling complaint.

Easing her grip on the child, Annie gently trailed her finger through the baby's curls. "Everything's all right, sweetheart," she murmured.

But it wasn't, and Madeline sensed it. The child kicked her pajama-covered feet and whimpered. Setting the chair to rocking, Annie began to croon a lullaby. "Hush, little baby, don't say a word. Papa's gonna buy you a mockingbird."

Darn it—the last thing Annie wanted to sing about was Madeline's papa, because she had no doubt it was Jake. The similarity in their physical appearance was too pronounced to be coincidental. She wished she could deny it, wished she could convince herself it was all a mistake, but deep in her soul, she knew it was true.

Annie deliberately revised the lyrics. "And if that mockingbird don't sing, Mama's gonna buy you a diamond ring."

But Annie didn't have the money for diamond rings— much less expensive custody suits. All of her money was invested in the ranch. Jake had certainly looked well-heeled, though. His suit had been expensive, and the watch on his wrist had probably cost as much as Annie's annual disposable income.

Madeline's eyes started to drift closed again. "And if that diamond ring turns to brass," Annie whispered, "Mama's gonna buy you a looking glass."

The baby's breathing resumed its deep, regular pattern. After a few more verses, Annie slowly rose from the chair, the baby limp and heavy in her arms, and carefully placed her in the crib. She tucked the pink baby blanket around the child, then bent and kissed her warm cheek. With a last caress of a ringlet on the child's forehead, she raised the side rail and tiptoed out the door.

The light in the hallway seemed unnaturally bright after the dimness of the baby's room. Annie blinked against the glare, but welcomed it all the same. Bright lights always comforted her when she got jittery or frightened.

But this fear was different than the kind that came from watching a scary movie or reading a murder mystery. This fear was alive—a loathsome, hungry creature, a creature intent on devouring her heart and consuming her soul. This fear concerned her daughter.

She felt alone, so alone. She longed to call Helen and Ben, but she didn't want to burden them with this the night before Helen's surgery.

Besides, she thought somberly, the advice she needed went beyond what a friend could give. She needed to talk to an attorney.

Henry. Annie froze in the hallway as the thought settled around her.

"Henry. Of course," she murmured. Henry Marlow would know what to do. An old friend of her grandfather's, Henry was retired now, but he'd practiced law up until a few months ago, when a stroke had forced him to move into the nursing home where Pearl lived. Henry had handled the probate on her grandparents' estate. He was no longer able to walk, but his mind was still sharp as a razor. Annie had talked with him just last week when she'd visited Pearl.

Why hadn't she thought of Henry sooner? She'd go see him first thing in the morning. She'd take Madeline with her and let Pearl keep an eye on the baby while she sought the attorney's advice.

A loud yap broke through Annie's thoughts. She looked across the living room to see Hot Dog standing by the back door, his long, skinny tail wagging.

"You need to go out, fella?" Annie crossed the room

and opened the door for the dachshund. The fat little dog waddled out onto the darkened patio. Annie flipped the light switch by the door, illuminating the back lawn.

With any luck, Annie thought, maybe Henry could shed some light on her situation as well.

Sunlight streamed through the windows of the sunroom at the Shady Acres Nursing Home the next morning, creating a sheen on Henry's bald head. The old man had always reminded Annie of Humpty Dumpty, with his large, egg-shaped head and small, thin-boned frame.

"Jake Chastaine," the elderly man muttered, staring at the business card Annie had just handed him. "Hmm."

Annie leaned forward on the yellow-and-green cushion that covered the white rattan sofa. "Do you know him?"

The old man nodded grimly, his bald head bobbing to the right. The stroke had weakened the left side of his body, so all of Henry's actions seemed unbalanced. "Know *of* him. He joined his father-in-law's firm a few years ago. Tom Morrison has one of the biggest law firms in Tulsa."

"Are they any good?"

Henry made a sound halfway between a harrumph and a cough. "Probably the best."

Annie's spirits took a nosedive.

"They specialize in corporate law. Mergers, acquisitions, that sort of thing. Tom Morrison has a lot of clout." Henry's mouth curved in a half grin. "Not to mention a knack for contributing to all the right judiciary campaigns."

Annie frowned. "You mean he's crooked?"

"Oh, no. Just well-heeled and well connected. He knows all the right people."

Annie felt a rekindling of hope. "So if they specialize

in corporate law, they probably don't know much about custody cases."

"I wouldn't say that," Henry cautioned. "A firm as large as theirs can provide full legal services. They'd bring in outside counsel, if need be. They'd do whatever it took to win." Henry ran his good hand across his jaw. "They don't so much specialize in corporate law as they specialize in winning."

Annie's shoulders slumped. Just her luck—Madeline's father was not only an attorney, but one of the meanest, baddest dogs in Tulsa's legal junkyard. She drew a deep, steadying breath. "So will you represent me against them?"

Henry's blue eyes were kind under his heavy lids. "I'm no longer practicing law, Annie."

"But you still can, can't you? You still have your license?"

"I'm still a member of the bar, if that's what you mean. But there's nothing to represent yet."

"There will be."

Henry's head wobbled as he nodded. "I'm afraid you're right." He shifted his weight in the wheelchair and peered at her closely. "Look, Annie—I'm no match for the likes of this firm. Hiring me to represent you against them would be like using a BB gun against an armored tank. You need someone who can play on the same field."

"I don't have a lot of money."

"You could mortgage the ranch."

Annie shook her head. "I already took out a mortgage to pay for repairs. The barn needed a new roof and the foundation of the house was badly cracked—then we had to buy a new hay baler, and I'm diversifying into alpacas, and I had medical expenses from having the baby that insurance didn't cover...." Annie's voice trailed off. She could go on and on, listing all the ways she'd spent the borrowed money. All of the expenditures had been necessary, but that didn't matter now. What mattered was that the money was gone, and she didn't have the income to qualify for a second mortgage. Annie swallowed. "I'm barely keeping my head above water now."

The right side of Henry's forehead knit in a frown. "Hmm."

Annie clasped her hands in her lap and steeled her spine. "Give it to me straight, Henry. What are my chances?"

"Depends on what you want."

"To keep things the way they are. To keep this man out of Madeline's life."

Henry's head gave a doleful, lopsided shake. "Well, then, I'm afraid they're not good. If he can prove paternity, he'll probably at least get joint custody."

A cold chill shimmied up Annie's spine. "I won't stand for that."

"You're likely to have no choice."

Annie's throat grew unnaturally tight. She gazed down at the bright yellow-and-green sofa cushion, a combination no doubt chosen for its cheerfulness. It sure wasn't cheering her now. When she spoke, the voice didn't seem to be her own. "What if Madeline and I were to move away?"

Henry regarded her keenly from his heavy hooded eyes. "You mean out of state?"

Annie nodded. "Maybe even out of the country. To someplace hard to find."

Henry shook his head. "Jake Chastaine has a lot of money, Annie—the kind of money that has long arms. I'm afraid you'd simply end up depleting your resources to no good end. And there's another issue to consider,

66

as well. You could end up looking reckless and unstable, uprooting the child and moving away for no reason. That's the sort of thing that could work against you in a custody battle."

"Work against me?"

"If Chastaine decides to go for full custody of the child, he'll try to prove you're an unfit mother."

Annie stared at Henry, her head reeling. Her whole life revolved around Madeline. From the moment she got up in the morning to the moment she fell asleep—not to mention any time Madeline awoke or murmured during the night—the child's well-being was Annie's chief concern. "How could anyone think I'm unfit?"

"No one who knows you would ever think that," Henry reassured her. "But that doesn't mean a judge couldn't be persuaded otherwise."

"But it wouldn't be the truth!"

"I hate to say it, Annie, but the truth doesn't always win out. It's all in how the facts are presented."

Annie's spirits slumped. The thought of sharing Madeline was gut-wrenching. The idea of losing her altogether was unbearable. "Do you think he could do that?"

Henry's eyes were grim. "It's not outside the realm of possibility. Especially for a firm like Morrison and Chastaine."

Annie stared at Henry numbly.

The man let out a heavy sigh and rubbed his head. "I hate to say it, Annie, but I've seen money influence the outcome of custody judgments in all too many cases."

"But Madeline's my flesh and blood. I'm her mother!"

Henry gave a lopsided nod. "And if the blood tests confirm it, Chastaine's her father. You told me yourself you thought he was."

Tears welled up in Annie's eyes. She blinked hard, trying to hold them back.

Henry leaned forward and awkwardly patted her shoulder. "Look, Annie. I know this isn't what you want to hear, but your best bet is to try to work out an amicable arrangement with this man."

Annie fought a childish urge to put her hands over her ears.

"Madeline could do a lot worse than Jake Chastaine for a father," Henry continued. "His money and connections could open a lot of doors for her on down the road."

"If I'd wanted to share my child with a man, I would have just gotten pregnant the old-fashioned way!"

The high-pitched whine of a hearing aid made Annie turn toward the doorway. Pearl stood in the doorway, leaning on the baby stroller, her curly white hair forming a wild white halo, her eyes round and wide behind thick plastic trifocals. She appeared for all the world to be eavesdropping.

Henry wheeled his chair to face the doorway as well. "Turn down your hearing aid, Pearl." Henry tapped his fingertip against his ear.

"All right, all right." Pearl fiddled with the gadget, and the screeching noise halted. Madeline kicked her feet against the footrest of the white and blue stroller and smiled gaily at Annie. Annie grinned and waved at her child.

"If you don't mind, Pearl," Henry continued, "this is a private conversation."

"Shucks. All the interesting conversations around here are private ones," Pearl grumbled. She looked at Annie. "I couldn't help but overhear you, dear. I know I'm not supposed to meddle in other people's business, but I haven't lived this long without learnin' a few things, and one of the things I've learned is that some old-fashioned ways don't need any improvin'. Makin' babies God's way is at the top of the list. Why, I remember when my husband and I were your age—my goodness, if we hadn't had to work to eat and eat to live, we would have been baby-makin' clean around the clock. Why, I remember one afternoon in particular, when—"

Henry made a choking sound that ended in a fit of coughing. At length he cleared his throat. "If you don't mind, Pearl, Annie and I are discussing a legal matter."

"We'll be finished in a few moments," Annie added. "Is Madeline behaving for you?"

"She's being a perfect angel. We're taking a little stroll down the hallway."

"I'll catch up with you as soon as Henry and I are finished."

"Guess that's my cue to leave, eh?"

Henry nodded.

The old woman teetered down the hall, leaning on the baby stroller as if it were a walker.

Henry's mouth curved in an apologetic grin. Annie tried to smile, but her lips refused to cooperate. She placed a hand on her side, where a sharp pain was developing.

Henry regarded her, his eyes kind but solemn. "As I was saying, Annie, you need to think of the child's best interests."

"I *am* thinking of Madeline's interests. That's why I chose to have her by artificial insemination in the first place."

Henry's right brow lifted quizzically.

Annie folded her arms around her stomach. "My parents had a lousy marriage," she explained. "I was married once myself, and that marriage was lousy, too. I'd love to have a marriage like Ben and Helen have or like my grandparents had, but those seem to be awfully rare. I know from personal experience how hard it is on chil-

69

dren when their parents don't love each other. Rather than put my child through that, I decided to have my baby without the complications of a man."

Annie sighed and gazed out the window at the courtyard. Two elderly women in wheelchairs rolled side-by-side across the patio toward a flowerbed of marigolds. "I thought I was making sure my child would never be caught in a tug-of-war between her parents. But now it looks like Madeline's going to be caught in the middle anyway."

Henry drummed his fingers on the arm of his wheelchair and regarded her solemnly. "I'll help you any way I can, Annie, but you need to give this matter some serious thought. I want you to go home and ask yourself if you really want to deprive your child of the love of a father."

"He doesn't love her. He doesn't even know her!"

"From what you told me, that's not his fault, is it?"

Annie hated to concede the point, but she had no choice. She glumly shook her head.

"You need to take that into consideration, Annie," Henry said gently. "And if Mr. Chastaine contacts you again . . ."

"Not if. When," Annie said bitterly.

"Well, when he contacts you, I advise you to be cordial to him, to talk to him and find out what he wants. Don't give him any reaction—don't agree or disagree or argue about anything. Your goal—your assignment, if you will—is to figure out what he's after. Then give me a call, and we'll work from there."

"Okay." The word came out on the tail of a sigh.

The right side of Henry's brow furrowed. "Are you all right? You don't look so well."

"I'm feeling a little under the weather," Annie admitted. "I didn't sleep very well last night."

To put it mildly. She'd tossed and turned all night, then awakened with a headache and a dull ache in her side. The pain seemed to be getting sharper, and now she was feeling queasy to boot. The stress of the situation was really taking a toll on her.

The intercom speaker overhead crackled to life. "Ladies and gentlemen, our weekly bingo competition is about to begin in the front parlor."

Annie rose from the sofa. "Thanks for your help, Henry. I'd better go get Madeline so Pearl won't miss her game." She stretched out her hand.

Henry gave it a warm squeeze. "I know this is upsetting, but it's going to all work out."

"I don't see how."

"It will, Annie. You just have to have faith."

Faith didn't seem like much of a weapon against a big gun like Jake Chastaine, Annie thought woefully. She headed down the hall to collect her child, suddenly anxious to hold her child, to feel the little girl's chubby arms around her neck, to inhale her sweet, milky scent. Madeline was her life, the very heart of her heart. The thought of a stranger laying claim to her knifed at Annie's soul.

And yet, against her will, Henry's words echoed through her mind—*do you really want to deprive your child of the love of a father?*

Chapter Five

The soft tinkle of silver and fine crystal greeted Jake as he entered the formal dining room of the Southern Oaks Country Club in north Tulsa that evening. His stomach tensed as he spotted Tom and Susanna at their usual table in the corner. He wasn't looking forward to telling them the news about the baby, and yet it wasn't something he could very well keep secret. His former in-laws were the closest thing he had to family, and Tom was his business partner as well. In the normal course of things, he already would have talked to Tom about the situation, but the older man had been at an out-of-town legal seminar for the past two days.

With a nod to the maitre d', Jake wound his way through the maze of linen-covered tables. He hadn't been here in a couple of years, yet the place was unchanged. The carpet was still so thick it felt like quicksand, the walls still hung with expensive oil paintings, the tables still set with glimmering votives and fresh flowers. It was fine dining in its highest form, the kind of place where the silver was real and the crystal had more lead in it than the James gang after their final shootout. The place was too staid for Jake's tastes, but it was one of Tom's favorite restaurants, and Jake had often dined here with his in-laws and Rachel.

They hadn't come here together since her death. Jake glanced toward the chair where Rachel had always sat, and was relieved to note that a waiter had removed it.

"Jake—I'm so glad you could join us." Susanna smiled up as he reached the table.

"I'm so glad you asked me." Jake had been surprised when his mother-in-law had called that morning and invited him to join her and Tom at the club. The woman had turned into something of a recluse since Rachel's death. Tom had privately complained to Jake that she seldom left the house, had no interest in seeing friends, and had dropped all of the civic work she had before cared so fervently about. According to Tom, Susanna sometimes didn't even get out of bed. Even when she did, she often spent entire days in her bathrobe.

On the few occasions when Jake had been to their home since the accident—holiday dinners and a couple of times when Tom had barbecued by the pool—Susanna had been as impeccably groomed as ever, but the sparkle had been missing from her eyes. Instead of actively joining the conversation, she'd sat quietly, only speaking when addressed.

After the last visit, Jake had asked Tom about it. "Is she angry at me?"

"Why would she be angry?"

Jake had lifted his shoulders in a nonchalant shrug, but he'd looked away, unable to meet Tom's gaze. "Well, if I'd gone to the airport to pick up my folks instead of asking Rachel to go, she'd still be here."

His father-in-law had patted Jake's shoulder in a paternal fashion. "Don't be ridiculous. Susanna doesn't blame you. Neither of us do."

"She sure acts distant."

Tom had given a sad smile. "Susanna's distant to everyone. Especially me."

Judging from the warm way she was smiling tonight, though, she was back to her old self. She looked like the woman Jake remembered—the one who loved life, who took an active interest in everything around her, and who always looked out for the comfort and welfare of others.

Jake bent and kissed her cheek, inhaling the scent of her White Shoulders perfume. Jake knew the name of her favorite fragrance because Rachel had sent him to purchase a bottle one year when it had been his turn to do the Christmas shopping. The memory brought a pang.

Jake hid it with a smile. "You look wonderful."

It wasn't just an empty compliment. Susanna was in her mid-fifties, but she looked at least a decade younger. Her figure was slim, her skin pale and unlined, her hair dark and pulled back in a stylish French twist. She wore a black dress with a pearl necklace. It was a simple outfit, but on Susanna, it looked expensive and stunning.

She treated him to a dazzling smile. "Thank you. So do you."

"It's good to see you out and about."

"It's good to be that way." Fingering her pearls, she leaned forward and spoke in a confiding tone. "My friend Joan dragged me to a doctor. He's been treating me for clinical depression, and, well, the medicine seems to be working."

"That's wonderful."

Tom made a sound deep in his throat. "It won't be wonderful if she gets hooked on that stuff."

Susanna turned and gazed at him, her dark eyes earnest. "The doctor assured me that antidepressants aren't habit forming."

"That's what they used to say about Valium, and you know what happened to my mother."

Jake looked at Tom, trying to hide his surprise. He'd never heard the older man refer to his parents before. All he knew about his father-in-law's family was that they'd lived up north and died before Rachel was born. Evidently an old skeleton was rattling around in the back of the family closet.

Susanna gave Jake an apologetic grin. "Tom thinks anyone with any type of mental illness is ready for the loony bin."

"You're not mentally ill, and you don't need that medicine," her husband said gruffly. "You just need to get out of the house. I've been after you to do it for months."

Jake didn't miss the wounded look that flitted across Susanna's face. "Well, I'm out now," she said softly.

Jake lifted his glass. "And I, for one, am mighty glad to see it." He gave the woman a smile, then turned to her husband. "How did things go in Denver?"

"Good." Tom took a long drink from his wine glass. "I made some new contacts that might come in handy on down the road."

"How was the meeting with Allco Petroleum?"

"Great. Looks like the merger will go through."

"No surprises?"

"Not until I got to the Tulsa airport." Tom glanced over at his wife.

"What happened there?"

"Susanna met me at the gate."

Jake's eyes widened. The airport was the last place he'd expect Susanna to go—especially on one of her first outings from the house in months. Rachel's accident had happened just outside the airport entrance.

Susanna lifted her shoulders and gave a sheepish smile. "I thought Tom would be pleasantly surprised. Instead, I'm afraid I alarmed him."

"Damn right," Tom growled. "I thought someone must have died."

Crimony, Jake thought, looking at Susanna's crest-fallen face. *And Tom thinks* I *need to brush up on my people skills.* He shot his mother-in-law a teasing wink. "Hey, now—Susanna is far too pretty to be mistaken for the Grim Reaper."

"That didn't come out quite right." Tom reached out and patted his wife's hand, but his grin didn't reach his eyes. "I was just surprised to see you, that's all. It was so out of character that I thought there must be some kind of emergency."

"I used to meet you at the airport all the time," Susanna said softly, turning her hand and squeezing his fingers.

"Yeah, well, it's been a while." He pulled away his hand and reached for his drink.

Susanna gazed at him, a wounded look in her eyes. Jake was relieved when the waiter stepped forward to take his drink order.

"Did anyone else from Tulsa attend the conference?" He asked to fill the silence after the waiter retreated.

Tom turned the glass in his hand. "Just, uh, Kelly Banyon. You know Kelly, don't you, Jake?"

He knew Kelly, all right. A curvacious blonde in her late thirties who worked at a competing law firm, she wore short skirts and the smile of a woman on the make. She and Tom had been on opposite sides of a hostile takeover attempt last month, and she'd spent a lot of time in Tom's office, working out the details of an agreement.

More time than was probably necessary, now that Jake thought of it. A current of alarm raced through him.

"That was the woman with you at the airport, wasn't it?" Susanna said.

"That's right." Tom took a long swig of his Chardonnay.

"She must be very amusing. You two were laughing like schoolkids when I saw you."

An odd look flashed across Tom's face. "She'd, uh, just told an anecdote about a fellow attorney."

A humorous anecdote was just what this party needed. "Who was it about?" Jake prompted.

Tom looked away. "Someone in her office. I didn't know him."

"So what was the story?"

Tom cleared his throat and shifted uneasily. "I don't remember, exactly."

Jake looked at him in surprise. Tom had the memory of an elephant, especially for amusing stories. It wasn't like him to forget one.

But it was even less like him to lie.

Susanna twirled her glass of sparkling water. "What firm is Kelly with?" she asked.

"Lancaster and Austin. She was opposing counsel in that drilling company takeover bid last month."

"She's very pretty."

Tom made a noncommittal grunt and polished off his wine in a single gulp.

That's odd, Jake noted. Tom usually nursed one glass all the way through dinner.

A jolting thought suddenly hit him. *Good Lord—were Kelly and Tom fooling around?*

Nah. No way. Tom and Susanna had been married

thirty-three years. They'd been college sweethearts and were each other's one and only love. They were a perfect match. Besides, Tom often called Susanna his biggest business asset.

It wasn't an exaggeration, either. Tom had Susanna to thank for his wide network of friends and contacts. She had a knack for bringing people together and making them feel at ease. She was the perfect partner for a man like Tom—a sparkling conversationalist, a gracious hostess, a devoted wife and mother, a dedicated community activist. True, she'd been withdrawn and quiet since Rachel's death, but still . . .

Jake shook off the suspicion. One of the things he'd always admired about this man was his sense of integrity. He wasn't the type of man who would renege on a promise—especially not one as solemn and sacred as a wedding vow.

Besides, Tom was a family man. He always had been.

The waiter brought Jake's drink and refilled Tom's Chardonnay. Susanna looked from her husband to Jake and smiled, her smile brighter than he'd seen it since Rachel's death. Apparently she didn't share his suspicions. Or if she did, she wasn't letting it show.

"It's so nice to be out with my two favorite men," she said.

Jake lifted his glass. "To Susanna—who's lovelier than ever."

Tom lifted his glass and took a long swig, then set it down and leaned back. "So, Jake—what's been going on for the last two days?"

It was the perfect opening, but Jake balked at taking it. Bringing up the fact he had a newly discovered daughter wouldn't open just a can of worms, but a whole vat of rattlesnakes.

Jake mustered what he hoped was an easygoing smile.

"Let's not ruin the evening by talking shop."

Tom was immediately wary. "Why? Has something happened?"

Jake's smile had evidently fallen short. He traded it in for a sardonic grimace. "Believe it or not, Tom, the office survived just fine in your absence."

Laughing, Susanna placed a hand on her husband's arm. "He's got your number, dear."

"And I've got his." Tom's gaze didn't waver from Jake's face. "Something's wrong."

Oh, damn. He really wanted to postpone this. He gave it another shot. "The office is fine. Our clients are happy and none of the staff has resigned."

"Well, that's good to hear." Tom's probing gaze scanned Jake's face. "But something's up. I can tell. What is it?"

"It's . . ." Jake started to say "nothing," but the word froze in his throat. Discovering that he was the father of a child was definitely something. He adjusted the knot in his tie. "It's, um, a personal matter. Nothing to do with business."

Tom's forehead creased with concern. "Oh, jeeze. Have you got a health problem?"

"Oh, no, no. I'll tell you all about it after dinner."

Tom's frown deepened. "Why can't you just tell us now?"

Jake sighed. The more he resisted, the harder Tom would push. It was the man's basic bulldog-with-a-bone personality, one of the reasons he was such a good attorney.

"If something's wrong, Jake, dear, we'd like to help." Susanna leaned forward, her delicate eyebrows knit with concern. "We're your family."

Hell's bells. They'd backed him into a corner. Jake fiddled with the stem of his glass and searched for a way to break it gently. "I, uh, got some rather, er, shocking news yesterday."

They looked at him expectantly. Jake drew a deep breath.

"You know the fertility clinic Rachel and I were using?"

They both nodded.

"Well, it seems our doctor . . . He, uh, apparently . . ." Jake hesitated. There was no easy way to say it, so he might as well just blurt it out. "He evidently used a specimen of my sperm to impregnate another patient."

Tom's eyes narrowed. Susanna's widened. Both of their mouths simultaneously dropped open.

Tom recovered first. He hunched forward over the table. "Some girl is pregnant?"

"Was pregnant." Jake shifted his weight on the chair. "The child is a little over a year old now."

"Yours and Rachel's?" Susanna eyes were bright, almost feverish, ablaze with irrational hope. "But—but—she hadn't had her ovum extracted yet. . . ."

"It's not mine and Rachel's. It's mine and . . ." Jake's throat was dry and tight. He swallowed hard. "Her name is Annie Hollister."

Tom's face turned red and blotchy. He set down his drink so hard that the table rocked, rattling the china. "You've got a child by another woman?"

An irrational burst of guilt shot through Jake. "I'd never met her. Not until today, that is. The doctor . . ."

Tom's palm slapped down on the arm of his chair. "We'll sue the son of a bitch," he hissed. "We'll bring that charlatan up on criminal charges. He'll be stripped of his license and thrown in the slammer, and publicly humiliated in the bargain."

Susanna face had gone pale. She was still apparently absorbing the news. "You have a baby?"

Jake nodded grimly.

"How do you know it's yours?" Tom asked.

"I've seen the medical records. And she looks just like me."

"She?" Susanna said. "It's a girl?"

Jake nodded. "Fourteen months old."

"You've seen her?" Tom demanded. "You know there's actually a child?"

Again, Jake nodded.

Tom muttered a low oath. "It's probably just a scheme to extort money."

"No. I found out by accident—at the clinic. They tried to cover it up."

"Start at the beginning," Tom said grimly. "I want to hear everything."

By the time Jake had finished explaining about his visit to the fertility center, Tom was already reaching into his jacket pocket for his cell phone.

Susanna placed her hand on his arm. "Who are you calling?"

"The D.A. He'll have that clinic shut down the moment it opens its doors in the morning. Whoever owns that place is going to find himself in the middle of the biggest damn scandal that's ever hit the health care industry. And as for that doctor—where did he get off thinking he could play God? I'll see that he rots in jail."

"That was my initial reaction, too," Jake said. "But then I thought about it. I don't want to pursue legal action."

"Why the hell not?"

"Because of the child."

"You don't intend to let that shifty-eyed bastard get off scott free!"

Susanna put her hand on Tom's arm. "Let him talk," she urged softly.

"I've got to think about the child's best interests." Jake leveled a steady look at his father-in-law. "If we pursue this, it'll be a huge news story. There's no way we can keep it quiet. And I don't think it's in the best interests of the child to have this dragged through the courts and the newspapers. I don't want her very existence labeled a mistake."

Tom stared at him, his lips pressed tight. "But it *was* a mistake, damn it!"

Jake struggled to keep his voice even. "Look—I can understand your reaction. But you haven't seen her. When I saw her, it changed things." How could he explain what had happened to him when he'd looked across that room and seen his own eyes looking back at him? He didn't understand it himself, much less know how to communicate it to someone else. "She's here. She's a child. She's *my* child. And I don't intend to let her think for one minute that she's not wanted."

Tom's eyes narrowed. "What are you saying?"

Jake drew a deep breath. He'd given this a lot of thought over the past two days. Hell, he'd hardly thought about anything else. Time and distance had tempered his initial desire to punish Annie for having the baby he'd intended to have with Rachel, but it hadn't weakened his resolve to play a key role in the child's life. "I don't give a damn about the doctor. I *do* care about my daughter. I'm not going to spend my time and effort trying to punish the man who helped create her. I'd rather spend my time and effort getting to know the child, getting to be her father. I intend to seek joint custody."

"*Custody?* Hell, son—the only kind of custody you need to worry about is getting that damned doctor in custody. And the sooner, the better. We can do it. I don't care what state he's moved to."

"I told you. I don't want to pursue that. I just want joint custody."

Tom gazed at Jake as if he'd lost his mind. "You don't even know the baby's yours. That woman might have gotten knocked up by someone else."

"The baby looks just like me."

Tom waved his hand in a dismissive gesture. "Hell. All babies look the same."

"No, they don't." Susanna frowned at Tom, then placed a soft, manicured hand on Jake's arm. "Tell us about this woman. You went to see her?"

Jake nodded.

"She probably said the baby's yours just to get you to pay child support," Tom said with a dark scowl.

"She didn't say it's mine."

"So, then, what makes you think it is?" Tom demanded.

"Give him a chance to tell us what happened," Susanna said. She turned back to Jake. "So what happened?"

Jake drew a deep breath. "Like I told you, I got her name and address off the computer at the fertility center. She lives about an hour-and-a-half away, not far from Bartlesville."

"So you just showed up at this woman's door and introduced yourself as the father of her baby?"

"No. She was expecting someone else. She mistook me for him."

Tom scowled. "So what is she—a hooker?"

"Tom!" Susanna gave her husband a shocked look.

"Well, what kind of woman expects a man she's never met to come knocking on her door?"

"Any woman with a broken air conditioner or a leaky faucet," Susanna replied.

Tom snorted. "I doubt Jake was dressed as a plumber."

"Well, maybe she thought he was an insurance adjuster or something. Let's give him a chance to explain." She turned back to Jake expectantly.

Now was not the time to disclose that Annie was a fortune-teller. The whole situation was enough of a shock as it was. "She was expecting a visit from the grandson of a family friend," Jake said. "I played along for a while, pretending to be him, so I could gather information about her."

"What did you find out?" Tom asked. "What's her story?"

"She runs the ranch herself, with the help of a foreman and some seasonal help. She evidently inherited it from her grandparents."

"Is she married?" Susanna asked.

Jake shook her head. "She's a single mother."

"So how did you get around to the topic of your visit?"

"Well, after letting on that I was her friend's grandson for quite a while, I hit her with the truth. I told her I'd just come from the fertility center, and that I had reason to believe her child was mine. She was shocked—so shocked she inadvertently confirmed that she'd been a patient there. She said I couldn't have seen the records, that sperm donors had to sign a contract surrendering all rights. I explained that I'd been a patient, not a donor. And then the baby woke up from a nap and came in. And when I saw her, well . . ." Jake leaned forward. "I knew. I just knew."

"What's her name?" Susanna asked.

"Annie Hollister," Tom said curtly. "He already told us."

"No. I meant the baby."

"Madeline." Jake pronounced it the way Annie had, with a long i in the last syllable.

"Madeline." Susanna said the name softly, experimentally, letting it roll slowly off her tongue. "That's pretty. Madeline."

Tom frowned. "Damn it, Susanna, you act like you're picking out a name for a future grandchild!"

Susanna turned and looked him. "I'm simply learning the name of the one that's already here."

Tom's jaw tightened. "She's not our grandchild, damn it!"

"Any child of Jake's is a grandchild of mine."

He stared at Susanna, his lips parted, then quickly clamped them together. "We don't even know for sure that it's Jake's child."

"A paternity test is easy enough to do," Jake said.

A nerve worked in Tom's cheek. "Did this woman agree to one?"

"Not exactly."

"Well, what *was* her reaction?"

"Like I said, she was upset. She thought the baby's father was an anonymous, voluntary donor."

"So how did you leave things?"

"Not very well." Jake ran a hand down his face. "I'm afraid I got steamed and threatened legal action, and she got all upset, and then her friend's grandson showed up. There was no point in trying to discuss things any further, so I just left. I told her I'd be in touch."

"So what do you intend to do?"

"Go back and see her. See if we can work something out. My first inclination was to try to get full custody of the child, but after thinking about it, I realized that might

85

not be in the baby's best interests. Besides, I don't want to alienate the mother. I want to be able to start spending time with the baby right away."

Tom drummed his fingers on the table. He gave an impatient sigh and slowly shook his head. "Sometimes the best thing to do, Jake, is nothing. Sometimes it's best to let sleeping dogs lie."

Jake felt his temper flare. His father-in-law sounded just like the doctor at the clinic. "This isn't a dog we're discussing here. It's a child. My child. I can't pretend I don't have a child if I do."

"The key word is 'if.' "

"The evidence is pretty damned convincing."

"Well, even if it *is* yours, it's not your responsibility."

"It sure as hell is! If I have a daughter, I intend to be a father to her."

Susanna reached over and patted Jake's arm. "That's perfectly understandable." She shot her husband a pleading look. "And any child of yours will be loved and welcomed by us. Isn't that right, Tom?"

Thank heavens the waiter had come and taken their dinner order when he did, Susanna reflected later as she climbed into the passenger seat of their Cadillac. She could tell by the way Jake's eyes had flashed that he was getting angry, and she'd feared Tom had been about to say something he'd regret. She'd tried to divert the conversation away from the topic of the baby for the rest of the evening, but the subject kept coming up, and the entire meal had been strained.

"I just can't believe it," Tom muttered as he guided their large car out of the country club's parking lot.

"It's amazing," Susanna agreed. "Imagine—Jake with a baby."

"Why the hell would Jake want to play father to the

child of some woman he doesn't even know?"

"Because it's his child, too."

"We don't know that."

"Jake seems awfully sure."

"That was supposed to be Rachel's child, damn it!" Tom's voice was sharp with bitterness.

"I know," Susanna said softly.

"That doctor ought to be drawn and quartered. Why, I have half a mind to go down to Florida, find the son of a bitch, and—"

"That won't change the situation."

The only sound was the steady whoosh of the car's air conditioner. Tom steered the large vehicle out of the stone gate onto the road. "How did we end up in this mess? Things weren't supposed to turn out this way."

Her husband's voice was angry and frustrated. Susanna stared out at the night, at the bright lights of a convenience store as they drove past.

"The damnedest part is I don't know what to do about it," Tom continued.

That would be the worst part for him, Susanna thought as she glanced over at her husband. Nothing bothered him more than a situation he couldn't control. Rachel had been so much like him. Both of them had a vision of how life ought to be, and both of them thought they should be able to mold the world to fit that vision. Both of them thought they could—and should—control everything in their lives.

The amazing thing was how often they'd succeeded. By sheer bullheadedness and dogged persistence, both of them usually managed to make circumstances to suit their wills. It was precisely because they usually succeeded that they took it so hard when they couldn't.

Rachel's infertility was a prime example. Susanna's daughter had planned out her whole life at eighteen, and everything had hummed along right on schedule. She'd completed college summa cum laude, and graduate school with high honors. She'd gone to work for a prestigious accounting firm straight out of school, then married her high school sweetheart. She and Jake had exchanged vows in an carefully choreographed and executed wedding, then waited two years before trying to begin a family—just as Rachel had always planned.

And then she'd run into an unexpected obstacle: her own body.

"It isn't fair!" Rachel had raged to Susanna after her gynecologist had diagnosed her with severe endometriosis. "There are teenage girls out there having babies right and left—babies they don't want and have no way to care for. Jake and I can offer a baby every advantage. There's got to be a solution."

And Rachel had set out to find it, attacking the problem as she'd attacked every other goal in her life: methodically, thoroughly, persistently. She'd consulted three different doctors and undergone a battery of tests. When the consensus was that endometrial tissue was obstructing her fallopian tubes, she'd researched the disease thoroughly. Her best chance of conceiving, she'd learned, was in-vitro fertilization. So she and Jake had become patients at the Tulsa Fertility Center.

It hadn't been easy, but Rachel was determined. She'd undergone a series of injections to make her ovaries produce eggs. The injections had made her irritable and ill, but she hadn't been deterred. She'd been scheduled to have the eggs harvested in an outpatient surgical procedure. Susanna had planned to accompany her daughter to the clinic on the appointed day.

Instead, Susanna had spent the day burying her, along with all hopes of ever having a grandchild.

Susanna's eyes filled with tears, blurring her vision,

turning the lights outside the car window into shapeless streaks. This was how life had looked for the past two years—dark and indistinct and surreal. Depression had smothered the life out of her, leaving her indifferent and detached, unwilling to tackle even the simplest of tasks.

She glanced over at her husband, taking in the way his forehead was bunched in a frown, and fresh tears filled her eyes. She'd been a burden instead of a comfort to Tom. He'd been suffering, too. He still was. His reaction to the news about Jake's baby showed how deeply he was still hurting.

Tom was the chief reason she'd finally agreed to seek help—him and her old high school friend, Joan. Joan had come back to Tulsa from Chicago last month to visit her ailing father. While she was in town, she'd called Susanna, wanting to meet her for lunch. Susanna hadn't felt up to going. Worried by the way she sounded on the phone, Joan had dropped by the house, bluffed her way past the cleaning lady and found Susanna still in bed at eleven-thirty in the morning.

Under a barrage of questioning, Susanna had admitted that she hadn't left the house in three months.

"Susanna—you can't go on like this." Joan's brown eyes had been warm and concerned as she sat on the edge of the bed. "You've got to get some help."

"No one can help me," Susanna had said, her tears splotching her silk pajama top. "No one can bring Rachel back. Nothing matters anymore."

"What about Tom? Doesn't he matter?" Joan had asked.

The question had startled Susanna. "Well, yes, of course."

Joan had taken her hand between her palms. "Tom needs you, Susanna. You've got to pull yourself together for his sake. He's lost a child, too. He needs you to be there for him." Then Joan had played her trump card: "It's not like you to let down the people you love."

It had worked. Susanna had agreed to see a doctor. Joan had called her father's internist, wrangled an appointment for that very afternoon, and taken Susanna to see him. The physician had diagnosed severe depression. He'd prescribed an antidepressant and scheduled weekly follow-up visits.

Joan had flown back to Chicago three days later, but she'd promised to call every day to make sure that Susanna was taking her medication. That had been six weeks ago. After two weeks, Susanna was feeling better. By four, she was shopping and lunching with old friends. By five, she was back to playing tennis.

"How's Tom?" Joan had asked on the phone just last week.

"Busy. Seems like I hardly ever see him," had been Susanna's answer. Her husband had been in the middle of a long, complicated, antitrust trial in Dallas when Susanna had first begun treatment, and he'd spent three weeks in Texas. When he'd returned to Tulsa, he'd immediately become embroiled in helping another client fight off a hostile takeover attempt, and he'd been so busy with work that he'd hardly noticed Susanna's improvement.

"Don't you think you need to do something to change that?" Joan had prompted, when Susanna had related that fact.

"What do you suggest?" She had asked.

"Well, for starters, get him back in your bedroom."

Tom had started sleeping in the guest room nine months ago, when Susanna's insomnia kept her up most of the night. At the time, it had seemed like a good solution; Susanna could read in bed and not disturb him, and he could get a good night's sleep. Lately, though, it had just seemed lonely.

But it had been lonely long before they took to separate bedrooms, Susanna thought with a painful twinge. Rachel's death had killed Susanna's interest in everything, including sex. Each time Tom had reached for her, she'd pulled away. After a while, he'd just stopped reaching.

"I'm no therapist, but separate bedrooms can't be very good for your marriage," Joan said.

"I know." Susanna had sighed into the phone. "Joanie, this is going to sound really stupid, but . . ." She hesitated, then just plunged ahead with the embarrassing confession. "I don't have a clue how to get him back in my bed."

Joan had laughed. "It's like riding a bike. It'll all come back the moment you start."

"So how do I start?"

"Well, you might try talking to him." Even now, riding in the car with her husband, Susanna could hear the smile in her friend's voice. "Tell him you've missed him. I bet he'll take it from there."

"I hope you're right," Susanna had replied. "Lately it seems like he's moved farther away than just down the hall."

It was Joan's turn to hesitate. "Do you think there's someone else?"

Susanna had been shocked. "Oh, no. It never entered my mind." Another woman? The idea was incomprehensible. "I just meant . . . well, we've lost touch. We hardly talk to each other. It's like we've become strangers."

"Well, then, get reacquainted," Joan had urged. "Tell him how you feel. And if that doesn't work, I'm sure you can come up with a way of showing him."

That had been her intention when she'd gone to the airport to meet Tom. She'd thought he'd be pleased to see her out of the house, glad to see her interacting with friends and family. She'd thought an evening of dinner and pleasant conversation with Jake would break the ice between her and Tom. She thought they'd joke and laugh on the drive home, then open the champagne she'd left chilling in the refrigerator, and before they'd each finished a glass, they'd wind up in each other's arms.

That had been the plan—until she saw Tom walk out of the jetway, a tall, attractive blonde at his side. Tom had been listening to the woman intently, his head inclined in that way Susanna knew so well, a way that meant his full attention was focused. He'd thrown back his head and laughed in a way she hadn't seen in a long time. It was a young, sexy laugh, rich and full-bodied, the way he had laughed when they were dating.

The laugh had struck her as odd. But the way he'd sucked in his stomach when the woman looked at him— sucked in his stomach and straightened his back, the way a man does when he wants to look his best—well, that had made the hair rise on the back of her neck.

She'd felt the strangest stab of alarm, uneasy and out-of-place, as if she were somehow intruding. She'd an almost overpowering urge to turn and leave before he saw her. But then Tom spotted her, and she felt like a Peeping Tom who'd just been caught red-handed outside a bedroom window.

Tom had quickly introduced her to Kelly, and the explanation seemed natural enough—the woman was a fellow attorney who had been opposing counsel on a recent case. They'd attended the same legal conference, and had coincidentally booked the same flight home. There was nothing truly unusual about the situation, nothing except for the odd, frightened feeling it left in Susanna's gut.

She'd never been the jealous type. In thirty-three years of marriage, Susanna had never once doubted Tom's faithfulness. He'd always been a wonderful husband.

But then, until lately, she'd always been a wonderful wife. Lately, she realized with sudden, sickening clarity, she hadn't been much of a wife at all.

"Is there someone else?" Joanie's words floated through Susanna's mind now, as Tom steered the car onto their elegant, oak-lined street in north Tulsa. A cold, achy fear gripped her stomach. She tried to shake it off, but it held her fast. Tom was different—distant, removed, remote.

He pulled into the long drive that led to their house, hit the automatic garage door opener, and slid the car into the garage.

She followed him into the house, through the kitchen door. He dropped the keys on the kitchen counter.

"I've got a bottle of champagne in the fridge," she ventured. "Would you like some?"

"Champagne?" He couldn't have sounded more incredulous if she'd offered him an armadillo.

She nervously twisted her fingers together. Throughout their marriage, they'd always shared champagne on special occasions—anniversaries, Christmas, New Year's. "I—I put it in to chill before I picked you up at the airport. I thought . . ."

She took a hesitant step forward, feeling unnaturally awkward.

Tom regarded her warily. She stopped and swallowed hard. "Look . . . I—I know I haven't been much of a wife to you lately. I haven't been myself. But the medicine is helping, and I'm better. I'm even sleeping through the night again."

Tom looked away. "Good. I'm glad to hear it."

Susanna's heart pounded hard. This was her husband, for heaven's sake. She had every right to make a pass at him.

Screwing up her courage, she took another step toward him, stopping at his side. She placed her hand on his chest. "I—I'd like it if you'd move back to our bedroom."

Tom stood stock-still, but she felt his heart pick up speed under her hand. He cleared his throat in that way that meant he was uneasy. "Gee, Suze, I don't think tonight's a good night for that. I'm upset about Jake's news. And I've, uh, got a headache." Tom's hand patted hers. His lips curved in a reassuring smile, but his eyes never quite met hers. "I'm afraid I'd just toss and turn and keep you awake. I don't want to set you back just when you're making progress."

A huge lump clotted her throat, making it hard to speak, much less to muster a smile. She tried nonetheless. "Okay."

He kissed her cheek, a soft, brotherly peck. Susanna's heart broke into a million pieces. She quickly turned her back to him, trying hard to hide the tears that sprang to her eyes. "Well, I'm going to turn in. Good night."

She hurried upstairs to the master bedroom, stifling back a sob, trying to stifle the fear clutching at her throat as well.

She'd already lost her daughter. And now—dear heavens—was she losing her husband as well?

Chapter Six

Jake mounted the steps to Annie's front porch, squinting against the glare of the early morning sun rising over the shake-shingle roof. He'd left Tulsa before dawn, hoping to catch Annie before she started reading tea leaves or grooming llamas or whatever the hell it was she did all day.

Besides, he'd been up anyway, awakened by another of the troublesome dreams that had been plaguing him ever since he'd learned he had a child. Babies and billboards, llamas and teacups had paraded through his mind all night in a solemn procession. But more alarming that that were the erotic images that had awakened him this morning—images of Annie and her luscious breasts swaying tantalizingly above him. With a muttered oath, he'd thrown back the covers and taken a cold shower.

He was only dreaming about that Hollister woman because of the child, he'd told himself as he stood under the stream of icy water. He'd had a baby with her, and his subconscious was processing the information. It didn't take a Ph.D. in psychology to figure out that it was his mind's way of sorting through data, of trying to make sense of the situation. So what if he'd dreamed about pulling that Tweety Bird ponytail holder out of her flame-colored hair and tasting her berry-tinted lips and touching the slopes of her generous breasts? That didn't mean anything. It didn't mean anything at all.

Hell, she wasn't even his type. He'd always gone for women like Rachel, women who were sleek and pulled together, whose physical appearance reflected their rational, logical, low-key approach to life. His only interest in this Hollister dame had to do with his child.

His child. The thought sent a ripple of amazement racing through him. It was an astounding concept, one that was difficult to absorb, even after two days. A child. A daughter. A dark-haired, dark-eyed little girl named Madeline, who was already fourteen months old.

He'd missed out on her first year. He'd missed her first tooth, her first smile, her first step. Well, by golly, he didn't intend to miss out on any more. It could take a year or longer to reach a permanent custody settlement, especially if this Hollister woman fought him on it. What he needed to do was come to some sort of temporary arrangement with her.

He rapped hard on the front door, then stepped back, eyeing the pot of pink geraniums on the ground beside it. He'd gotten off to a bad start with Annie the other day, but he was sure he could fix that. Once he apologized and smoothed things over, he was certain he could convince the woman to see things his way. After all, he was an experienced negotiator, and the law was on his side. If the paternity tests showed what he was certain they would, he was sure to end up with joint custody.

It would be better for the child, he intended to argue, if he were allowed to develop a relationship with her as soon as possible.

He knocked again on the heavy wood door. Inside, a dog yapped noisily, but Annie still didn't answer. Maybe she was out back, tending to the animals. He turned around, ready to walk to the side of the house, when the door slowly creaked open.

He turned to see Annie standing in the doorway, clad in a short pink print dress, clutching her stomach. Her face was pale, and her eyes held the look of acute pain.

Jake stepped toward her. "Hey—are you all right?"

"I—I'm ill. I can't talk to you now."

"What's the matter?"

"I have the flu or something. Please—would you just go away?"

It was more than the flu. She looked like she was in agony. "What hurts?"

"M—my stomach. And I'm nauseous and dizzy and . . ." The dachshund darted out the door, and the baby, dressed in a yellow and white two-piece playsuit, toddled out right behind. Annie reached forward to stop the child, then doubled over, her hand on her stomach. "Ohh!"

Madeline plopped down on the porch by the dog, right at Jake's feet. He turned his attention back to Annie. "You need to see a doctor."

She started to straighten, but it evidently caused her too much pain. "Please—just go away. I'm in no shape to deal with you today."

Jake started to tell her she was in no shape to deal with a baby, either, then thought better of it. "How long have you been feeling like this?"

"It started yesterday. It got worse in the night, and by this morning . . ." Her voice trailed off.

"I'll take you to the hospital," he said decisively.

"No. I don't want you to take me anywhere."

"Well, then, I'll call an ambulance. You're in no condition to drive yourself." He pulled a cell phone out of his pocket.

Annie stared at the man's phone, weighing his words. As much as she hated to admit it, he was right. Her stomach hurt so much that she couldn't even stand up straight. She felt weak and light-headed, as if she might pass out at any moment. She'd barely been able to lift Madeline out of her crib this morning.

But she couldn't go off in an ambulance. What would she do with Madeline? The only babysitters she'd ever used were Ben and Helen, and they were in Tulsa.

"Where's the nearest hospital around here, anyway?" Jake asked, opening the phone.

"Bartlesville."

He clicked the phone closed. "Look—it makes a lot more sense to let me drive you. I can have you at the emergency room before the ambulance could even get here."

It was her turn to hesitate.

A nerve flicked in his jaw. "Look, lady—we can stand here arguing until you pass out, or we can get you to a doctor while you can still tell him what hurts. If you want your daughter to grow up with a mother, you'd better get in my car and let me give you a ride."

He sure knew what button to punch, mentioning Madeline. "All—all right. But we have to get the baby's car seat out of my truck."

"Do you need anything else?"

"My purse. And the baby's bag. They're on a hook in the kitchen beside the garage door."

Jake nodded. "Okay. Let's get you to the car, then I'll get your things."

Annie turned loose of the door and took a step forward. A wave of searing pain rose up like heat from a summer pavement, making everything seem wavy and red.

She felt Jake's hand on her arm, steadying her. "Hey—you'd better let me help you."

His forearm was hard and sturdy under the starched white cotton of his shirt. Annie gripped it tightly. "Madeline. . . ." she muttered.

"She's fine. She's still sitting on the porch, trying to grab the dog's tail. I'll bring her to the car as soon as I get you settled."

The next thing Annie knew, he'd picked her up, one hand under her knees, the other under her back. Her cheek pressed against his. She felt the roughened smoothness of freshly shaved skin, and inhaled the faint scent of shaving cream.

He carried her down the steps and across the gravel drive, setting her down beside the car while he opened the door. He helped her into the seat, then strode to the porch and picked up Madeline.

The baby howled in protest as he carried her to the car. "In you go," he said to the child, placing her in the back seat.

Madeline immediately quieted, no doubt delighted at the novelty of being in an unfamiliar vehicle. "Stay here with your mommy. I'll be right back."

The next thing Annie knew, Jake had returned with the car seat, her purse, and the bag. It took him a couple of minutes to strap in the child seat, but he finally managed. Madeline protested loudly as he lifted her up and fastened her in.

Annie leaned her head against the headrest, trying

hard not to think about the knifelike pain slicing through her. Jake started the engine, put the car into gear, and headed out of the drive, kicking up a rooster tail of dust.

Annie closed her eyes against a fresh wave of nausea. She couldn't believe she was letting this man take charge like he was. Yesterday she'd considered leaving the country to avoid him. But she had no choice now. She was sick, so very, very sick. Sick enough to die.

Oh, dear God—if she died, what would happen to Madeline? The thought caused a surge of alarm. She couldn't die. She wouldn't. People her age didn't die of stomachaches in this day and age, anyway.

Did they?

Jake glanced over at her. "Do you have any family or friends you want me to contact?" he asked, as if he were reading her mind.

"No." Annie clutched her side as he turned onto the highway. The pain was excruciating.

"Well, is there a babysitter or someone you want me to call if you have to be hospitalized?"

Hospitalized—that was a very real possibility. The direness of her situation hit her hard. "I—I've never used a babysitter except my ranch foreman and his wife, and they're out of town for the next few weeks." A feeling of panic gripped her belly, along with a heightened sense of pain. Her lip trembled. "I—I don't have anyone to watch the baby."

"Yes, you do." His dark eyes flashed toward her, his expression grim. "You have me."

Oh, dear Lord—she couldn't leave Madeline with the man who'd all but threatened to take her away from her.

Still . . . what else could she do? Pearl couldn't manage the child, even if the nursing home would allow it. Annie sank back against the headrest and closed her eyes, feeling worse than ever.

* * *

Half an hour later, Jake sat in the empty emergency room waiting area, watching the baby toddle from green vinyl chair to green vinyl chair. He'd tried holding her on his lap, but the child had no more use for him than her mother did. Every time he got within three feet of the little girl, she screamed as if he were a three-headed monster.

The door that led to the examining rooms wheezed open. Jake rose as a short, gray-haired man in a white medical coat walked into the waiting area. An ID tag pinned to his jacket identified him as an emergency room physician. "Are you with Annie Hollister?"

"Yes."

"It's her appendix," the doctor said. "It needs to come out immediately. I've already sent her up to O.R."

Jake swallowed, absorbing the news.

"Dr. Meyers will be her surgeon," the doctor continued. "He's one of our best. He has thirty years of experience, used to work at a big hospital in Dallas. He was scrubbing up for an elective procedure when your wife came in. Since her condition's critical, he'll take her first."

Wife. The word hit him like a hard left to the jaw. "She's not . . ."

Jake stopped in mid-sentence. Doctors usually only gave information to the next of kin. He'd be better served by keeping his mouth shut. "She's not in any real danger, is she?" he amended.

"Not if her appendix doesn't rupture."

Crimony. Jake didn't like the grim set to the doctor's mouth. "Is that likely?"

"We hope not. But it needs to come out as soon as possible. It's extremely inflamed." The doctor pointed to an elevator. "The surgical waiting room is on the second floor. Dr. Meyers will look for you there after the surgery to tell you how it went."

"Okay. Thanks."

The doctor's gaze fixed on something behind Jake. "Your baby—she's, uh, eating dirt out of the planter."

Jake whirled around to find Madeline under a potted ficus, her face coated with black soil. He covered the distance in four long strides and picked her up. Angry at being interrupted, Madeline howled like an injured coyote, dribbling wet soil all over the front of Jake's white shirt.

Crimony—how was he supposed to deal with this? Juggling the child in one arm, Jake awkwardly felt in the pocket of his slacks for a tissue, but only came up with his keys and wallet.

The baby coughed, spitting more dirt on his shirt. Good grief—how much of that stuff had she crammed in her mouth? She was spewing soil like a volcano. He held her over his shoulder and patted her on the back, but then her cough deepened to an alarming gag.

He held her out and gazed at her. Her mouth was still caked with dirt. Panic flooded Jake's veins as she made a wet, choking sound.

Where the hell had that doctor gone? Where were the nurses? This was a hospital, for heavens' sake; where were all the medical personnel? "Nurse! Nurse!" he yelled.

Madeline gave a raspy wheeze. He had to do something; if he didn't clear the dirt out of Madeline's mouth and throat, she was likely to choke to death.

Desperate for something, anything, to use to clean the child's mouth, Jake yanked his shirttail out of his slacks. Plopping the baby on her back on the carpet, he used the end of his shirt to swab clumps of dirt out of the child's mouth.

Madeline gagged and sputtered, then sat up and let out an angry howl.

Relief, warm and sweet, rushed through Jake's chest. He picked up the screaming baby and held her against his shoulder. "Hey, now—don't blame me. You're the one who ate the darn dirt."

The baby yelled all the louder. Her tiny hands flailed at his chest and back, and her little feet kicked wildly. Jake walked around the room, trying to calm her down, but he only succeeded in making her screech all the more.

A heavyset woman in thick eyeglasses and green scrubs pushed a cleaning cart through the door. She smiled at Madeline in that soft, goo-goo-eyed way some women get when they look at babies.

"Oh, my—you're quite a mess, aren't you, sweetie?" the cleaning lady crooned.

The baby immediately stopped yowling and smiled.

"Do you have some paper towels I could borrow?" Jake asked.

"Sure." The lady grabbed a roll from her cart. "Here—I'll clean her little face."

The baby quietly let her do just that.

"We need to get those little hands, too, don't we?"

Madeline meekly let her wipe first one, then the other hand. "There we go. Much better." The woman's gaze raked over Jake. Her eyes twinkled with amusement behind her thick glasses. "My, my, my," she said to Madeline. "Looks like you got Daddy all dirty."

Madeline gave a gummy grin and laughed.

"Can I hold you while Daddy cleans up?" The cleaning lady held out her arms. Madeline eagerly went to the woman, cooing happily.

Jake didn't know which was more disconcerting—being called Daddy or having his child show such an obvious preference for a stranger. He stared down at his shirt and grimaced. Good grief, he looked like he'd just crawled out of a mud-wrestling pit. Grabbing a handful of paper towels, Jake mopped at the stains. Instead of improving the situation, his efforts only seemed to make it worse. The dirt spread and fanned out on his shirt like fine black powder.

"What kind of potting soil do you use around here, anyway?" Jake said, wiping at the smears on his chest.

The woman grabbed at her glasses as Madeline playfully pulled them off her face. "Oh, dear. That must be the volcanic ash our gardener has just started adding."

"Great. Just great." With a heavy sigh, Jake crossed the room to the trash receptacle, threw the paper towels away, then strode back, eyeing the baby. Madeline's playsuit was filthy, but she wore a huge smile on her face. At least her temperament seemed to have taken a turn for the better.

"Thanks for your help," Jake told the cleaning lady. He reached for the child, only to have Madeline throw her arms around the woman's neck and caterwaul.

The woman's eyebrows rose. The look she cast him was clearly appraising, as if she suspected he was a convicted child beater.

Jake pried the yowling baby's arms from around the woman's neck, shooting her a sheepish smile. She watched him carry the screaming child toward the elevator. "You're forgetting your diaper bag," she called. "You're sure to need it."

Jake hurried back and grabbed the item, trying not to think about what event would precipitate his need for it.

Madeline was still screeching when the elevator door opened on the second floor several moments later. Fortunately, the waiting room was right around the corner.

"Here you go," Jake said, setting the baby on her feet

just inside the entrance. Madeline immediately fell silent, putting all of her efforts into waddling across the room.

Jake followed, taking note of the room's occupants. Two elderly ladies in identical navy blue dresses sat together near the window. On the far side, a lanky young man, probably eighteen or nineteen years old, slumped in a chair, his head against the wall, wearing an expression of disdainful indifference. His left ear held more studs than a framing carpenter's pick-up. His hair was cut in a Mohawk and dyed the color of strawberry Jell-O.

Jake sat down near the baby. Madeline looked up at him, scrunched up her face, and gave a scream straight from a *Friday the Thirteenth* movie.

"What an adorable child," one of the elderly women remarked.

Her companion nodded. "Yes, indeed. Looks just like you, too."

"That's right," the first one agreed. "She has your eyes, and your hair color, and your chin."

"Not to mention the similarity in our shirts," Jake said dryly.

The white-haired woman gave a high-pitched titter that reminded Jake of a tropical bird. "Now that you mention it, you two are dirty as a pair of grave diggers. What happened?"

"Lilly!" the gray-haired one said in an appalled tone. "That's rude."

"Sorry." She turned back to Jake. "So what happened?"

Jake glanced down at his grime-covered shirt. He was chagrinned to realize that the tail was still hanging out, but he wasn't about to give these old biddies the satisfaction of seeing him tuck it in. He cleared his throat and watched Madeline toddle away from him. "The baby tried to eat some dirt."

The women giggled—both of them in that weird, high-pitched, birdlike cackle.

"Babies," said the gray-hair, shaking her head. "They'll put anything in their mouths that they can find. You have to watch them like a hawk."

"Like a vulture," the white-haired one piped in, apparently not wanting to be outdone.

The gray-headed woman flashed a pair of unnaturally white false teeth. "I'm Violet, and this is my sister Lilly. Is someone in your family having surgery?"

"Yes."

They looked at him expectantly. Jake sighed. He hated making conversation with strangers, but these two weren't likely to take a hint and leave him alone.

Sure enough, the older of the two leaned forward. "So who is it?"

"The, uh, baby's mother."

"Ohhh." Violet nodded sagely, then cast a meaningful glance at Lilly. "She must be the hot one."

Jake's eyes widened. "Excuse me?"

"The one with the hot appendix. That's medical talk. I heard it on TV."

Thank goodness. For a moment there, he'd been afraid the two old women had some dirt to dish on Annie. He turned and watched Madeline crawl under a chair. She was already filthy, so Jake supposed there was no reason to keep her off the floor.

"We just love medical shows," Violet was saying. "We watch them all."

Jake knew several elderly people in Tulsa who frequented the courthouse and attended trials for entertainment. Maybe these two did the same thing at hospitals.

"So . . . do you come here when there's nothing on the tube?"

The teenager coughed. Jake looked over, and the boy quickly looked away, but Jake was certain he saw a ghost of a smile cross the boy's face before he resumed his expression of studied disinterest.

Violet batted her eyes. "Oh, no. We're waiting on our sister Rose."

"Yes," the second one explained. "She's having a hernia fixed."

Jake was unaware that women got hernias, but he wasn't about to encourage the conversation.

"Of course, Rose's surgery has been postponed since your wife's condition is so serious," Lilly continued.

Jake squirmed. He was uncomfortable hearing Annie called his wife, but even more uncomfortable hearing about the severity of her condition. "Who told you that?"

"The O.R. nurse."

"That's slang for Operating Room," Lilly chimed in. "She said a young woman with a hot appendix needed surgery right away, and they were going to do her before Rose."

Some kind of apology seemed called for. "I, uh, hope the delay doesn't inconvenience your sister too much."

"Oh, no." Violet waved her hand in a dismissive gesture. "It'll just give her more time to enjoy the drugs." She leaned forward conspiratorially. "The doctor gave her a sedative first thing this morning, and she said it gave her a better buzz than two after-dinner sherries."

The teenager coughed fitfully. Jake glanced at him, finding the boy's efforts not to laugh aloud as entertaining as the two sisters' chatter.

"Rose is ninety-two years old," Lilly contributed. "I'm two years younger. Violet, here, is the baby. She's just eighty-nine."

107

The teenager's coughing attack worsened, requiring both hands to completely cover his mouth. Jake decided to try to make the teenager lose it.

He looked at the two women. "You two certainly don't look your age."

"We know." Violet stuck out her chest and smiled proudly. "It's hereditary. We come from a family of long livers."

Jake carefully kept his expression bland. "Is that related to cirrhosis?"

The teenager snorted.

"Oh, no," Lilly said earnestly. "Violet means our kinfolk live long lives. Our father lived to be a hundred and one, and our mother was a hundred and seven when she finally passed on. They were married seventy-eight years. Both of their fathers fought in the War between the . . ." Her voice broke off. "Oh, my! Your baby's gotten ahold of something."

Jake whipped his head around to see Madeline sitting under a chair, merrily sucking on a shiny object. He sprang to his feet, bolted across the room, and hauled the baby out into the open floor. The lower part of her face was smeared black, and her lips seemed to have disappeared. Jake yanked the object out of her mouth.

It was a large felt-tip marker.

"Oh, hell." Jake grabbed his shirttail again, and once more tried to swab out the baby's mouth. As before, the child screamed at an eardrum-piercing volume.

For all of his efforts, Jake wasn't making any progress. His shirt was gaining additional grime, but he didn't see any lessening of the blackness in the baby's mouth. It was black as pitch, and the blackness stretched all the way to the back of her tonsils—which she was showing to advantage as she yelped at full volume.

Alarm raced through Jake. "Hey—does anyone know if ink is poisonous?"

The pink-haired teenager squatted beside him and picked up the marker. "It says right here it's nontoxic."

Relief gushed through Jake. "Thank God."

Yanking away from Jake, Madeline threw herself at the teenager as if he were a life raft on a storm-tossed sea. Her crying stopped as she crawled onto his lap. She grinned up engagingly, her mouth looking like a coal mine at night.

The boy's eyes grew wide with alarm. "Hey! What's she doin'?"

"Sitting on your lap. She likes you," Lilly proclaimed.

The baby continued to grin. Despite himself, the boy smiled back. "Ya know, she looks kinda cool," he said. "She's kinda got a Goth look goin'."

"She's a sight, that's for sure," Lilly agreed.

No kidding, Jake thought. Her once-yellow playsuit was covered with marker smudge, ground-in volcanic ash and under-chair grime, and her mouth looked like a black hole.

He was going to have to be more watchful, Jake realized ruefully. It didn't take three seconds for the child to find trouble, and it took even less time for her to get smack in the middle of it.

"It might take a while, but that ink will wear off eventually." The gray-haired woman flashed her dentures in an encouraging smile. "My son got sprayed by a skunk once. It took three weeks, but it finally faded."

The teenager made a face. "Hey, man, speakin' of skunks . . . I think you need to do somethin' with her diaper."

Jake's spirits plummeted. Holy Moses—he didn't know anything about changing diapers. Maybe one of the elderly ladies would help him out. He looked over, about to ask, when the gray-haired one leaned over to her sister.

"Isn't it wonderful, Lilly, how involved fathers are these days? I think it's just marvelous, the way they take care of their little ones."

Lilly's white hair bobbed like a snowball as she nodded. "Things are sure different than they used to be. Nowadays, any dad worth his salt pulls his weight with child care. That's what all the TV shows say."

Ye gads. He sure as hell didn't want to explain to these gals why he'd never spent any time around his own child and didn't have a clue how do something as basic as changing a diaper. Besides, how the heck hard could it be?

Chapter Seven

A whole lot harder than he'd ever imagined, Jake thought twenty minutes later. Why the devil wasn't there someplace to change a baby in the men's room? He couldn't very well lay the baby down on the bare bathroom floor. The only other option was to change her while she was standing. That meant trailing after her and repeatedly trying to steer her away from the urinals, which seemed to hold a strange fascination for her.

"Come on, now, Madeline—hold still for a moment, would you?"

Madeline responded by tottering bare-assed across the room, back toward one of the three urinals. Jake hurried after her, diaper in hand. He'd managed to get her clean, thank heavens—although it had taken the entire box of wet wipes in the diaper bag to do it. What was eluding him now was the trick of taping the diaper so it would stay on. He'd accidently ripped one diaper while trying to refasten the tape, and he didn't want to strike out with the only other one he had. In the game of diapers, apparently each player got only one shot.

Madeline had nearly reached the object of her affection. Her pudgy hand was a split second from making contact with the urinal rim when Jake grabbed her around the chest in a modified wrestling hug and swung her around. As expected, she let loose a wail of protest loud enough to shatter glass.

"Come on, now, Madeline. Help me out a little." Working with one hand, he managed to get the diaper between her legs. He needed both hands free to fasten the tape, but the moment he loosened his hold on her, the child darted back to the urinal as fast as her fat little legs could carry her. The diaper fell to the floor behind her.

Jake picked it up and dashed in pursuit, vaguely recalling a magazine article that theorized people were motivated all of their lives by their earliest thwarted desires. If that was the case, then Madeline was probably destined to a life as a restroom attendant.

Grumbling under his breath, he tackled her again, and was once more treated to an ear-numbing shriek. Holding her between his knees, he got one side of the diaper fastened before the child broke free again. After another brief struggle, he taped the other side. His sense of victory was short-lived, however; the diaper drooped to her knees as she scurried back to a urinal.

Well, he'd just have to rely on her bloomers to hold the darn thing up. Now, if he could just get her legs back into those blasted things . . .

Ten minutes later, Jake emerged from the men's room, the pink diaper bag slung over his shoulder, a yowling baby in his arms, feeling like a war-weary soldier returning from the field of battle. He'd made it halfway down the hall to the waiting room when a warm sensation slithered wetly down his stomach.

"Oh, good *Lord!*"

He immediately thrust Madeline out at arm's length, where she proceeded to water his shoes. He gingerly set the dripping child down on the floor, only to have her look up and give an engaging, black-mouthed grin.

Jake felt a nerve twitch in his cheek. Drawing a deep breath, he picked her up under her arms and awkwardly carried her back to the men's room. There he peeled off her clothes and sponged her down with paper towels. The moment he released her, she headed straight back to a urinal.

Jake dashed after the naked baby. *What the Dow Jones am I supposed to do now?* he wondered. He'd used the last of the diapers, and her clothes were sopping wet. Holding the squirming, howling child under his arm, he rummaged through the diaper bag, hoping to find something he'd overlooked. All he turned up was a small flannel blanket printed with large yellow ducks.

He eyed it appraisingly. Babies had worn cloth diapers for centuries. The blanket was cloth. Hell, he could diaper her with it—if he could just figure out a way to hold it up.

Jake looked through the bag hoping to find some safety pins. No such luck—just a sandwich bag filled with Cheerios, an empty baby bottle, and two small jars of apple juice.

"Looks like we'll have to improvise, Madeline." Jake looked around the room, hoping to find something, anything with which to improvise. There was nothing—just toilet paper, paper towels, and soap.

He glanced down, and his gaze seized on his belt. "That's it!" Jake rapidly tugged it out of the belt loops of his slacks. It took fifteen minutes and countless sprints around the room—not to mention ruining his new Italian leather belt by poking an unsightly hole in the middle with the tongue of the buckle—but at last Madeline was clothed. Jake stepped back and surveyed his handiwork. He'd slung the blanket under the baby like a thong, then draped the top end over one shoulder and tucked it back between her legs. The belt was cinched around her waist, holding the whole thing in place.

From the standpoint of engineering, it was something of a marvel. On the up side, it worked. On the down side, the child looked like a duck-covered version of Tarzan.

Well, at least she was clean and dry—which was more than he could say about himself.

Maybe he could occupy the baby with some Cheerios long enough to allow him a chance to clean up. Jake spread a dozen paper towels on the floor, pulled the Cheerios out of the diaper bag and held them over the towels like bait. To his relief, the baby grabbed the sandwich bag, plopped down on the towels, and enthusiastically began shoving the cereal into her blackened mouth.

Jake turned to the mirror over the sink. The sight that greeted him there was not a pretty one. Using the hand soap, he washed off the front of his shirt the best he could, wringing the fabric in the sink. The volcanic ash and marker ink refused to budge, but at least he managed to rinse out the residue of Madeline's sprinkler system. Instead of improving the shirt's appearance, though, he only made it wetter and more wrinkled than it had been before.

He gazed down at his feet. His black socks were drenched, so he peeled them off and stuffed them in the trash. He rolled up the bottom of his slacks, rinsed his feet one at a time in the sink, then slipped back into his dress wingtips.

He'd just finished tying them when Madeline decided to make another break for the urinal. "Enough of this," Jake muttered. Hell, he'd been in here nearly an hour. Scooping up the loudly protesting baby, he grabbed the bag and headed back out into the hall. Madeline writhed and yelled as if he were stretching her on the rack.

The pink-haired boy met him in the hall. "Hey—you just missed the doc. Your wife is out of surgery, and the doc said she's askin' to see the baby."

Madeline screamed like a howler monkey, making it nearly impossible for Jake to hear. She stretched her arms out for the boy.

He looked at Jake questioningly.

"Please," Jake urged. "Be my guest. Go ahead and take her."

The baby settled in the boy's arms and began to coo happily.

"She doesn't seem to like you much," the boy remarked.

No kidding. Jake decided to ignore the observation. "So where's the doctor?" he asked.

"He had to go do the old woman's hernia. But he said your wife is fine. She's just waking up. He said you can go in and see her."

"Where is she?"

"In recovery. It's over there." He pointed to a set of double green doors.

Jake reached for Madeline. To his chagrin, the child shrieked and hid her head in the crook of the boy's neck.

Jake rubbed his jaw and jammed his hands in his pocket. "You know, Madeline really seems to have taken a shine to you. You must have a way with women."

The boy grinned. The expression gave his face an unexpectedly wholesome look. "That's what my girlfriend says. She's the one I'm waitin' on." He shifted Madeline to his other arm. "She's here havin' plastic surgery."

"Is that a fact." Jake couldn't help but wonder what part of her body was getting the plastic. Probably her breasts. From what he'd read, young women got implants as routinely as tetanus shots.

"It's her nose," the boy volunteered.

"You don't say." Jake shifted uneasily. "Well, I imagine a lot of people aren't happy with their noses."

"Oh, she liked hers just fine—until her nose ring got caught on a waitress's sweater at the Burger Barn."

Jake winced.

"Ripped her nostril right in two. The Burger Barn's payin' for the surgery, though."

Jake had had clients pay through the nose before, but never quite so literally. He watched Madeline merrily blow a bubble at the boy with her black mouth. "Listen—would you mind carrying the baby into the Recovery Room for me so her mother won't see her crying? I'll pay you ten bucks."

The boy looked at Madeline's black grinning mouth and shrugged his bony shoulders. "Okay. Sure."

Annie floated in a sea of grogginess, vaguely aware of bright overhead lights, a large white room, and a nurse in blue floral medical scrubs hovering over her. It was hard to keep her eyes open, but she fought to do so. "Is my daughter here yet?"

"I'm sure she'll be here any minute."

Annie struggled to sit up, but she couldn't. The nurse was at her side, adjusting her pillow. "It's going take a while for the anesthesia to wear off," she cautioned. "If you move around too much, you're likely to get a headache. It'll be best if you lie still and relax."

"I want to see my child."

"I'll let you know the moment she gets here."

Annie heard a noise on the far side of the room. The nurse smiled. "I bet that's her now."

"Madeline?" Annie called, turning her head on the pillow. Flat on her back like this, she had a limited range of vision.

"She's right here." The deep husky voice that responded from across the room could only belong to Jake. *Thank God.* Annie had been terrified that he'd taken off with her child while she was unconscious.

A familiar, babyish babble filled her heart with relief. "Bring her around here so I can see her," she said eagerly.

The nurse stepped back into her line of vision, her face drawn in a frown, her eyes worried. "On second thought . . . maybe you should wait and see the baby later."

Ignoring her, Annie craned her neck on the pillow, eager for a glimpse of her child.

The sight that greeted her was something of a shock. Blinking hard, Annie stared in disbelief, wondering if the anesthesia was making her see things.

It was a child, all right—*her* child, in fact. But instead of wearing the yellow two-piece playsuit Annie had dressed her in that morning, Madeline was clad in some sort of George of the Jungle costume. Most disconcerting of all, her lips were painted a light-absorbing shade of black.

Madeline squealed and gave Annie a wide grin. Oh, dear heavens—it wasn't just her lips. Her tongue and her gums were pitch black, too. The whole inside of her mouth, in fact, was dark as a bat cave. Her two bottom teeth looked like tiny, gray-tinged stalagmites.

"What—what have you done to my baby?" Annie gasped.

She pulled her gaze away from the child up to the

117

face of the person holding her, and her heart stopped in her chest. It wasn't Jake—it was an acne-riddled teenager with shaved sidewalls and a streak of pink hair that stood straight up on the top of his head, like the spine plate on a stegosaurus.

Jake's face appeared behind teenager's pink tufts. "She's fine. She just got hold of a felt-tip marker, that's all."

"She ate ink?" Annie said weakly.

"It was nontoxic. There's no need to worry."

No need to worry? Her baby's mouth was black as tar, she was dressed like Pebbles Flintstone, she was in the arms of a kid who made Charles Manson look like *GQ*'s man of the year, and all from being cared for by a man who wanted custody!

Annie gazed weakly up at Jake. "Where are her clothes?"

"She got them wet. She had a couple of diaper, er, situations."

"No joke," The boy muttered, rolling his eyes and wrinkling his nose.

Annie stared from Jake face to the boy, then back again. "And this is . . . ?"

Jake looked at the boy uncertainly. "Well, this is . . . uh . . ."

"Spike," the boy contributed. "I like to be called Spike."

"We just met," Jake explained. "In the waiting room. He's been helping me take care of Madeline."

Spike looked like he needed a caretaker himself. His pants were so baggy they looked in danger of falling off, and his left ear held more costume jewelry than most department stores even stocked. Madeline reached for a shiny gold hoop.

"Ow!" Spike howled. "Get her off my ear!"

Jake stepped forward and pried the child's fingers away from the earring. Madeline's hand immediately went back for more.

The boy ducked his head to the side, like a prize-fighter avoiding a punch. "Here—you take her." He shoved the child into Jake's arms. "I don't want my ears to end up like my girlfriend's nose."

Madeline complained loudly, her hand still outstretched for Spike's ear. The boy moved out of reach. "No way, kiddo. I'm outta here."

The teenager turned to Jake and held out his hand, palm up. Setting the baby on the floor, Jake rummaged in his pocket for a bill and handed it to the boy.

Madeline tottered over to Annie's bed and reached up as the boy left the room. Annie started to stretch out her hand, but was stopped by the IV tube. She settled for smiling down at her child. "Hello, sweetie."

"Ma-ma-ma-ma-ma."

"Did she just say Mama?" Jake asked in surprise.

"Yes." Annie grinned at her child, who was merrily blowing bubbles with her black mouth.

"She can talk?"

"She's learning to."

"Ma-ma-ma-ma-ma," Madeline repeated. Annie felt a wave of relief wash over her. Her child might look bizarre, but she appeared to be just fine.

Jake stepped forward and grabbed the baby as she tottered toward the IV stand. Annie gasped. He'd been standing behind Spike, and with the limited range of vision her flat-on-her-back position afforded, she hadn't yet seen his clothes. "Good heavens!"

The man who'd previously been expensively dressed and exquisitely well-groomed was wearing a wrinkled, filthy shirt with a blackened shirttail. His gray slacks were wet and rolled up, and he'd somehow lost his socks. He looked like a shipwreck victim from an episode of Gilligan's Island. "What happened to you?"

"Madeline happened."

"She did all that?"

Jake nodded grimly. "It looks worse than it is." He took a step toward her, his eyes dark and concerned. "The important question here is, how are you?"

Annie's heart pounded abnormally fast as he drew near. "Okay, I guess. The nurse said everything went just fine."

"Are you in any pain?"

"Not much. I'm pretty drugged up." Madeline's head poked up over the side of the mattress. Annie fingered the baby's curls. "They said I'll have to stay in here for a day or two."

"So I heard. I'll watch the baby for you."

Even in her woozy state, Annie knew her options were limited. Still, she didn't know which she felt more acutely, relief or worry. "I hate for you to do that. She can be a handful, and you have to watch her all the time. . . ."

"So I've learned."

Annie hesitated. "I want her to stay in familiar surroundings. I—I don't want you taking her to Tulsa."

"Okay. I'll keep her at your house."

Annie swallowed, her mouth dry. "What about your wife? Will she mind? Or will she come and help you?"

A cloud seemed to pass over Jake's face. "My wife is dead."

A rush of confused emotions poured over Annie. She was too full of anesthesia to think clearly, to figure out what this might mean to his pursuit of custody. All she knew was that she felt an undeniable sense of relief. She hadn't liked the idea of another woman in the picture, but she didn't know why. She'd sort it all out later. "I didn't know. I'm sorry."

Jake nodded and looked down at the baby, who was now examining the underside of the bed. "Tell me about the care and feeding of Madeline. What does she eat?"

Annie felt as if her brain was swaddled in cotton. She struggled to focus her thoughts. "Mainly finger foods— soft things that she can chew with her gums. There's a home-made chicken noodle casserole in the fridge at home that she likes, and there are several jars of baby food in the pantry. She likes applesauce and bananas and peaches and cheese and crackers . . . And she loves to snack on Cheerios. She drinks milk and juice. The pediatrician gave me a list of recommended foods for her age. It's on the refrigerator door."

"Okay. What else?"

"She takes a nap for about an hour and a half after lunch. She likes to be read to and rocked. And she likes to go for rides in her stroller, and to swing in the baby swing in the backyard."

Annie ran her free hand through her hair, wracking her fuzzy-feeling head. "She goes to bed at eight. She gets a bath first. Put the water up to her waist, not too warm or too cold, and don't ever leave her alone in the tub—not even for a second." She gave Jake the most serious look she could manage. "I mean it. If the phone or doorbell ring, either ignore it or pull her out and take her with you."

Jake nodded solemnly.

"She likes to play with her rubber duck and her boat, and she'll try to eat the soap if you're not careful." Annie closed her eyes. She was tired, so very tired. The anesthesia pulled at her, threatening to drag her back under its spell.

She forced her eyes back open. "Her pajamas are in

121

the top drawer of her bureau in her room. She likes to drink a bottle of milk before she goes to bed, and then you need to clean her teeth with a washcloth."

The nurse approached from the opposite side of the room and smiled at Jake. "I think you need to let your wife rest now."

The comment caught Annie off-guard. "Oh, he's not my husband."

The nurse's cheeks flamed. "Sorry. He looks so much like the baby, I just assumed he was the baby's father."

"I *am* the baby's father." He spoke to the nurse, but he looked straight at Annie.

The nurse froze, her pink-lipsticked mouth open. Her face colored. "Well, um, I'm still afraid you'll have to leave now. We limit visiting time in here. You can see your, um, *girlfriend* again once she gets settled in a room."

Annie reached out and gripped Jake's hand. It felt warm and strong, and she had a senseless urge to cling to it. "You'll take good care of Madeline, won't you?"

"I promise."

"Promise me one more thing." Annie's voice came out low and raspy. "Promise me you won't steal her."

"Steal her?" Jake's brow knit together.

Annie tried to nod. "I know you want custody, and . . ." She drew a deep breath. Henry had told her she needed to work out an arrangement with Jake. Now would be a good time to say she was willing to discuss it later, but she couldn't bring herself to say the words. She didn't want to share her child. She drew a shaky breath. "Madeline needs me. And I—I need her."

Jake's dark gaze settled on hers. For a moment, she thought his eyes softened. His hand tightened around hers. "I won't try to take her away from you. Madeline and I will both be here when you get out of the hospital."

Annie didn't know why, but she believed him. Releasing her hand, he bent down and picked up the child. Madeline wailed a protest.

"You just concentrate on getting well. I'll bring Madeline back to see you tomorrow."

Annie watched them turn toward the door. Madeline stared at her over Jake's shoulder, crying pathetically. Annie's heart turned over.

"She likes to be rocked and read to at bedtime," she called. "She likes lullabies, too."

Madeline's wails grew louder. Jake adjusted her in his arms and turned back to Annie. "Sorry—I couldn't hear that last part. What did you say?"

"She likes lullabies. And, Jake—she'll usually stop crying if you'll give her a Binkie."

The baby was crying at full volume, her mouth close to his ear. Jake stared at her so oddly that she wasn't sure he'd understood, but then he nodded and pushed the door open.

Chapter Eight

The dachshund sat below the kitchen table and eagerly wagged its tail, waiting for Madeline to drop more crumbs on the kitchen floor. The little dog's vigilance was soon rewarded.

"Slow down, Madeline," Jake said as Hot Dog's tongue mopped the floor. "No one's going to take it away from you."

Madeline gave Jake a big grin, exposing a mouthful of sponge cake and cream filling. The child's face was a mess and her pajamas were covered with crumbs, but Jake didn't really care. He was far too pleased by the fact that she was sitting in his lap and smiling.

Annie's parting advice as they'd left the hospital earlier in the day had been a real lifesaver, he thought, watching Madeline stuff another fistful of cake into her mouth. The baby had been wailing so loudly he hadn't been sure he'd heard her correctly, but he must have, because it was working like a charm.

124

"She'll stop crying if you give her a Twinkie." Who ever would have guessed that snack cakes were the key to a contented baby? He'd headed directly to a vending machine in the hospital snack bar and purchased a package of them as soon as he'd left the recovery room. Sure enough, Madeline had stopped crying the moment he'd ripped off the plastic wrapper and handed her one.

They'd worked so well that he'd stopped at the Wal-Mart in Bartlesville and bought four entire cartons of them, letting her eat another cake in the cart while he bought himself three changes of casual clothes, a razor, and a toothbrush. Twinkies didn't strike Jake as a particularly wholesome food, and they weren't on the pediatrician's list of recommended fare he found posted on Annie's refrigerator, but he'd talk to her about improving the child's diet later. Right now, he was grateful for anything that could sweeten up Madeline's attitude.

The cake had ruined her appetite for dinner, though— she hadn't touched the chicken and noodle casserole in Annie's fridge. Jake had eaten some and found it surprisingly tasty—hearty and earthy and satisfying, completely different from anything Rachel had ever fixed.

Rachel. The thought of his late wife sent a somber shadow over the warmth of the kitchen. She would have loved Madeline, he thought somberly.

"She should have been yours," Jake murmured into the night. He wondered if Rachel could hear him, wondered if she could see him here with Madeline.

The thought made him irritated. Crimony—what was wrong with him? Of course she couldn't see him. To believe in that would be to believe in an afterlife, to acknowledge that something bigger and more powerful was out there, implying that life had meaning and purpose. Jake didn't hold with that. Such ideas were for fools who couldn't deal with reality, who needed some kind of crutch, some kind of hope.

All the same, it was funny; being around Madeline had given Jake an inexplicable sense of optimism. It made no sense, but somehow the all-consuming task of caring for Madeline left him with a feeling of peace and purpose he hadn't felt in years. He was completely in the moment, he realized, not thinking about the past or planning for the future. He'd called his office once soon after arriving at the hospital to let them know he wouldn't be coming in, but after that, he hadn't given his work a second thought. Tulsa and the office and his life there seemed another planet away.

Thinking of the office reminded him that he'd better call his voice mail and get his messages. And he would, just as soon as he got the baby to bed.

"Ready to go night-night, sweetheart?"

Sweetheart—now there was a word he hadn't used in a while. He wasn't a pet-name kind of person, but he'd occasionally called Rachel that. It had always made her smile.

Just like Madeline was smiling now. Jake grinned back, lifting the baby in his arms as he rose from the chair. "Okay, kiddo. Let's go knock off those crumbs." He carried her across the kitchen to the sink, then bobbed her up and down over it until the crumbs tumbled off. Grabbing a paper towel off the roll suspended under the wooden cabinets, he dampened it and washed her face, then carried her to her bedroom.

He stood in the doorway, looking at the shadowy pink nursery. White lace curtains framed the windows in a froth of frills, a border of bunnies marched along the walls near the ceiling, and a giant white teddy bear sat in a child-sized chair at a tiny table. A wooden baby bed, a dresser, a large rocking chair, and two huge baskets filled with toys and books completed the room.

Still carrying the baby, Jake headed to the books and selected a couple. Annie had said Madeline liked bedtime stories. Just how the heck did a person read a bedtime story to a baby? Should he put her in the crib, then stand by the railing and read to her? He couldn't very well crawl in there with her. There was a lot to this baby business he didn't know.

"Let's start with Plan A," he said to Madeline, placing her in the crib. She grabbed a yellow pacifier from the corner, stuck it in her mouth, then promptly rose to her feet and grunted, her arms held out over the railing.

She wanted him to pick her up. After a day of screeching every time he came near, she actually wanted him to hold her. The realization warmed him like a cup of cocoa in February. "Well, okay, Madeline. Looks like you prefer Plan B."

Lifting her out, he carried her to the rocking chair in the corner. The baby settled contentedly against his chest, the pacifier firmly clenched in her mouth. Jake opened the book. " 'Baby bunny loves to hop,' " he began.

Less than ten minutes later, Madeline was fast asleep. Jake sat and rocked her, inhaling the sweet scent of her hair, feeling the child's chest rise and fall against his own, and his throat grew tight with emotion. An odd feeling swept over him, a feeling like the one he'd had when he'd visited the Grand Canyon.

Awe—that was it. It was a sense of awestruck wonder, of being confronted with something so immense and significant that he couldn't quite take it all in.

Here, finally, was something that mattered, something that counted, something worth living for. Something worth dying for.

A child. His child.

The rocker creaked gently, and out the window, cicadas and tree frogs sang a rhythmic evening chorus. Madeline's soft breath formed the pulse of the rhythm, a rhythm that encircled him, enclosing him like a heartbeat in a womb.

The wreck had taken everything from him. His wife. His parents. All of his family, all of his hopes, all of his dreams.

Finding Madeline was like getting a part of it back. Here was a key to the future, a link to the past. He needed this child in his life. Not just on the periphery, either, but right in the heart of it. He wanted to be a real father to her, an involved father—the kind of father Tom had been to Rachel, the kind he'd always wished he'd had.

In order to do that, Jake needed access to the child—more access than a court was likely to give him. And he needed it sooner, too.

He'd already missed out on the child's first year. He didn't intend to miss out on any more.

He gazed down at the baby, felt the rise and fall of her chest against his, and a sense of purpose, profound and deep, took root in his soul. He had to come to some sort of agreement with Annie. Over the course of the next few days, he intended to do just that.

Annie checked her watch for the tenth time in as many minutes, a sense of anxiety growing in her stomach. They were more than a half-hour late. She'd called her house at eight this morning, ostensibly to tell Jake what to fix Madeline for breakfast, but mainly to check and make sure he was still there. She'd spent the night tormented by strange, fragmented dreams. She vaguely remembered Jake and Madeline visiting her after the surgery, but it seemed like a bizarre hallucination. The baby had had a black mouth; Jake had looked like a homeless drifter; they'd been accompanied by a teenager with spiky pink hair. . . .

She had sighed with relief when Jake had finally answered the phone.

"Hollister residence," he'd said in that deep, sexy baritone. He'd reassured her that Madeline was fine. He'd held the phone to the child's ear, and Annie had smiled as Madeline had squealed into the mouthpiece. Then Jake told her that Madeline had eaten a good breakfast, and he'd assured her they'd be at the hospital by ten.

Annie looked at her watch again. It was already ten-thirty. Annie fretted the hem of the sheet with her fingers. Just because he'd been at the house when she called didn't mean she could trust him. He could have been there packing up the baby's things. For all she knew, he'd hung up the phone and headed straight to the airport. He could be en route to Timbuktu, and she wouldn't have the resources to track them down. She'd been nuts ever to have left her child with a man who'd told her he wanted custody.

And yet, what else could she have done? She'd been too ill to search out a babysitter.

A soft knock on the door made her pull herself up on the bed. "Come in."

A wave of relief poured over her as the door pushed open to reveal Jake, carrying Madeline. She was wearing a frilly pink dress with a white eyelet pinafore, which looked ridiculous with her yellow Big Bird sneakers and purple Barney socks. Her hair apparently hadn't seen a comb since the day before, but her mouth wasn't black anymore. It was a healthy shade of pink, and it was turned up in a huge grin.

"Ma-ma-ma-ma," she cried, struggling in Jake's

grasp. He awkwardly set her on the linoleum floor and she ran to the bed.

Annie started to reach out her hand to the child, then grimaced with pain. "Could you lift her up on the bed?"

"Aren't you afraid she'll hurt your incision?"

"I'll put a pillow over it."

Jake gave the child a boost up on the bed, then sat down on the edge of it beside her. Madeline threw her arms around Annie, and Annie buried her face in the child's soft hair. It smelled like baby shampoo. Evidently Jake had managed to wash it the night before.

"Madeline, baby," Annie crooned, holding her child.

"Bay-bay-bay," Madeline echoed.

Annie looked at Jake over Madeline's head. "I don't know how to thank you for watching her."

"Hey, I enjoyed it. It gave us a chance to get acquainted."

The words clutched at Annie's heart. She didn't like the idea of this man in Madeline's life, and yet here he was—in Madeline's life, and hers, as well. She swallowed hard and looked back at her child.

"Bay-bay-bay," Madeline repeated.

"You want to hear your baby song?" Annie asked. "Well, all right." She put her head against Madeline's and crooned in a singsong voice:

Baby, oh, Baby! Baby, oh, Baby! Baby, oh, Baby—
Oh!
Baby, I love you. Baby, I love you. Baby, I love you
so.

Madeline gave a gurgle-like laugh. "Bay-bay-bay."

Annie smiled softly. She looked up to find Jake watching her.

"Nice rhyme," he said.

Annie wrapped a finger around one of Madeline's curls, suddenly self-conscious. "The lyrics aren't exactly inspired, but that's as good as I get at two o'clock in the morning."

Jake's eyes were warm and interested. "When was that?"

"The first night I brought Madeline home from the hospital. She was crying, and I'd run out of lullabies, so . . ." She lifted her shoulders, only to discover that it hurt to shrug. "She likes it. I've sung it to her every night since."

He was looking at her with those dark eyes, those eyes that were so much like Madeline's. "Are you in much pain?"

"Some," Annie conceded. "Not as bad as from the C-section."

"That's how you had Madeline? By C-section?"

Annie nodded, then was immediately irritated at herself. Why was she giving this man any information? He had no right to any part of Madeline's life.

But good grief, his eyes were just like his daughter's. Except they were entirely male. And they were trained on Annie in a way that made her intensely aware that she was wearing only a thin hospital gown.

The door creaked open and a short, dark-haired man in a white jacket stuck in his head. "Mrs. Hollister? I'm Dr. Meyers, the surgeon who operated on you. You probably don't remember me."

Annie was relieved at the intrusion. There was something about Jake, something in the air between them, that made her nervous at being alone with him.

Annie smiled at the doctor. "It's nice to meet you."

"Nice to see you conscious. You were in pretty bad shape yesterday." He nodded pleasantly at Jake and stuck out his hand. "You must be Mr. Hollister. Sorry I missed you yesterday after the surgery."

"He's not . . ."

Jake abruptly rose and shook the surgeon's hand. "What she means is, I'm sorry I missed you, too. The baby here had a diaper emergency."

The doctor laughed jovially. "I remember those days from when my own children were small." He glanced down at the chart.

Jake reseated himself beside Annie on the bed, close enough that she could smell the shaving cream scent on his skin.

"Your wife had a close call," the doctor remarked, still reading the chart.

"I'm not. . . ." Annie began again.

Jake gripped her hand and squeezed hard. Annie was so surprised she stopped in mid-sentence and stared at him. His brow creased as he shot her a warning look. He obviously didn't want the doctor to know they weren't married.

"A hour or two later, and that appendix would have ruptured." The doctor finally closed the file. "Good thing you got her here when you did."

"It was hard to convince her to come."

The doctor set the chart on a chair and advanced toward the bed. "Well, let's take a look and see how you're doing this morning."

Jake rose from the bed and swung Madeline down, too. To Annie's alarm, the doctor seemed prepared to lift her gown and examine her right in front of him.

Jake cleared his throat and looked away. "I'll, uh, take the baby out in the hall."

"Oh, no need," the doctor replied. "This will just take a moment."

Annie's heart pounded. She couldn't very well tell the

doctor she didn't want Jake in the room while he examined her. Trying to correct his assumption that they were married would be more embarrassing than enduring the current situation.

To Annie's relief, Jake turned his back and lifted Madeline to look out the window. Annie kept her eyes on his broad shoulders as the doctor examined the small incision on her right side. "Looks like you're doing just fine."

He gently felt her abdomen, then pulled down her gown. Annie covered herself with the sheet as fast as she could.

The doctor picked up the chart. "If you promise to take it easy, you can go home this afternoon." He pulled a pen from his pocket and made a notation on it.

Jake turned back around. The doctor looked up and shot him a grin. "Of course, you'll have to wait on her hand and foot. She's not to do any heavy lifting. That includes the little one here."

Jake nodded. "I'll see to it."

"I want to see her in my office in three days, and we'll take out those sutures."

"I'll have her there."

The doctor jotted a final note, then closed the file. "Looks like you're in good hands, Annie. I'll sign the release papers, and you two can get out of here in an hour or so."

"Thank you," she said.

The doctor shook Jake's hand. "Take good care of her." With a final wave at Annie, he headed out the door.

She stared at Jake. "Why did you do that?"

"Do what?"

"Pretend we were married. Say you'd take care of me."

"I didn't pretend anything. I just didn't think a long,

convoluted explanation of our relationship was called for." He jammed his fingers through his thick hair. "And as for saying I'd take care of you and Madeline, well, I intend to do just that."

He sounded so darned confident, so damned in control. Dadblast it, she didn't want this man controlling anything about her or her child. She eyed him dubiously. "You're just going to drop everything and play nursemaid?"

Jake shrugged. "I have my laptop with me. I can work from your house."

The situation was appalling. Letting this man into her house and life while she was disabled was like letting a fox into a hen house full of crippled chickens.

But she needed help. She couldn't care for an active baby alone the day after major surgery.

She scanned the room for Madeline and spotted her beside the long window, still peering out. Annie followed the child's gaze to a large billboard across the street. It was an ad for a loan company, placed near a busy intersection for everyone in the town to see, but the message seemed solely aimed at Annie. Her grandfather's soft drawl reverberated in her head as she gazed at the words: "Sometimes we all need a little help."

The words seemed to grow larger as she gazed at the sign, and they transported her back in time, back to a warm April afternoon when she was six years old. She'd bought a kite with her own money and wanted to put it together by herself. The only problem was, she couldn't read the directions. She'd struggled and struggled, but only succeeded in making a mess. She'd finally burst into tears when it all seemed a hopeless tangle.

Her grandfather's hands had been gentle and sure as he'd unsnarled it for her, and his voice had been the same way. "Sometimes we all need a little help, girl.

There's no shame in taking it when we do."

He'd been right then, and he was no doubt right now. Annie closed her eyes, then breathed out a deep sigh. "Okay."

"Okay, what?"

Annie jerked her eyes open, surprised to discover she'd spoken aloud. "Okay. You can stay." Oh, dear— that certainly wasn't a very gracious way to thank someone who was going to put his life on hold to tend to her and her baby for the next few days. She swallowed back all of her uncharitable feelings and forced herself to look him in the eye, which gave her the oddest, funniest feeling in the pit of her stomach. "And—and thank you."

Jake pulled his eyes from the hilly road just outside of Bartlesville and glanced over at Annie. Her head was turned toward the passenger window and he couldn't see her face. She was being awfully quiet on the drive home. She'd hardly said a word since he had helped her out of the wheelchair the hospital had insisted she ride to the exit and into his car.

Madeline was quiet, too, but that was because she'd fallen asleep almost as soon as the car had left the hospital parking lot. Jake looked in the rearview mirror and saw the baby dozing in her car seat, her head drooping forward at an uncomfortable looking angle.

Maybe Annie was sleeping, too. Jake glanced at her again. She evidently felt his eyes on her, because she met his gaze, then quickly looked away.

"Are you feeling all right?"

"Not too bad. I'm sore and a little woozy from the pain medicine."

Now was obviously not a good time to get into a discussion about child custody. He was chomping at the bit to talk about it, but she wasn't in any condition to

135

make decisions. He needed to bide his time.

She winced as she shifted on the seat, angling her body more towards him. "You know, I really don't know anything about you."

"You knew enough to select me as the father of your child."

Annie's head abruptly turned away.

Damn. He was supposed to be gaining her trust, not ticking her off. "Hey—I'm sorry. I have a bad habit of shooting off my mouth. I'm working on it."

It was his turn to feel her gaze on him. "I take it you don't approve of single motherhood."

"I've never really thought about it. What I don't approve of, I guess, is someone having my child without my knowledge or permission."

"I didn't know *you* didn't know. I thought you were a regular donor." Annie stared straight ahead. "You act like I stole something from you."

"Well, I guess I kind of feel like you did."

"I'm as much of a victim of this situation as you are," Annie said stiffly. "I thought my donor had signed an agreement to stay out of my life."

"How did you choose me?"

"What do you mean?"

"Well, how does it work? Do they just give you a list of donor profiles and tell you to pick one?"

"Pretty much. But none of the ones on the list fit what I was looking for. Dr. Borden asked me to describe what I wanted. When I did, he said he had just the right person in mind. He mailed me your profile, and, well, he was right."

"So—what made you want *me?*"

Annie shrugged. "You had a good family health history. And your educational level and profession indicated a likelihood you were somewhat intelligent."

The dubious tone in her voice made him grin.

". . . And your physical description fit what I wanted."

Jake glanced over at her. "And what, exactly, was that?"

Annie looked down at her hands. "Someone tall, with dark hair and eyes."

"Why was that part of your criteria?"

Annie continued to study her manicure. Jake wasn't sure, but he thought her cheeks looked a little redder than before. She lifted one shoulder. "I don't know. I guess I just find it attractive."

Did that meant she found *him* attractive? Jake silently cursed himself for caring. She no doubt had some other guy in mind, some guy she was carrying a torch for. He bet he could even guess who it was. "I suppose your ex-husband fits that description."

Her eyes flew wide open. "Nate? Oh, no! Nate has light hair and blue eyes."

"Ah. So you were looking for his opposite."

"He had nothing to do with it. We'd been divorced for years."

"You just wanted a dark-haired child?"

"Oh, that wasn't really the issue."

"So what was?" He glanced at her curiously.

Annie lifted her shoulders and looked away. "Fantasy, I suppose."

"Fantasy?"

She nodded. He couldn't keep from pressing for additional information. "You mean the sexual kind?"

Her color heightened. "You're getting into a pretty personal topic here."

"The fact that we've had a child together is already pretty personal, if you ask me."

* * *

137

Jake was right. The thought that this man's sperm had been inside her was enough to make Annie break a sweat. There was something intensely primal about him anyway, despite his outward polish.

Why did he have to be so good-looking? It was impossible to look at him and not think about sex.

It had been a long time since she'd had any, Annie thought ruefully—too long, judging from the effect this man was having on her. What was wrong with her, having this kind of reaction to a man who posed such a threat to Madeline?

Well, maybe the threat wasn't really to Madeline, she mentally amended. He posed more of a threat to her— a threat to take away the life she'd envisioned and built, a life that contained only her and her child.

The thought put her on the offensive. "You have an unfair advantage over me in the personal information department. After all, I didn't pretend to be somebody else when we first met."

His right eyebrow shot up. "I didn't pretend anything. You assumed I was your friend's grandson and I just played along."

"Uh-huh. And you did the same thing with the doctor, I noticed. Too bad there wasn't a line on the donor form that described your ethics."

A nerve ticked in his jaw. The observation gave Annie a great deal of satisfaction.

"I don't like to play games." He spoke without taking his eyes from the road. "If you want to know anything about me, all you have to do is ask."

"All right. What happened to your wife?" Good heavens, what had made her start with that question? It sounded like she thought he'd bumped her off.

He was silent for so long that she thought he wasn't

going to answer. "She died in a car crash, along with my parents."

Annie's heart constricted. "Oh, how awful! Was it recent?"

"It happened a little over two years ago."

"Where?"

"Just outside the airport in Tulsa. A drunk driver ran a red light."

"Had you been married long?"

"Seven years."

"And . . . you were undergoing fertility treatments?"

Jake nodded. "Dr. Borden was her physician."

"Mine, too."

Jake shot her a dry look. "So I gathered."

Annie hesitated. "You said the mix-up at the fertility center was deliberate."

Jake nodded grimly. "According to the clinic's director, Dr. Borden was forced into retirement because he was caught doing the same thing with another couple. In that case, though, no pregnancy resulted."

"It's hard to believe he'd do something so unethical." Annie shook her head. "He seemed so nice—so intent on giving people just what they wanted."

Jake's lip curled in a mirthless smile. "That appears to be the problem."

"Can he be prosecuted?"

"Sure. If we bring charges."

"Do you think we should?"

Jake sighed. "That was my first reaction. My second, really. My first was to go to Florida and beat the guy to a pulp."

She looked at him curiously. "Sounds like you had a third reaction."

"Yeah." He gazed straight ahead through the windshield. "I thought about Madeline."

"And?"

He hissed out a harsh blast of air. "And this is the sort of thing that would get a lot of media play. I don't want her existence to be labeled a mistake."

I thought about Madeline. Dear Lord, he sounded like a father—a real father, the kind who put his child's best interests first. Annie didn't know if was the effect of the pain pills or the shock of the whole thing, but her throat grew thick with emotion.

As Jake steered the car into the drive of the ranch, Annie realized she had one more question, a question that was burning inside of her, although she didn't know why. She swallowed hard and asked just as he pulled the car up to the house, "What was your wife's name?"

His response was wary. "Why do you want to know?"

"I don't know. I just do."

He turned the key in the ignition. The motor died. "Rachel. Her name was Rachel."

His voice was hushed, as reverent as if in prayer.

Annie's throat grew thicker. He'd answered her underlying question, the one she had really wanted to know.

He'd loved his wife. He loved her still. She could see it in the fine lines of pain around his eyes, in the softening of his lips at speaking her name. Annie's heart ached in an odd, undefinable way.

She'd been a lucky woman, his Rachel. Not every woman got to be loved like that.

Madeline could be, her mind prompted. *A man who could love that deeply had the makings of a wonderful father.*

It should have been a comforting thought, but it wasn't. Everything about this man was unsettling. Jake made her want to run, yet at the same time, he held a dark fascination—a fascination that was as strong as it was disturbing.

Chapter Nine

"Steady, now." Jake tightened his grip on Annie's arm, but she still wobbled as he helped her up the steps to the porch.

"My legs feel like a couple of wet sponges." She took another hesitant step. "Sorry I'm acting like such a wimp. I promise not be so high maintenance once I get inside."

"You'd better be. The instruction sheet the nurse gave me says you're not supposed to walk without help for forty-eight hours."

"Oh, I'm sure I'll be able to get around just fine after a little rest."

"Not by yourself, you won't. I intend to see to it that you follow instructions."

Annie shot him a look. "Oh, no. You're not one of those follow-every-instruction-to-a-T kind of people, are you?"

"When it comes to some things, I am." *And appar-*

ently you're a bend-the-rules-all-over-the-place kind of woman. Jake thought grimly, pulling the key to the door from his pocket. *Great, just great. Just the trait I'd have handpicked for the mother of my child.*

The thought made him look for Madeline. She was doing a bow-legged strut down the porch, heading for the hanging wooden swing in the yard.

"Come on, Madeline."

The child ignored him.

"Come on, sweetie. Let's go inside," he called again.

The baby started to climb up into the swing. Jake hesitated, unsure what to do. He couldn't relinquish his hold on Annie—she was about as steady as a toothpick in a tornado. On the other hand, he didn't know how to get the child to cooperate, and he didn't dare leave her outside unattended.

Annie smiled over at the baby and motioned with her hand. "Come with Mommy, sweetheart."

"Ma-ma-ma-ma." Grinning broadly, the baby obediently tottered over to Annie's side.

"How the heck did you do that?" Jake grumbled, opening the door.

"You have to have the Mommy touch."

A low brown streak came charging out the door, startling Jake so much that he nearly bumped into the doorjamb. He turned around and realized it was Hot Dog, making a mad dash for the bushes to relieve himself.

"Looks like poor Hot Dog was practically crossing his legs, waiting for us to get home."

"Guess I don't have a Mommy touch with animals, either," Jake muttered. The fact of the matter was, it had been such a struggle to get Madeline dressed and out the door that morning that he'd completely forgotten about the dog. He realized Annie was probably expecting a modicum of remorse. If he expected to make her believe he could be a responsible parent, he'd better show a little.

"Sorry, there, pooch," he said as the dog came loping back, its skinny rat tail thumping. He glanced apologetically at Annie. "I, uh, don't know much about taking care of pets. I never had one."

"Never?"

"No."

"Not even as a child?"

Jake shook his head.

"Not even a guinea pig? Or hamster?"

"No."

"A lizard, maybe?"

He shook his head, then brightened. "I had some tropical fish in my office. But they all died."

Annie shot him a pitying look.

Damn. The last thing he wanted was to be pitied. "Can't say that I ever missed having pets," he said gruffly. "Animals are just a nuisance."

"You'd change your mind if you spent any time around them."

The matter-of-fact, assured way she made the statement grated on his nerves. So did the appealing way her waist indented and her hips flared under his arm. She lurched against him as she stumbled on the threshold.

He tightened his grip to steady her. His hand brushed her breast—a breast that felt surprisingly lush and full.

She gazed up at him, her blue eyes wide. A flicker of sexual awareness flashed between them, as sudden and bright as a just-struck match in a pitch-black room. A burst of desire shot through him, intense and unexpected.

Good grief. What a time and place to have his libido pull a Lazarus. He drew his hand back as if it had been burned.

Annie steadied herself on the door frame. "Sorry. The

medicine seems to have made me a little dizzy."

"Well, then, we'd better get you to bed."

Crimony. It was a completely normal thing to say to someone just released from the hospital, but it sounded so suggestive.

"My room is the one next to Madeline's."

"The one with the covered wagon?"

Jake had seen it last night when he'd walked through the house after putting the baby to bed. The house was filled with curious antiques, but none were more curious than Annie's bed.

"Isn't it great?" Annie said.

"It's certainly unusual," Jake said cautiously, guiding her through the foyer.

"The canopy is made from the frame of a real Conestoga. And not just any old Conestoga, either. It's the very one my great-great grandfather used when he moved from Missouri to Kansas."

"It must have looked pretty odd moving across the prairie, covered with all that pink and green floral fabric," Jake said dryly, helping her through the doorway of her room.

Annie grinned. "I'm not a purist when it comes to antiques. I like to add my own special touch to things."

She sure did, Jake thought, as he helped her toward the bed—and her touch was more than a tad eccentric. It wasn't without its charm, though. The room brought to mind a gypsy tent, romantic and exotic and cozy. It smelled like Annie—soft and powdery. It looked like her, too—a colorful mix of rosy cinnamon and sage green, done in a hodge-podge of florals and stripes and plaids. Nothing in the room matched, but it somehow all went together. If anything could actually go with a Conestoga top.

The bed creaked softly as Annie sat on the edge of it.

Her brow furrowed and her eyes creased with pain.

"Are you okay?"

She nodded, but she was clearly hurting. Jake hauled the sheet of medical instructions out of his pocket and scanned it. "It's time for your pain medicine. It says you need to take it with food. And it looks like you're on clear liquids for the rest of the day."

"There's some chicken broth in the freezer."

"Frozen soup?"

"It's homemade."

Jake didn't know anyone who made homemade soup. It seemed like a waste of time, considering you could just open a can.

"What do I do with it?"

"Just take off the lid and zap it in the microwave." She winced as she turned and reached for a pillow.

"Here." He reached out and adjusted the pillows against the headboard, accidently brushing close against her, close enough to inhale the soft scent of her hair. Once again, a flash of sexual awareness flickered through him, fast and hot as lightning.

He cleared his throat. "Do you need anything else?"

She gingerly leaned back against the pillows. "Could you get me a nightgown? They're in the top drawer of the dresser."

"Sure." He strode to the bureau against the wall and opened it, then swallowed hard. It was filled with sachet-scented lingerie—silky panties and matching bras in all the colors of the rainbow. Good grief—it looked like a Victoria's Secret catalogue. It was enough to make his mouth go dry, thinking of her in that exotic lingerie.

"The nightgowns are on the right," she said.

He awkwardly pawed through the lacy stuff, feeling like a voyeur, and pulled out something that looked like a gown. It was dusky rose, and when he pulled it out, he saw that it was short, no longer than mid-thigh, held together with the narrowest of straps. He felt like an idiot, handling it as she watched. He tossed it to her.

"My robe is on a hook on the back of the closet door. Could you get it, too?"

Nodding, he strode to the closet and pulled out a silk floral kimono.

"Thanks," she said as he handed it to her.

"No problem." The thought of her changing into the skimpy clothes made his voice come out husky and low. He couldn't wait to escape from the room. "Well, I'll go see to the soup." He turned toward the door.

"There's, uh, one more thing."

He turned back around. Her expression was oddly embarrassed, and she didn't meet his eyes. "I hate to ask, but I don't think I can undo my dress. It buttons up the back. The nurse had to help me get it on."

Jake blew out a slow breath. "Okay." She shifted on the bed, and he moved behind her. He had to lift her hair to reach the top button. It was silky and thick, and the clean, herbal scent of her shampoo filled his nostrils. His fingers seemed large and clumsy as he fumbled with the button.

He realized he was holding his breath. He breathed deeply, and felt her shoulders fall and rise as he undid the next button. Either she'd been holding her breath, too, or she was breathing in sync with him. Either thought was decidedly disconcerting.

Her skin was smooth and fair. He tried not to touch it, but as he struggled with the button, his fingers brushed against her flesh. It was even warmer and softer than he'd imagined. Frowning, he tried to focus his attention on unfastening the next button, then the next. The pink-flowered fabric gapped open, low enough to reveal that she wasn't wearing a bra.

He slowly undid the fifth, then the sixth buttons. The opening now revealed the curve of her waist, the bow of her hips. His mouth went dry. Good heavens, but she was beautiful. Maybe it was the way the light filtered over her, making her skin look as if it were glowing, or the way the fabric played hide-and-seek with her curves. He'd never realized that a woman's back was such a feminine, seductive part of her body.

One more button—his upper lip beaded with sweat as his hands awkwardly worked to free it. Oh, dear heavens. She wasn't wearing any underwear! Under the thin linen sheath, she was completely naked.

Well, it was no wonder. He hadn't thought to bring her any clean clothes while she was in the hospital. It was his fault.

The thought should have made him feel guilty, but the fact that he was the cause of her nakedness only heightened his arousal.

He heard a hitch in her breath. Was she feeling it, too? It seemed impossible that she wouldn't. Sexual awareness lay thick and heavy over the room, like fog over a summer lake. He saw her tremble, and reached out to rub her arms to warm her. He stopped himself abruptly. Hell; he'd be the one to heat up if he touched her again, and he was overheated as it was.

He dropped his hands. "You seem cold. You'd better get changed and under the covers."

Holy Moses. What the hell was the matter with him, getting all turned on by this woman? Especially under the circumstances. She was fresh out of surgery, in pain from her incision, for God's sake.

He turned to the baby, who was still sitting on the floor, batting at the dog's tail. "Come on, Madeline."

The baby ignored him.

He motioned to the door. "Let's go, sport. Let's go fix Mommy some lunch."

The child looked up and grinned, then turned her attention back to the dog. Not knowing what else to do, he bent down and picked her up.

Madeline burst out with a shriek of protest, her face growing red as a tomato.

"Put her down and call the dog," Annie suggested.

"Huh?"

"Hot Dog will follow you more readily than Madeline."

Jake stared at her blankly. He was having a hard time getting past the fact her dress was drooping over one shoulder and he knew for a fact she was stark naked underneath it. "I don't care about the dog. It's Madeline I need to keep an eye on."

Annie gave a maddeningly patient smile, the kind one might use with a half-wit. "Madeline will scream bloody murder for half an hour if you move her against her will. She's very stubborn. But if Hot Dog follows you, Madeline will, too. And she'll think it's her idea."

"Oh." It was such a clever plan, it irritated him he hadn't thought of it himself. Jake released the protesting baby and strode slowly to the door. "Hey, Hot Dog—let's go."

The dog eagerly followed him out of the room. Sure enough, Madeline scampered along behind.

There were a lot of tricks to this parenting thing, Jake thought, and Annie seemed to know them all. He had to hand it to her—she had a real knack for keeping the baby calm. The problem was, he thought ruefully, she apparently had an equal talent for getting him overly excited.

* * *

Madeline was crying. Annie opened her eyes, surprised to find morning light streaming through her bedroom window. The bedside clock was directly in her line of vision.

Nine o'clock. Dear heavens, she hadn't slept this late since Madeline had been born! The baby usually woke at six. The poor dear must be starving to death. In fact, it sounded like she'd somehow already made her way to the kitchen.

Annie tried to sit up, only to be slammed back against the pillow by a hard fist of pain. It all came flooding back. *Appendicitis. Surgery.*

Jake.

The thought of him made her pulse skip a beat. She heard the dog bark, heard the deep rumble of his voice. Madeline's crying quieted. A second later, she heard the baby's squeal of delight.

Annie leaned back on the pillows and closed her eyes. He was surprisingly good with the child. And with her, she silently admitted. Her stomach did a loopy little free-fall. He'd tended to her during the night. Her memory was foggy from the pain medication, but she remembered him by her bedside, handing her pills and water. He'd been wearing sweatpants and no shirt, and at first she'd thought she was dreaming. Then he'd leaned forward and helped her sit up, and his touch had jolted her fully awake. She'd been keenly aware that his bare arms were hard and muscled, his chest covered with dark hair, his face beard-shadowed and soap-scented.

Annie tossed back the covers and slowly pulled herself upright, despite the pain. She rested a moment, letting herself adjust to the new position, then swung her legs off the bed. Her stomach was sore—so very sore. But she didn't want to lie around and feel helpless. Besides, the doctor had said she was supposed to get up and move around.

She haltingly made her way to the bathroom, where she brushed her teeth and ran a brush through her hair. Taking care to cinch her robe high above her incision, she padded barefoot to the kitchen.

She found Jake at the sink, rinsing off a plate, and Madeline seated in her high chair, polishing off a banana. The baby spotted Annie in the doorway and banged the tray loudly with her fist, grinning hugely. "Ma-ma-ma-ma-ma!"

Annie smiled at the child. "Good morning, sweetheart."

Jake turned from the sink, his eyes startled, as if he'd thought she'd been talking to him.

Annie felt tongue-tied and awkward, like an intruder in her own home. "Good morning. I was, uh, talking to the baby."

He nodded. "Morning." He looked away, then, but not before his gaze swept over her, making her acutely aware that she was only wearing a nightgown and a brief kimono. "What are you doing up?" he asked.

"The smell of coffee drew me in."

Jake shut off the sink and turned around, drying his hands on a dish towel. The motion was slight, but his arms were so muscular that it made his biceps bulge in his T-shirt. She couldn't help but remember how he'd looked without it. "You're not supposed to be up without assistance," he said.

Annie lifted her shoulders and grinned. "If you don't call the rules police, it can be our little secret."

His eyebrows knit in a frown. He opened his mouth as if he were about to say something, then abruptly shut it, as if he'd thought better. He slung the towel over the edge of the sink. "So how are you feeling?"

"Not too bad, considering." She stepped further into the kitchen.

He moved to her side and pulled out a chair. "Here. Have a seat and I'll pour you some coffee."

She slowly lowered herself into a chair beside Madeline's, trying not wince from the pain. She distracted herself by looking at his legs. He was wearing a pair of shorts, and his legs were every bit as appealing as his chest—brown and muscled, and covered with dark hair. She turned to the baby. "How are you doing today, Madeline?"

The baby banged on the tray of her high chair and gurgled merrily.

"Is this her breakfast or a mid-morning snack?"

"From the way she's attacking that banana, I'd say it's her second breakfast. She ate her first one when she got up around six."

Annie nodded. "She's an early bird, all right."

"Maybe she gets that from me."

Annie's heart jumped in her throat. It was going to take some getting used to, this concept that she'd had a child with this man.

It was so odd. Here they were, the three of them—a biological family—having breakfast together in a kitchen. It could be a scene from any normal household in America.

Except she and Jake weren't married. They weren't even lovers. They'd made a baby together, but they hadn't so much as even kissed.

Unbidden, her gaze went to his mouth as he moved toward her, the cup of coffee in his hand. She glanced up, and their eyes locked. For a fraction of a second, they both stared at each other, and an unmistakable charge of awareness surged between them. It was just a look, but it was as clear as a spoken word, as tangible as a touch.

He cleared his throat and looked away. Her stomach did a nervous somersault as he set the coffee down in front of her.

"Thanks." She took a sip. It was hot and strong, and she welcomed its bracing heat. She searched for something to say, for something, anything, to neutralize the odd charge in the air. "And thanks for handling the nursing duties in the night."

"No problem."

Madeline banged her tray again, flinging smashed banana on Jake's shirt. He turned back to the sink and picked up the towel, using it to wipe his shirt. "She's awfully hard on clothes," he griped good-naturedly. The baby grinned and kicked the legs of the high chair, making it scoot backward on the floor. "Not to mention furniture."

Annie smiled. "She can't hurt that piece. It's sturdy as the oak tree it was made from. It's been in my family for three generations. My grandfather made it before my dad was born."

Jake ran a hand over the carved wooden back. "Nice work. I used to do some carpentry and woodworking myself."

Annie's eyebrows rose in surprise. "You don't look like a do-it-yourself kind of person."

"I guess I'm not. Not anymore, anyway. But I used to enjoy it."

"So why did you stop?"

Jake lifted his shoulder. "My handiwork didn't go with my wife's décor. Besides, it made more sense to spend my free time on golf and tennis—things that could help my career."

"I thought the whole point of free time was to do what you wanted."

"There are only so many hours in the day. In order to get ahead, you have to maximize your use of time."

Spoken like a real workaholic, Annie thought. Not that she was surprised; she'd pegged him for the type. She took another sip of coffee. "What kind of things did you used to build?"

"Oh, just simple stuff. A game table, a bookcase, a bench."

"Do you still have them?"

"Nah. It was all junk."

Annie smiled. "One man's junk is another man's treasure. That's what my grandmother always used to say."

"Your grandfather was evidently a lot better at woodworking than I ever was."

"That's because he took his time. It took him eight months to make that high chair."

"Is that right?"

Annie nodded. "He started making it the day he found out Gran was pregnant. He planned to surprise her with it when the baby was born. When she was eight months along, though, she burst into tears one day because her stomach was so large she couldn't reach her feet to pull on her socks. Grandpa helped her with her shoes and socks, then went out and got the chair, hoping to cheer her up." Annie smiled. "She was so touched, she just cried harder. Grandpa thought she was about to go into labor."

Jake grinned. "That's a nice story."

"They had a nice marriage." Annie gazed down at her coffee cup. "I always dreamed of having a relationship like that, but it didn't work out."

Annie looked up and saw a pained look in Jake's eyes. He must have had a nice marriage, too. An odd wistful twinge passed through her, one she couldn't quite define.

"Grandpa did all kinds of woodworking," she continued, wanting to smooth over the awkward silence, to erase the strained look on his face. "He built the cabinets here in the kitchen, the table in the dining room, and Gran's bedroom vanity. His tools are still out in the barn."

"Maybe I can take a look at them sometime."

Annie took another sip of coffee, but the lump in her throat made it hard to swallow. She needed to accept it; Jake was going to be a part of their life—a major, ongoing part of their life. The prospect was still alarming, but it was no longer as chilling as it had seemed at first. He'd said he didn't intend to take Madeline away from her. He was good with the baby, and he'd been incredibly kind and helpful in a crisis. She'd never planned on having Madeline's father in the picture, but here he was, and she needed get used to it.

She nodded and forced a smile. "Sure. Maybe you can even try them out the next time you come visit Madeline."

"Hold still, Madeline."

The baby squirmed on the changing table as Jake tried to fasten on a diaper. It had been two days since he'd brought Annie back, and he'd gotten perhaps a little better at changing their child.

"Come on, girl. We've got to take your Mommy to the doctor and we don't want to be late."

The baby twisted around completely so that she was up on her knees. Jake gently flipped her on her back like a turtle. The child laughed, then struggled to get back on her stomach.

"I swear, Madeline, the next time I have to change your diaper, I think I'll gag and bind you first."

"I hope that's not what the duct tape is for."

Jake turned his head to see Annie in the nursery doorway, gazing worriedly at the roll of silver tape nearby. She was wearing a loose sundress with sunflowers printed all over it. Her hair was pulled back from her face with two tortoiseshell combs, and tiny gold earrings sparkled in her lobes. If she hadn't been frowning, she would have looked like a ray of sunshine.

As he watched, the crease between her eyebrows deepened. "You wouldn't really tie up the baby, would you?"

"Of course not."

"So what's with the duct tape?"

"It's for the diaper. If I mess up, it gives me another shot at getting it on." Jake struggled to hold Madeline still while he tugged the diaper under her bottom. "In case you haven't noticed, getting a diaper on this kid is harder than putting a saddle on a rattlesnake."

Annie grinned and stepped up beside him, close enough that the disconcertingly erotic scent of a soft, flowery perfume filled his nostrils. Madeline kicked her legs and smiled broadly. "Ma-ma-ma-ma-ma."

"I'm right here, sweetie." Annie reached down and expertly fastened the diaper on her first try.

Jake shot her sardonic grin. "You're just trying to make me look bad in front of the baby."

Annie laughed. "Not at all. You're doing a good job of that all by yourself."

Jake couldn't help but laugh. He picked up the child and swung her to the floor. Her mother eyed the child appraisingly. "Looks like she's ready for the next size of diaper. I don't know what you've been feeding her, but she seems to have gained weight since I've been sick."

Jake swallowed guiltily. Annie probably wouldn't appreciate learning that the child had been living on a steady diet of Twinkies. He gave them to her whenever she threatened to cry, which to his way of thinking was alarmingly often. They worked like a charm, but they spoiled her appetite for actual meals.

Madeline reached out her arms. "Ma-ma-ma-ma."

"Oh, sweetie, I'm not supposed to pick you up yet." Annie sighed, casting a rueful glance at Jake. "It breaks my heart to refuse to hold her."

The baby was obviously attached to Annie, and it was no wonder. For all of her eccentricities, she was a loving and devoted mother. She'd turned her sickbed into Madeline's playground, using it to read storybooks, play games, and sing songs to the child. She'd given Jake a long list of instructions, and she was constantly questioning him to see whether or not he'd followed them.

"Ma-ma-ma-ma."

"Could you support her weight while I give her a hug?"

"Sure." Jake lifted Madeline, her back to his chest, one arm around her stomach, the other forming a seat under her bottom. The child's arms snaked around Annie's neck. Annie hugged the child back. The only problem was, the position put the back of Jake's hand directly against Annie's right breast. It was warm and soft and lush, and he had the most inappropriate urge to turn his hand and fill his palm.

The thought disturbed him. Abruptly breaking the hug, he placed Madeline on the floor. "We'd better get going if we're going to make Bartlesville by eleven."

"Okay."

Jake helped Annie and Madeline out the front door and into the car, then strapped Madeline into her car seat.

"We'll need to take the baby's bag," Annie said as Jake climbed into the driver's seat.

"It's in the back. I loaded it with fresh diapers and juice this morning."

"Did you put in her Binkie?"

Jake looked at her blankly. "Binkie?"

Annie nodded. "Her pacifier. In case she cries."

Binkie, not Twinkie. The pacifier was called a Binkie. Oh, Christ. And here he'd been shoveling snack cakes at Madeline as if they were the mainstay of a baby's recommended diet.

"I, uh, think I left it in her crib," Jake hedged. "I'll go get it."

He returned to the house and retrieved the pacifier. Opening the car's back door, he handed it to the baby. Sure enough, she stuck it in her mouth and happily sucked away.

Annie smiled at Jake as he crawled in the driver's seat and started the engine. "You've really caught on to this parenthood business."

He'd caught on, all right—to the fact that Madeline would do anything for a Twinkie. He only hoped Annie never caught on to his mistake.

Twinkies instead of Binkies, he thought, inwardly wincing. *Jumpin' Jehohasphat.*

"Madeline has really taken a liking to you," Annie was saying.

Jake cast her a sideways glance. He'd better take advantage of her good opinion of him while it lasted. "Look—we're both quite sure I'm Madeline's father. But I'd still like to have the DNA test done."

The gaze Annie shot him was wary. "Why?"

"Well, because it would prove that I am with a ninety-nine point nine percent probability of accuracy or prove for certain that I'm not."

Annie's eyes grew scared. "Why do you need proof?"

"Because I want to be as sure as it is possible to be." He angled a glance at her. "If you were in my shoes, wouldn't you?"

She gave a reluctant nod. "I suppose."

"It's really very simple." He stopped at the end of the driveway, then pulled the car out on the road and headed north. "We can do it today. I made a few phone calls, and there's a lab near the doctor's office in Bartlesville."

Annie stared out the window as they pulled out on the highway. "And if the tests say you're Madeline's biological father, then what? What do you want to do with the information?"

Jake met her gaze. "Annie, I want to be a part of Madeline's life."

Annie stared out at the passing pastureland, her heart pounding, her palms damp with anxiety. The last few days had given her a lot of time to think about things and to watch him with Madeline.

Just last night she'd walked in to the nursery to find Jake dancing with the baby in his arms, crooning a low-key rendition of "Inagodadavida." Annie had ducked back into the hallway, not wanting to ruin the moment, her hand over her mouth to suppress a laugh.

"Bay bay bay," Madeline had cooed as he finished.

Annie had leaned against the wall, listening to his response. "Do I hear a request from the audience? You want your mommy's baby song? Well, it's not in my usual repertoire, but let's see what I can do."

Jake's deep baritone had begun to sing:

"Baby, oh, baby! Baby, oh, baby! Baby, oh, baby— Oh!" To Annie's amusement, he'd put a James Brown-type yowl on the last syllable.

"Baby, I love you. Baby, I love you. Baby, I love you so!"

Jake had sung the last verse like an Elvis impersonator. Madeline had squealed with laughter, and something in Annie's heart melted.

Jake's words brought her back. "If the test is positive, I want to be a father to her," he was saying.

Annie slowly nodded. "I can understand that. I've even come to accept that it could be good for Madeline. But . . ."

"But what?"

"I don't want to be separated from her."

"Annie, I'm not planning to take Madeline away from you."

She searched his face, trying to search his heart. "You threatened to."

"That was before I got to know you."

Annie's eyes narrowed. "And now that you know me, you've changed your mind?"

Jake rubbed his jaw. "Well, when I first met you, I thought you were a real head case."

Annie's chin tilted up. "Thank you for that astoundingly flattering assessment."

Jake shot her a cajoling grin. "Oh, come on—you have to admit, you came across as something of a flake. You mistook me for someone else. You force-fed me tea, then started reading my fortune. You told me your dead granddad talks to you through billboards, you were dressed like a fur-covered street urchin, and you had a sign by the road advertising pecks of llama poop. . . ."

"Alpacas," Annie corrected. "They're alpacas."

Jake heaved a sigh. "The point is, you came across as less than stable."

"And now you've decided I am?"

Jake's grin was teasing. "Well, I wouldn't take it that far."

Annie couldn't keep from smiling back.

"You're a good mother. Madeline loves you, and you obviously dote on her." Jake pulled his eyes from the road and gazed at her. "I know she needs you."

Annie's chin was still tilted at a combative angle, but her eyes softened.

"But I also think every child needs a father." Jake searched her face. "I'll be good for Madeline, Annie."

Annie drew a slow breath, then nodded. "Okay. You can come see Madeline anytime you like. But I don't want you taking her away for weekends or anything until she's older."

"How much older?"

"I don't know."

At her words, the attorney in Jake wanted to respond, to negotiate, to press the advantage. But another part warned him off.

This was a start. Annie had just made a major concession. He didn't want to scare her by forcing the issue. He'd get the legal proof, then he'd have it if he needed to use it. "So what about the paternity test?"

He heard Annie suck in her breath.

His brow wrinkled with concern. "What is it? Does your incision hurt?"

"No. That billboard. . . ." Her voice broke off.

Oh, jeeze. "Your grandfather's talking to you?"

She sheepishly nodded.

Christ. Maybe she *was* a head case, after all. Jake peered at the sign. "He's saying *'Turn here for gas?'* "

"No. The other sign."

"*'Give blood?'* "

"Not that part. Read what's under it."

"'*You know it's the right thing to do,*'" Jake read aloud. "'*So go ahead and say yes.*'"

Annie nodded. "Well, I guess you have your answer about the test."

It was one thing for her to tell him her grandfather spoke to her through billboards. It was another to be there when it happened. "When your grandfather talks," Jake asked carefully, "Do you actually hear him?"

"Yes."

"I didn't hear anything just now."

"Well, of course not. He doesn't actually *speak.*"

"But you just said—"

"I don't hear him with my ears. I hear him with my heart." Annie looked over, her eyes half-amused, half-worried. "You think I'm crazy, don't you?"

Jake considered the question, his fingers tightening on the steering wheel. Hell. Some people believed in the power of pyramids and crystals. Other people believed in seances and channeling and good luck charms. That didn't mean they were ready for a padded cell.

What the heck. When it came to paranormal happenings, having a dead granddad give advice through billboards was probably preferable to a lot of options.

"Admit it," Annie prodded. "You think I'm nutty as squirrel bait."

"Well," Jake said at length, "you're definitely a little eccentric. But as long as Grandpa's on my side, I guess it's not too bad."

The smile she flashed him was so warm and genuine that it seemed to bore right into him, right through the muscle of his chest, right through the hard rock of his heart. And before he knew it, against all his better judgment, he found himself smiling back.

Chapter Ten

"A baby he didn't know about, by a woman he'd never met," Susanna's friend Joan murmured through the phone. "This is incredible, Suze. It's like something from the *National Enquirer*!"

Susanna twirled the kitchen phone cord around her finger. "I know. And Jake seems enamored with the child. I can't wait to see her."

"What's Tom's reaction?"

"He's mad enough to spit nails."

"Why?"

Susanna sighed. "That's a good question. He says Jake is being disloyal to Rachel, but I think the unfairness of it all is what's got him upset. You know how much Rachel wanted a baby."

"Yes." Joanie's voice was soft. "I can understand how he might see it like that."

There was a pause. "So how are things between the two of you?"

Susanna sighed again. "Oh, I don't know."

"That doesn't sound good."

"It doesn't feel very good, either." Susanna pulled a glass from the cupboard and carried it to the sink, stretching the phone cord behind her.

"So what happened the other night? Besides finding out about Jake's news, I mean."

Susanna turned on the faucet and filled the glass with water. "Well, I picked Tom up at the airport, just like I used to do. It used to be a little ritual of ours—a way of letting him know that I'd missed him while he was gone, and that was I eager for him to be home, eager to . . . well, you get the picture."

"And?"

"And he got off the plane with a woman—a very attractive woman. Apparently she's an attorney, too, and she'd attended the same seminar in Denver. She was . . ."

"What?"

"Oh, I don't know, maybe I'm just paranoid, but it seemed like she looked at Tom like she wanted to just eat him up, then looked at me like she wanted to scratch my eyes out."

"Uh-oh. Did you ask Tom about her?"

"Well, he introduced us. Evidently they'd worked on a case together a few months back—they were opposing counsel. They'd run into each other at this seminar and just happened to be on the same flight home together. He acted like they only knew each other through work."

"But you don't believe him?"

Susanna set the glass on the kitchen counter and pushed back her hair. "Oh, Joan, I don't know what I believe."

"How are things in the bedroom between you two?"

"Nonexistent. I mean, I tried, but . . ." She trailed off.

"You tried to seduce him?" Joan prompted.

"Well, I don't know that I'd call it seduction, exactly."

"So what *did* you do?"

"I asked him to move back into our bedroom." Susanna felt her voice waver. "He turned me down. He said he was afraid he'd disturb my sleep, that he didn't want to set me back just as I'm getting well."

"Is it possible he just didn't get your drift?"

"I don't know. I guess anything's possible. He's been so different since Rachel died." Susanna twirled the phone cord around her finger, her chest tight and heavy. "And I feel like it's all my fault. I mean, I'm the one who withdrew."

"You were ill. Depression is an illness."

"Ill, depressed, crazy—all I know is that the whole rhythm of our lives is off. We barely see each other. He leaves for the office at dawn and gets home late. There's a huge gulf between us, and I hate it."

"Well, then, you need to bridge it. Try again. Be more direct this time."

"What if he just flat-out rejects me? I don't think I could stand that."

"Can you stand letting things go on the way they are?"

Susanna hesitated. She missed more than the physical intimacy. She missed the emotional closeness, the private jokes, the special, wordless way they used to connect across a room. "No," she said softly. "No, I can't. But I don't want to confront him about it, either. Not yet, anyway."

"Why not?"

"I'm afraid he'll leave." Putting her deepest fear into words made it suddenly seem more real. "I want a chance to fix things, to show him I've changed. I want a chance to win him back."

Joan was silent at the other end of the phone for a

long moment. "What are you going to do?"

"I don't know. Somehow, I need to find a way to make him fall in love with me all over again."

Tom pulled his Jaguar into the driveway and killed the engine. It was nine-fifteen at night, but from the lack of light inside his house, it might as well have been midnight.

Odd. Susanna was usually a night owl. A month or two ago, he would have assumed she'd already gone to bed, but lately she'd started keeping her old hours again.

Maybe she'd gone out with some friends. She knew he hadn't planned to be home for dinner, because she'd called and asked. He'd told her that he had a racquetball game scheduled and that he'd grab a bite at the gym afterwards.

She'd assumed he was playing with his usual partner, Gary, and he hadn't volunteered any information otherwise. He saw no point in telling her his partner had been Kelly.

A twinge of guilt pricked his conscience as he unbuckled his seatbelt. He tried to push it away. He had nothing to feel bad about. He wasn't cheating on Susanna.

Not anywhere but in his imagination, that was. Nor would he. It went against his grain, against his ethics. He wouldn't get physically involved with another woman unless he'd ended things with Susanna first.

The thought brought a fresh burst of guilt, sharper than before, and he heaved out a sigh that seemed to come from the center of his gut. He was considering it. God help him, he was. For the first time in thirty-three years, he was actually contemplating divorce.

He sighed and speared his fingers through his hair. Susanna had been his first love, and he'd always thought she would be his last. Over the past two years, though, things had changed.

She had changed. He had changed. Their lives had changed. It felt as if the supports had been knocked out from under them, as if the very foundation of their marriage had crumbled.

He didn't know if it could be rebuilt. He didn't know if he even wanted to try. The whole thing felt like such a convoluted mess, such an awful burden. Maybe they'd both be better off if they just cut their losses and walked away. That way they could each make a fresh start without having to sit around and sift through any more pain.

He was so damned tired of all the pain. He'd done nothing but grieve and hurt and work since Rachel died. Susanna had been so depressed that it depressed him to be around her. He'd started getting up in the morning before she awoke and coming home late. When he was home, he buried himself in paperwork in his study.

He couldn't stand to see Susanna hurting and not be able to do anything about it. She wouldn't let him do anything, wouldn't let him try to comfort her, either. The helplessness of it all was crushing him. It had made him feel impotent and old and useless.

And then Kelly had entered the picture. From the first time she'd shown up at his office with two other attorneys to discuss a corporate merger, something about her had made him feel more alive than he had in ages.

She'd radiated something—interest, awareness, flirtatiousness. It had been there in her eyes from that very first day, from the moment she'd first shaken his hand and held it a second or two longer than necessary. During the hour-long meeting that had followed, he'd felt the heat of her gaze on him across the long conference table. When he'd glanced up, she hadn't looked away.

Instead, her lips had curved in a slight, knowing smile, a smile that was suggestive and inviting.

That smile had sent currents of shock rippling through him. That was when he'd first noticed, on more than a cursory level, that she was attractive—extremely attractive. Long legs, a slim waist, generous breasts, shoulder-length blond hair . . . good heavens, she was a knockout! The realization startled him. It had been a long time since he'd thought of a woman other than Susanna in terms of sexual attractiveness.

It had been even longer since a woman had thought of *him* in those terms, he thought darkly. Susanna had lost all interest in sex after the death of Rachel. She hadn't even wanted to be held or comforted. She'd rejected all physical contact, wanting to curl up in a ball and just be left alone.

At first he'd been suspicious of Kelly, thinking she might be a decoy, part of a tactical plan by opposing counsel to keep him distracted and off-guard. The ploy wasn't unheard-of in the world of high-stakes negotiations. In the case of a friendly merger like this one, though, it made no discernible sense. Besides, she wasn't just an ornament; she was lead counsel for her legal team.

"It's been a pleasure," she'd purred, offering her hand as she left the office at the end of the meeting. "I look forward to our next meeting."

She'd called and invited him to lunch the following week. Thinking it was strictly business and the other attorneys assigned to the case would be present as well, he'd taken Jake along to get his perspective on a tricky financial issue. He'd been surprised to discover that she was alone, and she hadn't bothered to bring a single document with her.

Jake had seemed surprised, too. He'd made several

pointed references about Susanna, as if he wanted to make sure Kelly knew that Tom was married. If she took the hint, she didn't show it.

Over the last couple of months, Tom had seen Kelly frequently. She dropped by his office when a phone call would have been easier, and she continued to give him that sexy, secret smile whenever she caught his eye. Tom found himself smiling back. It gave him a heady feeling, this flirting business. After months of rejection at home, it felt good to indulge in something light-hearted and frivolous, something that boosted his ego and lifted his spirits. It was all perfectly innocent, he told himself, just good, clean fun. And it probably would have stayed that way, too, if Kelly hadn't gone to that conference in Denver.

He'd run into her the first night at the opening reception. They'd gone to dinner with a group of other people, but by the end of the evening, they'd ended up alone in the hotel bar. He told her about Rachel's death, and she told him about her divorce two years earlier. She'd asked about his marriage, and the next thing he knew, he'd spilled out all of his frustrations and worries about Susanna. The conversation drifted to sports, and they'd discovered they both liked to ski and play racquetball. He told jokes and laughed at hers and drank more than usual, and then she'd begged him to dance.

That had been the turning point. Holding her against him, swaying to a slow samba rhythm, feeling her breasts against his chest and her breath on his neck—it had all conspired against him. During the brief duration of the song, she'd infected him like a virus, weakening his resistance, making him feverish with desire. In the span of just a few minutes, she went from being a woman he was flirting with to a woman he longed to bed.

It had taken all of his resolve not to kiss her, not to follow her to her room. He might even have tried if two of his friends from Texas hadn't entered the bar and invited the two of them to join them for a drink. After a quick nightcap, Tom fled to his room.

The close call scared him. He'd avoided Kelly the rest of the trip. But then she'd sat beside him on the plane on the way home, and it was there again—the strong pull of attraction, the heady sensation of wanting and being wanted. Tom had tried to keep the conversation neutral, but every topic seemed laden with innuendo.

She'd called him twice in the past two weeks, and both times he'd turned down her invitations to lunch. But she'd caught him at a weak moment this afternoon. He'd had a crummy day—he'd not only lost a case, but argued with Jake over that damned baby—and when she had suggested a game of racquetball that evening, he'd agreed. He deserved a little pleasure in his life, he thought belligerently. Life shouldn't be all work and worry and problems. He liked the way he felt when he was with her—witty and smart and younger and, well, sexy. Hell. He might be a little gray around the temples, but he still liked to feel like a man.

So they'd played ball and eaten fat-free chicken Caesar salads at the club's snack bar. And then, as she polished off her bottle of Evian water, she'd looked him straight in the eye and said it: "I want to go to bed with you."

His mouth had gone dry, despite the fact he'd just taken a drink of diet soda. "I—I'm married."

"So?" She ran her foot up the inside of his calf.

"So . . . I don't believe in cheating."

Kelly's lips curved in a mocking smile. "From what you've told me about your wife, she'd probably think I was doing her a favor."

Hell—he knew he shouldn't have talked about his

169

wife so freely that night in the bar. "Kelly, I'm not the kind of man who can do that."

"Have you thought about leaving her?"

Tom had drawn a deep breath, then slowly it had hissed out. "It's crossed my mind."

"Well, maybe you should give it a trial run." She'd reached out and placed her hand over his. "We both love jazz and Creole food. Can you imagine what a great time we could have if we went to New Orleans together? The national corporate attorneys' convention's going to be held there this year, isn't it?"

"Kelly—" He'd begun to stop her short, but she cut him off.

"Don't say no. Just think about it."

Tom had pulled back his hand and checked his watch. "I—I've got to go."

"Me, too. I'll walk out with you."

He'd walked her to her car, started to give her a friendly peck on the cheek, but at the last moment she turned, and the kiss landed on her lips. Her hands had wound around his neck, and she'd pulled his head closer. He hadn't meant to, but he'd found himself kissing her back, kissing her like a hormone-crazed teenager until he was as hard as flagpole, right there in the health club parking lot.

The memory sent a fresh surge of guilt through him. It hadn't meant anything, he told himself as he climbed out of his Jaguar. He hadn't intended to do it. Hell—it was just a kiss, nothing more. One little kiss didn't mean he'd betrayed Susanna or his marital vows.

Not yet.

"Damn it. Damn it all." Grabbing his gym bag, he slammed the car door harder than necessary, wishing he could shut off the cloying sense of guilt as easily. He knew he was playing with fire, but he couldn't seem to help himself. Kelly made him feel alive. And lately he'd felt so dead—dead and flat, dead and colorless, dead and dry, like an old, crumpled leaf.

Juggling his gym bag in one hand and his laptop in the other, he unlocked the door and pushed it open, then stopped cold in his tracks.

Oh, Christ. Soft music wafted through from the stereo, and candlelight flickered from the dining room. Susanna appeared in the foyer, wearing a fitted black pantsuit he'd never seen before.

She smiled brightly. "Hi."

"Uh—hi." Tom stared from her to the flickering candles. "Is the electricity out?"

"No." Her smile widened. "I just thought candlelight might be . . . festive."

Festive—good God. She hadn't cooked up some sort of surprise party, had she? He ran a rapid mental inventory. It wasn't their anniversary, it wasn't his birthday, and it was six months before hers. Tom peered cautiously into the dining room. "What's the big deal?"

"No deal. I just thought it might be romantic if you and I had a glass of wine by candlelight."

Romantic—aw, hell! She was in the mood for romance, and he had Kelly's kiss fresh on his lips. He turned away and set his gym bag on the credenza in the hallway, shame gathering in his chest like storm clouds in a summer sky. "Not tonight." His voice was gruffer than he intended. "I've, uh, got some work to do." He avoided her eyes, not wanting to see that he'd hurt her, knowing damn well that he had.

There was a long, pregnant pause. She gave a little laugh, one that rang a little too brightly, was a little too brittle. "Well, surely you can spare me a few minutes. I haven't seen you all day."

Tom drew a deep breath and stifled the urge to blow

171

it out in a sigh. Hell. There was no way he could refuse without flat-out being a son of a bitch. "Okay."

"Can I pour you some wine?"

"No, thanks. I think I'll have a beer." Tom headed into the kitchen and flipped on the overhead light, glad to dispel the intimacy of the candlelight. Plopping his laptop on the counter, he opened the refrigerator and pulled out a bottle.

She leaned a slim hip against the counter. "How was your day?"

"Not great. I lost the LaMarr case."

"Oh, that's a shame. But you'll win on appeal."

"I hope so." Tom twisted off the cap and took a long swig of brew.

"Want to come in the living room and get comfortable?"

"Nah. I'd just as soon sit right here." *In the light. Where I don't feel like a fly about to be trapped by a spider.*

"Okay." She shimmied up on a bar stool beside him. "Was Jake back today?"

The thought made Tom scowl. He took another long pull on the bottle. "Yeah. He was back. Full of stories about that baby."

"The mother must still be recovering from surgery. Who's helping take care of the baby?"

"Jake hired a private nurse." Tom shook his head in disgust. "If he didn't have the big Steelco meeting this afternoon, he probably would have stayed out there in the sticks for another two weeks and played private nurse himself. He's completely besotted with this whole fatherhood thing."

"Well, you can't very well blame him."

"Yes, I can. He doesn't even know the mother."

"But it's his baby."

"Maybe." He twirled the bottle, staring at the wet circle it left on the white countertop. "Maybe not. He'll know for sure next week."

"He got a paternity test?"

Tom nodded. "If it's positive, I bet that floozy nails him but good for child support."

"I doubt that she's a floozy."

"Any woman who has a child and doesn't know who the father is ranks as a floozy in my book."

"It's not as if she slept around," Susanna said. "She had artificial insemination—a medical procedure. She must have wanted a child very badly."

Tom took a long pull from the bottle, not wanting to listen to reason. "Say what you want, but I bet she expects Jake to pay through his nose for the rest of his life."

"Well, it doesn't sound like Jake would mind. After all, he said he wants joint custody. This whole thing could turn out to be a wonderful blessing."

Tom snorted. "Being saddled with an illegitimate bastard and payments to a money-hungry broad for the next eighteen years sounds a lot more like a curse to me."

Susanna's lips parted in surprise. She leaned forward. "Tom, are you feeling all right? This isn't like you." Her brow was creased with worry. "You haven't been acting like yourself lately."

You're a fine one to talk. It was all he could do not to voice the thought aloud. He tilted back the bottle. "Sorry."

She placed a soft hand on his arm. He didn't have to look at her to know her eyes were troubled. "I think you've been working too hard lately. It would do you good to take a break. Why don't we get away? We could take a trip to Hawaii, or maybe book a cruise to the Caribbean."

173

Aw, hell—just what he needed. Until now, he'd done his best to keep his feelings bottled up, to try to be the stalwart one for her sake. But he couldn't do that tonight. He was too bitter—so bitter his insides felt like scorched earth.

Bitter—and angry. He was angry at her, and that made him angry at himself, because it was a completely unreasonable emotion, and he knew it. Hell, he knew she'd been hurting. She and Rachel had been closer than most mothers and daughters. He'd tried to comfort her, tried to help her, tried everything within his power, but all she'd wanted to do was push him away.

Well, she'd damned well succeeded. She'd pushed him away, all right—right toward someone else. And just as he'd about decided to go for it—to do what *he* wanted to do for a change, not what was best for the firm or his family or a client—she did a complete one-eighty. What was he supposed to do, just forget how she'd rejected him for the past two years?

Well, he couldn't do it. Just thinking about it made his blood boil. Where had she been all those nights when he'd needed her, when he'd longed to affirm that life was worth the trouble of living, that love was more than a heartache waiting to happen, that something bigger, more enduring than the pain inside of him actually existed? Where had she been when her body could have given him solace, when he'd longed to hold her and be held, to share in her grief, to have a safe place to pour out his own? He knew it was wrong to feel this way, knew it was petty and vindictive, but damn it all, he felt it anyway. He felt it so strongly he thought he was about to explode, like an over-filled canister of volatile gas.

She had no right to pop a few antidepressant pills and do a complete about-face, to suddenly become all sweetness and light, and expect him to act like nothing had happened. Plenty *had* happened, by damn!

His mouth tasted like burned toast. He reached for his beer, hoping to wash it away, only to realize he'd already drained the bottle. He stood, the barstool screeching on the cream-colored ceramic tile.

"Look, Suze, I'm snowed under right now. I can't even think about a trip." He tossed the bottle in the trash. "I've got to tackle these briefs now or else I'll be up all night." He gave her a brotherly peck on the cheek. As he did, he inhaled her perfume, the soft, subtle scent she'd worn for years, ever since he'd told her it made him think of sex.

She hadn't worn it in a long time. It set off something inside of him, some deep, aching, primordial ooze of emotion, one too embedded to be explained. His anger softened, and his voice did, too.

"Well, I'd better get to work."

Her brown eyes played over his face like searchlights. "I love you, Tom."

She must have said the words a million times in the past thirty-three years, and he had always responded the same way. Not to do so now would upset her. He didn't want to create a scene, didn't want to launch a big discussion. Above all, he didn't want to hurt her.

He swallowed hard. "I love you, too."

Then he grabbed his laptop and retreated to his study, not sure if he'd told the truth or a lie, not sure if he even knew the difference anymore.

Chapter Eleven

"Up! Up!"

Annie turned from the rosebush she was inspecting in the backyard to see Madeline lift her chubby arms above her head.

"Up!" the baby pleaded again.

"Oh, sweetie—you learned a new word!" Annie reflexively reached down for the child.

"You're not supposed to lift her yet," the home care nurse cautioned. "Not for three more days."

Annie sighed. "That's the hardest part about this whole recovery process—not being able to pick up my child."

"You can sit down and let her climb on your lap."

"I know, I know, but it's not the same."

"Up!" Madeline insisted. "Ma-ma-ma up!"

Annie smiled ruefully down at her child. "Honey, I'm sorry, but Mommy's boo-boo still hurts."

The nurse, a kind-faced woman named Mrs. Forest,

bent and picked up Madeline. "Let's go back to the patio, honey," she said to the child. "Mommy can sit down and hold you there."

Annie turned toward the house, just as Jake strolled around the corner. Her heart jumped into her throat.

Mrs. Forest spotted him at the same time. "Oh, look, Madeline!" She gave the baby a little bounce. "There's your daddy!"

"Ink! Ink! Ink!" Madeline cried, squirming in the nurse's grip. Mrs. Forest put her down, and the baby raced toward Jake, her arms out.

A smile broke over Jake's face as he scooped the child up. "Hello, there, sweetheart. Are you glad to see me?"

"She sure seems to be," the nurse affirmed.

Jake settled the child in his arms, his smile widening. It was the first heartfelt smile Annie had seen him give to the baby, and it was so much like Madeline's that her throat tightened.

He turned his attention toward her. "Hi, Annie."

Annie's pulse fluttered. "Hi."

He glanced at the nurse. "Mrs. Forest, do you think Annie's well enough for a little outing? I'd like to take her and the baby out to lunch, if she's up to it."

"I believe she is. In fact, I think an outing would do her good."

"Great. This will give you a break, too."

"Oh, good. I could use an hour or two to run a few errands."

"You go right ahead."

Mrs. Forest headed for the house, leaving them alone.

Annie gave Jake a teasing grin, her heart pounding erratically. "When a person issues an invitation, it's customary to address the person one is actually inviting."

"I know. But I didn't want to run the risk that you'd say no. I knew you'd go if it was under nurse's orders."

Annie grinned. He grinned back. Sexual tension stretched between them, tightening like a kite string on a windy day.

She felt his gaze rove over her. Self-consciously she smoothed her short denim dress.

"You look great," he said. "How are you feeling?"

"Better every day."

"That's good."

He held her gaze a second too long, looking away only when Madeline fidgeted.

Annie felt fidgety, too, but for an entirely different reason.

"It's getting close to Madeline's lunch time," she said. "She's probably getting hungry."

He set the baby on the ground. "Well, then, let's go."

The only restaurant in Lucky was the Cowbell Café, a ramshackle diner that had been a truck stop before the interstate diverted traffic away from the two-lane state highway that ran through town. Jake shifted Madeline to one arm and opened the door for Annie with the other, causing the cowbell over the door to jangle. Every head in the restaurant swiveled toward the door.

Jake nodded at the sea of curious faces and ushered Annie toward a booth near the window, pausing to grab a highchair along the way. A disconcerting silence followed as every pair of eyes in the place watched them walk. A buzz of conversation began as they sat down.

"Guess they don't get many strangers in here," Jake remarked as he tried to place Madeline in the highchair.

"I guess not," Annie replied.

"Do you know these folks?"

Annie shook her head. "I recognize a few faces, but I'd be hard-pressed to put names to them. Everyone around here knew my grandparents, though, so they all know who I am."

I'll bet they do. And I'll bet an attractive, single woman raising a baby and a herd of alpacas by herself is pretty good conversational fodder. Jake finally managed to get Madeline's legs through the opening in the highchair. He slid the seat up against the table, then slipped into the booth opposite Annie.

"When I come to town, it's usually just to go to the grocery store or the nursing home," Annie said. "I don't get out much."

"Even for dates?"

She smiled ruefully. "Especially for dates. I haven't been out on a real date in nearly three years."

Three years. That was well before Madeline had been conceived. He didn't care what she'd done before she'd gotten pregnant, but for some reason, he was extremely relieved to discover she'd been dateless since. There was nothing personal to it, he told himself. He just didn't like the idea of the mother of his child out cattin' around, that was all.

Madeline pounded a chubby fist on the tray. "Ink! Ink! Ink!"

Uh-oh. The baby was staring at him, hoping to score a Twinkie.

"It sounds like she wants her Binky," Annie said. "Check and see if she has one in the diaper bag."

Jake reached in and pulled out the yellow plastic pacifier. He set it on the table in front of the baby, only to have Madeline quickly snatch it and toss it to the floor. "Ink! Ink! Ink!"

Annie's brow knit in bewilderment. "I wish I knew what she was saying."

And I hope you never find out.

Jake retrieved the pacifier as a big-haired waitress approached. She set a basket of crackers and two glasses of water on the table, smiled a greeting, then reached into the pile of teased hair on her head to pull out a pencil. "The blue-plate special today is spaghetti and meatballs."

"Sounds good to me," Annie said.

Jake doubted that anything at a dive like this was likely to be very good, but he might as well go along. "I'll have the same."

"And could you please bring us an extra plate for the baby?" Annie asked.

"Sure thing."

Annie reached for a package of crackers, opened it, and handed a Saltine to Madeline. "I'm pretty sure you didn't drop everything and drive to Lucky just to sample the blue-plate special."

"No."

Annie's eyes locked on his, her face tense. "You've gotten the test results, haven't you?"

"Yes." He reached into his pants pocket, pulled out a folded yellow paper and placed it in front of her. "It's right here."

Annie stared at the paper, but didn't reach for it. "I'd prefer just to hear."

"It's positive." Jake couldn't repress a smile. The news made him feel like he was walking on air. "I'm Madeline's father."

Annie sagged back against the booth. "I knew it."

"I did, too, but the test confirmed it. The DNA markers all matched. The accuracy rate is ninety-nine point nine percent."

Annie slowly nodded.

Jake gazed at her, trying to read her expression. "So . . . are you upset?"

Annie sighed and leaned forward, her elbows on the

table. "I don't know. A week ago, I would have thought it was the end of the world. But you've been so kind during my illness. . . ." She reached for her water glass and took a sip, eyeing him over its rim, as if she were trying to see into his soul. "Of course, I realize it's to your benefit to be that way."

Jake's stomach tightened. "What do you mean?"

"Well, I didn't just fall off the turnip truck. It's pretty obvious you want to win me over so I'll willingly share custody of Madeline."

Her bluntness was disarming—the complete opposite of the fencing and dodging he was accustomed to dealing with on a daily basis. He decided to respond just as bluntly. "So how am I doing?"

To his relief, she grinned. "Pretty well, actually."

Jake smiled back. That blast of heat surged between them again, radiating back and forth. A person would always know where he stood with Annie Hollister, Jake thought. He liked that. He liked that a lot.

She reached for another pack of crackers. "But just because you're relatively nice doesn't mean I'm ready to sign any papers." She pulled open the cellophane and handed the crackers to Madeline. "I still don't know much about you."

"So what do you want to know?"

"Everything."

"That's a pretty broad topic."

She twisted the cracker wrapper as if she were wringing it out. "Well, for starters, tell me about your family. Does Madeline have any extended family? Any aunts or uncles or cousins?"

Jake leaned back against the vinyl booth. "I'm an only child. As for family, it's pretty much just me."

"Tell me about your parents."

"Well, they were both neurologists."

Annie's eyebrows rose high. "Both of them?"

Jake nodded. "They lived and breathed neurology. They specialized in research. They were obsessed with unlocking the secrets of the human brain."

"Wow. So Madeline's grandparents were a pair of geniuses."

Jake gave a wry grin. "Pretty much. Sometimes I think the only reason they had me was to combine their genes and produce the ultimate neurologist."

"What made you decide not to become one?"

"I was a disaster at science. I nearly blew up the high school chemistry lab, and the poor frog I dissected in biology looked as if he'd been on a bad date with Jack the Ripper."

Annie smiled.

"They tried not to show it, but I know my folks were disappointed," Jake found himself saying.

"Oh, surely not."

"Trust me. They were." Annie's eyes filled with something that looked suspiciously like sympathy, making him anxious to change the topic. "What was your family like?" he asked.

Annie looked down and sighed. "Well, we didn't have what you'd call a happy home life. My parents fought like cats and dogs. Like a typical kid, I thought it was all my fault. They stayed together for my sake, but they were miserable."

"After coming from a home like that, you'd think you'd be gun-shy about marriage."

Annie gave a dry smile. "I wish I had been. I got married right out of college, when I was still in the trying-to-please-my-parents phase, thinking it was my job to make them happy. Nate was a topic they both agreed on. He was smart, well educated, from a good family. . . ." She looked down at the cracker wrapper.

"Unfortunately, he was still in love with someone else, and he married me on the rebound. As he got over the girl that got away, he got over me, too."

Jake drew his brow together. "That must have been rough."

She gave a single nod. "We didn't quite make it to our first anniversary. He said our marriage was a mistake, that he didn't love me as I deserved to be loved." Annie gave a small smile. "He was right, of course, but that didn't make it hurt any less."

"You loved him." For some reason, he found the thought distressing.

Annie lifted her shoulders. "I thought I did." She untwisted the cracker wrapper, then started twisting it the other direction. "As time passed, though, I realized I loved the idea of putting down the roots I never had as a child, of having a quiet, peaceful relationship. Nate seemed like a good bet because he was nonconfrontational. We never argued. Of course, we never really talked, either—not in a deep, meaningful, heart-to-heart, soul-to-soul kind of way. I was always worried about not rocking the boat." She gave a wry smile. "I'm talking more freely to you right now than I ever did to him."

Before he could quite figure out whether that fact pleased or alarmed him, she turned the conversation around. "What about you? What was your marriage like?"

Jake shifted uneasily on the vinyl booth. "Great."

Annie rested her chin in her hands and sighed wistfully. "You were one of the lucky ones, huh?"

"That's not how it feels now."

She regarded him somberly. "No, I suppose not. So, are you dating anyone now?"

The question jarred him. "No."

"Why not?"

"Well, there's no point. There will never be another Rachel."

"No, but there could be someone else."

"Anyone else would just be second-rate."

Annie gazed at him for a long moment. "So you don't intend to ever have another relationship?"

He shook his head.

"But what about . . . you know . . ."

"What about what?"

Annie shot a surreptious look at the baby, who was munching a cracker, and leaned forward. "What about sex?" she whispered.

Jake stared at her. "What about it?"

"Well . . . are you going to live the rest of your life without it?"

What a depressing thought! "I, uh—I don't think about it in those terms." Or, he hadn't until now. Crimony—why had she had to put it that way? He'd come here so happy. Now he was seriously bummed. "I take it a day at a time."

"So what do you do when you're . . . you know . . . ?"

Good Lord, but she was nosy. He glared, irritated at her for raising the spectre of lifelong celibacy, ready to put her in her place. "When I'm horny?"

She should have blushed, but she didn't. "Yes."

"I take care of myself," he said belligerently. "What about you?"

"I . . ." She at least had the grace to look down at the plastic cracker wrapper in her fingers. "Well, I do the same."

Unbidden images flashed through his mind—hot, steamy images of Annie, naked in her bed, her hands running over her own body. Jake's pulse roared in his ears, and his mouth went dry. "Well, then, I guess we're in the same boat."

"For the time being, I suppose." She twirled the cracker wrapper around her pinkie. "My knight hasn't ridden up on a white charger yet, but I still have hope." She gave the wrapper a final twist, then looked up, her eyes filled with something that looked suspiciously like pity. "It must be awfully sad not to have any hope."

How in blue blazes had they gotten on this topic? Jake took a long gulp of water, using the glass as a shield from eyes that seemed to see too much, then set it down on the Formica tabletop harder than he'd intended. He was relieved when the waitress arrived and set two heaping plates of spaghetti in front of them, along with an extra plate for Madeline.

He watched Annie cut a meatball into baby-sized bites. It was time to steer the conversation to the purpose of his visit. "Now that we know I'm definitely Madeline's father, I'd like to draw up a custody agreement."

Annie froze, her knife in the air. "We don't need anything in writing. You can just come see her whenever you want."

"That's what you say now, but situations change." He leaned forward. "I want to be a real father to her. I don't just want my name on her birth certificate—although I definitely do want that."

"What else do you want?"

"Joint custody."

She looked at him, her eyes round and scared, her face white. "What does that mean? That she'd live with you half the time?"

"Well, not exactly half. The custodial parent—that would be you—has the child the majority of the time. All throughout the school year, for example."

"But you'd have her for weekends and summers and holidays?"

"Well, we'd have to work all that out."

Annie stared at him. "You want me to spend several months of every year without my child?"

Jake moved his plate to the side and folded his hands on the table. "Annie, be reasonable. I'm her parent, too. She deserves to grow up knowing both of us. And, of course, I intend to provide child support."

"I don't need your money."

"From the stack of bills sitting in your kitchen, I'd say otherwise."

Her eyebrows rose. "You looked through my bills?"

He shrugged. "They were right by the phone. Sorry."

She looked like she was about to take the child and bolt. He decided to back off. "Look, we don't have to do this right now," he said.

"What would you do with her while you're at the office? Leave her with a nanny? Put her in daycare? Why would you want a stranger taking care of your child, when she could be with her own mother?"

Jake raised his hands in a placating gesture. "We wouldn't have to split physical custody right away. She needs you. I can see that. I just want to be as much a part of her life as possible."

"Well, you're welcome to come see her whenever you want."

"I appreciate that. And that's fine for right now."

"So why don't we just leave it that way?"

"Because things change. You might remarry or move away. . . ."

"I'm not moving anywhere."

"You say that now, but who knows what may happen in the future? You just said you'd like to meet Mr. Right." He reached out and covered her hand with his. It was a calculated gesture, one he used often with female clients to persuade them to see things his way, but this time, it backfired. The feel of her warm, soft hand

186

was lessening *his* resolve. "Look—this is for the protection of both of us. Why don't I draft up a preliminary agreement, just something to use as a starting point, then you can show it to your attorney and think about it. I won't push you to sign anything you're not comfortable with." He tightened his fingers around hers. "Okay?"

She looked down at their intertwined hands, then slowly pulled back her hand. Her eyes took his measure for a long moment, then she breathed out a sigh. "If you draw something up, I'll look at it. I can't promise I'll sign it, but I'll look at it."

"Good." He wasn't about to tell her he had the papers already drafted and sitting in a folder in the backseat of his car. Some issues needed to be broached bit by bit, baby step by baby step.

Thwak! Something warm and wet suddenly hit Jake smack in the middle of his forehead. He reflexively raised his hand and touched his face. When he pulled it back, he was alarmed to see it covered with spaghetti sauce.

Madeline giggled gleefully, and Annie gave a snort of laughter.

"What just happened?" Jake asked.

"Madeline stole a meatball off your plate and lobbed it at you."

Jake looked down at his lap. Sure enough, a meatball sat damply on his navy slacks, wedged suggestively between his thighs. He gingerly picked it up and plopped it on the tabletop. "Good one, Madeline."

Annie covered her mouth and sniggered.

Jake picked up his napkin and wiped the sauce off his face. Annie scooted the metal dispenser of paper napkins toward him. He pulled out a handful and attacked his white shirt. "What's the deal with this kid and my

187

clothes? Every time I take her out in public, she covers me with dirt, food, or bodily fluids."

"Maybe she's trying to decorate you."

"Like a Christmas tree?"

"Maybe." Annie's smile was blinding. "Or maybe she's just trying to get you to loosen up."

"I don't need loosening up." He stopped wiping his shirt, looked up, and quirked an eyebrow. "Do I?"

"Maybe a little."

It was ridiculous that such a benign remark should prick his pride, but it did. "In what way?"

Annie's lips curved. "Well, you have to admit you're a little too structured."

"Structure isn't a bad thing to have in your life." *In fact,* Jake thought darkly, *you ought to try it some time.*

"Neither is the ability to trust other people and go with the flow." Her full, sexy lips curved in a teasing smile. "I bet if I frisked you right now, I'd find an itinerary outlining how you plan to spend every minute of your day, complete with goals and objectives."

The idea of being frisked by Annie held a disturbing appeal. "Planning your day is the best way to prioritize your time."

The curve of her lips made him realize how completely stuffy he sounded. With a noncommittal grunt, he resumed wiping his clothes.

"Babies don't fit into a Day-Timer," Annie said. "They're messy and time-consuming and prone to accidents. Especially our baby."

Our baby. There was no reason a simple possessive pronoun should make his heart beat like a judge's gavel in a disorderly courtroom, but it did.

Annie, too, seemed hit by the significance of her unwitting remark. Her eyes widened and met his across the table, and the moment came and went when one of them should have looked away.

Our child. It was a weighty concept to grasp. He and Annie were inextricably bound together by the cherubic imp at the end of the table who was now merrily finger painting on her plate with tomato sauce. Before he'd ever met this woman, his seed had impregnated her womb, his heritage had fused with hers, and their futures were irrevocably intertwined.

But they were complete opposites. In the normal course of events, their paths probably never would have crossed, and if they had, they never would have given each other more than a cursory glance. He would have considered her much too free-spirited and Bohemian, and she would have thought him too rigid and stuffy. The only reason they were sitting here together now was because they'd made a child.

That had to be the only reason he was feeling such a strong, hot pull of attraction toward her. He was pretty sure it wasn't just a one-sided thing, either. He could feel heat sizzling between them, bouncing back and forth, firing off so many sparks it was a wonder the restaurant wasn't filled with smoke.

They'd made a baby, but they hadn't made love. They'd skipped an important step in the natural order of things. That must be why they were so physically aware of each, so sexually curious. After all, people who made babies together were lovers. He didn't even know what Annie looked like naked.

But, boy, I'd sure like to. The thought made him jerk his eyes away from her in alarm.

Annie quickly averted her gaze, too. Picking up a napkin, she busily wiped Madeline's chin, then pushed Jake's plate far out of the baby's reach. "You'd better watch out, or she's likely to resume pitching practice."

Jake gave a weak grin, thinking that the baby was the least of his worries. Madeline might throw meatballs, but Annie threw him for a loop.

"The nurse's car is still gone," Jake said as he pulled into the drive of Annie's house. "I'll stay with you until she gets back."

For some reason, the thought of being alone with Jake made Annie's stomach quake. "You don't need to do that."

"Maybe not, but I'm going to anyway." He softened the words with a smile as he braked the car and killed the engine. "Stay put and I'll get the door for you."

He circled the automobile and helped her out, then opened the back door and gazed down at the sleeping child. "Looks like the meatball hurler is down for the count."

Annie smiled as Jake unfastened the strap of the baby's carseat. He carefully lifted the child out, nestling her against his shoulder, so that her head rested against his. A lump formed in Annie's throat. Their dark hair was a perfect match.

Annie followed as Jake carried the child into the nursery and gently placed her in her crib, then she covered the sleeping baby with a blanket. Her shoulder brushed Jake's, and a current of attraction rolled through her, along with a strong feeling of déjà vu.

She suddenly knew why. This was the scene she'd imagined so many times in her fantasies. Over and over, she'd pictured herself here at her grandparents' ranch, standing beside a crib, smiling down at a baby, a handsome man by her side. She'd never envisioned the man's face in her fantasies, but if she had, it would have been Jake's.

That thought made her freeze. She needed to stop letting her imagination run away with her. Jake was emotionally unavailable. Hadn't he just told her he had no interest in a relationship, that no one could ever measure up to his late wife?

She gave the blanket a final tuck, then quietly left the baby's room, wanting to leave the disturbing thoughts behind. Jake followed her to the kitchen.

"Want some coffee?" she asked.

"Sure. Here, I'll do it for you." He headed for the refrigerator and pulled out a bag of freshly ground coffee. It was disconcerting, how this man was invading her space. He'd fathered her baby, he'd stayed in her house, and he knew his way around her kitchen, yet she knew very little about him.

Well, that was something she could change. She glanced over at him as she filled the coffee maker's pot with tap water. "What made you decide to go into law?"

Jake pulled a measuring cup out of a drawer and carefully poured in some coffee grounds. "I guess I figured that if I couldn't save the world by fighting neurological illness, I'd do it by fighting injustice." He poured a half-cup of grounds into the coffeemaker. His lip curled in an ironic expression that was more grimace than grin. "That was back when I was young and idealistic and believed justice actually existed."

"You don't now?"

Jake gave a derisive snort.

"Not too jaded, are you?"

He shrugged. "Let's just say I've seen the scales tipped by the weight of a wallet a few times too many. Corporate law isn't exactly a bastion of fairness."

"You could always do something else." She switched on the coffeemaker.

"Like what?"

"You tell me. What did you want to be when you were a boy?"

Jake leaned against the kitchen counter. "Batman or Superman. But they didn't offer superhero training as a major in college."

Smiling, she rested a hip against the walnut cabinet beside him. "You wanted to be one of the good guys."

Jake met Annie's gaze. He'd never thought of it that way. This woman had an uncanny way of seeing things that he'd never realized about himself. "Yeah. I guess so."

"Have you ever thought about being a prosecutor?"

"I've done more than think about it. I was assistant D.A. in Tulsa for two years."

"How was it?"

Jake thoughtfully rubbed his jaw. "Frustrating as hell. It was like fighting a war that'll never be won. But it was somehow rewarding, too. I looked forward to going to work every day." He looked away, vaguely embarrassed to have said so much.

She nodded slowly. "It was a war worth fighting."

"Exactly." There it was again—that uncanny ability of hers to know what he was feeling.

"So why did you switch to corporate law?"

Jake lifted his shoulders. "My father-in-law's partner retired. Tom had been after me for some time to join his firm, and my wife . . ." He trailed off. Rachel had resented the long hours he put in as D.A., for little pay. She'd been jealous of his job, as if it had been a mistress. And in a way, Jake mused, he supposed it had been. Jake blew out a breath as he ran a hand through his hair. "It was the logical thing to do."

Annie looked at him, just looked at him, her gaze

cutting him no slack. "Sometimes logic isn't the best criteria for decisions."

"What is? Tea leaves?"

"No. Your heart."

Jake rolled his eyes.

"You said you used to look forward to going to work everyday. I bet you can't say that now."

"How do you know how I feel?"

She waved her hand, dismissing the question. "I'm right, aren't I?"

She was. Tension hummed between them. The air grew thick with it, thick and still and heavy. "Okay, fortune-teller. What else do you see in your crystal ball?" He was stepping into quicksand, venturing onto dangerous ground, but he couldn't resist the question.

She gazed up at him with those blue, blue eyes. "That you don't let people close. You keep your distance because you don't want to get hurt, but the very distance you think will protect you is hurting you."

Jake deliberately stepped closer, wanting to prove her wrong. "You think I'm hurting?"

She nodded. "I think you're lonely."

Hell, she made him sound as pathetic as a homeless hound. His eyebrows knit in a hard scowl, and his voice lowered to a deep growl. "You offering to change that?"

Annie's eyes widened.

He didn't know what demon seized him, but it was a dark one. Two years of heartache bubbled up and boiled over. He'd show her, by damn. He'd teach her what came of trying to psychoanalyze him and pry into his soul. He'd wipe that pitying look off her face if it were the last thing he did.

He reached out and pulled her to him. She stared up, her eyes wide, as he caught her face in his hands. She was still staring up when he slanted his mouth over hers.

He'd intended to give her a short, hard, I'll-show-you-not-to-feel-sorry-for-me kind of kiss, but all coherent thought fled his brain the moment his lips met hers. All that remained was the kiss.

Soft. Her mouth was so soft, softer than anything in recent memory—soft and pliant and willing, soft and lush and salty-sweet. He wanted to drown in that softness, to dive in and be surrounded by it, to let it soothe away all of the sharp, rough edges of his soul. His hands skimmed down the top of her arms. Her skin was soft, too—as soft as her lips.

And warm. His hand slid down to her back, and suddenly the heat between them ignited. She gave a soft little moan and fitted herself against him, winding her arms around his neck, pressing her breasts against his chest, snugging her pelvis against his. His body responded. She moaned again and moved against him.

Good Lord, he was on fire, ablaze, blind to everything but the scent of her hair, the feel of her body, the taste of her mouth. He was consumed by an aching need, a need so great that it overpowered all reason and shrank the world to nothing but Annie—Annie's skin, Annie's warmth, Annie's lush, soft woman's body.

His hand slid down and cupped her breast. It was full and heavy and warm, and she groaned with pleasure as he ran his thumb across the tip. Her responsiveness inflamed his senses. He deepened the kiss, and her fingers threaded through his hair, pulling him down, urging him on.

A soft noise seemed to come from a far distance. Jake would have ignored it, but Annie abruptly pulled away. The noise sounded again. This time Jake realized it was a discreet cough.

"Mrs. Forest—hello." Annie's voice sounded startled and unnaturally high.

Jake opened passion-glazed eyes to see the middle-aged nurse standing in the kitchen doorway, her jowl-lined cheeks beet red, an embarrassed smile on her face. She lifted two fingers in a tiny wave.

"I, uh, just wanted to let you know I'm back," the woman warbled. "I'll be in the back of the house if you need me." She turned and fled as fast as her rubber-soled shoes would take her.

Jake dropped his hands as if they'd been scorched. Good God in heaven, what was the matter with him? He'd never done anything so irrational in his life.

Folding her arms across her chest, Annie rubbed her upper arms, as if she were suddenly cold.

Jake looked away. "Hey—I'm sorry. I—I didn't mean for that to happen."

Annie ran her hands up and down her arms. "I didn't, either."

Jake awkwardly rubbed his jaw. What the devil had he been thinking? He *hadn't* been thinking, that was the problem. He cleared his throat. "I don't know what got into me. I hope you'll forgive me."

She nodded. "It's okay. It was just one of those things."

Jake nodded uncertainly. He couldn't help but wonder what kind of a thing she thought it was. He shoved his hand in his pocket. "Well, look—I'd better be going."

"All right." She walked him down the hall to the door. "Well . . ."

"Yes. Well . . ."

They stared at each other. Jake started to hold out his hand, but that seemed ridiculous, considering they'd just been swapping saliva.

Hell. He might as well just address the situation head-on. "Look—I really don't know what just happened here. I'm not in the market for a relationship, so it was really stupid of me to . . . to . . ."

"Kiss me." The words came out soft and hazy and inviting. Her eyes looked that way, too.

"I beg your pardon?"

"It was stupid of you to kiss me. That's what you were trying to say, isn't it?"

"Well, uh, yes. . . ." For a moment there, he'd thought she was asking for another kiss, and damned if he wasn't ready to oblige.

"You're not the only one at fault, you know." Her voice was soft. "I was kissing you back."

The admission did nothing to make him feel better. In fact, it made him feel aroused all over again. He clenched his fists at his side, determined to regain his self control. "Well, you don't have to worry about it happening again."

Without another word, he hurried out the door and to his car, anxious to put as much distance as possible between himself and this impossible woman. The only problem was, he had an unsettling feeling that distance alone would not solve the problem.

Chapter Twelve

"Hi, Ben! How's Helen?"

"Annie, girl—hello!" Ben's voice crackled over the cell phone. "She's doin' great. The doc says we'll be able to come home next week."

"That's terrific." Cradling the phone between her chin and shoulder, Annie stood under the large pecan tree in her back yard and pushed the swing suspended from its lowest branch.

"She's gonna be sorry she missed your call," Ben said. "Our daughter just took her to physical therapy. The therapist says Helen is her star pupil."

"Tell her to keep up the good work. Sounds like she's going to have you out square dancing before you know it."

"I'm afraid she might at that. How are you doin'?"

"Fine."

"Is that nurse still stayin' with you?"

"Yes. She'll be here a few more days, until it's all right for me to pick up Madeline."

Annie pushed the swing again. The baby giggled gaily.

"I hear the little scamp laughin'," Ben said. "What's she up to?"

"Swinging in the backyard. I'm on the cell phone."

Annie could picture Ben's frown. "I hear those phones can fry your brain."

"Too late. Mine is already scrambled. Besides, I've got other things to worry about."

"Like that Tulsa attorney, I imagine."

Annie sighed. The last time Ben called, she'd told him all about Jake's unexpected appearance in her life.

"Has he been giving you more problems?" Ben asked, his voice was low and somber.

"Only if you count lost sleep."

"Why's that?"

Because his kisses are hotter than fresh-picked jalapeños. Annie tried to push the thought out of her mind, but it swung back just as predictably as Madeline's yellow toddler swing.

She'd tried to put that kiss into perspective, she really had. She'd tried to reason it away, to tell herself it was nothing more than an impetuous gesture, but she couldn't reason away the way it had felt.

All consuming. All encompassing. Absorbing. Exceeding the boundaries of what it was. Never before had a kiss done the things to her insides that Jake's kiss had done. Jake's kiss had changed things.

It had changed *her*. But for the life of her, she couldn't explain it or understand how.

It all had to do with the fact that they'd made a child together, she told herself. Although that didn't explain the instantaneous attraction she'd felt the moment she'd first set eyes on him.

"Annie? You still there?" Ben asked.

"Yes."

"So what's new with this paternity business?"

Annie shifted the phone to her other ear. "The blood tests say that Jake is Madeline's father."

A long silence followed. "I know it's not what you wanted," Ben drawled, "but it might not be a bad thing for Madeline, Annie. A father can be a big asset to a child."

"I know." The words came out soft and grudgingly.

"Seems to me that the key to it all is both of you havin' the child's welfare at heart. Last time we talked, you told me he's good with Madeline."

"He is. He's gentle and patient, and he makes her laugh. She's taken a real liking to him."

"Well, dogs and babies are pretty good judges of character. I take it Hot Dog hasn't run him off either, huh?"

Annie snorted. "The way Hot Dog follows him around, you'd think he bathed in chicken livers."

Ben chuckled. "Well, then, there you go. This Jake fella seems to get along with everyone—except maybe you." There was a meaningful pause. "How *do* you two get along?"

Physically, all too well. Annie gave Madeline's swing another push. "Personality-wise, we're pretty much opposites. He likes everything planned out and written down. He's pretty structured."

Ben chuckled. "I can imagine how well that sets with you."

"Well, like I said, we're opposites."

"Maybe that's good. Between the two of you, you'll provide a good balance for Madeline."

"I suppose." Annie sighed again. "But, Ben, I can't

tell you how much I hate the idea of sharing Madeline."

"Is that what he wants?"

"He wants joint custody. And Henry says he's likely to get it."

"You're not still worried he might try to take her away from you altogether?"

"Now that I've gotten to know him, I can't imagine him doing that. He knows how attached Madeline is to me, and he really does to seem to care for her."

"How does he feel about *you?*"

"Me?" Annie's voice rose along with her eyebrows. "What does that have to do with anything?"

Ben's raspy chuckle rocked over the phone line.

"How the heck would I know a thing like that, anyway?" Annie asked.

Ben laughed again. "Same way you gals seem to know most things. He's single, isn't he?"

Annie's stomach knotted. It was exactly the train of thought she was trying to avoid. "He's a widower. But he's not looking for a relationship."

"No man is ever looking for a relationship, but most men can't help just plain lookin'. You're not too hard on the eyes, Annie-girl." Ben paused a moment. "A little romance between you two would sure solve a lot of problems. Stranger things have happened."

Annie had been trying hard not to think the same thing. "No way. He told me no one could ever compare to his wife, and I'm not interested in playing second fiddle. I did that in my first marriage." She shifted the phone to her other ear. "Besides, we're too different."

"Well, you know what they say about opposites. And the way I figure it, he can't be too ugly, if he looks just likc Madclinc."

"Oh, he's not ugly at all."

Ben chortled again. Annie's face heated as she realized she'd guilelessly taken his bait.

She was relieved to see Mrs. Forest step out on the patio. Annie covered the receiver with her hand and looked at the nurse inquisitively.

"I hate to disturb you, Annie, but you have a guest," the woman said.

"I've got to go, Ben," Annie said into the phone. "Someone's here."

Annie said her good-byes and clicked off the phone. "Who is it?"

"Susanna Morrison."

The name drew a blank. "Did she say what she wanted?"

"No. Just that she wants to see you and Madeline."

"Did she say why?"

Mrs. Forest's eyes grew baffled behind her bifocals. "She said she's Madeline's grandmother."

"Madeline's grandmother?" Jake's mother was dead, and Annie's mother was in Europe.

Annie must have looked as confused as she felt, because the nurse's eyes widened. "Well, she did say something about being an unofficial grandma or something. I thought she might be your stepmother. It did strike me as odd, though, because I didn't think you had any family, from what your husband said when he hired me. . . ."

"He's not my husband," Annie replied automatically.

The furrows of consternation between Mrs. Forest's brows deepened. "Oh, dear. I meant to say ex-husband."

Annie didn't bother to correct her. It was all too complicated. A lifetime of similar complications suddenly seemed to loom before her, a tangle of misunderstandings and tedious explanations. She heaved an exasperated sigh. "It's all right. Would you watch Madeline?"

"Sure."

Heading to the house, Annie entered the kitchen and walked through the foyer to the front door. She opened it to find a tall, dark-haired woman in an expensive black linen pantsuit, a warm smile on her lovely face.

"Hello," the woman began. "I'm Susanna Morrison. Jake's mother-in-law." She held out her hand.

Annie took it, her mind fitting the information together. "Your daughter was Jake's wife."

"That's right."

"I'm Annie Hollister. It's nice to meet you." If Rachel had looked like her mother, it was no wonder Jake was still in love with her. Susanna was a strikingly attractive woman—beautiful in a cool, polished, pulled-together way that Annie had always admired. "Jake told me about the accident. I'm so sorry."

Susanna nodded. For a moment, her eyes grew somber, then she drew a breath and smiled. "I know it's odd, me dropping in on you like this, but I wasn't sure if you'd see me if I called."

"Why wouldn't I?"

"Well, the whole situation is so . . . unusual. I'm not sure how you feel about Jake, much less about how you'd feel about meeting Jake's family." Susanna smiled. "I'm not a blood relation, of course, but Jake is like a son to me."

This woman was so warm and sincere, it was impossible for Annie not to like her immediately. "I'm glad to meet you. Won't you come in?" She held the door wide and stepped back.

Susanna followed her through the foyer and into the living room, looking around admiringly. "What lovely antiques!" She ran her fingers gingerly over an heirloom sidetable.

"Thank you. They belonged to my great-grandparents."

The woman stopped before the apothecary case and gazed at the contents. "This is fascinating—like something from a museum."

"My great-great grandfather ran an apothecary in Salina, Kansas, in the 1800s. The stuff in here is from his store's inventory."

Susanna leaned toward the case, peering at its contents. "There really was such a thing as Spring Tonic?"

Annie smiled. "I'm afraid so. My grandmother used to say she remembered her mother making her take it."

"My goodness. Soaps and salves and lotions—and just look at the assortment of teas!"

Annie nodded. She wondered if Jake had told Susanna about her family tradition of reading tea leaves. Deciding not to volunteer the information, she gestured to the sofa. "Won't you have a seat?"

"Thank you." Susanna perched on the edge of the sofa, her long legs folded neatly beneath her. "I want to apologize again for just dropping in on you. I was just so thrilled to learn that Jake has a child." Her brown eyes were warm and friendly. "Jake and Rachel had been trying to have a baby for years. Learning that Jake had this child . . . well, it was jarring at first, I have to admit. But then I realized this was as close as I was likely to ever come to being a grandmother. So I screwed up my courage and came to see you."

"I'm glad you did." And she was. Susanna emanated a warmth that made Annie feel like they were already friends. Besides, her visit was a perfect opportunity to learn more about Madeline's father. "So, how long have you known Jake?" she asked, seating herself in the wingback chair.

"Oh, goodness—for nearly twenty years, I guess."

Annie's eyebrows rose in surprise. "Twenty years?"

Susanna nodded. "Jake and his parents used to live next door to us. They moved in when Jake and Rachel were in their early teens."

"I didn't realize that."

"Oh, yes. They were high-school sweethearts."

For some reason, the news left Annie with an odd, hollow feeling. "I suppose you knew Jake's parents well, too, then, if they were neighbors."

Susanna nodded. "We all belonged to the same country club, and I chaired several fundraisers for neurological research projects that Jake's parents initiated."

"So you were close friends."

Susanna hesitated. "We were friends, but I don't know that you'd exactly call us close. I don't think anyone was really close to them. They were both very career-oriented. They didn't socialize much. And they traveled a lot, doing research and such."

"That must have been hard on Jake."

"I think it was. He wanted their approval more than anything in the world, but I don't know that he ever felt he got it. They were just so busy. . . ."

Annie thought of Jake's determination to spend time with Madeline. Something in her chest started to ache.

"Jake spent a lot of time at our house as a teenager," Susanna continued. "He was always a very serious young man, always determined to excel at whatever he did. Rachel was very goal-oriented, too. She was just like her father that way."

"Was Rachel an attorney, too?"

"No. She was an accountant—a C.P.A. She was a very practical, pragmatic sort of person. She liked things to always add up the same way. She thought law was frustrating because there are too many loopholes, too many variables." Susanna smiled. "She's the only teenaged girl I know who had a business plan for her life. She had it all written out—what she wanted to achieve by what age. And she did it, too."

"She must have been a remarkable person."

Susanna nodded, blinking hard. "She was. She was very intense, very focused. It was almost as if she had a sense that she didn't have much time." Despite her apparent efforts to hold them back, two tears coursed down Susanna's cheeks.

Without a word, Annie moved onto the sofa beside Susanna and patted her hand. The woman grasped Annie's fingers as another tear escaped. "Forgive me. Lately I seem to cry every time I talk about her."

"That's perfectly natural," Annie said softly.

"That's what my therapist says." Susanna opened her purse and pulled out a tissue. "After the accident, I couldn't cry. I just held it all in. It felt like it was too deep, like it would just tear me up if I let it out."

Annie's heart filled with sympathy. "It must have been awful."

"It was. A friend finally dragged me to a doctor, and I'm much better now." Susanna gave a rueful smile. "It doesn't always seem like it, though. I cry at the drop of a hat."

"My grandmother always said a good cry was healthy."

"Is that right? Your grandmother was a wise woman. My grandmother taught my mother and me that a lady never shows any emotion. She was a very proper Southern lady from Charleston. A lady, she said, is always pleasant and reserved. Not to mention well-groomed and hospitable."

Annie grinned. "Don't forget trustworthy, loyal, and brave."

Susanna laughed. "Are we talking about ladies, Cub Scouts, or labrador retrievers?"

"Probably all three."

Susanna smiled. "I'm not sure Grandmother would have approved of the bravery part. That implies that a lady might have some spunk, and I'm sure spunk was considered an undesirable trait."

"I happen to think it's highly desirable."

"So do I, dear." The woman smiled at her. "So do I. And I can tell you have a lot of it."

"You do, too. Otherwise you wouldn't have come here."

She grinned. Annie grinned back. They might have just met, but Annie felt completely at ease with the older woman, as if she'd known her all her life. "Would you like to meet Madeline?" she asked impulsively.

"Oh, I'd love to!"

"Then follow me. She's out in the backyard."

"Oh, Tom, she's so adorable! You just can't imagine." Susanna leaned forward, her voice filled with enthusiasm as she told him about her encounter earlier that afternoon with Madeline. "She looks just like Jake. She has his thick dark hair and his brown eyes. And her smile! It could charm the raisins out of a cookie."

Tom's eyebrows rode low over his eyes. He hunched over his mahogany desk and drummed the eraser of a pencil on the desktop, his displeasure almost palpable. "I can't believe you went to see her."

Susanna's spirits sank. "Why not? She's Jake's baby."

"A baby conceived behind his back, by a woman he'd never met."

"Well, that's certainly not the child's fault. And Annie was no more to blame for the mix-up than Jake was. It was entirely the doctor's fault."

"Damn it, Susanna, it doesn't matter whose fault it is. What matters is that the whole thing is a mistake—a mistake that you're compounding by trying to drag this total stranger and her child into the bosom of our family."

"It's not a mistake. It's a child."

"You sound like a damned bumper sticker."

"And you sound like a damned ass!"

Tom stared at her. Susanna's hand inadvertently flew to her mouth. It was the first time in her life that she'd ever used the word.

Her husband's lips tightened, and a nerve twitched in his jaw. "I'll assume that you didn't mean to say that. I'll give you the benefit of the doubt, and presume that was the Prozac talking."

Anger flared in Susanna's chest. "That wasn't Prozac. That was me."

Tom's knuckles blanched around the pencil. "The Susanna I know doesn't talk like that. You sounded just like my mother after she'd popped a few too many pills."

"Antidepressants don't impair judgment like your mother's tranquilizers did," Susanna replied. "If anything, they help people think more clearly."

Tom's lip curled. "Oh, so clear thinking was what led you to call me an ass?"

"I didn't say you *were* an ass. I said you *sounded* like an ass. And when it comes to the topic of Jake's baby, you're certainly behaving like one."

"That's quite enough, Susanna."

"Yes. I suppose it is."

Rising from the leather chair, Susanna whipped out of his office and down the hall. She'd nearly made it to the reception area when she collided with a tall blonde coming from the opposite direction. The impact made the other woman drop her purse.

"Oh, I'm so sorry!" Susanna knelt down and helped the blonde collect the scattered contents. "I should have been paying more attention to where I was going." Susanna retrieved a lipstick, a gold key ring and a plastic box of breath mints from the burgundy carpet. She handed them to the woman, whose shoulder-length hair swung forward, obscuring her face. "Here you go," Susanna said. "I think that's everything. Oh, wait—there's one more thing by your foot."

Susanna reached out and picked up a shiny plastic packet. She realized it was a two-pack of condoms as she placed it in the woman's hand. Susanna felt her face flame. "I'm so sorry," she murmured again, starting to rise.

The blonde dropped the condoms in her purse, then straightened and flung back her hair. Recognition poured over Susanna like a glass of icy water.

It was Kelly—the woman from the airport. The woman she'd seen with Tom. She was wearing a fire-engine red suit with a short skirt and a fitted jacket, and she looked hot as a five alarm fire. Susanna's stomach tightened like a neck in a hangman's noose, but years of training forced her to smile. "Kelly. How nice to see you again."

"Yes." Kelly snapped her bag closed and hung it on her shoulder.

"I'm sorry about running into you."

"No harm done." Kelly gave a tight smile.

"Are . . . are you here to see Tom?"

"Yes." Kelly tossed her hair, then adjusted a heart-shaped pendant that swung between the lapels of her suit to nestle in her decolletage. "We have some business to discuss."

I'll bet you do. With two condoms in your purse. The thought sent a wave of shock crashing through her, leaving her feeling seasick. Susanna fought it off with a brave attempt at a smile. "Tom told me you worked together on the LaMarr case."

"Yes."

The woman added nothing more. She didn't say she had come by to tie up loose ends or that they were working on another case. She didn't offer any explanation for today's visit, or give any reason for her presence in Tom's office. She simply looked at Susanna, her eyes cold and vaguely hostile.

Tension hung between them, awkward and out of place. "Well," Susanna finally managed. "It was nice seeing you."

"Yes." Without another word, the blonde turned and continued down the hall, her slim hips swaying as she went.

Susanna turned toward the reception area, her heart somewhere in the vicinity of her knees. Her only thought was to leave the building before she burst into tears.

And then she heard Jake's voice behind her. "Susanna! My secretary said you were looking for me earlier."

Susanna slowly turned around, her stomach tightening again. Jake stood in his office doorway. His forehead creased into a worried frown. "Are you all right?"

"Fine," she said in strangled voice.

Jake's frown deepened. He stepped forward and took her by the arm. "Come on into my office."

He led her to a chair opposite his desk, then sat beside her. "What's wrong?"

"It's . . . nothing." Susanna looked down at her lap. She was embarrassed to bring up the topic of Kelly.

"Something's wrong. Is it the baby?"

Susanna had called Jake that morning, told him of her plan to go to Lucky, and gotten directions to the ranch. She reached out now and patted his hand. "Oh, no! Madeline is beautiful, Jake—just beautiful! She looks exactly like you."

Jake smiled in a way Susanna hadn't seen since Rachel's death, a way that lit him up from the inside out.

"And I really liked Annie, too," Susanna continued. "She's very warm, very easy to talk with. She seems like a wonderful mother."

Jake nodded, his eyes still aglow. "She adores Madeline."

"And Madeline adores her. It looks like your child has a wonderful home."

Jake's smile faded. "Yes. I suppose she does. And as much as I want to be a part of her life, I don't want to mess that up."

"I'm sure Annie will work with you," Susanna said. "She seems very flexible." Her mouth tightened. "Unlike someone else I could name."

"Tom?"

Susanna nodded.

"I take it he's not happy you paid a visit to Lucky."

"He's furious. He doesn't want me to have anything to do with Annie or the baby. He doesn't want you to, either."

Jake leaned back in his chair and sighed. "I know."

"Well, he's wrong. Don't pay any attention to him."

Jake leaned forward. "I appreciate your support, Susanna. But I don't want to be the cause of problems between you and Tom. That's why you're upset, isn't it? You argued about the baby."

"That's not the problem. Not the main one, anyway."

"Then what is?"

To Susanna's chagrin, tears sprang to her eyes. She reached up and wiped them away.

"Come on, Susanna," Jake gently urged. " 'fess up. You told me your therapist said suppressing your feelings isn't healthy."

She drew a ragged breath and slowly nodded. She *did* need to talk. But more than she needed to talk, she needed to know the truth. "I ran into Kelly in the hallway."

Jake's eyes immediately grew wary. "Kelly Banyon?"

"Yes." Gathering her courage, she forced herself to look him in the eye. "Jake, I'm going to ask you a question, and I want you to tell me the truth, no matter how much you think it might hurt me. Is something going on between Tom and her?"

Jake went still. "Why do you ask?"

"Because I need to know."

"Susanna, I can't imagine Tom being unfaithful to you."

"I couldn't, either, until the last few weeks. But lately, I've been picking up on something. There's something different about him. And that woman . . ." She hesitated. "Well, I get very weird vibes from her."

"Weird, how?"

"I don't know how to describe it. Hostile, like she hates me. She doesn't even know me!"

Jake shifted uneasily on his chair.

"Is there a business reason for her to be seeing Tom?" Susanna pressed.

Jake nodded. "They're working out an addendum to the LaMarr merger agreement."

That, at least, was reassuring. "Does she come here a lot?"

Jake hesitated.

Susanna slowly exhaled a long breath. "I was afraid of that."

Jake leaned forward. "Susanna, I don't think anything is going on. Tom is not that kind of man. But Kelly . . ." He raked his hand through his hair and blew out a breath. "Well, she's not above trying."

Susanna's spirits plummeted.

Jake reached and patted her hand. "Look, you have nothing to fear. You're a beautiful woman. Tom loves you. You've been his whole world for . . . how many years have you been married?"

"Thirty-three."

". . . for thirty-three years," he continued. "I know you didn't ask for my advice, but I'm going to give it to you anyway."

Susanna managed a wan smile. "I suppose you really can't help yourself. After all, you're an attorney."

Jake grinned back. "My advice is to go home and forget about Kelly. Before you know it, she'll quit sniffing around and go track easier game."

Susanna reached out and softly patted Jake's cheek. "You're a dear man, Jake. No wonder Rachel adored you."

"Tom adores *you*. Remember that. Now, go home, forget about all this and concentrate on keeping your home fires burning."

Susanna forced a quick nod and ducked out the door, a lump the size of Texas in her throat. She didn't have the heart to tell Jake her deepest fear: that her home fires had grown too cold to be rekindled.

Jake rapped briskly on Tom's closed office door five minutes later, then sauntered in without waiting to be invited. He found Tom seated behind his desk, a contract spread out before him. Kelly stood close beside him, her arm stretched over his, her breast all but resting on his shoulder as she pointed to something on the paper.

Tom looked up and as Jake entered. "Yes?"

"We need to go over a few things," Jake said.

"All right. I'll drop by your office as soon I finish up here."

"That's okay. I'll just wait." Jake deliberately plopped himself in a chair opposite the desk.

Tom drew back from Kelly. She leaned closer, her long red fingernail tracing a line on the contract. "This is the part I'd like you to reconsider," she murmured.

Tom adjusted his tie and nodded. "I'll, uh, look it over and get back with you."

"Why don't we discuss it over lunch tomorrow?" Kelly suggested. She leaned forward, exposing an eyeful of cleavage.

Tom rubbed his jaw. "Well, I . . ."

"Oh, gee," Jake interjected. "Don't you have that museum trustee luncheon tomorrow, Tom?"

Kelly shot Jake a poisonous smile. "What are you—his personal Palm Pilot?"

A muscle twitched in Jake's cheek. "No, but it looks like *you're* applying for the job."

Tom cut a sharp glance at Jake, then turned back to Kelly. He cleared his throat uneasily. "I'm afraid I'm tied up for lunch tomorrow."

"Well, then, I'll call you in the morning and see what your schedule is. Perhaps we can get together later."

"Why don't you just buzz his secretary and get her to fax you the changes?" Jake suggested. "That way you won't have to take up any more of Tom's time."

If looks could kill, Jake would have been a goner. "There are some fine points that need to be ironed out," Kelly said carefully. She pulled her purse off the desk and turned toward the door.

Tom politely rose from his chair and rounded his desk. "Thanks for coming by."

"My pleasure. I'll talk to you tomorrow." The blonde's hips swayed provocatively as Tom walked her to the door.

" 'Bye," Jake called, deliberately remaining seated despite all of his upbringing to the contrary.

Judging from the disdainful look she shot him, Kelly didn't miss the slight.

"Close the door behind you, would you?" Jake called.

Kelly's lips pulled in a distorted simulation of a smile as she pulled the door closed.

Tom eyed Jake warily as he strode back behind his desk. "What was all that about?"

"Just doing you a favor."

"Favor?"

"Yeah. I was saving you from the jaws of a man-eating piranha."

Tom gave a scoffing snort. "Kelly's a good attorney, but I think I can hold my own against her."

"I'm not talking about her legal skills."

Tom froze as he lowered himself into his chair. "Then what the hell *are* you talking about?"

Jake leaned forward and picked a silver letter opener off Tom's desk. "Come on, Tom. She's a sexual predator. She sets her sights on a man and goes after him like a big-game hunter. She wants to add you to her trophy case."

"If you're trying to be amusing, you're missing the mark."

"I'm not trying to be amusing. I'm trying to be a friend." Jake paused, letting the words hang in the air. "To you . . . and to Susanna."

A reddish stain crept up Tom's neck. "A woman like

214

Kelly doesn't need to pursue men. She probably has to beat them off with a stick."

"I'll bet that's not what she uses."

"Very funny, Jake. Very funny."

"I'm trying not to be funny." Jake looked Tom right in the eye. "Look—the scuttlebutt around the courthouse is that her conquest list includes a senator and a former governor. She has a thing for married men who are rich, powerful and older."

Tom gave a sardonic smile. "Well, then, that eliminates me."

"No, it doesn't. It fits you to a T."

Tom's expression grew grim. "Just what the hell do you want me to do, Jake?"

"Nothing. I want you to do absolutely nothing." *And I mean that literally.* "I just want you to be aware of her reputation, that's all."

Tom shifted in his chair. His gaze struck Jake as tellingly evasive. "Okay. Consider me aware."

"Good." Jake looked at him for two long beats. "You should know that Susanna saw her here this afternoon, too. She was upset."

It was Tom's turn to pause. Then he shook his head. "Susanna wasn't upset about that. She was upset because we argued about her little field trip to the boonies to see that—that *woman* and her baby." Tom tapped a pen on his desk and fixed a cold eye on Jake. "I don't want Susanna involved in this mess of yours. That woman and her child are not a part of this family."

It was a familiar technique of Tom's—going on the attack whenever he felt defensive. It worked well in court, but it wasn't going to work now.

Jake slowly rose from his chair. "That's my child, and that makes her part of *my* family." His voice was low and soft, but it was strong as tempered steel. His gaze was equally hard and unrelenting. "I've always considered you and Susanna family, too, and I don't want that to change. But you need to understand something: I have a child now, and I intend to be a father to her. From here on out, Madeline will be a part of my life, and that means she'll be a part of the lives of the people close to me. Susanna understands that. She accepts that, and she's ready to welcome Madeline with open arms. I hope you'll decide to do the same." Jake turned and strode out the door.

Tom watched him go, his chest as heavy as a bag of gravel. He had the awful feeling that everything he cared about was slipping away, like sand under his feet in an outgoing tide. He leaned back and turned his chair toward his credenza, only to have his gaze snag on a series of photos.

Rachel at the age of eight, sitting on his lap in this very chair, gazing up at him adoringly. Rachel holding up a wide-mouthed bass she'd caught in a father-daughter fishing tournament at Lake Tenkiller when she was twelve. Rachel wearing a black gown and mortarboard, proudly holding up her college diploma.

Rachel. A lump big as a golf ball formed in his throat. She'd been the light of his life, the axis of his world, the sweet, soft, candy-nougat center of his heart. No achievement, no possession, no personal accomplishment could ever rival the pride or joy his daughter had given him.

And now Jake had a daughter. Did he really want to deny Jake the experience of fatherhood? Hell, even if he did, did he think he actually could? Tom leaned his head back in his chair and closed his eyes. "Susanna's right," he muttered. "I *am* a damned ass."

He swiveled his chair back toward his desk and leaned

forward on his elbows. He couldn't expect Jake to ignore his own flesh and blood. Besides, the baby wasn't really the problem, anyway.

The baby's mother was the problem. The woman—this Annie Hollister—was the one who was usurping Rachel's place. What Tom needed to do was figure out a way to get her out of the picture. He needed to find a way to help Jake get full custody.

Everyone had some kind of skeleton in the closet. If he dug around long enough, he was sure to unearth one in this gal's.

Leaning forward, he punched a button on his sleek black phone. His secretary's voice crackled over the intercom. "Yes?"

"Call Jeff Blade's secretary and get the name and number of the private investigator he used on the Henderson case." His friend and fellow attorney, Jeff, had said he'd found a man guaranteed to get results.

"He's a real bloodhound," Jeff had said. "He can find a bug under every rock."

Tom's secretary's voice buzzed through the speaker again. "Yes, sir. Anything else?"

"No." Tom tapped his pen on top of his desk. "Just get me that name and number. I'll take it from there."

Chapter Thirteen

Madeline pulled yet another empty pan from the bottom shelf of the kitchen cupboard. Ignoring the loud clanging, Annie sat at the kitchen table and concentrated on the leaves at the bottom of Helen's teacup. "An obstacle has been cleared away," she said. "I see new zest and vitality and activity." She grinned up at the older woman. "Everything in your life seems to be on the upswing."

The round-faced, snow-haired woman beamed. "It didn't take tea leaves to tell me that, but it's great to hear it all the same." She reached over and patted Annie's hand. "It's so good to be home."

"It's so good to have you back." Ben had brought Helen home from the hospital two days ago, and he'd dropped her off at Annie's house for a visit while he tended the livestock.

A loud clatter made Annie jump. She glanced over at Madeline, who had just discovered the musical possibilities of banging two pots together. The baby giggled in delight and banged them again.

Annie winced. "I'm sure things were a lot quieter at your daughter's house, though."

"In more ways than one," Helen said with a smile. "Sounds like I missed a lot of excitement around here." She helped herself to a blueberry muffin from the basket on the table and looked Annie curiously. "So, tell me—what's this man like?"

Just the thought of Jake made a swarm of butterflies set flight in Annie's stomach. She reached for her mug of coffee. "Well, at first he comes across as curt and abrupt, but then he kind of grows on you. I think his brusqueness is just a protective shell. He's actually very kind. And he adores Madeline." Annie picked up a large box on the seat of the chair next to her and handed it to Helen. "Look what he sent yesterday."

Helen lifted the lid. The box was filled with designer baby clothes from an exclusive children's clothing store in Tulsa. Helen's eyes grew large. "He's certainly generous."

Annie nodded. "When I asked the home nurse for her bill, I learned Jake had already paid it."

"How nice!"

"Of course, as soon as I have the money to pay him back, I will."

Helen leaned forward, her brow furrowed. "That nurse was here to help you care for Madeline. There's nothing wrong with letting him share the financial responsibility, Annie. After all, he's the child's father."

"I know. I just. . . ." She sighed, then looked up at Helen. "I'm just afraid of getting too many strings attached to him."

Helen waved a hand toward Madeline. "I hate to say

219

it, honey, but there's a pretty big string sitting right over there with a pan on her head."

Annie gave a reluctant grin. "You're right. And I know he's going to be a big part of her life. I just don't know how much of a role I want him playing in mine."

"Madeline's life and yours are very intertwined right now," Helen pointed out. "They will be for several years."

Annie nodded. "I just don't want to become dependent on him. And if I start to let him do things for me, I might."

"Why would that be so bad?"

"If I start depending on him, I might start needing him. And if I need him . . . well, then it gets into a whole other thing."

"You mean you might start to care about him?" Helen asked gently.

Annie stared down at her coffee mug. "Maybe."

"And what would be wrong with that?"

Madeline banged two pans loudly together. Annie picked up her mug and rose from the chair. "He's not available, Helen. Not emotionally. He still loves his late wife, and he says no one will ever compare to her. I don't have any intention of getting into a situation where I'd have to compete with some idealized memory."

The telephone rang, adding to the din of clanging pans.

"Take the call in another room," Helen suggested. "I'll stay here and supervise Madeline's concert."

"Thanks." Annie scurried to the living room and picked up the cordless phone.

"Annie?" said a woman's voice on the other end. "This is Priscilla at Cimarron Pediatrics."

"Priscilla!" Annie smiled into the phone. The receptionist at Madeline's pediatrician's office had a child nearly the same age as Madeline. The two women compared notes every time Annie's daughter went in for a well-baby check up. "How are you? How's Nathan?"

"He's fine, thanks. Listen. I'm calling because we've had a couple of strange phone calls about Madeline, and I thought—well, if it were me, I'd want know about it."

A buzz of alarm rushed up Annie's arm. "What kind of phone calls?"

"Well . . . A man with a really deep voice called here this morning and said he needed copies of all of Madeline's medical records because you were considering changing insurance carriers."

Annie gasped. "I'm doing no such thing!"

"I thought it was odd. I'd never heard of the company before—Worldwide Global Health, I think he said it was. Anyway, I told him I couldn't release the records without approval from you. He got very annoyed and hung up."

Annie's head reeled. Jake was the only person who could possibly want Madeline's records. But why? And why wouldn't he just ask her for a copy? Why resort to such an underhanded stunt?

"There was another call, around noon," Priscilla continued. "I was at lunch, so the bookkeeper took it. I think it might have been the same man—she said his voice was really deep. Anyway, this time the caller said he was with the state's social services agency, and he was investigating a report of neglect."

"Neglect!"

"That's what he said. He said he needed to look at Madeline's records to determine if there was any basis for going ahead with the investigation. She told him we couldn't release the records without your permission. And then he said . . ." Priscilla hesitated. "Annie, he said there would be a hundred dollars of reward money in it if she would bend the rules a little."

"He offered a *bribe?*" Annie's voice rose an octave. "Why, of all the sneaky, lying . . ."

"You know who this is?"

"I'm afraid I do."

"Is it a custody battle or something?"

Annie's jaw was clenched so tightly it was hard to speak. "Yes."

"You poor thing," Priscilla's voice was sympathetic. "I hope everything works out for you."

"Thank you. And thanks for the call." Annie hung up the phone, her heart thumping hard against her rib cage, her hands balled into fists at her side.

"He's a snake," she muttered. "A sneaky, lying, two-faced snake."

She'd thought he was warm and caring and sincere. He'd said he wasn't in any hurry to pursue a permanent custody arrangement, that he didn't want to take Madeline away from her. She'd believed him. She'd trusted him. Good heavens, she'd even kissed him!

And all the time he was plotting to take Madeline away from her.

Anger boiled in her veins. He'd played her for a fool. Well, by golly, she wouldn't be fooled again. She strode purposefully back to the kitchen.

Helen's eyebrows flew up as she glanced at her. "My stars, dear—what happened? You look upset."

"Upset doesn't begin to describe it." Annie quickly filled her in.

"You need to talk to Henry," Helen said when she finished.

Annie nodded. She'd been thinking the same thing.

"I'll come with you," Helen offered. "I'll watch Madeline while you two talk."

"Thanks. I appreciate the moral support." Annie grabbed the diaper bag off a hook by the door, her mouth set in a determined line. "Jake may think this is a custody battle, but as far as I'm concerned, it's all-out war."

The late morning sun streamed into the nursing home sunroom half an hour later as Annie finished telling Henry about the phone call. The old man rubbed his head with his good hand and sighed. "I hate to tell you, Annie, but he's been here, too. I was going to call you this afternoon."

Annie leaned forward. "Jake has been here?"

"It wasn't Jake. It was a private investigator named Bill Hawk. I recognized him from a case I worked on three years ago. I saw him as he was leaving about an hour ago." Henry gave his head a lopsided shake. "I've got to tell you, Annie, he's an unsavory sort."

Annie felt as if she'd been socked in the stomach. "Did you talk to him?"

"No. He didn't recognize me. Guess I look quite a bit different than I did before that stroke."

His voice sounded wistful. Annie reached out and patted his hand.

"He evidently talked to Pearl and Myrtle," Henry continued.

"Myrtle?" Annie moaned. "Oh, no." Myrtle was the nursing home busybody. She loved to gossip, but her memory was shot and she couldn't keep anything straight.

"Afraid so. He told them he was an old friend and he was putting together a 'This Is Your Life' surprise birthday party for you. They were eager to help. And of course they swore to say nothing to you."

"Oh, no."

"Oh, yes." Henry rubbed his jaw, his eyes rueful. "He was very interested in your, uh, more unconventional activities."

"What do you mean?"

"Pearl told him all about your tea-leaf reading. And about the billboards and your grandfather."

"Oh, dear."

"I'm afraid it does make you sound rather odd. I understand he was also interested in your alpacas."

Annie knit her brow in bewilderment. "The alpacas?"

Henry nodded. "He tried to get Pearl to say that you talk to them."

"Well, of course I do," Annie said defensively. "They're animals. There's nothing odd about talking to animals. It calms them down."

"Apparently he tried to get her to say you thought they talked back."

"You're kidding."

"Afraid not. He has Myrtle convinced you do. She said you thought they were Dalai Lamas and they told you what to do."

Annie shook her head incredulously. "If this weren't so frightening, it would be funny."

Henry nodded. "He's fishing, Annie. Dragging a net, trying to see what muck he can rake up. What worries me most is that this guy is not above baiting some hooks and dragging those as well."

"Surely no one would believe Pearl and Myrtle!"

"Maybe not by themselves. But if he's offering bribes, it's only a matter of time before he finds a few takers who'll substantiate their claims."

"I don't know anyone who would betray me for a bribe."

"It doesn't have to be anyone you know. He just needs to find someone who'll claim they saw you leave your baby unattended in your car, or someone who'll say he saw you strike Madeline across the face, or—"

Annie raised her hands to make him stop. "Please. I can't bear to even hear those things. To think I might be accused of doing them to my baby . . ." Annie's voice shook. She twisted her hands in her lap. "Henry, what can I do?"

"Well, for starters, I thought we'd investigate this investigator. If we can discredit him, it'll go a long ways toward discrediting any information he gathers. I've already made a phone call to another P.I. in Tulsa who owes me a favor. He's digging up all he can about the illustrious Mr. Hawk."

"What about trying to discredit Jake? I'm sure he's the one who hired him."

Henry shook his head. "I did a little checking into his background when you first told me he was Madeline's father, and he looks solid as a rock." Henry wheeled his chair closer. "My advice, Annie, is still the same. You need to work out an amicable custody agreement with him."

"I thought I was. I mean, I thought we were getting along. This is coming out of the blue."

Henry slowly shook his head. "*Try again*, Annie. The best thing you can do is work this out with Jake."

"The best thing I can do, Helen, is put as much distance as possible between myself and Jake." Annie pushed a pink teddy bear into the black duffel bag she was packing on the floor of the nursery. Madeline handed her a large Winnie-The-Pooh doll, thinking the packing was a game.

It had been only twenty-four hours since Annie had learned about the private investigator, but it seemed like a lifetime ago. The discovery had turned her entire world upside down.

Helen watched her from the rocker, her eyes mournful. "But, Annie—this is your home!"

"This might be my home, but Madeline's my child. If it comes to losing one or the other, it's no contest."

Helen nodded sadly. "But, Annie—this is so sudden! And New York is so far!"

"That's the idea." Annie pushed a striped zebra into the bag, then reached for a green gorilla. "The farther away I am, the harder it'll be for Jake to get his hands on Madeline."

"You hated living in the city before."

"I know. But I hate the idea of sitting here, being a sitting duck, all the more. And New York is where I can make the most money."

She'd called her old boss at the ad agency, and he'd jumped at the chance to rehire her. Next she'd called an old friend, who'd offered to let Annie and Madeline stay at her place while she searched for an apartment.

Helen's forehead creased with worry. "Annie, is this really a solution? Running away seldom is."

Annie pushed a lock of hair from her eyes. "I know. But the ranch is barely breaking even. If I'm earning a salary, I'm in a better position to fight this thing financially. And if I've moved out of state to take a well-paying job, Jake can't claim I moved just to avoid him or because I'm unstable."

Helen sighed and slowly nodded. "I can't say I wouldn't do the same thing if I were in your shoes." The grandfather clock in the foyer chimed twelve times.

Helen rose from the rocking chair, leaning heavily on her cane. "I've got to go. Ben is driving me to Tulsa this afternoon for a follow-up appointment with my doctor. What time does your flight leave tomorrow?"

"Three in the afternoon." Annie rose and walked her friend to the door. Madeline followed along behind.

Helen turned at the door. "I'm going to miss you, Annie."

"I'll miss you and Ben, too." Annie gave her a tight hug. When she pulled away, both women's eyes were wet.

Helen wiped her cheek and pasted on a warm smile. "I'll come by tomorrow morning to help you finish packing."

The doorbell rang the next morning as Annie dabbed a blob of applesauce off Madeline's chin. "Come on in, Helen," she yelled. Madeline banged her covered sip cup on her high-chair tray, splattering drops of milk everywhere, then laughed delightedly at her handiwork.

Annie eyed her with mock exasperation. "You really want to put me through my paces this morning, don't you?" Annie turned toward the sink to grab a dish towel.

"Ink! Ink!" Madeline yelped, her chubby legs kicking the high chair excitedly. "Ink! Ink! Ink!"

Only one person got Madeline that excited. Annie turned around, a feeling of dread in her chest, to see Jake standing in the kitchen doorway, grinning at the baby.

"Good morning, sugar." He crossed the room and kissed the baby's plump cheek, then straightened and smiled at Annie. "Morning, Annie."

No man had the right to look so handsome. Against her will, she felt a flash of attraction. His gaze was so direct, his smile so sincere that it disarmed her. If she didn't know better, she'd never believe he was plotting behind her back to steal her child.

Annie realized she was standing like a statue, staring at him, a blue dish towel in her hand. She shouldn't let on that she knew about the detective, she thought. "Good morning. I, uh, wasn't expecting you." She quickly knelt and began wiping up the splattered floor.

"I have a meeting later in Bartlesville, so I thought I'd swing by." Eyeing her quizzically, he grabbed a paper towel and knelt beside her to help. "What's with all the suitcases in the entry hall?"

Annie kept her head down as she rose and turned to the sink. "Nothing."

"Sure looks like something to me."

Annie rinsed out the dish towel, trying to decide what to tell him. She didn't expect to be able to hide from him. She did, however, hope to get out town before he discovered her plans. If he found out she was leaving, he'd try to find a way to stop her.

Jake looked at her warily. "Looks to me like you're planning a trip."

There was no point in denying it. The suitcases were irrefutable evidence. "Oh—well, yes, I am. I'm, uh, going to California for a few days to visit an old friend."

"Looks like you've packed enough to be gone a month or two."

Annie shrugged. "I've never been a light packer. I've always thought more is more."

"Madeline's going, too?"

"Of course."

"Where in California?"

"Oh, the, uh, southern part."

Jake's eye's narrowed. "Where, exactly?"

"Ummm . . ." Oh, dear. If she told him the name of a town, he was likely to check it out. "It's a little town. I can't remember the name of it. My friend is picking us up at the L.A. airport."

Jake's lips flattened. His eyes were skeptical. "This is kind of sudden, isn't it?"

"Umm, yes. My friend's, er, brother died. I'm going for the funeral."

"Is that right."

"Yes."

"That sounds a little different from just going for a visit."

"No." She was speaking too fast and sounding defensive. She needed to slow down, to act casual. "I mean, not really. I'm going to visit her." Annie turned to the sink, unable to look him in the eye. "To—to comfort her."

"You're a rotten liar, Annie. What's really going on?"

Something in her snapped. She whirled around and faced him directly, her hands on her hips, the towel still in one hand. "Why don't *you* tell *me.*"

"Tell you what?"

Annie slapped the towel down on the counter, anger and indignation rising inside her. "I know about the private detective, so you can cut the wide-eyed, innocent act."

"Detective?"

"Yes, detective."

His brow furrowed, and his dark eyes looked so baffled that for a moment, Annie almost thought she herself must be mistaken.

Almost, but not quite. "I suppose you have no idea what I'm talking about," she scoffed.

"You're right about that."

"Oh, please." Annie rolled her eyes.

"Come on, Annie. What the hell is going on?"

She put her hands back on her hips. "I suppose someone *else* hired a private detective to try to bribe my pediatrician's receptionist into releasing Madeline's records. Not to mention snooping around all over town, spreading tales about how crazy I am and how I call my alpacas Dalai Lamas and think they talk like Mr. Ed."

"*What?*"

Annie blew out an exasperated breath. "Oh, you're good. You're very good. You'd have a bright future in Hollywood." She pointed to the door. "I want you to leave."

"Not until I figure out what the deuce you're talking about."

"You know good and well what I'm talking about."

"All I know is what you just told me."

"Well, then, I'm afraid I'll have to leave you in ignorance. If you have any further questions, you can talk to my lawyer."

"I'd love to. What's his name?"

The request caught Annie up short. She hesitated, but only for a moment. What the heck—let him talk to Henry. At least then he'd know she didn't intend to take this lying down. Besides, it would get him out of here and give her a chance to get to the airport.

"Henry Marlow."

Jake whipped a cell phone out of his pocket and flipped it open. "What's his number?"

"He can't be reached by phone."

Jake cocked a leery eyebrow. "And why is that?"

"Because he's in a nursing home."

"Your attorney is in a nursing home." He shook his head, his gaze incredulous. "And you think I'd need to hire a private eye to prove you're nuts?"

Annie experienced her first real moment of doubt.

"What's the name of this nursing home?" Jake demanded.

"Shady Acres."

Jake strode across the kitchen with unerring certainty, straight to the drawer where Annie kept the phone book. He pulled it out and looked up the number, then grabbed the phone and punched some buttons. He spoke to a nursing home staff member, and within minutes, had Henry on the phone.

"Mr. Marlow, this is Jake Chastaine. I understand you represent Annie Hollister." There was a brief pause. "Yes, that's right. The DNA results were positive." Another pause. "That's not why I'm calling. I'm here at Annie's house, and she's very upset about some business involving a private investigator. I've tried to tell her I knew nothing about it, but she wouldn't listen. She suggested I call you. Can you tell me what's going on?"

A longer silence. "I assure you, I never hired Mr. Hawk."

Tires crunched in the driveway. Jake strode to the window and peered out, the phone still to his ear. "Can you describe him? A man has just pulled up in Annie's drive, and I have a hunch it's our boy."

Jake thanked Henry and hung up, then turned to Annie, who was lifting Madeline from the high chair.

"Well?" Annie asked.

Jake's mouth was set in a grim line. "Looks like Mr. Hawk is paying us a little visit. Better let me handle him."

Annie eyed him warily. "Why? So you can stage a cover-up?"

His eyes flashed with annoyance. "So I can get to the bottom of this. Keep Madeline out of sight, would you? I don't know what this jerk might try."

Alarm shot through Annie. Clutching the baby she hurried to the dining room, where she could listen without being seen. She heard the doorbell ring, heard Jake open the door. She peered around the corner and saw an overweight man in his mid-fifties standing in the doorway.

"I hope I'm not disturbing you," the man said, baring

yellow teeth in a smile. "I'm here about your poop."

"My *what?*"

"I saw a sign that says you sell 'paca poop."

"Oh. Uh, yeah."

The man's eyes darted around. He craned his neck, trying to peer into the house. "I'm interested in buying some. How much poop is in a peck?"

"Huh?"

"The sign says 'Pick a Peck of 'Paca Poop.' "

"Oh. Right." Jake looked the man up and down, his eyes skeptical, his gaze raking over the man's cheap blue suit. He stepped forward, blocking the man's view of the interior of the house. "You don't look dressed for scooping it. This is a you-scoop-it operation."

The man backed up and gave another horsey smile. "I see. Well, I guess I'll have to come back later. While I'm here, though, would you mind if I walk around and take a look at the animals?"

Jake stepped out onto the porch with the man, closing the door behind him. Annie hurried to the window, where she had a clearer view.

"If you're so interested in the alpacas," she heard Jake say, "I'm sure you'll want to see the Dalai Lamas, too."

The man froze. He stared at Jake, his eyes cagey.

"No?" Jake growled. "Well, how about the Dolly Partons?"

Before either Annie or the man knew what was happening, Jake had grabbed the man's arm, twisted it behind his back, and bent him over the porch railing.

"Hey! Hey! Ouch! Let me go!" the man yelped.

"I know who you are, Hawk." Jake's voice was low and menacing. "And you're not going anywhere until I find out is who hired you."

"Hey, stop! You're hurting my arm."

"I'll hurt more than that if you don't tell me who hired you," Jake snarled. "Who was it?"

"T—Tom M—Morrison. At Morrison and Chastaine."

Jake muttered an oath. "What are you doing here?"

"Just checkin' things out." The man squirmed. "Come on, man—I told you what you wanted to know. Let me go!"

Jake loosened his grasp so abruptly the man nearly fell over. Straightening, the P.I. turned frightened eyes on Jake.

Jake pointed to the man's vehicle. "Get in your car and get the hell out of here, and don't even *think* about coming back. I'm the Chastaine in Morrison and Chastaine, and you can consider yourself fired."

The man raced to his car, climbed in, and sped away, gravel flying beneath his tires.

Jake stormed back into the house, his face a mask of anger. Annie followed him to the kitchen and watched him pick up the wall phone.

"Who are you calling?" she asked.

"Tom."

"Why? To cook up some other scheme to prove I'm unfit?"

"Annie, I swear I didn't know."

"He was hired by your firm." Annie clutched Madeline to her chest, her heart pounding furiously. "Why should I believe you?"

A nerve ticked in his jaw. "No reason. No reason at all." He punched some numbers into the phone. "Listen in on this conversation, if you want. Maybe that'll convince you."

Annie hesitated, then carried Madeline to the living room. She set the child down, sank into a chair and picked up the extension just as a man's voice answered.

"Tom, it's me," Jake said brusquely. "I want to know what the hell's going on with Bill Hawk."

Annie heard a man clear his throat on the other end of the line. "I was going to tell you about that," said a voice that sounded as if it belonged to an older man. "Look, Jake, I can't talk. I should be on my way to the airport now."

"When were you going to tell me?" Jake demanded.

"When I had some information to pass on to you. After I got back from Geneva."

"What the hell do you think you're doing?"

"Helping you. You need to know what kind of woman you're dealing with here. And from what I hear, you've got a good shot at sole custody."

"I don't want sole custody. I don't think that's in Madeline's best interests."

"Oh, come on. You think it's in her best interests to be passed back and forth like a football? This Hollister woman is a mental case. Did you know she thinks she can tell fortunes? And she thinks her dead grandfather talks to her through billboards! Hell, she even thinks her llamas give her advice."

Annie bit back a sharp retort. She'd learn more, she told herself, if Tom didn't know she was listening in.

Jake spoke up on her behalf. "They're alpacas, and that's a bunch of bull. I want you to call Hawk off. I don't know where you found him, but he's a sleazebag. He's making up a pack of lies, spreading rumors, offering bribes—he's ruining her."

"I didn't tell him to do anything like that."

"Well, it's what he's doing." Jake's voice was as tight and dangerous as a bear trap. "Listen, Tom—This is my life, my child, my personal business, and I want you to stay out of it. Annie is the mother of my child, and I won't let you treat her this way."

Tom heaved a sigh through the phone lines. "Okay. I'll tell Hawk he's off the job."

"Do it now."

"All right, all right. I'll make the call before I leave."

Jake hung up the phone so abruptly that he was in the living room before Annie had even replaced the receiver in its cradle.

"Well?" Jake demanded. "Do you believe me now?"

Annie gazed at him uncertainly. "You could have staged all that."

"Staged a spontaneous phone call?"

Annie lifted her shoulders. "For all I know, you could have made arrangements to have this conversation if I got wind of what you were up to. You're clever enough to have thought of it."

Jake's jaw tightened. "Well, I'm glad you think I'm as farsighted as I am devious."

"Ink! Ink! Ink!" Madeline stretched out her arms to Jake.

He turned to the baby, his expression softening until it completely changed his appearance. "Hey, there, sweetheart." His voice was warm, his eyes even warmer as he bent and picked up the child.

Their child.

Annie heaved out a long sigh. Dadblast it. Believing the worst of Jake was somehow easier than accepting that he was telling the truth.

And he was. She knew it, knew it deep in her gut.

He turned his eyes on her, his gaze straightforward and clear. "Believe it or not, Annie, I want what's best for Madeline."

Annie nodded, a lump in her throat. She gazed down on the kitchen floor.

"So where are you going?" Jake asked.

Annie looked up, surprised.

Jake jerked his head toward the foyer. "The suitcases."

"Oh." Annie looked away again, unable to meet his gaze. "Well, I guess I'm not going anywhere now."

"You were running away." It wasn't a question. It was a statement of fact. "You were going to take Madeline and leave."

Annie didn't respond. Jake waited for two beats. She could feel the heat of his glare, feel it bore right through her skin. "Well, this is a hell of a situation."

Annie silently nodded her agreement.

"You don't trust me. I can't trust you."

Annie ventured a glance up, and the intensity in Jake's gaze nearly nailed her to the wall.

"There's only one thing left to do," he said tersely.

"What's that?"

"We've got to get married."

Chapter Fourteen

"Married!" Annie gaped at him, her eyes as round as blue marbles.

Jake gave a decisive nod. "That's right."

"You're out of your mind."

"I probably am, but listen to me anyway." *Keep your friends close, but your enemies closer.* The old advice flitted through Jake's mind as he sank down on the sofa beside Annie and settled Madeline on his lap.

The child twisted around and toyed with a button on his shirt, her four teeth gleaming in a grin. He inhaled the soft, baby-powder scent of her hair, and his heart filled with a desperate, aching love.

She was so guileless, so genuine, so honestly right here in the moment. A button was a fascinating toy, the sight of a human face a reason to smile. She was the purest, most undiluted life form he'd ever encountered.

She was a miracle—the child he had thought he would never have. It was a miracle that she existed, a

237

miracle that he'd found her, a miracle that such a sweet, beautiful creature would light up with joy when he walked into a room.

He knew he didn't deserve her, but oh, dear Lord, he didn't want to lose her! And if Annie moved away and launched a battle for custody, he would. Maybe not for summer visits and alternate holidays, but for all the everyday little things, the things that made a life. Her first sentence, her first taste of ice cream, her first visit to a zoo. Knowing how to make her laugh or how to comfort her when she cried. Teaching her to ride a bike. Watching her board a school bus her first day of kindergarten.

Most of all, he'd miss just being there, being a key part of her life—especially now, when she was forming her earliest thoughts and memories. This was when her personality was being shaped, when she was developing the traits she'd carry into adulthood, when she was learning how to deal with frustration and fear and all the other emotions that were part of being human. This was when she was forming her strongest attachments, the ones that would sustain her for a lifetime.

More than anything, Jake wanted to be one of those attachments. Nothing was more important, and he'd do anything—anything at all—to make it happen. Including marrying Annie.

He glanced over at her. Her eyes were huge and her lips were parted, parted in a way that reminded him of how they'd opened under his during that kiss. He abruptly looked away, annoyed at the thought. He didn't *want* to marry her, for Pete's sake. He had no choice. It was the only way he could make sure she didn't take the child and bolt the state.

Annie was eccentric and full of surprises, but there was one area of her life where she was entirely predict-

238

able. When it came to Madeline, Jake knew she'd always put the child's best interests first. If he could convince Annie that Madeline needed him, that the father-daughter bond between them was so strong that Madeline would be harmed if it were disrupted, his worries would be over.

In order to form that kind of bond with his daughter, though, he needed time and access. Marrying Annie was the perfect solution.

He bounced Madeline on his knee and angled another glance at Annie. "It wouldn't be a real marriage, of course. It would just be a temporary arrangement. And it would be the perfect solution for everyone."

"Perfect . . . how?"

"Well, I want a chance to get to know my daughter, and you want assurance that I'm not going to do anything underhanded to get sole custody. I can't do anything too nefarious if I'm married to you, can I?"

"I-I guess not," Annie grudgingly conceded. "But . . ."

Jake held up a hand. "Please—hear me out on this. The person who would benefit the most is Madeline. If you and I are married, even for a little while, it'll make her life a lot easier in the long run. It'll be much simpler for her to explain parents who are divorced than to explain sperm banks and artificial insemination. And whether you like it or not, this is a conservative community, and a lot of folks around here have some old-fashioned ideas. Madeline is likely to face a lot of teasing and even some discrimination for having parents who never married."

Annie's eyes were still as round as Moon Pies, but she appeared to be listening.

Jake shifted the baby on his lap. "It'll be easier on us, too. Think of all the years of teacher conferences and PTA meetings, all the situations where our relationship

239

will need to be explained. It'll simplify everything if we're each other's ex."

There was another, more immediate advantage, too, Jake thought grimly. Tom wouldn't dare try to prove Annie was an unfit mother if she were Jake's wife.

Annie's lips parted again as she stared at him. She had such beautiful lips, Jake thought distractedly—full and ripe and pouty, the kind of lips a man could just lose himself in. The memory of how they'd tasted poured over him. Disconcerted, he turned his gaze to the baby.

"It wouldn't be a real marriage, of course," Jake continued. "We wouldn't—wouldn't . . ." Confound it, why was it so hard to say it out loud? Probably because he'd thought about it so often, he thought with a rush of guilt. He cleared his throat, but the words still came out sounding strangled. "We wouldn't sleep together."

Annie's mouth opened further. Was it his imagination, or did her eyes hold a shadow of disappointment?

Christ, he was really losing it, thinking a thing like that. He had no reason to think she was interested in him romantically—no reason at all, except for that kiss.

She *had* kissed him back. She'd even admitted it.

A burst of irritation shot through him. He didn't *want* to marry her, damn it. She was forcing him into it. And yet here he was, in the untenable position of having to talk her into it.

He pushed down his aggravation and struggled to keep his voice even. "There's another thing to consider here, too. I want my name on Madeline's birth certificate. I also want her to take my last name, and it would simplify things if you had it, too."

"This is crazy." Annie's eyes were wide and dazed. She pushed back her hair from her forehead, only to

240

have it fall forward again. "The craziest part is that it actually seems to make sense."

"So you'll do it?"

Annie's head swam like a school of goldfish in an over-crowded bowl. As insane as it sounded, Jake was right: a short-term marriage would make life easier for every-one in the long run. She'd already encountered several occasions where explaining or not explaining her rela-tionship to Jake had been downright awkward. She could only imagine what Madeline would face as she grew up—a childhood of taunts and schoolyard whispers, a lifetime of clumsy explanations. Her heart ached at the thought.

The name issue was a consideration, too. Annie didn't want to deprive Madeline of her father's last name, but at the same time, she hated the idea of having a different last name than her daughter. Marrying Jake would solve all of those problems.

"Will you do it?" Jake repeated.

There were lots of good, solid, logical reasons for de-ciding to accept Jake's proposition, Annie told herself. The fact that just the sight of him made her heart race a mile a minute had nothing to do with any of them. In fact, her physical reaction to him was a reason to be cautious.

"How long would we have to stay married?" she asked.

Jake lifted his shoulders. "A year ought to do it."

"A *year?*" Annie shook her head. "Oh, no. That's way too long."

"Well, then, how about nine months?"

"That's not much better. What about three?"

"Six," Jake countered.

"Five," Annie replied.

"Five months, two weeks and three days."

"Five months, and not a day more," Annie stated firmly.

Jake's grin was rakish and unexpected. "Sold."

Annie couldn't help but grin back. Their eyes locked, and a jolt of attraction, unbidden and unwanted, surged between them. Annie was relieved when Madeline grabbed Jake's tie in a hangman's hold, and he had to turn his attention to disengaging the baby's grip.

"So it's settled," he said, setting Madeline on the floor. "We'll get married right away, and stay married for five months. At the end of that time, we'll divorce."

Annie felt as if she were having an out-of-body experience. "How soon is 'right away'?"

Jake stood and straightened. "Well, what are you doing tomorrow?"

Good grief. How could he be so casual about it? They were talking about getting married, not going out for a pizza.

But then, this wouldn't be a real marriage, she reminded herself. It was strictly a matter of convenience, a way of simplifying Madeline's life.

Ignoring her pounding heart, she tried to match Jake's air of nonchalance. "Tomorrow? Well, I'd planned on mopping the floor, playing several rounds of patty-cake and preparing a fabulous meal of stewed peaches. I'll take another look at my schedule, though, and see if I can find time to squeeze in a wedding."

"Do you, Jake, take this woman, Annie, to be your lawfully wedded wife . . ."

Annie looked around the oak-paneled judge's chambers at the Tulsa County Courthouse the next afternoon. This was a far cry from the setting she'd always envisioned for her next wedding—her real wedding, as she'd always privately thought of it. Her first wedding had been her mother's production—a garden party extravaganza so elaborate that Annie wouldn't have been surprised if singing midgets had popped out of the wedding cake.

She'd mentally pictured a beautiful church lined with stained glass windows, not a dark, stuffy office. She'd imagined flickering candles, not a spastic fluorescent light, and in her mind's eye, the air had been scented with flowers, not musty law books. She'd wanted a small, intimate ceremony, but she'd always thought there would be more than four guests, and she'd always thought they'd be seated, not huddled together in a cramped space between two bookshelves at the side of a judge's large desk.

The only notable thing about the room was the window—or, more specifically, the billboard visible through it.

It was an ad for a water park, and it showed a gleeful child rocketing down a long water slide. When Annie had first seen it, she could have sworn she'd heard her grandfather chuckle as his voice read the message: *Go Ahead. Take the Plunge.*

Well, it was good to know that Grandpa approved, Annie thought dryly. When she'd called her old boss and friend in New York to explain her change of plans, the two had both thought she'd lost her mind. Ben and Helen certainly had their doubts.

"Annie, dear, this is so sudden!" Helen had exclaimed when she'd heard the news yesterday afternoon. She and Ben had come by the house to help Annie pack, thinking they were going to drive her and Madeline to the airport. Instead of loading Annie's bags into the truck, Ben had been introduced to Jake and told of their plans to marry.

Ben had scowled at Jake, as if he were considering

doing the man bodily harm. "Is this some kind of shyster lawyer trick to get Madeline all for yourself?"

"I telephoned Henry," Annie said quickly. "He thinks getting married is a great idea. He says it's in Madeline's best interests. Mine, too."

"Hmph." Ben had turned a worried gaze to Annie. "One minute you're ready to pull up stakes and hightail it back to New York because you don't trust this man, and the next you're plannin' on marryin' him? I can't say that I follow your reasonin'."

"Jake didn't hire that private investigator." With Jake's help, she'd rapidly explained the situation.

"Hmph." Ben had eyed Jake, his eyebrows beetling in a suspicious frown. "Gettin' married is a big step. I haven't heard you say anything about love."

Jake and Annie had agreed to keep the real nature of their marriage to themselves. Ben and Helen would be upset to learn that she was entering into a sham of a holy institution, and there was no point in giving Tom a new reason to interfere.

"We both love Madeline," Jake had told Ben.

Helen had placed her hand on his arm. "A lot of folks have gotten married for a lot worse reasons," she said softly. "In the old days, love often came after marriage."

Ben had heaved a sigh, then slowly shaken his large head. "I'd say you're puttin' the cart before the horse, but seein' as you two had a baby before you even met . . ." He rubbed a large, calloused hand across his balding skull. "Heck, I reckon the cart has already been to town and back, and the horse hasn't even left the barn." He'd held out his hand to Jake. "You've got yourself a fine woman there. Treat her right, and we'll get along."

Susanna had been a much easier sell. Jake had been worried about how his mother-in-law would react to the news, but his concerns had proven unfounded. She'd insisted that Jake put Annie on the phone immediately.

"I'm so happy for you, dear!" Susanna had said. "Welcome to the family."

Annie had been touched by the older woman's warmth. "Thank you."

"Jake says you're getting married tomorrow."

"Yes. We, uh, decided to do it as soon as possible."

"Well, I want to come to the wedding," she'd said. "And I'd love to watch Madeline while you two honeymoon."

Honeymoon—now there was a startling concept. Annie had been too shocked to respond. Even now, she couldn't bring herself to imagine what Susanna thought they were going to do for a honeymoon. She'd packed a bag for Madeline, because Jake had convinced her to let Susanna keep Madeline after the ceremony. Annie had packed a bag for herself, as well, because they were going to spend their wedding night at Jake's house.

Wedding night. The phrase made goosebumps rise on her flesh. Not that anything was actually going happen, Annie reminded herself. She and Jake were just going through the motions, trying to look like a normal, newly married couple.

The sleeves of the judge's black robe billowed out like the wings of a bat as the courthouse air conditioner kicked into high gear. He raised his voice to be heard over it. "For better or for worse, for richer or for poorer, in sickness or in health, as long as you both shall live. . . ."

Or five months, whichever comes first. It was the time limit Annie and Jake had agreed upon. Jake had assured her that an amicable divorce, with both parties in agreement, could be finalized in a matter of days. Getting divorced would be almost as easy as getting married.

And that had been surprisingly easy. Jake had called a judge yesterday and scheduled the wedding. He'd picked Annie and Madeline up early this morning and driven them to Tulsa. They'd stopped at a medical lab and taken premarital blood tests, then headed to the Court Clerk's office to purchase a marriage license. The next stop had been a jewelry store.

Annie had selected a plain gold band. When she tried to buy a matching one for Jake, he'd refused.

"I don't want a ring," he'd said.

"Oh, come on. If I'm going to wear one, you should, too."

"No."

Annie had smiled persuasively. "You know the old saying—what's good for the goose . . ."

A nerve had flicked in his cheek, and his mouth had firmed into a stubborn line. "Drop it, Annie. I'm not wearing a ring, and that's all there is to it."

The flash of obstinance was the only genuine emotion Jake had shown all day. He'd put his arm around her waist as he'd escorted her into the judge's chambers, but Annie was certain that was only for the benefit of Ben and Helen and Susanna, who'd followed them into the small room.

Jake turned toward her now, his eyes dark and inscrutable. "I do."

"Do you, Annie, take this man, Jake," the judge intoned, "to be your lawfully wedded husband?"

Annie stared at Jake, her stomach tightening. Why, oh why did he have to be so handsome? Just being in the same room with him made her feel oddly short of breath. Her gaze locked on his lips. The memory of how his mouth had moved over hers, gentle yet demanding, soft

246

and firm all at the same time, hit her with a force that left her weak-kneed.

Dear heavens. What was she doing? It was one thing to marry the man. It was entirely another to allow herself to be attracted to him.

"To have and to hold. . . ."

Oh, mercy, she *wanted* to have him, all right. And to hold him—just like she had during that kiss.

A feeling of panic welled up inside of her. She knew what it was like to fall for someone who was still in love with someone else. That had been the story of her first marriage, chapter and verse. It was a mistake she'd vowed to never make again. Hadn't she learned the hard way how lonely a one-way love affair was?

" . . . to love and to cherish, for better or worse, for richer or poorer, in sickness and in health, from this day forward, as long as you both shall live?"

Annie felt as if her throat were paralyzed. Her eyes fastened on Jake's face. If only he weren't so attractive—not to mention smart and funny and so endearingly tender with Madeline.

And sexy. Had she mentioned sexy? Goodness gracious, he was sexy! How could she marry him, when she was so physically attracted to him?

"You're supposed to respond, 'I do,' " the judge whispered.

But it wasn't the judge's words she heard; it was the words printed on the billboard out the window behind him. Her grandfather's voice, urgent and insistent, again whispered in her ear, "Go ahead. Take the plunge."

Annie drew a deep breath, closed her eyes, and dove heart-first into waters that were dark and turbulent and way over her head.

"I do."

* * *

Jake cut a sideways glance at Annie as he pulled away from the curb of the French restaurant where Susanna had insisted on taking everyone after the wedding. He'd thought he would be relieved to get away from Susanna and Ben and Helen, that he would feel more at ease when he no longer needed to act as if he and Annie were starry-eyed newlyweds, but being alone with Annie was even more unnerving than keeping up any pretense.

He'd thought the wedding would be nothing more than a simple exchange of vows. Dadblast it, he'd forgotten all about the obligatory kiss at the end of the ceremony. He should have had the foresight to prepare for it. If it hadn't taken him by surprise, surely it wouldn't have rattled him so much.

But it had, it rattled him down to the soles of his wingtips. When the judge had said, "You may kiss the bride," Jake had had no choice but to comply. After all, everyone in the room—including the judge, who was not only Jake's friend, but Tom's—thought they were committing to a serious stab at marriage.

Jake had intended to just brush Annie's lips with his, but somehow, that plan never stood a ghost of a chance. The moment he entered her airspace, he was pulled down by a force as compelling as gravity. The scent of her perfume, the warmth of her breath, the softness of her lips moving under his, they had all conspired to turn a perfunctory kiss into a lava-hot lip-lock that had left them both gasping for air.

Crimony. He'd meant to put on a convincing performance, not completely lose his head. Why was it that every time he kissed Annie, losing his head was exactly what happened?

Annie's voice drew his thoughts back to the present. "It was sweet of Susanna, offering to watch Madeline tonight," she was saying. "She told me she's already bought a baby bed and that she's turning a spare bedroom into a nursery so that Madeline can visit often."

"Oh, that'll go over well with Tom," Jake said sarcastically.

Annie looked at him with curiosity. "Doesn't he like children?"

"He likes children. He just doesn't like this situation."

"What kind of person is he?" Annie asked. "I have him pictured as some kind of monster, but I can't imagine Susanna with a man like that."

Lately Jake had been having a hard time knowing what Tom was like, either. He changed traffic lanes, considering the question. "He's not a monster. He's acting like a jerk about this, but it's not the way he is about most things." Jake pressed the accelerator and passed a slow-moving minivan. "He was a wonderful father to Rachel. They were close—really close. He was very involved in her life. He was the kind of father I always wished I'd had." Jake guided the car back into the right lane and glanced at Annie. "I guess if I had a role model of the way I want to be with Madeline, Tom would be it."

Jake felt Annie's eyes on him, warm and intent. "It must have been hard on him when Rachel died," she said softly.

"It was. It was hard on all of us." He braked for a traffic light.

"What's Tom like?"

"He's always been a salt-of-the-earth kind of guy— someone you could count on to level with you, to come through in a pinch. I can't name the number of people that Tom has helped, personally, professionally and financially. He used to be really involved in the community, too. He used to serve on the boards of all kinds of charities and causes."

"Used to?"

Jake nodded. "Susanna was always the impetus behind that. After Rachel died, she barely left the house, and Tom began to focus all of his energy on work." The light changed, and Jake guided the car through the intersection. "He's been working like a demon ever since. I think he's overextended himself. He's taken on too many big cases, accepted too many speaking engagements, and won't accept enough help from me or anyone else. I'm worried about him. He's on the verge of burnout. He's stressed and edgy and not acting like himself. He's not seeing this whole situation with Madeline rationally."

Annie nodded slowly. "He probably feels like Rachel got cheated."

Jake glanced over, surprised that she understood. "That's it exactly."

"He's going to hate the fact that we got married."

That was putting it mildly. "He'll come around." At least, Jake hoped he would. "Tom's always been the voice of reason," Jake explained. "If you push him up against a wall, he'll scratch and claw and do his best to tear it down, but when he finally realizes the wall won't budge, well, he accepts it and goes in another direction. That's why he's so good at his job."

"I hope he comes around. He sounds like a formidable opponent."

Jake made the turn onto the highway, and they drove in silence for a while.

"I know we just left her, but I already miss Madeline," Annie remarked.

"She'll be fine with Susanna."

"I know. Madeline seems to adore her." Annie gazed out the window at the passing lights. "It's just . . . aside from when I was in the hospital after the appendectomy,

I've never spent a night apart from the baby."

"What about when was she born?" Jake asked.

"She stayed with me in my hospital room. I couldn't bear to be apart from her." In the light of street lamp, Jake saw a soft smile flit across Annie's face. "I'd dreamed about her for so long, it was hard to believe she'd finally arrived. I just completely fell in love.

"It was like—oh, I don't know—like I was getting to hold a part of my very own heart. She was my *baby*."

Annie wrapped the word in warmth, like an infant in a blanket. Jake's chest grew oddly tight. "What was your pregnancy like?"

"Oh, it was great. I loved being pregnant. Madeline was really active. You should have seen the way she kicked."

I would have liked to, Jake thought. The thought left him with an uneasy sense of guilt. "When did you first learn you were pregnant?"

"Exactly thirteen days after the insemination. I couldn't wait to see if I was late, so I did a home pregnancy test a day early. I used the kind that shows a plus or a minus. It was a plus. I couldn't believe it. I was ecstatic. I only wished . . ."

She cut herself off abruptly, as if she'd thought better of what she was about to say.

He braked at another stoplight, then looked directly at her. "What?"

She lifted her shoulders. "Nothing."

"Tell me what you were about to say," he urged.

"Just that I wished I'd been able to share the news with the baby's father."

I wish so, too. The words formed so clearly in Jake's mind that for a moment he was afraid he'd said them aloud.

He wouldn't have wanted to know, of course—not at

251

the time. When Madeline was conceived, Rachel had only been gone a month or two, and his grief had been fresh and raw.

And yet, deep in his gut, in an odd, inexplicable way, he was sorry he hadn't been there to share the experience with Annie.

"Did you have morning sickness?"

"A little. But not always in the mornings. It happened any time I got hungry." Annie grinned ruefully. "My solution was to eat around the clock. I gained seven pounds the first trimester."

Jake smiled.

"It was an easy pregnancy," Annie continued. "The only part that was a little difficult was at the end. It was hard getting around. My stomach was always in the way."

Jake grinned at the image. "Was Madeline a big baby?"

"Eight pounds, four ounces."

A burst of paternal pride filled Jake's chest. "Did she arrive on schedule?"

Annie shook her head. "She was ten days overdue. The doctor was planning to induce labor if she didn't arrive in a couple of days. I was out in the barn, feeding the alpacas, when my water broke. Ben and Helen drove me to the hospital. Helen was my labor coach."

He had wondered if anyone had been with Annie when she delivered. "Why did you have a Caesarian?"

"Madeline was in the breech position. The doctor said it was safer to deliver that way."

Jake pulled into the driveway of his house and hit the automatic garage door opener. "Were you awake?"

Annie nodded.

"You must have been scared."

"Only that Madeline wasn't going to be all right."

Annie's eyes took on that soft look again. "I can't describe the way I felt when I first heard her cry. And then they put her on my chest, and I got to hold her." She gave a deep, heartfelt sigh. "It was the most wonderful, most amazing moment in my life."

Jake's heart squeezed in his chest, regretting all that he'd missed. He pulled the Volvo into his garage.

Annie looked over at him as he killed the engine. "Speaking of Madeline, I told Susanna to call if she had any trouble with her. Do you think she will?"

Jake hit the opener again. The garage door rumbled down. "I doubt it. Susanna thinks it's our wedding night."

Wedding night—good grief, now there was a sexually loaded term. It might as well be called "copulation night" or "night of wild marital nookie."

The mention of it made the air grow hotter. Annie looked like she felt it, too. They sat there and stared at each other, sexual awareness humming between them like a current through a power line.

Annie moistened her lips with her tongue and gave a small smile. "I guess our kiss looked pretty convincing."

"I'll say. It nearly convinced the hell out of *me.*"

Jake had meant the remark to be flippant, but it came out sounding alarmingly suggestive. The garage light shut off, plunging them into darkness. Jake quickly opened his car door, making the light inside the vehicle flip on.

"You're a really good actor," he added, wanting to diffuse the tension.

"You, too."

I wasn't acting. The troublesome thought ricocheted through his head like a Ping-Pong ball, bouncing from one disturbing memory to another. He realized they were leaning toward each other. He forced himself to look away, to get out of the car, to deliberately steer his mind back to the reason they'd gotten married in the first place. "Let's go in and give Susanna a call. You'll feel better if we check up on Madeline."

Annie hung up the cordless phone ten minutes later and turned around to find Jake lounging against the black granite kitchen countertop, watching her.

"Everything okay?" he asked, handing her a glass of wine he'd opened while she was on the phone.

Annie took a tentative sip. "Fine. Madeline fell asleep in the car on the way home from the restaurant. She barely woke up when Susanna changed her and put on her jammies, and now she's down for the night."

"That's good."

"Yes." Except that Madeline had always served as a buffer between them. Without the child here, there was nothing to diffuse the tension that stretched between Annie and Jake like a tightrope. Annie took another sip of wine and looked around. "Your home is lovely."

"Thanks. I'll give you the grand tour."

She followed him through the kitchen and breakfast room, taking in the way it was all done in black granite and shining chrome, very high-tech and sophisticated. "It's very striking. Who designed it?"

"Mainly Rachel. She worked with an architect and an interior designer, but she had specific ideas of what she wanted."

Annie followed Jake into the dining room. It, too, was stark and modern. The focal point was a long, black-lacquered table surrounded by twelve white upholstered chairs. A tall, Oriental silk flower arrangement sprawled dramatically in the center. An enormous abstract painting of cubes and rectangles supplied the only note of color in the room.

Baby, Oh Baby!

The black-and-white theme continued in the living room. Two black leather sofas faced each other in front of the imposing white-marble fireplace. An enormous glass-topped coffee table, a pair of zebra-print chairs, a shoulder-high wrought iron candle holder, a large abstract sculpture, and a plush black-and-white, geometric-patterned rug completed the room.

The house looked like a showplace, not a home. It wasn't just the stylized décor, Annie realized; it was the fact that everything was picture perfect. Every pillow was fluffed, every tabletop neat. "How do you keep it so spotless?" she asked.

"I have a housekeeper come in once a week."

"She must have just been here."

"Actually, she's due tomorrow. I, uh, don't spend much time at home."

Apparently not. Annie looked around, her attention drawn to a collection of oil paintings that looked like Rorschach tests hung over a low buffet against one wall. An array of steel-framed photographs sat below them.

Annie crossed the room and picked one up. Jake, looking about ten years younger, stood in front of a Christmas tree with his arm around a smiling brunette. Annie's stomach twisted. "This must be Rachel."

Jake nodded.

"She was lovely."

"Yes."

Annie gazed at the attractive young woman in the photograph. She had Susanna's sleek hair, the kind of hair Annie herself had always envied. Unlike her own unruly curls, Rachel's locks gracefully fell to her shoulders in a sleek, obedient wave. The woman had a slight tan, even though it was the holiday season, with not a freckle anywhere in sight. An irrational stab of inadequacy cut through Annie's chest. The only way she

255

could get a tan was if her freckles all collided.

Carefully replacing the photo, she picked up the one next to it. A teenaged version of Rachel and Jake smiled back. They were riding in an open convertible, waving to a crowd. Rachel wore a crown and a white evening gown, and Jake wore a football jersey. A banner on the side of the car read "Homecoming King and Queen."

Annie gazed at the smiling couple, suddenly feeling strangely wistful. Rachel and Jake had a long, shared history. Like plants that had been potted together, their roots were deep and intertwined. It was something she would never share with Jake—or any man, for that matter. "Were you two an item all the way through college?"

"Nah. We went our separate ways after high school— Rachel went to Emory in Atlanta and I went to Harvard. But we both ended up back in Tulsa. We got back together at one of her parents' parties. We married a couple of years later."

Annie nodded silently, a large lump in her throat. The next photo made the lump grow bigger.

Rachel, resplendent in a long white wedding gown, a gown that was sleek and fitted and stunning in its simplicity. Her hair was pulled back in a chignon, and she was holding a sophisticated bouquet of white calla lillies.

The next photo showed Jake beside her, looking handsome as a movie star in a tuxedo, smiling down at his bride as together they cut together an enormous, multi-tiered wedding cake. But it wasn't Jake's clothes or even the warmth of his smile that drew Annie's eye; it was the wedding ring on his finger, clearly visible as his hand covered his bride's.

"You used to wear a wedding ring."

Jake nodded.

A flash of insight stabbed Annie's heart. "I'll bet you

were the kind of man who never took it off."

Jake looked at her. She could tell she'd hit home by the guarded look in his eyes.

"It was a part of you," Annie whispered. "Just like she was."

Jake looked away, but not before she saw the flicker of pain in his eyes. An odd emptiness filled her chest.

She placed a hand on his arm. "I'm sorry. I should have realized . . . I mean, I shouldn't have tried to push you into getting a ring this morning."

"Forget about it. It's no big deal." He stepped back and gestured to the next room, apparently eager to change the subject. "Let me show you the rest of the house."

Annie followed him through the other rooms—a home office with two desks, obviously a his-and-hers arrangement. An upstairs TV room, filled with more pictures of Jake and Rachel. Two pristine guest rooms, each with their own private bath.

And a large, unfurnished room located across from the master suite. "What was this?" Annie asked, looking at the blank white walls.

"It was going to be the nursery."

The nursery—and it was completely empty. As empty as Rachel's arms, as empty as her womb. As empty as Rachel's death had left Jake's heart.

Annie's throat grew tight with emotion. Jake flipped off the light, plunging the room into darkness. Annie stood there for a moment, blinking back the tears that crowded her eyes, not knowing if the tears were for Jake or Rachel or herself.

She drew a deep breath and followed Jake into the next room—the master bedroom suite. Spacious and airy, with tall ceilings and a pair of French doors, the room was all done in white. The tall posts of the king-sized iron bed were draped with a gauzy white fabric, giving it a feminine look. More photos of Jake and Rachel covered the tops of two matching dressers.

The house was a shrine to Rachel, Annie suddenly realized. Jake hadn't changed a thing. He was living there in the house, keeping everything just as it had been when she was alive, with virtually nothing changed.

Nothing, that was, except his whole life.

Annie fought a sudden urge to flee. She didn't belong here. She was an intruder, an invader in another woman's home. She'd known that Jake was clinging to Rachel's memory. She just hadn't known how tightly.

Not that it mattered, she told herself. She'd known Jake didn't love her, known she wasn't entering into a real marriage. Still, a tiny little corner of her heart had secretly, inexplicably hoped . . .

What? Annie asked herself derisively. *That he was going to fall in love with her?* She knew better than to set herself up for disappointment like that. She knew better than to pine after an emotionally unavailable man. And any man who flatly stated that he had no interest in ever getting involved again because no woman could possibly compare to his late wife was emotionally unavailable.

Still, he hadn't kissed her like a man who was pining for another woman. He'd kissed her like a man who'd wanted *her*. Twice.

She glanced across the bed, only to discover that he was staring back at her, looking for all the world as if he wanted to kiss her again. A shock of sexual awareness rolled through her.

She looked away, and her gaze fell on the French doors. She walked toward them. "What's out here?"

"A balcony. It overlooks the backyard." Jake unlocked and opened the doors, and Annie stepped through them, onto a wide wooden deck.

Jake joined her at the railing. The night was warm, and the air felt soft after the hard chill of the air conditioning. Annie peered into the night, but it was too dark to make out anything but shadows. "I hear some frogs. Are you near water?"

"There's a landscaped fishpond at the back. I can go downstairs and turn on the lights, if you want to see it." Jake turned to go.

"Oh, don't bother." Annie reached out her hand to stop him, and it landed on his chest. It was a small, inconsequential gesture, one she'd made without thinking, but the simple touch set off an odd chain of events.

Jake froze. Annie did, too. They looked at each other, their eyes gleaming in the night like those of a pair of wild animals. She awkwardly started to lift her hand.

His hand came down on top of hers, trapping it against his heart, and then his eyes trapped her gaze, as well. Their eyes held a wordless conversation, speaking eloquently of hunger and need and desire. And then she was in his arms, and his lips covered hers in a kiss.

And oh, dear Lord, what a kiss it was. It started out gentle, but then his tongue slid between her lips, and the next thing she knew, his mouth was doing urgent, delicious, lascivious things to hers, and she was doing them back. Desire, hot and demanding, seized her like a bodysnatcher. She pressed against him and felt the hard proof of his desire pressing back. A moan drifted through the night air, and she realized, on some vague, less-than-conscious level, that it had come from her own throat.

Jake's hands slid down to her bottom. She fitted herself against him, grinding shamelessly, on fire with desire. She wanted him to pick her up, to carry her inside,

259

to strip her down, to stretch her out, and to spend the whole night making wild, fierce, uninhibited love to her in that big, iron bed.

Except . . . the bed would be the one he'd shared with Rachel. The thought hit her like a splash of cold water. Dear Lord—what on earth was she doing? And why was she doing it in Rachel's own house?

Annie abruptly pulled back. Jake pulled away, too. He ran a hand down his face and blew out a harsh breath. When he finally looked at her, his eyes were full of remorse. "Good God, Annie—I-I'm sorry. I didn't mean for that to happen."

"Me, neither."

"We—um—must have had too much to drink."

"We must have." But it was a lie, and they both knew it. Annie walked stiffly back into the bedroom as Jake closed and locked the doors. She pretended a deep interest in a candlestick on the bureau.

"I—I'm really sorry," he stammered.

"Forget it. It's no big deal." She faked a yawn. "I'm ready to turn in. Where do you want me to sleep?"

"I don't care. In here, if you want."

Annie looked up, startled. Surely he didn't mean . . .

Jake cleared his throat. "I, uh, sleep in a guest room these days. So you can have this room, if you want."

He couldn't bear to sleep alone in the bed he used to share with Rachel. A huge lump formed in Annie's throat. "No, thanks. I'd rather sleep in the guest room, too."

Jake's eyebrows arched upward.

Annie's cheeks grew hot. "I mean, the *other* guest room."

"Oh. Okay. Sure. Wherever you'd be most comfortable." Jake's Adam's apple moved as he swallowed. "I'll, um, go get your bag from the car."

260

He turned and strode from the room, leaving Annie to stare at the large iron bed—the bed where Jake had made love to Rachel, where they'd tried to make a baby, where Jake no longer slept now that Rachel was gone.

The bed looked empty, but it was crowded with memories, and there was no room in it for her. A quiver of pain shot through Annie's chest.

It was just like Jake's heart.

Chapter Fifteen

"Married? Are you out of your *mind?*" Tom loomed over Jake's desk the following Monday, his hands planted firmly on the desktop.

Jake leaned back in his swivel chair. He'd known his father-in-law would be upset about his marriage, but he hadn't expected Tom to come completely unhinged. The man had stormed into his office like a S.W.A.T. team trooper two minutes after Jake had settled behind his desk.

"When Susanna told me what you'd done, I couldn't believe my ears. I couldn't believe you'd do such an idiotic thing, and I especially couldn't believe you'd do it behind my back."

Jake deliberately kept his voice calm and controlled. "I didn't do anything behind your back. You would have been invited to the wedding, but you were out of the country."

"You did this because you were angry at me for hiring that detective!"

Jake turned a pen in his fingers as he looked up at Tom. "I *am* still angry about that. You had no right to interfere. But that had nothing to do with my decision to marry Annie. I married her because it's the best thing for our child."

"How do you figure that? You can't love this woman."

"I love my child."

"You didn't marry the child, for Christ's sake!"

"That's right. I married her mother, and now Madeline has a family." Jake deliberately used the low, even, voice of reason he used in court to make an opposing counsel's argument sound histrionic.

That seemed to inflame Tom further. "Oh, and I suppose you spent the last three nights with that woman—first at your house, then out at her so-called ranch—just cementing your family ties?"

Jake felt a muscle tick in his jaw. He had no intention of telling Tom that he and Annie had slept in separate bedrooms. He fixed the man with a stony gaze. "That's right."

Tom's face was already red with rage. It darkened to a mottled purple. "It doesn't bother you one bit that you're making a mockery of your marriage to Rachel?"

"This has nothing to do with her."

"Bringing in another woman to take her place has nothing to do with her?"

"That's not what this is about."

"It most certainly is. You're being disloyal to Rachel's memory."

Jake rose from his chair, his temper blazing to life. "*You're* a fine one to talk."

Tom's scowl deepened. "What the hell is that supposed to mean?"

"I'm referring to Kelly."

"Kelly?" Tom straightened, his expression wary. "What does she have to do with this?"

"She disqualifies you from talking about loyalty."

Tom's eyes widened, then narrowed. He took a step back. "Nothing's going on between Kelly and me."

"No?"

"No."

"Well, the way you two are carrying on, it's just a matter of time." Jake glared at the older man. "Don't you dare come in here and lecture *me* about loyalty. Now, if you don't mind, I've got work to do."

Jake abruptly sat down and swiveled his chair toward the computer on his credenza, turning his back on the whole situation.

Silently fuming, Tom strode down the hall to his own office, where he slammed the door and loosened his tie. Damn it! He didn't understand how Jake could go off and marry that woman. What was he thinking? He stalked to his window and stared out, unbuttoning the top of his shirt. And what about Susanna? He sure as hell didn't understand how she could have aided and abetted Jake with this cockamamy scheme.

He'd arrived home last night, exhausted and jet lagged, only to have Susanna cheerily tell him that during his absence, Jake had remarried. Just as shocking had been the fact that Susanna had been a party to it.

Tom's blood boiled at the thought. What the hell had his wife been thinking? She'd not only attended the wedding, but she'd hosted a wedding dinner and kept the child overnight so Jake could spend the night alone with that woman. And Jake had evidently taken her directly to Rachel's house.

To Rachel's bed.

Tom slammed his fist on his desk at the thought. Damn it! Susanna was so besotted with the idea, the thought of playing grandma, that she'd lost all her common sense. She'd even gone and gussied up a guest bedroom with all kinds of baby paraphenalia. And then she'd had the temerity to suggest that the child might be good for their own marriage.

"She's such an adorable child," Susanna had said. "I can't wait for you to see her. She's just what this family needs."

"What this family needs is for you and Jake to get your heads examined," Tom had curtly responded.

What the hell was wrong with the two of them? Was he the only one who hadn't forgotten about his daughter?

The intercom buzzed. He jabbed a finger at it. "Yes?"

"Kelly Banyon on line three."

Great. Just what he needed—especially after Jake's remark. Tom expelled a harsh sigh. He'd decided while he was in Geneva to quit toying around with Kelly. He was old enough to know that if one played with fire long enough, one was likely to get burned. The mature thing to do was to focus his attention on sorting out the situation with his wife.

But, hell—that promised to be painful, and Kelly offered a respite from pain. When he was with her, he felt vibrant and desirable and sexy. Powerful, even—not like a limp-willied Viagra candidate. When he was with Kelly, he didn't feel impotent against life.

With a sigh, Tom lowered himself into the chair and punched the telephone button. "Hi, Kelly."

"Hi." Her voice was a low, sultry purr. "How was your trip?"

"All right."

"You don't sound like everything's all right."

He rubbed the bridge of his nose between two fingers. "The trip was fine. Everything here seems to have gone to hell in a handbasket while I was gone, though."

"Sounds like you need some cheering up. Why don't you meet me for a game of racquetball this evening?"

"I don't think that's wise, Kelly."

"Oh, come on. Physical exercise will do you good. It'll clear your head and help you unwind."

Tom hesitated. Like any good attorney, Kelly pressed her advantage. "It's just what you need. Meet me at the club at six."

It sure sounded a lot more appealing than going home and arguing with Susanna about Jake and the baby.

"It's just a game of racquetball," Kelly cajoled.

"Are you sure that's all we're playing?"

Kelly laughed, her voice deep and throaty. "That ball, counselor, is entirely in your court."

Tom smiled. Damn, but he liked the way Kelly made him feel. Powerful, manly, sharp, in control.

He was strong enough to control this situation. What the hell could a game of racquetball hurt?

"Okay," he relented. "See you at six."

The summer had gained momentum as June stretched into July, the days growing hotter with each passing day. As Jake walked toward Annie's barn four weeks later, his shirt clung damply to his back, even though it was early evening and the sun hung low in the sky.

He topped the hill to see Annie, her back toward him, brushing out the gray alpaca inside the corral. The animal stood perfectly still, as if it were enjoying her ministrations. Hell, Jake thought with an absurd burst of envy, why wouldn't the beast? Annie's hands were playing over its body, her voice murmuring softly in its ear.

She was wearing a brief pair of khaki shorts and a blue tank top, and her copper hair glistened in the waning sunlight. A burst of attraction shot through Jake. Ever since that kiss on the balcony the night of their wedding, Jake found it impossible to look at Annie without a surge of desire.

He walked closer, watching her stroke the animal's neck, then pause to clean out the brush and stuff the fur into a burlap sack. "Thanks a lot, Smoky Joe," he heard her murmur. "That was a lovely bit of wool you donated today."

Jake smiled at the polite way she talked to the animal. He'd learned that Annie's infatuation with alpacas had a practical side: their fleece was extremely valuable. She had discovered a niche market of specialty stores that catered to weaving and knitting enthusiasts, and she sold the harvested fleece directly to them. There was a lot more to Annie than he had initially assumed. She was eccentric—there was no doubt about it—but she also had a very good head on her shoulders.

The alpaca pulled back his velvety lips and showed his teeth before he ambled a few feet away.

"If I didn't know better, I'd think that creature was smiling at you," Jake called.

Annie whipped around, the curry brush in her hand. Her face lit with a smile that made his heart pound a herky-jerky beat. "Jake! I didn't expect you this evening."

He hadn't really expected to be there, either. The arrangement they'd agreed upon was that he'd visit on the weekends and stay in Tulsa during the week. Since this was Wednesday, he wasn't due for another two nights.

In the four weeks that they'd been married he'd found himself coming up with more and more excuses to spend more and more time at Lucky.

He told himself it was because of the tension between Tom and him at work. A distinct frostiness now characterized their relationship, and Jake avoided spending any more time around the man than necessary. He'd consequently quit working late hours at the office, but that left him with nothing to do with his evenings. He hated going home to rattle around that big empty house by himself.

He much preferred being here on the ranch. He loved being with Madeline, making her laugh, watching her learn new skills, hearing her add new words to her rapidly expanding vocabulary. He loved being outdoors, too. He'd forgotten how good it felt to feel wind on his face and the sun on his back. He'd even started playing around out in the barn with some of the woodworking equipment that had belonged to Annie's grandfather. There was something satisfying about turning a block of wood into an object he'd pictured in his mind. He loved the sawing and sanding and polishing, loved the solid feel of wood in his hands. He'd found a stash of high quality oak, and he'd begun making a rocking horse for Madeline.

But there was another reason he liked being here at the ranch, a reason he was uncomfortable admitting, even to himself. He liked being around Annie. He liked it a lot.

Her grin widened. "What brings you all the way out here in the middle of the week?"

Stooping down, Jake climbed through the rails of the fence and strolled toward her. "I had a meeting in Broken Arrow. Since I was on the far side of Tulsa anyway, I figured I might as well drive on over."

Annie nodded. She was always gracious enough to pretend his lame excuses were perfectly logical. "Madeline will be glad to see you."

What about you? Jake rubbed his jaw, wishing he could rub away the inappropriate question, rub away the attraction that burned behind it. He didn't *want* to be attracted to Annie. It complicated everything. Try as he might, though, he couldn't erase the memory of how sweet her body had felt, or how eagerly her lips had clung to his.

"Where is the little squirt?"

"Looking at a baby calf in the back field with Ben. Here they come now."

Jake looked where Annie pointed and saw the large man top a grassy hill in the distance, Madeline perched on his overalled shoulders. Jake lifted his arm and waved. The baby grinned widely and began bouncing on Ben's shoulders. "Ink! Ink! Ink!"

Jake's smile felt like it began in a warm spot of his chest and expanded outward.

"I told you she'd be glad to see you," Annie said.

"She probably thinks I brought her another toy. I'm afraid I'm empty-handed today."

"You don't have to bring a toy every time you come. You underestimate your appeal."

"With Madeline, or with you?" The remark was out before he considered the wisdom of making it. Annie did that to him—made him toss out remarks without weighing his words. It was a dangerous trait, considering how physically attracted he was to her. When he was with her, he found himself talking more freely than he had with anyone since Rachel. The thought made him frown.

Annie grinned at him. "Don't look so worried. You have immense appeal to the world at large."

"Ha! I doubt that Tom would agree with that." He unlatched the corral gate and held it open for Annie.

She stepped through it. Together, they started walking toward Ben and Madeline, who were still a good distance away. "Things are still strained between you and he?"

"To put it mildly."

"Susanna was afraid that was the case."

Jake's eyebrows rose as he looked at her. "You've talked to Susanna?"

Annie nodded. "We talk regularly. In fact, she's coming out to see Madeline in a week or two."

A stab of guilt shot through Jake. He hadn't talked to Susanna since the wedding. He made a mental note to call and invite her to lunch later in the week. Just because Tom was behaving like a jerk was no reason to let his relationship with her suffer. "How's she doing?"

"She's staying busy—seeing old friends and heading up two new charity events. She's even joined a tennis team." Annie hesitated. "I get the impression you're not the only one having trouble with Tom, though. It sounds like things are pretty strained between the two of them as well."

Ben and Madeline were drawing near. The older man set Madeline on the ground, and the toddler scampered toward them, the cat face on her red playsuit bobbing as she ran. "Ink! Ink!"

Jake scooped her up in his arms and swung her around. Madeline giggled gleefully. Jake's heart felt as full and warm as his arms.

"I hope you can stay for dinner," Annie said.

"I was hoping you'd ask."

An hour later, Annie grinned at Jake across the remnants of a baked chicken. "I have a surprise for you."

270

"Oh, yeah?"

"Yeah." Annie's eyes flickered mischievously. "I've discovered your deepest, darkest secret."

Jake tensed. Oh, damn—surely she hadn't discovered how much he wanted her. He eyed her warily.

Her smile widened. "It's something you've probably wanted every time you came out here, but didn't think you could have."

Oh, Lord. He grinned uncertainly.

"You have no idea what I'm talking about, do you?"

"Afraid not."

"Well, close your eyes."

What was she going to do? Surely not a striptease—not in front of the baby! All the same, his palms grew damp and his heart thumped hard in anticipation.

"Close your eyes," she repeated.

He did as she requested. He heard her chair scrape back and heard the pantry door open, then close. He felt her arm brush his shoulder and smelled the enticing scent of her perfume as she placed something on the kitchen table in front of him.

"Okay. You can open your eyes now."

Jake blinked. Sitting in front of him was a plate piled high with Twinkies. Two, four, six . . . good grief, there were a half-dozen stacked there on the plate!

Annie stood back, her arms folded, looking very pleased with herself. "I found two empty cartons of Twinkies boxes in the pantry, along with one that was still half full. I hadn't realized you had such a sweet tooth, but since you apparently do, well, I want you to feel free to indulge it."

For a brief moment, he considered eating them. It would probably be easier to force down six Twinkies in one sitting than to tell her the truth.

Just then Madeline caught sight of the snack cakes

and frantically kicked her legs against the high chair. "Ink! Ink! Ink!"

The gig was up. Jake drew a deep breath. "Um, Annie, I have an embarrassing confession to make."

Annie patted Jake's shoulder and shot him a reassuring smile. "Hey, it's okay. Lots of people are secret junk food junkies. It's nothing to be ashamed of. Go ahead. Dive in." She picked up an empty platter and carried it to the sink.

From the corner of his eye, Jake saw the baby straining toward the Twinkies, her hands outstretched, her brow furrowed with determination. "I've been meaning to tell you this, Annie, but . . ."

Madeline had worked up a full head of steam by now. Kicking furiously, she banged her tiny fists on her tray and screeched, "Ink! Ink! INK!"

Oh, jeeze. He'd better hurry up and just spit it out. "When you were in the hospital and Madeline was crying, you said to give her a Binky. I—I'm afraid I misunderstood."

Annie's back was toward him, but he saw her freeze. Madeline was now screaming at the top of her lungs, her face an alarming shade of red. Jake quickly placed two Twinkies on her tray. She stopped in mid-yowl, grabbed one in each hand and crammed them both in her mouth.

Jake used the ensuing silence to finish his confession. "When she says 'Ink,' she's trying to say Twinkie. The truth is, she's a Twinkie addict, and I'm her supplier."

Annie still stood at the sink. He wished she would turn around so he could he could see her expression.

"I'm really sorry." His words tumbled out in a rush. "I know you go to a lot of trouble to make sure she eats healthy foods. I haven't given her any in weeks—not since I figured out you were talking about her pacifier.

I wanted to tell you, but it was such a numbskull thing to do, and I didn't want you to think I was totally incompetent when it came to caring for her. . . ."

Annie just stood there, her back toward him. He wished she would say something. He rose and walked toward her. "Aw, Annie, it couldn't have done any real harm. Come on, now—don't be mad at me." He put his hand on her shoulder.

She turned toward him. She wasn't angry, he realized with relief. She was cracking up with laughter. She leaned against him, laughing until tears ran down her face.

She finally drew a breath and wiped her eyes. "Well, you get points for coming clean about it."

He looked at her accusingly. "You knew."

The remark set off a fresh round of giggles. Annie looked at Madeline, who was holding the stubs of two snack cakes in her fists, her cheeks stuffed like a chipmunk's. "Madeline gave it away. She went nuts when I found the Twinkie boxes in the pantry."

Jake rubbed his head, feeling like an idiot. "I should have told you," he admitted. "It was just such a stupid thing to do. . . ."

Annie's eyes danced. "It would have been stupider if you'd sat there and actually eaten six of them to keep me from finding out."

Jake grinned back. "You would have let me do that, too, wouldn't you?"

"*I* would have. But I didn't think Madeline would."

He laughed and gazed into her eyes—into her laughing, impish, blue eyes—and felt an almost overwhelming surge of attraction.

"Twinkie." Annie cocked her head as she said the word, as if she were testing it on her tongue. "You know,

273

I kind of like the name. Maybe I should start calling you that, too."

"Don't you dare."

"I just might, just to see what you'll do."

"I know what I'd *like* to do." His words came out low and husky and full of innuendo. The ever-present chemistry between them began to smoke. He gazed at her, and she gazed back. The air in the room suddenly grew several degrees warmer and strangely harder to breathe. "Annie . . ." he murmured.

"Ink! Ink! Ink!"

The jarring interruption made them both turn toward the high chair, where a cream-covered Madeline was straining to reach the plate of remaining Twinkies.

Annie scurried to the table and picked up the plate. "That's more than enough, sweetheart," she told the baby. She turned to Jake. "Since you're the one responsible for the layer of cream filling Madeline's wearing, I think you should be the one to wash it off. So why don't you take over bath duty tonight"—she shot him a mischievous smile—*"Twinkie?"*

By the time Jake got the baby out of the tub thirty minutes later, he was nearly as soaked as she was. He'd managed to carry her to the nursery, dry her off and put on her diaper, but his hair was still dripping in his eyes as he squatted on the floor, struggling to work the child's arm through her nightgown. Annie walked into the baby's bedroom and smiled.

"What did she do—pull you into the tub with her?"

"Almost." With a final tug, he managed to get the night gown on the squirming toddler. Madeline immediately waddled over to a basket of stuffed animals and began pulling them out onto the floor.

Jake started to rise from his crouched position, then

froze as something soft touched his head. He looked up to find that Annie had picked up the towel and was using it to dry his hair. The gentleness of her hands jolted him.

It had been a long time since someone had touched him like this. A handshake, an occasional pat on the back, a kiss on the cheek from Susanna—those were the only types of physical contact he'd had since Rachel had died. He'd never realized how important the sense of touch was, until it was suddenly missing from his life.

"How did you get so drenched?" Annie asked.

Her fingers were weaving a spell. Her breasts were just above eye level. Jake found it hard to breathe, much less to talk. "Madeline hit me with a loaded sponge toy."

Annie's breasts swayed mesmerizingly above his forehead. He tried to focus on what he was saying, but all he could think about was the beauty of those breasts, so close to his face. He could lean up and kiss them. He could reach up and touch them. He wondered what she'd do if he did.

Annie gave his hair a final tousle, then stepped back, the towel in her hand. "There. That's better."

No, it's not. It was much better when you were touching me.

Madeline toddled over, a stuffed toy dachshund in her hand. "Aw Dah," she announced.

Annie looked at Jake, her eyebrows raised in surprise. "Did you hear that?"

"What?"

"She just said 'Hot Dog.'"

Madeline gave a gummy smile and waved the stuffed toy. Jake looked from the child to Annie and shook his head. "You're imagining things. She's just making baby sounds."

"No, she said it. She misses Hot Dog since he's gone back home, now that Ben and Helen are back." Annie

275

crouched down beside the child and gave her an encouraging smile. "Who have you got there, Madeline? What's the name of your puppy?"

"Aw Dah."

"See?" Annie's face beamed with pride. She scooped the child into a big hug. "What a smart girl, Madeline! That toy looks like Hot Dog, doesn't it?"

"Aw Dah," Madeline confirmed.

"She *did* say it!" Jake exclaimed. "She said Hot Dog, clear as day." Jake jubilantly lifted the child in his arms and swung her around. "You're one smart little cupcake, aren't you?"

Madeline grinned up. "Aw Dah."

Annie caught Jake's eye and laughed. Madeline did, too. Jake's heart filled to bursting. His fifteen-month-old daughter had said hot dog! He couldn't have felt prouder if he'd won the Nobel Peace Prize, snagged a Pulitzer, and finished first in the Boston Marathon, all at the same time.

This is what it's like to be a family, he thought.

The thought made him pause. The three of them *were* a family, at least biologically and legally. But they weren't a real family, not in the real sense of the word.

He and Annie were married, but the marriage was just a matter of convenience. They'd made a child together, but they'd never made love.

Love—that was the key ingredient. That was what melded people into a family, not marriage contracts or bloodlines.

A rush of confusion and something close to panic poured through Jake's veins. There was no place for love in this relationship. Love was emotional, and emotions muddied legal issues. The whole point of this marriage was to work out a legal custody arrangement—that, and to give Madeline a simple, normal, easily explainable family history.

Annie lifted Madeline from Jake's arms. "Are you ready to go to bed, sweetie pie?"

I sure am. The thought was so clear that for a moment, Jake was afraid he'd said it aloud. Crimony, he was really losing it. He needed to get out of here before he did something he regretted. "I'd better go. I've had a really long day."

"You're welcome to stay and spend the night."

Awareness pulsed between them. "In the guest bedroom, I mean," Annie added quickly. "Like usual."

Sexual energy hung in the room like volatile vapors, dangerous, capable of igniting at any moment. It was growing between them, every time he saw her. Jake needed to leave before the sparks between them set off an explosion.

"I need to get back to Tulsa. I have a meeting first thing in the morning." He leaned in and kissed Madeline. As he did, he got a delectable whiff of Annie's soft perfume. He started to kiss her on the cheek as well, then decided against it.

Her eyes held a funny light as he drew away. *She knew,* he thought uneasily. *She knew he'd almost kissed her.* He wondered if she knew why he hadn't—that he didn't trust himself to stop with just a friendly peck.

He took a step toward the nursery door and lifted his hand. "Well, I'll see both of you on Friday."

"Okay. We'll look forward to it, won't we, Madeline?" Annie lifted the baby's arm. The baby gave an engaging grin, but it was the picture of Annie's face as she watched him leave that haunted him on the drive back to Tulsa—her lips parted, her eyes filled with wistful yearning.

Chapter Sixteen

Annie was closing the door to Madeline's room Friday evening when she heard the sound she'd been waiting for—the crunch of car tires in the drive. Her heart picked up speed. She quickly checked her appearance in the hall mirror, then chided herself for being foolish. Jake was coming to see Madeline, not her. Still, she'd taken an inordinate amount of time with her appearance—showering after dinner, donning a casual sage-green sundress with crisscrossed straps in the back, putting on makeup.

She was falling for Jake. She told herself that she was heading for a major heartache, that she was being ridiculous, that he wasn't interested in a long-term relationship, but her heart wouldn't listen to reason. It still raced like a greyhound as a knock sounded at the door.

Annie opened it. She knew Jake would be on the porch, but she was unprepared for the physical impact he had on her. When he smiled, she was hit by a knee-

278

weakening, breath-catching bolt of magnetism that struck her square in the solar plexus. He'd obviously come straight from the office; he was wearing dress slacks and a blue shirt that was unbuttoned at the neck. A large cardboard box sat at his feet on the porch.

He seemed to feel the attraction, too. She saw it in his eyes, in the way his pupils dilated. For a moment they just stood and looked at each other.

"Hi," she finally said.

"Hi, yourself." His gaze roamed over her, then returned to her face. It was an awkward moment, a moment when friends kiss cheeks or strangers shake hands. Jake made no move to do either. "You look really nice."

"Thanks." She opened the door wider. "Come on in."

He picked up the box and followed her into the living room. Setting the box on the coffee table, he seated himself beside her on the sofa.

She needed to focus on something, anything besides Jake and the almost palpable current between them. *The box,* she told herself. *Focus on whatever is in the box.* She gestured towards it. "What's this?"

"A surprise for Madeline."

The package seemed to shift slightly on the table. Annie glanced at it curiously. She was dying to know what was in it, but Jake's guarded expression made her hesitant to ask. "Oh, gee, she just fell asleep. I guess you'll have to wait until morning to give it to her."

"Well, this is probably the kind of surprise that's best in the morning, anyway. It's likely to get her pretty wound up."

Annie thought she saw the box move again. "Madeline loves surprises."

"I figured she would. I wasn't so sure about you, though."

"Oh, I like surprises, too. If they're pleasant ones."

Jake rubbed his jaw. "Well, now, that's where this whole situation gets iffy."

A suspicious snuffling noise emanated from the box. Annie shot him an amused glance. "Are you going to make me wait until morning, too?"

Whatever was inside the box began scratching at the cardboard. Jake gave a wry grin. "I don't think I can. This present is about to open itself."

He pulled his gift onto the sofa and set it between them, then folded back the top. Annie peered in. A tiny russet dachshund puppy not much bigger than Jake's hand gave a joyful yap.

"Oh—how adorable!" she exclaimed. The creature wagged its long, thin tail as Jake reached in and gently lifted it out. Annie held out her arms.

Jake passed it to her. "If you don't want to keep it, I'll take it back to Tulsa and keep it there. I just thought that Madeline would like to have a dog of her own."

"I'd love to keep him. Madeline will be crazy about him. *Is* it a him?"

"Actually, it's a her. The lady at the kennel told me females were easier to train than males, unless the males were neutered."

Annie grinned. "That rule doesn't only apply to dogs."

Jake winced. "I hope you aren't getting any ideas."

Oh, I'm getting ideas, all right. But they don't have anything to do with neutering. Annie forced her attention back to the dog. "She's beautiful."

"Yeah." Jake reached across Annie's lap and stroked the dog. "She reminded me of you."

Annie's pulse quickened. She tried to hide it under a dry smile. "Now there's a backhanded compliment if I ever heard one."

Jake laughed. "I meant her coloring. Her coat is almost the exact same color as your hair." He lifted a strand of Annie's hair from her shoulder and draped it across the dog's coat. "See?"

I see that your slightest touch makes me quiver. I see that you have a five o'clock shadow I'd love to touch. And I see that your lips look like they were just made for kissing.

The puppy leaped up and licked her on the chin. *The dog*, Annie reminded herself. *I'm supposed to be focusing on the dog.*

Picking up the puppy, Annie rose to her feet. "I'll bet she could use some water."

Jake stood, too. "I've got food and water bowls for her in the car—along with some other supplies. I'll go get them."

He returned with a large wicker pet bed, a red dog pillow, a huge bag of puppy chow, and a big plastic bag of toys and other accessories.

"We can fix her up in the kitchen," Annie said. "I have a baby gate we can use to keep her in there until she's house-trained."

While Jake fixed the puppy a bowl each of food and water, Annie stretched the white plastic gate across a section of the kitchen by the back door and spread newspapers on the floor. The puppy gobbled up its chow, then eagerly slurped some water.

"She probably needs to go outside," Annie said.

She opened the back door and stepped out into the night, the little dog at her heels. Jake followed them onto the flagstone patio.

Overhead, the stars glowed like Christmas lights in December. A chorus of crickets and tree frogs sang a throaty, seductive song. The scent of honeysuckle wafted on the light breeze, making the air seem thick and sweet. The night offered a feast for the senses, but

it was a sixth sense that set Annie's heart to pounding—
a sense of mutual awareness, of mutual attraction. The
night seemed full of possibilities.

The little dog ran along the fence, investigating her
surroundings. Annie eased herself into the wooden porch
swing and let her eyes adjust to the dark. The seat
creaked as Jake sat down beside her. He stretched his
arm along the back of the swing, his hand near her hair.
Annie fought the urge to lean back against it.

The dog, she reminded herself, forcing her thoughts
back to it like a mantra. "Madeline will love her new
puppy."

"I hope so. I probably should have called and asked
your permission, but I don't have a great track record
of getting people to agree to keep pets."

They set the swing to rocking, keeping perfect time
with each other. "You told me your parents wouldn't
allow you to have any pets."

"Rachel wouldn't go for the idea, either. She said a
dog wasn't compatible with white carpeting."

Annie started to say that white carpeting wasn't compatible with life, then thought better of it. It would sound
like a criticism of Rachel, and she didn't want to do that.

The little dachshund trotted across the patio and
through the partially open door into the kitchen. Annie
craned her neck, but couldn't see through the door. "Is
she going back for more food?"

Jake turned and peered through the panes of the window behind him.

"No. It looks like she's going to bed."

Maybe we should do the same. Annie drew in a deep,
steadying breath. *Focus on the dog*, she silently ordered
herself. "Is the carpeting the reason you still don't have
a dog?"

"Nah. I'm not home much. I don't think it's good for

dogs to be alone for long stretches of time."

"It's not good for people, either," Annie said softly.

Jake looked at her, and the intensity in his gaze made her heart skip a beat. "Sometimes people don't have a choice."

"Sometimes they do, but they just don't realize it."

Awareness hovered in the air, thick as the scent of honeysuckle. It was getting harder and harder to think of anything but Jake and the way his mouth had felt when he'd kissed her.

Annie forced herself to look away, forced herself to direct the conversation back to the animal kingdom. "So did you just figure me as a sucker for puppies?"

Jake lifted his shoulders. "I was hoping that if you saw her, you'd have a hard time saying no."

His eyes gleamed in the soft light from the kitchen window. He was gazing at her lips. When he raised his eyes to hers, she could no longer ignore all that was zinging back and forth between them.

Attraction. Hunger. Need. Desire. It was all there, exposed in his gaze, naked and irresistible.

"I'd have a hard time saying no to you, Jake, about anything," she found herself saying.

She'd spoken in a low whisper, but the meaning came through loud and clear. The swing quit moving. The air grew still. Even the tree frogs seemed to hold their breath.

Jake's eyes moved over her face, hot and close, reading her eyes, searching her expression. Whatever he was looking for, he evidently found. His lips moved, and one word came out. "Annie."

And then she was in his arms. He smelled of shaving cream and Juicy Fruit gum, a combination that was unexpectedly erotic. His arm on the back of the swing came down to her hair, his other arm moved around to her back, and his mouth angled down over hers in a hungry swoop. And then she was lost, hopelessly lost, in a kiss so full of passion, she never wanted to be found.

Everything about the kiss was hot and wet and compelling—the slick feel of his lips on hers, the slide of his tongue inside her mouth, the way it made her insides melt and turn to liquid flame.

She wound her hand around his head and threaded her fingers in his hair, holding him to her, not wanting to give him the option of letting go. She'd wanted to kiss him like this ever since she'd first set eyes on him, before she'd even known who he was. And now that she was in his arms, she never wanted to leave.

His breath was hot against her neck. His hand reached around the back of her dress, to the straps that crisscrossed her spine, his fingers gently burrowing under the strips of fabric. Never had a touch felt so hot, so intense. He kissed her again, a deep, plundering kiss, and eased the strap off one shoulder, pulling it down, exposing her breast.

"Ah, Annie," he murmured, his gaze caressing her. "You're almost too beautiful to touch."

"Touch me anyway," she urged.

He lowered his head and took her nipple in his mouth. Sensation, warm and exquisite and deep and needy, shot from her breast straight through to the center of her being, to the womb that had carried his child.

She wanted to touch him, too—wanted to feel his skin against hers. Her hands trembled as she unfastened the buttons of his shirt—trembled not with nerves, but with eagerness. She pushed back the shirt and ran a hand over his chest. Flat and hard-muscled, it was covered with rough-textured hair. Her hand moved lower, to the buckle of his belt.

"Slow down, angel," he groaned.

"I don't want to go slow."

The next thing she knew, he was standing, and he'd scooped her up in his arms. He carried her through the open kitchen door, kicking it closed behind him. And as she clung to his neck, inhaling the scent of him, feeling his chest hair against her cheek, he carried her to her room and placed her on the bed.

He peeled off his unbuttoned shirt. His eyes were dark and hungry, and they never left her face. Her hands moved to the other strap of her dress. He knelt on the mattress and covered her hands with his, stopping her. "No. Let me do it."

His fingers eased it down. The soft, sage-green fabric pooled at her waist.

His eyes drank her in. "You're even more beautiful than I imagined."

The thought that he'd imagined her naked excited her almost as much as the feel of his hand cupping her breast, and his thumb flicking against the sensitive tip. His mouth followed his fingers. She stretched back on the bed, giving herself up to the pleasure of his beard-shadowed skin on her flesh, of his lips trailing hotly across her breast. When he took her nipple in his mouth and suckled, a shiver of pleasure shot through her, pooling into hot, molten pleasure between her thighs.

She ached to be touched there, and he seemed to sense it. Still kissing her breast, his hand moved higher. Slowly, slowly, with infinitely tormenting slowness, his fingers inched up the soft cotton of her dress. She moaned as he langorously stroked the bare flesh of her inner thigh.

She reached down, wanting to touch him as well, but he moved lower, raining kisses on the underside of her breast, down her belly, all the while pushing up the hem of her dress.

285

His touch glided to the edge of her silk bikini panties. He ran a finger slowly along the elastic edge, first one side, then the other. Just when she thought she couldn't stand it, his finger slid right down the center, pressing the silk first against her swollen nub, then against the wet, aching center that throbbed to be touched and filled. She moved against him, groaning.

"Easy, sugar," he murmured.

"Please. *Please . . .*" she begged.

He moved up and reclaimed her mouth, all the while continuing the exquisite stroking. She reached up and unfastened the button on his slacks. He gave a low, throaty moan, then rose and quickly shed his clothes.

He returned to the bed, immensely aroused. She reached for him, but he moved low on the mattress, slowly tugging her dress down, then off. Tantalizingly slowly, Jake pulled off her panties. His hand ran from her breasts to the top of her pubic mound, pausing to trace the horizontal scar just above her curls.

"Your C-section?" he asked.

"Yes," Annie murmured, moving her hand to cover it.

He caught her hand and eased it away. "It's beautiful." He bent his head and feathered kisses along the scar—long, slow, adoring kisses. Annie's heart opened like a freshly cracked safe.

Jake's lips moved lower, and his fingers followed. Slowly, he began a torturous teasing, inciting her until she was wet and pulsing and moaning with need.

"Jake—Jake . . ."

His mouth urged her on, and his fingers drove her over the edge. She spiraled past a point of no return, into a star-strewn dimension that was bright and hot and urgently sweet.

She shuddered, pulsed, cried out.

She clutched at his head, all but dragging him upward by the hair. She ached for him to be inside her, ached for him to fill her, ached to complete the circle that had begun before they'd even met.

"Easy, sugar. Easy."

"I want . . ."

"Tell me what you want."

"You. I want you." Her voice was a breathy whisper. "In me."

He could hold back no longer. Hovering above, he plunged into her sweet heat. She moved against him, meeting him thrust for thrust, her hands pulling him closer, urging him deeper, pushing him higher. She felt her muscles tighten again, felt herself quiver, felt herself scale the wall. But this time he went with her, into a honey-kissed place of mutual surrender, a place where their two hearts pounded in a single humming rush, drumming so hard and fast and perfectly in sync that there were no spaces between beats.

Chapter Seventeen

A high, plaintive yip pulled Jake from the depths of a deep, sated sleep. He burrowed his face in the pillow, not wanting to awaken. He was having the most amazing dream—hot and erotic and so real he thought he could actually smell a trace of perfume. He'd been making love to Annie, and . . .

Annie. His eyes flew open, and he found himself inside a floral covered wagon. It had been no dream. He was in Annie's bedroom, in Annie's bed. A shot of pleasure raced through him, quickly followed by a chaser of fear.

Dear God. What had he done? Sex complicated everything. This marriage was supposed to simplify everyone's life, to keep Annie from bolting off to Timbuktu with the baby, to give Madeline a readily explainable family history. He hadn't intended for things to get physical. Sexual involvement always made things emotional, and when things got emotional, reason and logic went right out the window.

He sat up in bed, trying to shake the fog from his brain, trying to remember how it all had happened. Where the hell *was* Annie, anyway? And what was that weird yapping sound down the hall? It sounded like a dog.

The dog. The details of the previous evening came back in a rush. One moment he and Annie had been talking about dogs, and the next thing he knew, they'd been in each other arms. He wasn't sure exactly how one thing had led to another, but once they'd started kissing, there had been no turning back. The events of the evening had taken on a life of their own, rushing downhill with the momentum of a freight train, a momentum against which he had been entirely, completely powerless.

Jake squeezed his eyes shut and muttered a low curse. If there was one thing he hated, it was being out of control, and he'd definitely been that last night. He'd made love to Annie not just once, but three separate times. And if she'd been beside him in bed this morning, he'd no doubt have done it again. Hell, he had an erection right now just thinking about it.

Mumbling another oath, Jake threw back the covers, rose from the bed, and searched for his clothes. He located his slacks and underwear on the floor and quickly scrambled into them. Damage control was always most effective when it was launched immediately after a mistake, and last night had definitely been a mistake.

Annie was his complete opposite. Opposites might attract, but they didn't make for good lifelong partners—anyone with a lick of common sense knew that. The reason he and Rachel had gotten along so well was because they'd been so alike in so many ways. Their temperaments, ideology, approach to problem-solving—all of the important stuff—had been practically identical. He and Annie shared none of those things. They had no hope for a viable marriage, and neither one of them was the type for a casual sexual relationship.

He'd screwed up, big time. He needed to talk to Annie and set things straight as soon as possible.

Pulling his pants on with some frustration, he headed across the room for his shirt, which had somehow landed against the opposite wall. Donning it, he started down the hall, only to be stopped by a cheerful cooing coming from Madeline's room.

"Ah ah oooh ah."

He peered in the doorway and found the baby lying on her back in her crib, pulling on her toes, musically crooning to the ceiling.

Madeline's cheeks puffed out in an enormous grin as she spotted him. Scrambling to her chubby feet, she grabbed the crib railing and did a couple of deep knee bends. "Ink! Ink!"

Jake grinned and walked to the side of the crib. "Good morning, sweetheart."

"Good morning, yourself," called a feminine voice behind him.

Jake whipped around to see Annie leaning against the wall, wearing a short pink robe and a smile. Her hair was a tousled mass of red curls, and her eyes were bright and blue.

A surge of interest shot through him. He tried to tamp it down. "Hi."

"Hi. Did you sleep well?" she asked.

Sleep was not the most memorable part of his evening. He cautiously nodded, afraid to commit to anything. "You?"

She raised her arms in a sensuous stretch. "Wonderfully, until the puppy decided it was time to begin the day."

Jake knit his forehead in a frown. "Oh, hey—I meant to get up with her. Sorry you had to."

"It's okay. Madeline has me accustomed to early mornings."

"Ooh ah," the baby agreed, gripping the railing and bouncing on the mattress.

The corners of Annie's eyes crinkled sexily as she smiled. "Besides, you looked like you needed some sleep. Especially after that last little interlude at three-thirty."

Jake swallowed hard. "Annie . . . we need to talk."

Her smile rapidly evaporated. "Uh-oh." She folded her arms protectively across her chest. "Whenever people say 'we need to talk,' they never mean about anything pleasant."

Hell. He hadn't even said anything, and he'd already hurt her.

Madeline's bouncing grew more agitated. Her mother quickly strode to the crib and lifted the child out.

"Annie . . ." Jake began.

She cut him off, her voice thick. "Not right now, Jake, okay? Madeline needs a dry diaper, and I need some coffee. Why don't you go make us a pot? You and I can talk while Madeline plays with the puppy." Her back was toward him as she carried the baby to the changing table, but he caught a brief glimpse of her profile, long enough to detect the glimmer of something that looked suspiciously like a tear on her cheek.

Annie's heart was heavy as she followed a gleeful Madeline and a rowdy puppy out to the patio fifteen minutes later. Jake was right behind her, carrying two mugs of coffee.

It was a beautiful July morning—painfully so. The sun shone in a brilliant blue sky, songbirds tweeted on every branch, and the honeysuckle climbing the back-yard fence filled the air with a lush, heady scent. It had started out as a perfect day. When she'd awakened and felt Jake curled beside her on the bed, her heart had been dancing on tiptoe, pirouetting in the air.

And then Jake had said, "We need to talk," and her joy had crashed to the ground like a duck with a shat-tered wing.

Holding her spine rigid, Annie walked past the porch swing to the wrought iron patio and sat under the large green-and-white striped umbrella as Madeline merrily chased the dog across the lawn. Jake set a mug of coffee before her, then lowered himself into the adjacent chair.

Annie took a sip and closed her eyes. For one last moment, she pretended that everything was the way it had seemed when she'd awakened—that she and Jake were not just married, but really husband and wife. That they were lovers, in love. That they were a family, with no end in sight.

Jake cleared his throat. "Madeline seems to like the puppy."

Annie opened her eyes and nodded. "She loves him."

"I'm glad it worked out." Jake looked at her, then quickly looked away. His dark eyes were troubled. He was having a hard time saying whatever it was he had to say.

Annie decided to help him out. "But *we're* not going to work out. Is that what you're trying to say?"

Jake kept his eyes on the iron mesh tabletop. "An-nie . . ."

"You've got a case of buyer's remorse."

Jake's gaze jerked up quizzically. "What?"

"Buyer's remorse. After making a big purchase, sometimes people feel like they've made the wrong decision. Especially if they made the purchase impulsively. You've got buyer's remorse about last night."

"Jeeze, Annie—you make it sound like I bought a leaky boat!"

She forced a smile. "I'll bet you wish that's all you'd done."

Jake's mouth twisted into a rueful grin.

"Do you feel like you're cheating on Rachel?" she asked softly.

Jake avoided the question. "I didn't mean for things to get so out of hand." He ran a hand through his hair and blew out a harsh breath of air. "Look—I really like you. And I'm attracted to you like crazy. Last night was incredible. But . . ."

"But I'm not Rachel."

Annie's soft words hung in the air. Jake stared into his coffee. The only sound was the nearby squeal of Madeline and the distant caw of a bluejay.

He ran a hand through his hair and looked up, his eyes dark. "You and I, we're just too damned different, Annie. Too different for things to work out for very long."

"Different isn't necessarily bad. Not physically, anyway."

The corners of Jake's mouth quirked up, but the smile was short-lived. He fiddled with the handle of his mug. "Annie, there's more than just you and me involved here. There's a child who needs stable parents in a stable relationship. In the long run, things like similar beliefs and compatible goals are what hold couples together. We don't have that stuff going for us. We just have . . ."

"Sex." Annie supplied softly. "Hot, lusty, incredible sex."

She saw his throat move as he swallowed. "It *was* incredible."

"And hot."

"Very hot." His voice was an octave lower than normal.

Their eyes locked, and for a moment, Annie thought he was about to haul her into his arms and kiss her. And then the puppy darted by and Madeline dashed after him.

"Aw Dah!" she called.

Jake's eyes followed the toddler as she headed back across the lawn. He blew out a hard sigh. "If we continue down this road, Annie, we're going to end up hurting each other. And if we hurt each other, well, it's almost inevitable that we'll hurt Madeline, too."

Annie sat very still. If she didn't move, maybe she could hold back the pain.

She knew he was right. It had hurt her immensely, having parents who argued and fought and tried to wound each other.

"I think we need to stick with our original agreement," he said. "I think we need to go back to having a platonic relationship."

Annie forced a smile she didn't feel. "That's going to be awfully difficult, now that I know what you look like naked."

Jake looked at her longingly. "Not half as difficult as it'll be for me, Annie. Every time I look at you, I . . ." He stopped himself and shook his head.

"What?"

His mouth turned up in a rueful, sexy smile. "If we want to have a platonic relationship, I'd better not tell you."

"Who said that was what we want?"

Jake's eyes were pleading. "Annie . . . don't make this any harder than it is."

Annie turned her hands palm up on the table. "So what do you suggest we do? Pretend that last night never happened?"

"Yes."

Annie shot him a skeptical look.

"The way I figure it," he continued, "it'll be easier to stop things now than to continue on and get all emotionally involved."

Too late, Annie thought silently.

Jake drained his mug, then rose to his feet. "I'm going to get another cup of coffee. Would you like one?"

Annie shook her head. What she wanted was another night like last night, and another hour like the one when she'd first awakened this morning—an hour when her future with Jake seemed to stretch on indefinitely, when life held joy and promise, when love finally, finally seemed to have arrived.

"I've never had my fortune told," Susanna told Annie four weeks later as she leaned against the counter in Annie's kitchen. The older woman had driven over from Tulsa and played with Madeline that morning, then treated Annie and Madeline to lunch at the Cowbell Café. In return, Annie had offered to read her fortune while the baby took an afternoon nap.

Annie set the kettle on the burner and smiled. "In that case, I'm going to use Granny's special blend—one she kept for special readings."

Annie headed to the old apothecary case in the living room, rose on tiptoe, and slid her hand along the top of the old piece of furniture. Her fingers closed around a rusty key. She used it to open the hinged glass doors and pulled out an enormous tin box from the very back.

"This is very old and stale, so I'm afraid it doesn't have the best flavor," Annie said. "But Granny swore it was the best tea for readings. It's called 'China Seer.' "

"China Seer," Susanna echoed. "What a romantic name."

The two women traipsed back to the kitchen. Annie carefully pried the lid off the tea container and placed a heaping serving in the teacup. When the teapot whistled, she poured in the steaming water, then crossed the room and retrieved a small piece of ice from the freezer.

"That'll help the tea leaves settle at the bottom," she said, dropping in the ice. She carefully carried the cup to the breakfast table and set it in front of Susanna. "There. Now drink it down until there's nothing left but about a teaspoon of liquid."

Susanna took a sip. "Do you read your own fortune every morning?"

"Oh, no. Gran said the gift is only to be used for others—never for selfish reasons, and never for money. She said it's impossible to accurately read your own fortune."

Susanna took a deeper drink. "But you read Jake's. Since you two are married now, your fortunes should be the same."

"Not necessarily." To her dismay, Annie's voice cracked on the last syllable.

Susanna leaned forward and placed her hand on Annie's. "Annie, dear—is everything okay between you two?"

"Yes." The concern in Susanna's gaze was so warm and genuine that tears formed in Annie's eyes. "No."

Susanna gently patted Annie's hand with her own. "If you don't want to talk, I'll certainly understand. But if you do, well, I'm a good listener, and I know how to keep a confidence."

Annie blinked back a tear. "Jake doesn't want Tom to know any details about our marriage, and I don't want to ask you to keep a secret from your husband."

Susanna smiled sadly. "Tom and I seem to have gotten very good at keeping secrets from each other lately."

Annie looked up questioningly. The other woman patted her hand again. "If you need a friendly ear, I'm here for you. And you can rest assured that nothing you tell me will be repeated to anyone."

The urge to talk to someone had been building like steam in a teakettle. Susanna's sympathetic offer made it all come boiling out. "Oh, Susanna—I'm falling in love with him!"

"And that's bad?"

Annie nodded miserably. "We got married to simplify Madeline's life and quiet down the small-town gossips and give us all the same last name. We agreed to stay married for five months. It's supposed to be platonic, but . . ."

"You're for falling for Jake." She squeezed Annie's hand and gave her a consoling smile.

Annie nodded, rubbing away a tear. "And he's still in love with Rachel."

"That doesn't mean he can't love you, too. The human heart has an enormous capacity for love."

"Do you think so?"

"Oh, yes. Look around—you see it all the time. Why, my great-aunt was married for thirty years. When my uncle died, she was certain she'd never love again. But about a year later, she remarried, and she and her new husband had twenty wonderful years together." Susanna gazed down the teacup, as if she were seeking inspiration. When she looked up, her eyes were bright. "Maybe what you and Jake need is a change of pace. I'll keep

Madeline for a weekend, and give you a chance to be alone together, as a couple."

Annie shook her head. "Jake says we should avoid being alone together."

"That's a good sign. That means he finds you hard to resist." Susanna grinned and took a long draught of tea. "Leave it all to me. I'll find a way to corner him into it."

A seed of hope took root in Annie's heart. Maybe, just maybe, there was a chance. It frightened her, how intensely she hoped it was true. She squeezed Susanna's hand. "Thank you."

"Don't mention it. It's in my best interests to keep you two together to make sure that grandbaby stays nearby." She took another sip of tea, then peered over the rim of the cup. "You don't mind if I think of Madeline as a grandchild, do you?"

"I'm honored," Annie answered honestly. "Madeline is fortunate to have you in her life." She smiled softly at Susanna. "I am, too."

Susanna's eyes grew suspiciously moist. "Oh, dear, I'm about to puddle up again." She picked up her cup. "I better get busy and drink my tea before Madeline gets up from her nap."

A few sips later, she handed over her cup. Annie cradled it in her palm, swirled it clockwise three times, then carefully turned it upside down on a saucer. She silently counted to seven, then set it right side up and peered inside.

Susanna leaned close. "What do you see?"

Annie gazed at the wet leaves. Oh, dear—her grandmother had always cautioned her about giving people bad news, and Susanna's leaves did not bode well. She hesitated.

"Tell me." Susanna's voice was soft but firm. "I want to know."

Annie drew a steadying breath, and began with the tea leaves nearest the handle. "Something precious is slipping away. Something—someone—is trying to take it from you."

"My marriage?" Susanna whispered.

Annie turned the cup. "It has to do with love, and it's very close to your heart."

Susanna's eyes were large, her voice just above a whisper. "Is Tom being unfaithful?"

Annie peered into the cup. "You still have loyalty in love—but there's a turn ahead. If you don't do something to change the course of events, you will lose it."

"What can I do?"

Annie frowned down at the leaves. "The symbol for war is in your sphere. You'll need to wage a battle. You'll have to fight to keep the one you love."

"Fight?" Susanna's expression fell. "I don't know how to fight."

"Well, you need to learn." Annie stared into the tea-cup. "You'll have to fight to keep love loyal. The message is there, as plain as day."

"But I don't know how!" The older woman's lovely face was drawn, her eyes distressed. "Conflict upsets me. I was raised to be polite, to get along with people, and it's just too ingrained. Besides, every time I've ever disagreed with Tom, he just walks out. It makes me feel so bad that I always give in."

"Maybe you're not supposed to fight *with* Tom. Maybe you're supposed to fight *for* him. I see the letter *K*. Annie looked from the cup to Susanna. "Do you know anyone whose name starts with a *K?*"

Susanna's face grew pale. "My Lord. This is eerie."

"I take it that's a yes."

Susanna nodded. "Kelly. She's an attorney. I've suspected for several months that she's after Tom."

"The leaves show that your intuition is very strong in this matter."

"What am I supposed to do?"

Annie continued to gaze at the cup. "Follow your intuition."

"Are there any clues? What am I supposed to fight with?"

Annie turned her palms up. "I'm sorry. The leaves don't give the answers. They just help point the way."

Susanna's eyes were pleading. "Is there anything else? Anything that might indicate what I'm supposed to do?"

"I don't see anything else. I'm sorry." A thought struck her. "Wait! There's one trick my grandmother used once. She said that sometimes there's a clue for the reader in the saucer."

She picked up the saucer she'd drained the teacup into and gazed at it.

Susanna leaned forward. "What do you see?"

Annie stared at the leaves matted on the side of the saucer. "A claw."

"What does that mean? That I'm supposed to scratch her eyes out?" Susanna gave a wan smile. "Can't you just see me in a catfight?"

Annie grinned at the idea of the refined, ladylike Susanna in a knockdown, drag-out brawl. She shook her head. "The saucer is meant to aid the reader, so this message is for me. It's supposed to help me guide you." Annie closed her eyes for a moment and let her mind drift. *A claw. A scratch.* She let her thoughts free-associate, until an image formed, an image circled in light. She abruptly opened her eyes.

"I've got it! Come with me." Her chair screeched on the wooden floor as she rose from the table and headed back to the living room. Once again she reached for the key on top of the tall apothecary case, and once again she unlocked the glass doors. She pulled out a small, rusted tin can, no bigger than a quarter, and handed it to Susanna, then carefully relocked the case.

The older woman held the tin at arm's length to read the tiny label. "Itching powder?"

Annie nodded. "Grandma's mother gave this to her on her wedding day. She said that if Grandpa ever got an itch to wander, she should give him something to scratch."

Susanna laughed. "How very appropriate. But what am I supposed to do with it?"

Annie shrugged. "I don't have a clue. I only know you're supposed to have it."

Susanna closed her hand around it. "Maybe it's a good-luck charm. A reminder to follow my intuition."

"And to have the courage to fight for what you love," Annie added.

"Sounds like a reminder you could use, too." Susanna smiled at her as the two strolled back to the kitchen. "I'll call Jake as soon as I get back to Tulsa. I'll tell him you two need some time together as a couple, and I'll insist that he let me have Madeline for the weekend. That way you two will have some time alone."

The thought made Annie's heart race. She watched Susanna pick up her purse and slip the tin of itching powder inside. "What should I do once I get him alone?" Annie asked.

Susanna pulled the purse on her shoulder and grinned. "I'm sure you'll think of something."

Chapter Eighteen

Tom plopped his glass down hard two mornings later, sloshing his orange juice on the green linen place mat. He frowned across the breakfast table at Susanna. "I will *not* sit down to dinner with that—that *hussy!*"

Susanna adjusted the sash on her silk robe. "Annie isn't a hussy. She's a perfectly lovely young woman. She and Jake are going to be in Tulsa this weekend, and it would be a nice gesture for us to invite them to dinner."

"She's a hussy in my book."

"Tom, we've been all over this. She's done nothing wrong."

"Oh, no? She hoodwinked Jake into marrying her less than a month after they met."

"That was Jake's idea."

"Hogwash. He has better sense than that. At least, I thought he did." Tom swilled his juice, looking like he wished it were bourbon.

Susanna leaned forward. "You're letting this ruin your relationship with Jake. Annie is his wife now. If you met her and gave her half a chance, I'm sure you'd like her."

Tom's lip curled in a snarl. "I wouldn't like her if you told me she was Mother Teresa reincarnated."

"Tom, just listen to yourself. You're being completely unreasonable."

"I can't just sit by and watch this woman try to take Rachel's place."

"She's not trying to take anyone's place."

"What's the matter with you?" Tom leaned forward and glowered. "Has that shrink and those damned pills you're taking addled your brain so much that you've forgotten your own daughter?"

The venom in his voice hurt even more than the words. Susanna rose from the table, picked up her cup, and calmly strode to the coffeemaker on the counter. "This isn't about forgetting, Tom. This is about letting go and letting life go on." Susanne lifted the pot from the burner. "It's interesting that you'd mention my 'shrink,' as you call him, because he says this unreasonable anger of yours is fear in disguise. Fear of facing your own mortality." She splashed some coffee into the cup. "He thinks you're scared to die."

"He's full of bull."

Susanna moved to the refrigerator and pulled out a carton of skim milk. She carefully poured some into her cup. "You know, maybe he *is* wrong. I don't think you're afraid to die. I think you're afraid to live."

Tom's eyes jerked up to hers, his expression first surprised, then wary. "What the hell is that supposed to mean?"

She moved back to the table and sat down opposite

him. "You won't be betraying Rachel, Tom, if you're happy again. If *we're* happy again."

He raked a hand through his hair and blew out a harsh sigh. "Happy? What the hell is that? I don't think I even remember what it feels like. So much has changed."

Susanna placed her hand on his. Her eyes searched his face. "One thing hasn't. I still love you, Tom."

She needed, desperately needed, to hear him say that he loved her, too. She waited, then waited some more. The words didn't come. The only thing that stirred was the ceiling fan overhead. The silence grew thick and threatening, darkening the sun-filled breakfast room like an ominous thundercloud.

Tom gazed at her, his eyes troubled. "Susanna . . ."

Suddenly she knew he was about to say something that would change their lives forever—something like "I want to leave" or "there's someone else" or "I don't love you anymore." She knew, deep and instinctively, that if the words were spoken, their marriage would be over.

She couldn't let him say it, whatever it was. "Oh, Tom, let's get out of here for a while." Her words tumbled out like water over rapids, rushed and jumbled. "Maybe we could take trip to Europe, or go to Hawaii for a week, or . . ."

"I told you before. I don't have time for that. My schedule is full."

Susanna picked up her spoon and vigorously stirred her coffee. "Well, the national corporate attorney's convention is coming up soon. I can go with you to that."

Tom stared straight into his juice glass. "You wouldn't enjoy it, Susanna. I'm on the conference committee this year. I've got something scheduled just about around the clock."

"Oh, I'll find plenty to do. After all, it's in New Orleans. While you're in meetings, I'll go see the sights with the other wives."

~~Tom~~ cleared his throat. "I don't think very many spouses are going this year. You shouldn't plan on it."

Until Rachel's death, Susanna had always gone to the convention with him. She'd become good friends with the wives of other attorneys who always went, too.

Oh, dear Lord—that look was back in his eye. He was trying to get up the nerve to say something, something she didn't want to hear. She rose from the table, her cup in her hand, and quickly changed the subject.

"Well, about this weekend . . . I won't ask Jake and Annie to dinner. But I've already offered to keep the baby Saturday night."

Tom's eyes followed her as she flitted to the sink and poured her newly poured coffee down the drain. He sighed, then pushed back his chair. "Do what you want. I'm playing in the legal association's annual corporate cup golf tournament this weekend, so I won't be around much."

I hadn't thought you would be. Susanna seized on the topic, eager to keep the conversation on neutral ground. "You and Jake played in that last year, didn't you?"

Tom brow knit in a displeased frown. "Yeah. And he should be playing in it this year, too. Our firm is one of the sponsors. I couldn't believe the lame-ass reason he gave for not participating, either. He said weekends were for his family." Tom shook his head, his expression full of disgust. "*We're* his family, damn it! I tell you, this woman is brainwashing him. Hell, the other day he said he'd like to start taking on some different types of cases—consumer cases, children's advocacy cases." Tom shook his head. "He's not the person I used to know."

Neither are you. Susanna thought. *Neither am I. Ra-*

chel's death has turned us all into strangers.

Tom glanced at the clock on the kitchen microwave and sighed. "I'd better get dressed and get to the office."

Susanna watched him head for the stairs, relief and fear mingling in her heart. She'd managed to avert disaster this morning, but how long could she keep him from speaking the awful, fateful words that would end their marriage?

Annie's words floated through her mind: *You'll have to wage a battle. You'll have to fight to keep the one you love.*

Tom was drifting away—she could see it, she could feel it. She had do something to turn the tide, and she had to do it soon. Somehow, some way, she had to find a way to pull him back before he'd drifted beyond reach.

"This is so much fun!" Annie's face flushed with excitement as the roller coaster roared into its final turn at the Tulsa County fairgrounds on Saturday.

It sure is, Jake thought, tightening his arm around her. The ride gave him the perfect excuse to touch her, to inhale the scent of her perfume, to feel her hair brush across his skin. A wave of regret washed over him as the ride squeaked to a halt.

"Let's do it again!"

Jake had been thinking the exact same thing ever since the night they'd made love, but it wasn't a roller-coaster ride he'd had in mind. The memory of making love to Annie was torturing him, taunting his thoughts morning, noon and night.

Especially at night—and especially at Annie's house. It was excruciating, lying in the guest room down the hall from her, just yards from the bed where they'd given and taken such pleasure in each other. It killed him, knowing that she was lying alone under that crazy covered-wagon canopy, that all he had to do was walk down the hall.

He'd made the logical decision, he told himself over and over. He'd been absolutely right, insisting that their relationship go back to the platonic stage. After all, continued physical involvement would eventually create the type of gut-wrenching divorce experience they both wanted to avoid. And yet, all the logic in the world couldn't keep him from wanting Annie, and all the arguments his lawyer's brain could invent couldn't keep a creeping tenderness from winding into his heart, twisting and binding little bits of her to him, like the tendrils of a vine.

The chemistry between them was strong and combustible, and over the last few weekends, he'd done his best to avoid being alone with her. When he was at the ranch, he went to his bedroom immediately after putting the baby to bed, using the excuse that he had work to do. But instead of studying the piles of legal briefs he brought with him every weekend, he'd sit and listen to the sounds of the night, listen and remember, replaying the sweet way she'd tasted and smelled and felt.

Later, as the night drew on, he'd listen to the sounds of Annie moving through the house, getting ready for bed. He'd hear the shower running, and imagine her taking off her clothes. In his mind's eye he'd see the swell of her breasts, the curve of her waist, the erotic surprise of her red-gold curls. He'd envision her stepping into the water, envision the wet spray splashing over her smooth, fair, naked skin. She'd torment him with her mere proximity until he was in a white-hot lather.

Annie tugged as his arm. "Come on, let's ride it again."

"Okay. We'll have to get some more tickets."

The ticket booth was at the far end of the midway.

Jake followed her off the loading platform and into the jostling crowd, into a cacophony of voices and loud music and barker calls, into a scented sea of corn dogs and nachos and cotton candy. The sun was setting, and the midway lights were beginning to gleam.

Jake put his arm around Annie to pull her out of the way of a hot-dog vendor's cart. She glanced up, smiled and looped her arm around his waist in response. He knew he should draw away, knew he should disengage from the intimacy that came with her touch, but she felt too good against him.

"I'm having a great time," she said.

"Me, too." A better time than he ought to be having, he thought guiltily. He'd tried to weasel out of spending the weekend alone with Annie, but Susanna had shamed him into it. "Your marriage doesn't stand a chance unless you put some effort into it," she'd said. "You and Annie need some time alone."

To appease Susanna, Jake had agreed. It would be easier for her to accept their divorce if she thought he'd tried to make the marriage work. Jake had thought he could spend the day working and Annie could spend it shopping or sight-seeing, and Susanna would never know the difference. But then Susanna had presented them with two tickets to the Tulsa State Fair and a gift certificate to a luxury hotel.

"Annie told me she loves carnivals and fairs, so I thought it would be the perfect place for you to take her," she'd said.

"What's with the hotel gift certificate?" Jake had asked.

"You two never had a real honeymoon. I thought it would seem like more of a special occasion if you spent the night away from home, so I made reservations for you for tonight. There's a gift certificate for dinner at the hotel restaurant, too. It's supposed to be very nice—very romantic." She'd patted his arm. "You two go and have a good time. I'll look forward to hearing all about it when you pick up the baby on Sunday."

Susanna had him over a barrel. He didn't want to tell her the truth about his relationship with Annie, but he was incapable of telling her a bald-faced lie. So here he was, against his better judgment, spending the day with Annie, enjoying himself more than he had any right to do.

"Susanna said you're missing out on a big golf tournament this weekend," Annie remarked as she and Jake passed a concession that required contestants to guess which plastic cup hid a golf ball.

He shrugged. "I wasn't that eager to spend time with Tom."

How about spending time with me? Annie wondered. She prayed that Susanna was right—that the reason Jake was keeping his distance was because he was drawn to her. Tonight she intended to find out.

The thought made her stomach knot. She directed her thoughts back to Tom. "From what Susanna told me, it sounds as if things have gotten pretty tense between you and him."

"That's putting it mildly." Jake shook his head. "Lately he's been completely unreasonable."

"About what?"

"Everything."

"Our marriage?"

Jake sighed. "The marriage. Work. Life in general."

"His relationship with Susanna?"

Jake shot her a keen glance. "That, too."

The line of people buying tickets was long and slow moving. Talking to Jake suddenly held a lot more appeal than taking another ride. Annie looked up at him. "You know, I don't think I've got another roller-coaster ride in me after all. I'm famished, and all the noise and lights and smells are about to give me sensory overload. Why don't we go use Susanna's gift certificate for dinner?"

"Sounds good."

They walked to the car, their arms still looped companionably around each other. Jake opened the car door for her, then settled behind the wheel and started the engine.

She gazed over at him, her heart tripping at the sight of his handsome profile. "Aside from things with Tom, how are things at work? Have you got any interesting cases?"

"To tell you the truth, none of it is very interesting anymore." He pulled the car onto the road, steering it toward the interstate, then glanced at her. "I've been doing a lot of thinking about what you said, about practicing another type of law."

"Oh, yeah?"

"Yeah. I even talked to Tom about it. I told him I'd like to expand the kind of cases we take, to take on some consumer law cases, maybe even do some pro bono work for battered women and abused kids."

"What did he say?"

"That it would damage the firm's reputation."

"Is he right?"

"Maybe. He said, 'If you needed a triple bypass, would you choose a cardiologist who only does heart surgery, or would you choose one who also treats ingrown toenails?' It was a valid point." Jake looked in the rearview mirror and changed lanes. "I've got to make some kind of change, though. I can't stand the thought of doing nothing but acquisitions and mergers for the rest of my life."

Annie stared at the taillights of the car ahead of them. "That's exactly the point I'd reached when I decided to leave advertising. The final straw came when someone asked what I liked best about the business, and I couldn't come up with an answer."

Jake shot her a sidelong glance. "Why did you decide to go into it?"

"Actually, I didn't. It was my father's decision. He thought he knew what was best for me, and I went along with it, wanting to please him." Annie gazed out the window at the passing lights. "There comes a point when you have to stop trying to please other people and set your own course. Nobody knows what's best for another person. Sometimes we don't even know ourselves. We have to find out as we go along."

Jake pulled off the highway and guided the car toward a large high-rise hotel. He glanced over at her. "How did you get so wise?"

His gaze was warm, and it sent a current of heat sizzling through her. "Oh, I'm not wise. I mostly learn by making mistakes."

Jake grinned as he pulled into the parking lot. "That's what I like about you."

"What? That I make a lot of mistakes?"

"You don't pretend to have all the answers. It's so damned refreshing."

Annie's heart felt full and ripe and heavy, loaded with love, the way her belly had felt when she was pregnant with Madeline. She gazed at Jake as he parked the car and turned off the engine. "Is that all you like about me?" she found herself asking.

His gaze locked on hers like a patriot missile. Tension crackled in the air, along with an acute sexual awareness. "No." His voice was very soft, very deep. "Oh, no." His eyes were hot and aware and hungry, and they set Annie's heart to thumping against her rib cage.

It was time for her to make her move. Slowly, deliberately, Annie reached her arms around his neck and pulled him toward her. Slowly, deliberately, her eyes open the whole time, she fitted her mouth to his.

She needn't have worried about how he'd respond. The kiss went from zero to sixty in a matter of mere seconds. He kissed her back, ravishing her mouth and neck and face, kissing her as if he were starved for her taste.

"That was even more thrilling than the roller coaster," Annie murmured long moments later when they surfaced for air, hot and panting.

"A lot more thrilling." His voice was low and smoky, throbbing with desire. "But, Annie, honey, it's a lot more dangerous, too."

"So let's live dangerously." She gently drew her fingers through his hair. "I want to make love with you, Jake. I want to feel your hands on me and your mouth on me, and I want to put mine on you. I want to feel the weight of your body on me." Her voice lowered to a breathy whisper. "I want to feel you inside of me."

"Good God, Annie. . . ."

"I've been thinking about you, wanting you until I thought I'd lose my mind."

He pulled her into a kiss so hot she thought she'd melt, drawing her as close as the gear box would let them get. It wasn't nearly close enough. "Let's go in and get a room," he murmured.

Annie's heart did a fast, giddy dance. Their arms around each other, she and Jake crossed the parking lot and walked through the brass double doors.

As they entered the lobby, they nearly collided with a short, blond-haired man. The man glanced at Jake, then stopped short, his ruddy face creasing in a smile. "Jake—Jake Chastaine! Why, I haven't seen you since our ten-year high school reunion."

Jake dropped his arm from around Annie as if she were a hot potato. "Smitty—good to see you." The two men shook hands.

Smitty glanced at Annie with open curiosity, then looked back to Jake.

"How are your folks?" Jake asked.

"Fine, fine. They recently moved to Arizona. How are yours?"

A shadow passed over Jake's face, as if a gate had clanked shut. "They're dead."

Smitty looked stunned. "Oh, wow—I'm so sorry. When did it happen?"

"Two years ago. An auto accident. Rachel . . . well, Rachel was with them."

Smitty's mouth fell open. He rapidly closed it. "She's . . ." His voice held a question mark.

Jake nodded, his face grim.

"Oh, man. I'm so sorry. I didn't know. I've lived in Dallas for the past five years, and . . ."

"It's okay."

Smitty cast another curious glance at Annie. Jake cleared his throat. "Annie, this is Darrell Smith, an old friend from high school. Smitty, this is Annie—Annie, er, Hollister."

Hollister? Her last name was Chastaine now. She glanced at Jake questioningly.

"Nice to meet you," Smitty said, shaking her hand. "Any friend of Jake's is a friend of mine."

Annie smiled at him, wanting to correct the error. "Actually, we're . . ."

Jake took her arm and gave it a warning squeeze. "We're, uh, just going in for dinner," he interrupted.

"Well, I won't keep you. It was great seeing you." The man shook Jake's hand again, and nodded at Annie. "Nice meeting you." His eyes creased in a sympathetic frown as he turned back to Jake. "Hey—I'm really sorry about Rachel and your folks."

Jake nodded somberly. Smitty headed out through the brass doors, leaving Annie and Jake alone in the bright, marble-floored lobby.

"You didn't want him to know we were married," she said bluntly.

"No." Jake raised his hand to his cheek. "It seemed too awkward."

"It was awkward anyway."

Jake sighed, avoiding her eyes. "He knew Rachel. We all went to school together. For me to have remarried so soon after her death. It seems, well . . . disrespectful. As if I didn't love her."

An ache started deep inside of Annie and expanded outward, growing keener and sharper as it reached the surface. When she spoke, her voice came out sharp, too. "I didn't know you were so hung up on appearances."

Jake's jaw firmed into a stubborn set. "I am when it comes to Rachel."

"I don't suppose it occurred to you to just tell him the truth."

"Look—I hadn't seen Smitty in five years. I didn't feel like getting into a discussion about infertility treatments and donated sperm."

It was understandable, of course, but it didn't make Annie feel any better.

His voice softened. "You're hurt."

Annie didn't deny it. Hurt seemed like a paltry word to describe the raw ache she felt inside.

"Hey, I didn't mean to upset you." Jake's eyes were remorseful. "I just didn't think any good would be

314

served by giving him a bunch of unnecessary details."

Was that how he viewed their marriage—as an unnecessary detail? A fresh wave of hurt washed over her. "Do you intend to keep our marriage a secret from all your friends and acquaintances? If that's the case, I don't know why we bothered getting married at all."

"For Madeline. We did it for Madeline."

Of course. How could she have forgotten? How could she have been so foolish as to think, for even a minute, that they could have a real marriage, a union with love between the two of them as well as between each of them and their child? How could she have been so moony-eyed as to think Jake might actually grow to care about her, might even fall in love with her as she'd fallen in love with him?

"Be sensible, Annie. As time goes by, it'll become easier to explain. All anyone will ever need to know is that you and I were briefly married and that we have a child together."

It made perfect sense. It was logical and reasonable. But Annie didn't feel reasonable. She felt heartsick and hurt.

It was an exercise in futility, trying to win Jake's heart. Jake would never love her as he'd loved Rachel. Annie would never fill Rachel's shoes. She would always be second best. What she and Jake had wasn't a marriage; it was an arrangement.

She'd known that, going into it. She'd been an idiot to think she could change his mind.

"Would you like to get some dinner and talk it over?" Jake asked.

There was nothing to talk about. She'd hoped that this weekend would be a turning a point, that she and Jake would become lovers, that they could turn their sham of a marriage into the real thing. Now she could see it was a lost cause.

Jake didn't want a future with her. In his mind, she was already a thing of the past. His words burned painfully in her mind: *All anyone will ever need to know is that you and I were briefly married and that we have a child together.*

Tears welled in her eyes. She struggled to blink them back.

"Let's go get some dinner," he urged.

She shook her head. "I'm not hungry. I'd like to just check in and go straight to the room."

"Well, okay." Jake's expression was clearly bewildered. "But I thought, after what just happened, that you wouldn't want to. . . ."

Good grief—he didn't really think she was suggesting *that,* did he? She pulled herself to her fullest height. "It'll be easier if we spend the night in separate places," she said in her frostiest tone. "You can pick me up here tomorrow afternoon, and we'll go get Madeline together."

Jake's eyes were somber, his expression pained. "I didn't mean to hurt your feelings, Annie. If I did, I'm really sorry."

"So am I, Jake. So am I."

Chapter Nineteen

"I don't see what the big deal is." Kelly looped a strand of blond hair around a long red fingernail and recrossed her legs, flashing a tempting stretch of thigh. "You've told me you haven't slept with your wife in over a year. Surely she can't expect you to stay celibate indefinitely."

It wasn't Susanna who expected celibacy, Tom thought guiltily, fiddling with a pen on his desk. For the last few months, she'd made it more than clear that she wanted him back in her bed. And she'd sure made it tempting—parading around in slinky lingerie, making sure he caught her in various states of undress, giving him that come-hither, I-want-you look that had always made his libido work overtime.

And damn it all, it was still effective. He wanted his wife like crazy, despite the fact he was mad as hell at her. And that, in turn, made him angry at himself.

What was wrong with him? If he were a normal, red-blooded man, he'd be panting after Kelly. What fifty-five-year-old male wouldn't be flattered and turned on by a beautiful young woman who was actively pursuing him?

Hell, he *did* feel flattered and turned on; his libido was revved up and rarin' to go, and he felt as randy as a sixteen-year-old boy. The strange thing was, all of his thoughts and fantasies centered on his wife. The closer he'd gotten to convincing himself that he was within his rights to leave her, the more his body seemed to crave her.

It must be force of habit, he thought moodily. Thirty-three years of making love to the same woman must have programmed an automatic response. If he got aroused, he wanted Susanna. Sexually, he was Pavlov's dog.

Take this weekend, for example. Dear Lord, but he'd wanted his wife over the weekend. He'd come home from that golf tournament to change clothes for the evening's dinner, and he'd found her sitting on the kitchen floor, rolling a ball back and forth with that baby. She'd been laughing, and she'd looked so much like she had when Rachel was young that it had taken his breath away. It was like walking through the door and stepping back thirty years. And for a moment, all of those good times, all of the hopeful, youthful exuberance, all of the joy and fun and passion, all the best parts of his life— they were all there, right there in the room, so tangible he could touch them.

Could touch *her*.

For a moment, he'd had an almost overpowering urge to put the baby in her crib, carry Susanna upstairs, and make slow, fast, passionate, tender love to her. For a fleeting moment, he had been certain that if he could just bury himself in Susanna, he could bury all of the pain between them. It was ridiculous, of course—an overly simplistic solution. Besides, even if he'd wanted to give it a try, he wouldn't know how to start. He'd allowed such a distance to grow between them that he had no idea how to bridge it.

So instead of making a move on Susanna, he'd focused on the baby. He'd thought he'd feel indifferent to the child, but she'd charmed the socks off him. The baby was the spitting image of Jake, and she had such a winsome, appealing smile that it was impossible to look at her and not smile back. She'd toddled over to him, a picture book in her hand, and looked up at him with her father's brown eyes. Before he knew it, Tom had found himself sitting on the floor, the child in his lap, reading nursery rhymes.

Kelly shifted her legs again, deliberately hitching her skirt even higher. "I've registered for the New Orleans convention."

"That's a good career move. I'm sure you'll get a lot out of it."

"I hope so." Her lips curved in a slow, sexy smile. "I had my secretary call your secretary, and we're booked on the same flight."

Oh, Christ. Tom swallowed.

"I got my reservation in late, though, and the hotel is sold out."

"So where are you going to stay?"

"I'd like to stay with you."

Tom's heart began to pound. "Kelly . . ."

"I'll be discreet. No one but the hotel maid will know what room I'm in."

"Kelly, it's the convention hotel. People would see us getting on and off the elevators together."

"So? They'll just think we have rooms on the same floor. No one would believe you'd have the nerve to have a lover stay right in the room with you." She

319

smiled. "The secrecy of it will make it all the more exciting."

Tom squirmed on his chair. "Look, Kelly—I'm a married man. I can't do anything like that until I've severed things with Susanna."

"So sever them."

"It's not that easy."

Kelly shifted forward. Her jacket gaped open to reveal a glimpse of cleavage. "You'll probably find it a whole lot easier after a weekend in New Orleans with me." She ran a finger down her decolletage. "Besides, you're looking at things all wrong. If we have an affair, you'll be doing your wife a favor."

"How the hell do you figure that?"

Her lips pulled back in a kittenish smile. "You'll give her the satisfaction of being the wronged spouse. The fact of the matter, Jake, is that she'll probably be just as relieved to end the marriage as you will. I'll bet she's just as unhappy as you."

Tom tapped his pen on his desk blotter. Kelly might be right, but he didn't like hearing it.

She leaned over further, making her breasts strain against her low-cut gray silk blouse. He could see the black lace at the top of her bra. "I've been dreaming of the things I'll do to you, Tom. Of the things we'll do together. We'll have a good time. A really good time."

A knock sounded on the door. Tom looked up to see Jake standing in the doorway. Jake's eyes went to Kelly, then his mouth hardened into a tight, displeased line. "Sorry. I didn't know you had company."

A hot rush of guilt washed through Tom. "Kelly and I were just, uh, discussing some business."

Jake's eyebrows rose. "I thought you'd settled the LaMarr case."

"We did. We were just discussing the conference in New Orleans."

Kelly shot him a smile, apparently hoping to win him over. "Are you going, Jake?"

"Not this year."

Tom scowled. This was news to him, and he didn't like it—not one little bit. He started to say as much, but Kelly rose from her chair. He automatically rose as well to see her out.

"Thank you for your time." Kelly's voice took on a professional tone for Jake's benefit. "I appreciate your advice about the conference."

"I'm sure you'll enjoy it."

"I'm counting on it." Her lips curved in a catlike smile. She sauntered to the door, her hips swaying. Tom held the door open and watched her leave.

Jake's eyebrow quirked up as he sat down across from Tom's desk. "She's chasing you all the way to Louisiana?"

"She's not chasing me, for Christ's sake." Tom circled the desk and sat down. "She's planning to attend a national professional conference for attorneys in her specialty. Which, I'd like to point out, is exactly what you should be doing."

Jake placed his elbows on the arms of the chair and folded his hands. "That's kind of what I came by to talk about. I'm still interested in changing the focus of my practice."

"I told you my thoughts on that. As far as I'm concerned, the subject is closed."

"But I've got a way we can satisfy both of our objectives." Jake leaned forward, his eyes earnest. "We could form a whole separate division devoted to consumer law. We'd want to do it first-class, of course—

bring in a couple of attorneys who already specialize in that area, and . . ."

Tom leaned over his desk, the tendons in his neck tightening. "I told you no, damn it."

"Come on, Tom. It's a reasonable, workable plan."

"Not to me." Tom's fist clenched his pen so fiercely it nearly snapped in two. "This firm handles corporate law—period. Not charity cases or worker's comp or ambulance chasing. Corporate law. It's our specialty, our only specialty. It's been that way for twenty-five years, and I intend to keep it that way."

"Well, then, what would you say about me setting up a separate practice on the side?"

"I'd say you can't hold two full-time jobs and do them both justice. If you want to increase your caseload, believe me, there's plenty of work out there. I turned down two major accounts last month."

"Tom, this isn't a whim. I've given this a lot of thought. I'm burned out. I went into law because I wanted to work for justice, to make a difference, to help people. To tell you the truth, I don't feel like I'm helping anyone but a bunch of fat cats get fatter."

Tom stared at him. He hardly knew this boy anymore. He'd loved Jake like a son, but Jake had changed to the point that he seemed like a stranger.

Or maybe it was himself who'd changed. Maybe the person Tom no longer knew was Tom.

He brushed a pile of papers to the side of his desk with the back of his hand, trying to brush away the unsettling thought. "This doesn't sound like you. It's that woman, isn't it? You've let her turn you into a friggin' bleeding heart."

Jake's eyes glittered, hard and cold as ice. "I'd rather have a heart that bleeds than no heart at all."

"You're out of line there, son."

"No. *You're* out of line. With your priorities, with your attitude, and with your ethics."

"My ethics have never been questioned."

"Well, I'm questioning them now. I see what's going on with Kelly. I might be a bleeding heart, but I'm not blind." Jake glared at him hotly. "Neither is Susanna."

Tom's heart constricted. So did his hands on the desk. "That's enough."

"You're right." Jake rose stiffly from the chair. His voice was hard, the look in his eye even harder. "It's more than enough. I resign. I no longer care to be your partner." He strode to the door, then turned and paused. "Or your friend."

"You quit?" Annie's eyes were wide. She stood in the flower bed at the front of her house, a spade in her hand, a Chinese-style straw hat on her head, wearing short denim cutoffs and oversized cowboy boots. She looked ridiculous.

She looked adorable. Jake's heart had done a funny little leapfrog when he'd pulled into her drive moments ago and seen her bent over, industriously planting periwinkles. She'd looked up when she'd heard the car, and the way her face lit up at the sight of him had made his pulse leapfrog again.

Madeline ran up to Jake, a plastic spade and bucket in her hand, a huge grin on her face. "Ink! Ink!"

Smiling, Jake, bent down and picked her up.

"What are you going to do?" Annie asked.

"Well, first of all, I'd like to take a week or so off and spend some time with Madeline." *And you*, he silently added. "If that's all right."

Annie wore a slightly stunned look. "Sure."

"Then I thought I'd explore my options. I'll network with other attorneys, talk to my old friends at the D.A.'s office, maybe visit with a district judge or two. I might even explore the possibility of teaching at a law school."

"You'd be good at teaching."

"I don't know how good I'd be, but it sounds a lot more satisfying that what I've been doing lately."

Annie smiled. "This calls for a celebration."

"Quitting my job is a reason to celebrate?"

"Darn right." She grinned. "This is the first completely spontaneous action I've ever known you to make."

"No, it's not."

"It's not?"

"No. Kissing you was."

Annie's face turned a deep shade of red. "That's something we're better off not discussing."

"I agree. It's far better just to do it."

He leaned around Madeline and kissed her, full on the lips. The baby giggled. Even with a pint-sized chaperone between them, Jake felt the kiss all the way to his toes.

"There," he said. "Another spontaneous act."

He'd been thinking about Annie obsessively ever since he'd kissed her that night in Tulsa, thinking about how she'd told him she wanted to make love with him.

Knowing that she harbored such thoughts about him had been keeping him awake at night, tossing and turning, aching with desire. It didn't help that she'd said she was doing the same. Her words kept echoing in his mind: "I've been thinking about you," she'd said. "Wanting you until I thought I'd lose my mind."

He angled his head, wanting to taste more of her. Annie's lips were so soft, so sweet, so warm. He stepped closer, and then a tiny hand grabbed his nose.

"Hey!" Jake jumped back. The baby chortled gleefully, exposing her four tiny teeth and a wide expanse of gum.

Jake readjusted his grip on Madeline and fixed her with a mock-serious glare. "I'll remember that, young lady. When you're sixteen years old and your prom date tries to kiss you at the front door, it'll be payback time."

Annie laughed, but her cheeks blazed, and her eyes held an odd, confused expression. She stepped away and pulled off her gardening gloves. "Would you mind watching Madeline for a little while?"

"Mind? That's why I'm here."

"Good. If I'm going to pull a celebration together, I'd better go inside and get started."

It turned out that Annie's idea of a celebration was a festive dinner in the dining room, complete with candles, her grandmother's fine china, and guests. Ben and Helen were invited, along with Henry and Pearl. Annie drafted Jake to grill some steaks outdoors while she drove into town to pick up the elderly guests from the nursing home. "It looks like it's going to rain," she said. "We'd better get the outdoor cooking done while we can."

Sure enough, Jake had no sooner finished grilling the meat than the skies opened and rain poured down in sheets. He was relieved when Annie at last pulled her four-door truck into the garage. To his surprise, he discovered that she'd not only brought the aging attorney he'd spoken with on the phone and a poodle-haired elderly woman, but also Spike and a young brunette with a rose tattooed on her shoulder, a nose ring, and a pierced eyebrow.

Annie unfolded Henry's portable wheelchair and helped him into it as she introduced him to Jake. "You remember Spike, don't you, Jake?" she asked as they all moved into the living room. "He got a job in the kitchen at Shady Acres, and his girlfriend, Lauren, works there as a nurse's aide. They were both finishing their shifts, so I invited them along."

"Good to see you, Spike," Jake said, stepping forward.

"Yo!" Spike lifted his hand and gave Jake a high five. "How's it hangin'?"

The dark-haired girl poked him sharply with her elbow. "When you're a guest at someone's house, you don't ask, 'how's it hangin'.'"

The elderly woman shuffled forward on a metal walker, her eyes bright as bird's. "Well, don't you want to know? I always do. My guess is he's hanging left. My husband always hung to the left, and this fella reminds me of him." Pearl leaned on her walker and stared pointedly at Jake's fly. "Yessirree, I'm certain he's hanging left. You can always tell, because—"

Annie abruptly took her by the arm. "Pearl, sweetheart, why don't you have a seat, and we'll get you a drink."

The old woman looked at Annie, not at all perturbed to have been interrupted. Apparently it happened a lot. "All right, dearie. Make mine a double."

She settled on the sofa beside Helen. Annie introduced Jake to Henry, and Spike and Lauren to Ben and his wife. Two minutes later, Pearl leaned forward and pointed at Jake. "Tell me again, who's the fella with the hot bod?"

Annie threw Jake an amused glance. "Jake. He's my husband."

"Oh, my, aren't you lucky. Is he any good in the sack?"

Helen's generous cheeks turned a bright pink. She patted the old woman's hand. "Pearl, dear, that's not a question for polite company."

"Aw, shucks. The good ones never are."

Henry cleared his throat. "They've changed her medication again. She always gets like this when they change her medication."

Across the room, Spike grinned at Jake. "The old gal's a real trip, isn't she?"

Lauren elbowed her boyfriend again. "Don't talk about people where they can hear you." She rolled her eyes, which made the ring in her pierced eyebrow rise and fall, and she glanced at Annie apologetically. "Guys can be such dorks."

Pearl adjusted her hearing aid. "Dorks? Is that another word for stud muffins?"

Annie reached down and patted the old woman's shoulder. "That's right, Pearl. That's exactly what it is."

Everyone laughed. Annie turned to Jake. "Why don't you fix our guests a drink? I think Pearl would like a lemonade. I'm going to change into an honest-to-goodness party dress."

She returned in twenty minutes, her air damp from the shower, her skin glowing. She wore a long sleeveless apricot print dress that made her skin look like peaches and cream.

"You look gorgeous," Jake said.

He was pleased at the way she smiled, pleased that he had the power to make her cheeks pinken and her eyes brighten.

She turned away, as if she didn't want him to see how he affected her. "Spike, since you're a pro in the kitchen, maybe you can help me with the salad."

"Sure."

The rain continued to pelt on the roof as they gathered in the dining room. The meal was simple and delicious, the conversation lively and punctuated with frequent laughter. Jake looked up from his plate of steak, pasta primavera, and Annie's homemade bread, and gazed around the table. Six months ago, he never would have imagined he'd be dining with such an odd assortment of people—a pink-haired teenager and his tattooed girlfriend, a dotty old woman with a raunchy tongue, an attorney who practiced law out of a nursing home, and an overall-clad rancher and his wife who looked like they'd stepped straight out of a rerun of Green Acres. Even more amazing, he was having the time of his life.

It was all because of Annie, he thought. Only Annie could bring such a bizarre group of people together and meld them into friends. She was really something— funny, wise, quirky, sweet, endearing, sexy. . . .

His thoughts snagged on the last word, and his gaze returned once again to Annie. He found it hard to take his eyes off her.

At the end of the meal, Annie raised her glass. "We forgot to make the toast. Here's to Jake—for taking a bold step forward on the pathway to his dreams."

"Hear, hear!" Pearl cried. The clink of crystal filled the air.

Helen raised her glass. "And here's to Jake and Annie—who are celebrating four months of marriage this evening."

Jake glanced at Annie. He could tell from her expression that she'd forgotten, too. Four months. Only one to go. For some reason, the thought seemed to dampen the evening more than the rainstorm raging outside.

"Oh, my." Pearl's face wore a sly smile and her eyes held a mischievous twinkle. "A newlywed anniversary. We'd best clear out of here and let the newlyweds do what newlyweds do best."

Annie nearly choked on her wine.

"I hate to say it, but this storm may keep us stuck here all night," Ben remarked.

"Why's that?" Henry asked.

328

"The creek rises fast. In a hard, fast storm like this, it tends to overflow the road."

"Maybe we should try to catch a weather report on TV," Helen suggested.

Jake flicked on the television in the living room, and they all gathered around it. Sure enough, a weather advisory crawled across the bottom of the screen, announcing that a flash flood warning was in effect for a three-county area. The rain was expected to last for several more hours.

Ben strode toward the kitchen. "I'll drive down and check the creek. Everyone just stay put."

He was back in twenty minutes, his cowboy hat dripping. He pulled it off in the garage before he stepped into the kitchen, where Annie and Jake and Helen were cleaning up the dishes. "The road's covered. I'm afraid no one's going anywhere tonight."

Spike and Lauren just shrugged their shoulders.

"I hate to make you put us all up, Annie," Helen fretted.

"It's no trouble. I've got Gran's stash of extra toothbrushes, and you know I have three guest rooms."

"How are we going to divvy them up?" Pearl asked.

"Well, Ben and Helen will take one," Annie began.

"And Henry and I can shack up together," Pearl said spryly. "Boy, won't that give 'em something to talk about back at Shady Acres!"

Henry's expression was clearly alarmed.

"How about if Henry and Spike share a room," Annie quickly suggested.

"Well, okay," Pearl agreed. "Then Lauren and I can bunk together. I'm dying to see all her tattoos and body piercing. I've been thinking about getting some myself."

Jake couldn't suppress a laugh.

"Where do you want Spike and me?" Henry asked.

"You two would probably be most comfortable in the room at the end of the hall," Jake said. "It has two beds."

It was the room where Jake always slept. Annie glanced at him, her eyes wide.

The electric lights flickered, then went out. The room was dark except for the candles on the dining room table.

Pearl looked around a confused expression on her face. "Is it last call already?"

"No," Jake explained. "The power just went off."

Pearl gazed at Jake blankly. "Who are you again?"

"I'm Jake."

"And where will you sleep?" she asked.

"With Annie, of course," Helen said. "They're married, remember?"

Pearl smacked her forehead with her palm. "Oh, that's right. They're going to make nookie."

"Pearl!" Henry admonished.

She put her hand over her mouth and stifled a girlish giggle. "Sorry." She cut her eyes at Jake. "Sometimes I say things I shouldn't. It's my age, you know." She leaned conspiratorially toward Spike. "It's the best part about getting old."

Annie felt like she was having a senior moment herself when she stepped inside her bedroom an hour later, a candle in her hand, to find Jake, barefooted and shirtless, resting against the headboard of her bed. The sight of his bare chest made her knees go weak and her heart flutter like a firefly's light.

"Is everyone settled in for the night?" he asked.

"I think so." Annie had doled out towels, toothbrushes and flashlights. The candle in her hand flickered as she closed the door.

Jake's mouth curved in a smile. "I've got to hand it

to you, Annie. When you throw a celebration, you sure make it interesting."

"I'm afraid I can't take credit for the special effects."

Jake grinned, but then a long pause stretched between them. The candlelight and the sound of rain on the roof made the room seem as secluded as a cabin in the woods.

"It was a nice party."

Annie placed the candle on the dresser. "It's important to celebrate the big moments in our lives. Deciding to quit a job so you can pursue your dreams is a big moment."

Jake gave a mirthless smile. "It would be an even bigger moment if I had a clearer idea what those dreams might be." He shook his head and exhaled a breath, leaning back on the pillows. "Annie, do you think a person forfeits the right to his dreams if he's ruined someone else's?"

Annie looked at him quizzically. "Whose dreams do you think you've ruined?"

"Tom's. Susanna's. Rachel's. My parents'."

Annie's heart turned over. "Why do you say that?"

"Because of the accident. I've never told you this, but I was supposed to be driving." Even in the candlelight, she could see lines of pain radiating out from his eyes. The bed creaked as Annie turned toward him. She didn't say a word, just sat, waiting for him to continue.

After a long moment, he did.

"My parents were returning from a European medical conference and I had told them I'd pick them up at the airport. I got tied up in a meeting. It was Rachel's day off, so I called her and asked her to do it for me." A gust of wind blew the rain hard against the window. Jake stared up at the covered-wagon canopy. "*I* was supposed to be in that car, not Rachel. Rachel should still be here,

331

not me. Tom and Susanna should still have a daughter."

Annie put her hand on his arm. "Oh, Jake—I'm sure they've never thought of it that way."

"They've never said it, but how could they not think it? I think of it every day."

"And now you're feeling guilty about leaving Tom's firm." So much was falling into place now, so much was making sense. Her fingers stroked his forearm. "Jake, the wreck was an accident. You can't blame yourself."

"Sure I can. I do every day." His voice held the old bitter edge, the edge it had held when she first met him.

Annie's hand slid down his arm. "You're feeling survivor's guilt. I know a little about that." She reached for his hand. Her fingers intertwined with his. "I was at college when my father had his heart attack. I used to feel guilty that I wasn't at home when it happened. I knew how to do CPR. If I'd been there, maybe I could have saved him."

"That's different, Annie. You were where you were supposed to be."

"And you were, too." Her eyes burned as brightly as the candle on the dresser behind her. "Almost everyone who loses a loved one suddenly feels guilty. You wonder, 'Why should I be alive when this person I love is dead? What could I have done to prevent it?' It's normal to think that. But the answer is always the same: Nothing."

Jake sat very still for a long moment, letting her words curl around his heart, letting them creep like smoke into the hollow crevices and empty spaces. He didn't know why, but they soothed him like a balm.

"You want things to make sense," she said softly. "Well, some things just *don't*. Not from our perspective, anyway, because we can't see the big picture." She tucked a leg underneath her and angled more fully towards him. "See, the way I figure it, life is God's tapestry, and each person is a thread. When we look around, we can't see a pattern. We just see a bunch of other threads, all going every which way. We have to trust that a wiser hand is guiding the weaving, and that later on we'll understand why our thread went where it did."

Jake shook his head. "I don't know that I believe in God."

"That's okay." Annie squeezed his hand. "He believes in you."

Jake smiled; it was impossible to be around her for any length of time and not end up doing so.

"I believe in you, too," she whispered. Her eyes were soft, as soft and bright as the candlelight. "I believe you're a good man. And I believe that if you'd known that accident was going to happen, you'd have given your life to prevent it."

It made no sense that such simple words would choke him up, but they did. His voice grew thick. "Thanks."

"No thanks needed. I didn't do anything."

"You made me feel better."

Annie lifted her shoulders. "You just needed to talk. Talking helps."

"*You* help." He reached out a finger and gently traced the line of her jaw. His chest felt strangely tender, like a sore muscle that hadn't been used in a long time. His finger trailed up to the curve of her cheekbone.

Her eyes were warm and soft, her lips full and slightly parted. The memory of how her lips tasted pulled him toward her. She leaned forward, until she was so close he could feel her breath on his face. Their lips were just inches apart, their eyes crooning a love song.

Jake wanted to kiss her so bad it hurt. But most of all, he didn't want to hurt her. "Annie—honey, I don't want to take advantage of this situation." His voice came out low and husky. "It's your call. If you want me to sleep on the floor, I will, and I'll leave you completely alone. But if you want . . ."

He heard her breath hitch in her throat.

He swallowed and tried again. "I'll do whatever you want, but you have to tell me. Where do you want me?"

Her eyes glimmered in the candlelight, two hot blue flames. "Right here," she whispered. "Right now."

The fervent way she said it set him afire. He drew her into his arms and down on the bed. The kiss started out slow and sweet, but soon they were plundering each other's mouths, frantically tugging down zippers and unfastening buttons, pulling off each other's clothes as if they were peeling bananas. He stripped her down to a dusky-pink bra and matching bikini panties. She stripped him down to nothing.

He grinned at her. "You appear to be overdressed for this occasion."

"Well, then, why don't you do something about it?"

He unhooked her bra. Her breasts were full and pink-tipped, and they hardened into tight buds as he ran his thumb across the nipples.

He bent and pulled a sweet tip into his mouth. He teased first one, then the other breast, until Annie's breath came in hard little pants and her head tossed on the pillow from side to side. All the while, he slowly slid his hand up her calf along the silky, sensitive flesh of her thigh.

Her hand splayed across his chest, then moved down his belly. When she closed her hand around him, he thought he'd died and gone to heaven.

"Annie, sweetheart . . ."

She gasped as he worked his way up to her panties, then slid a finger inside. She was slick and hot and ready—so very, very ready. He tugged her panties down and off, revealing soft titian curls.

"You are so beautiful," he said. He lay beside her, his fingers skimming over her flesh, not quite touching, making her strain toward his hand. "I've thought about this, about how you look naked, about how you feel, until I thought I'd go crazy."

"Me, too," she murmured. "I've been burning up, remembering how . . ." She gasped as his finger gently stroked the wet, sensitive center of her womanhood.

"When do you think those thoughts?" he murmured.

"All the time. But mostly here, alone, at night."

"Oh, yeah?" His hand moved back up her body. "When you think those thoughts, do you ever do anything about them?"

"Sometimes."

"Show me." He took her hands and guided them down. His hands hovered lightly over hers. Slowly, hesitantly, she touched herself.

It was the most erotic sight Jake had ever seen. He touched her then as she'd shown him, circling her swollen nub. "Like this?"

"Yes. Oh, yes." She drew her legs further apart, giving him greater access. She reached for his other hand, directing his finger to her most secret spot. "And here. I touch here, and I think about you. And I want . . . Oh, Jake . . ."

He stroked her as she'd done, and her arousal fed his own, until he was feverish and aching. She looked up, her eyes glazed and heavy-lidded. "Jake . . . Jake, please. *Please* . . ."

She reached for him, pulling him to her, lifting her hips, straining closer. He hovered over her, watching her face, the need to please her greater even than the need for his own pleasure.

"Come here." She grabbed his buttocks and urged him toward her, into a hot, tight heaven where the pleasure was too keen for words, where sighs and moans were the only language needed. She moved under him, matching him stroke for stroke, a perfect fit in perfect rhythm.

It was as if they'd been born to be lovers. They shifted positions fluidly, finding each other's sweet spots, intuitively knowing just how to touch, where to stroke, what to kiss, and when.

He felt her muscles tense, heard her breathing quicken. When rhythmic spasms rocked her and she cried out his name, he followed right behind, diving headfirst off the ledge, into the sublime depths.

Long moments later, when his senses floated back to earth, he was aware of the rain pattering against the window. It seemed as if the drops formed a soft refrain, a chorus that echoed in his heart as he lay holding Annie. *Home. This is home.*

Annie awoke the next morning to find herself cradled against Jake, spoon-fashion. His arm was wound around her, his hand curved under a breast. One of his legs was wedged between hers, and his breath was warm atop her head.

She closed her eyes against the daylight shining through the window, not so much wanting to shut out the day as to cling to the night. It had been the sweetest, most splendid night of her life. She wanted to clutch it tightly, to squeeze it to her heart, to press it into her memory like the wedding flowers pressed in Gran's Bible.

She loved Jake. She'd known it for some time, but she hadn't wanted to admit, even to herself, just how deeply her heart was involved. She loved who he was and what he was, what'd he'd been and who he was becoming. She loved him with a depth and intensity that was sure and true and timeless.

She loved him in the same way he still loved Rachel.

The thought stabbed her heart. She squeezed her eyes, trying to hold back the tears, but two eked out anyway. She turned her face into the pillow to hide them.

The movement woke Jake. His leg stirred between her thighs. "Good morning," he breathed in her ear.

" 'Morning." She rapidly wiped her cheek with her fist, still keeping her back toward him.

His hand opened, then closed around her breast. Arousal shot through her. She pulled away. "I—I'd better get up and get dressed. We have a houseful of guests."

"Let them fend for themselves." His thumb flicked across her nipple, then his hand moved lower—to the place where her breast met her rib, then down to the curve of her belly.

Annie struggled against the whirlpool of heat he was inciting inside her. "Madeline will be awake soon, and she's not old enough to be fend-worthy. And then there's Hot Dog Junior—I'm sure she needs to be let out—and . . ."

"All right," Jake said with a reluctant sigh, releasing his hold. She sat up, trying to cover herself with the sheet, keenly aware of his eyes on her. Jake pulled himself to a sitting position, too, and leaned against a pillow on the headboard. "But before we leave this room, there's something I want to say."

Annie's heart lurched to a standstill, then beat a wild, hopeful double-time. Maybe, just maybe, he was going to say he loved her. *Please, please, please, oh please,* she prayed.

He lightly trailed his finger across her shoulder. "Last night was incredible."

All Annie could do was dumbly nod.

"And I've been thinking. You and I . . . well, we have more going for us than a lot of couples. We get along pretty well, we make each other laugh, and we're great in bed together."

Annie's mouth went dry. *Please, please, please.*

"So there's really no reason get a divorce. Why don't we just continue on the way we're doing?"

Annie waited, but the longed-for words didn't come. Hope swirled out of her like water down an unplugged drain. "It's not a marriage without love," she finally said.

He reached out and took her hand. "We both love Madeline."

"That's not enough." Annie struggled to keep her voice from cracking. "My parents both loved me, but that didn't hold their marriage together. And their unhappiness made me miserable."

"We're sensible people. If it ever gets to the point we can't get along, well, that's when we'll divorce."

He made it sound so logical, so orderly. But her feelings for him weren't orderly at all; they were strong and deep and emotional. "Marriage doesn't work that way." Her voice wobbled slightly, but she forced herself to continue. "Marriage is about love and commitment. If you don't have that, then everything else will eventually fall apart."

"I don't see why we can't just give it a try."

"Because . . ." *Because I've been in a one-sided marriage, and I know how bad it hurts. Because I love you, and you're still in love with your late wife.*

She pulled the sheet free from the foot of the bed and gathered it around her, gathering up her courage as well. "I'm not willing to settle for that. I want a no-holds-barred, not-holding-anything-back, in-it-with-everything-I've-got kind of love. That's what I have to give, and that's what I want in return. I want a man who'll love me with his whole heart and pledge to be with me his whole life. I don't want to be second best or second rate or anybody's second choice."

Jake stared down at the covers. She saw his Adam's apple move. She hurried on before she lost her nerve.

"Besides, it'll be easier for Madeline to grow up with us already divorced, than for her to get used to us being together and have us split up later. She won't miss what she's never had."

Jake heaved a heavy sigh.

Annie's eyes filled with tears. She blinked them back, determined to see this through, for Madeline's sake and for her own. The longer this went on, the longer she let herself love him, knowing he didn't love her back, the harder it would be when it ended. "I think we should stick with our original plan. We said we'd stay married for five months. Well, that will be up soon. We ought to end this then."

Silence stretched between them. Out the window, a blue jay cawed and a cricket chirped. "Are you sure that's what you want?" Jake asked.

No, her heart shouted. *What I want is for you to love me.* "Yes," she whispered softly.

He sighed again. "Okay. I'll draw up the papers. Joint custody, with you as the custodial parent."

They sat there in silence for another long moment. Annie fought the urge to cry.

"What will we do about the holidays?" Jake asked.

"You can come here. You're welcome any time you want. A big advantage of divorcing now is that we can keep it friendly."

"How friendly?" He gave a slow, sexy smile, his finger tracing a sizzling path up her arm. "Is there any chance we could still—"

339

Annie put her hand on his, stopping its treacherous path toward her breast. "You told me that when things get physical, they get emotional, and when they get emotional, they get messy. That's exactly what we're trying to avoid, isn't it?"

"I suppose." He looked at her, his eyes full of longing and regret. "Damn."

Annie gave a sad smile. "My sentiments exactly."

Wrapping the sheet around herself like a toga, she rose from the bed. "I'd better get dressed. Madeline will be up any minute."

She strode to the master bathroom, her back toward him. She managed to close the door before her tears began to escape. Dropping the sheet, she stepped into the shower and turned it on, muffling her sobs with the stinging spray.

Chapter Twenty

Susanna's high heels clicked on the polished floor of the Tulsa airport concourse as she hurried toward the gate. She was running late. She'd thought she'd timed things perfectly, but she hadn't counted on it being so hard to find a place to park.

Oh, dear—she hoped they hadn't boarded the plane yet. The airline they were flying didn't have assigned seating or a first-class section, so she hadn't been able to request a seat by her husband. She'd practiced how she might handle things, but she didn't have a clue what she'd do if Tom and Kelly were already seated together on the plane.

Her palms grew damp and her stomach bucked queasily. She was tempted to just turn and run, to abandon this whole scheme and flee back to the safety of her home.

But it was her very home she was struggling to save, she reminded herself. Her life with Tom. Her marriage.

And this was war. Only a yellow-bellied coward ran from a confrontation on the field of battle. Annie had said she'd have to fight to keep what she loved, and by golly, Susanna was ready to fight with all she had.

She'd made the decision three days ago, when she'd met Jake for lunch at a trendy suburban bistro. She'd flat out asked him the question that had been gnawing at her heart.

"Tell me the truth, Jake. I need to know. Are Tom and Kelly having an affair?"

Jake had looked miserably ill at ease. Blowing out a hard sigh, he'd looked away, but when he'd looked back, his gaze had been straightforward. "I don't think so. At least, not yet. But she seems to have made Tom her mission." His gaze had met hers, his eyes somber. "She's going to the convention in New Orleans, and I don't think she's attending to sharpen her litigation skills."

Susanna could no longer ignore it, could no longer afford to sit by and hope the situation would resolve itself. Her home was under attack, and she had to strike back.

Jostling through the foot traffic of a disembarking plane, she craned her neck around the crowd and finally spied her gate, only to have her spirits plummet. Darn—the waiting area was nearly empty. Tom and Kelly must already be on the plane.

Her heart pounded like an unbalanced washing machine. She'd just have to brazen it out. She was going to have to fight her way through a lot over the next few days, and she might as well get started. She'd decided to lead with her strengths—her ladylike charm, her polite southern upbringing, but most of all, her mother's advice on how to handle adversaries. "Kill them with kindness," she used to say. "Remember, Susanna, you'll

342

trap more flies with honey than vinegar." Well, she intended to trap a fly, all right—the one right on the front of her husband's trousers.

By the time Susanna got her boarding pass, the last of the passengers had trudged down the gateway. She squared her shoulders and resolutely did the same.

She'd no sooner entered the jet's cabin than she saw them, seated in the third row. Tom sat on the aisle, his head cocked at an attentive angle, and Kelly sat beside him, touching his arm as she talked.

Tom seemed to feel her gaze. He looked up, and for a fraction of a second, the expression on his face told it all. It was a look of pure guilt—the transparent shame of a child caught red-handed with the lid off a cookie jar. The look in Tom's eye zinged an arrow straight through her heart.

She'd already known, of course; but now she *knew*.

Her husband quickly regained his composure. His jaw tightened and his chin tilted up. Susanna had lived with him long enough to know what that meant. When Tom was cornered, he lashed out. She couldn't give him a chance to launch an attack.

She forced her brightest Southern belle smile. "Surprise!"

Tom's eyes were wary, his expression displeased. "Susanna—what arc you doing here?"

She kept smiling. "Well, honey, we've both been so busy lately that we've been like ships passing in the night. I know you were worried that I'd be bored at the conference, but I decided to surprise you and come along anyway. I know you'll be busy, but at least we'll have the flight and our nights together."

She glanced over at Kelly, as if she were just noticing her. She forced her mouth to continue smiling, even though she felt as if her face would crack from the effort.

"Why, Kelly—how nice to see you! Are you going to the conference, too?"

The blonde's eyes were full of venom; she didn't bother to reply.

"The best way to treat a slight is to pretend it didn't happen," Susanna's mother used to tell her. She used the advice now. "Well, how delightful. I'm sure we'll see a lot of you there."

A slender flight attendant materialized in the aisle behind Susanna. "Excuse me, ma'am, but you need to take a seat."

"Why, certainly." Susanna determinedly kept smiling. "Kelly, dear, would you mind moving over so I can sit by my husband?"

Kelly shot Tom a glance so sharp it could have shaved his whiskers without a nick. All the same, she sullenly complied.

Tom rose, too, apparently intending to move over and sit between the two women. Susanna had no intention of allowing that. She rapidly handed him her black carry-on bag. "Honey, would you please put this in the overhead bin for me?"

When he stepped out into the aisle, Susanna scooted into the center seat. She took far longer than necessary fastening her seatbelt so that she didn't have to converse with Kelly.

A final pair of late-boarding passengers came through the door. To Susanna's relief, she recognized them as a prominent local attorney and his wife.

"Bob—and Barbara!"

The woman, a trim, middle-aged blonde, smiled brightly. "Susanna—it's wonderful to see you! It's been so long."

"Yes. Too long." Susanna smiled up. "I think the last

time we got together was at our holiday party three years ago."

"I believe it was. That was a wonderful affair."

"Tom and I will be holding another one this year. I hope you two can come."

"Oh, we wouldn't miss it! Your party was the highlight of the season!"

Bob clapped Tom on the shoulder as they edged past. "Glad you convinced your better half to join us in New Orleans. Barbara was disappointed when I told her Susanna didn't plan to come."

So Tom had been telling people she wouldn't be coming. The news sent another arrow into Susanna's heart.

"I surprised him at the last moment," she volunteered.

"I'm sure you made him a very happy man." Bob winked at her husband. "We'll all have to go out to dinner together while we're in New Orleans. It'll be like old times."

"Oh, that sounds marvelous," Susanna said gaily. She placed her hand on top of Tom's, knowing he wouldn't pull away in front of a friend. He would do anything to avoid a scene. "Doesn't it, dear?"

He cleared his throat and stiffly nodded. "Sure."

The flight attendant came on the intercom and began the liturgy of preflight instructions. Susanna leaned back and sighed. She'd won the first round. But she didn't kid herself. The Battle of New Orleans was still ahead.

"What is *she* doing here?" Kelly demanded two hours later, as she and Tom waited in line at the boarding gate of their connecting flight at Houston Hobby Airport.

Tom glanced over at Susanna, who was holding an animated conversation several yards away with the wives of two other Tulsa attorneys also bound for the convention. He lifted his shoulders. "She just showed up. I was as surprised as you."

"Well, can't you send her home?"

"Now, Kelly, you know I can't very well do that. I'm not going to cause a scene in front of my colleagues."

The woman's eyes narrowed with displeasure. "What am *I* supposed to do?"

Act like an adult, Tom thought irritably. "We agreed we'd be discreet. Since so many people we know are on the flight, we'd have needed to sit separately on this leg of the trip anyway."

"I'm not talking about that. I mean once we get to New Orleans. Where am I supposed to *stay?*"

"Well, obviously not with me."

"Great. Just great." Her mouth twisted into a pout. "I don't have a reservation and the convention hotel is sold out."

"I'm sorry, Kelly. I told you I wasn't comfortable with this arrangement from the beginning. It was all your idea."

"You didn't exactly tell me no."

That was true. He'd handled things badly. It wasn't fair to lay all the responsibility on Kelly. "I'm sorry. I really am. But the fact is I'm a married man."

"Maybe not for long."

Something in her voice sounded an alarm in Tom's mind. He'd talked to Kelly about the problems in his marriage; he'd even talked to her about leaving Susanna. But her remark didn't sound like a reflection on those conversations.

It had the sly, ominous hiss of a threat.

He smiled down at her in what he hoped was a placating manner. "I'm sure the conference registration staff will be able to help you find a place to stay."

Kelly sniffed haughtily. "I have no intention of staying at an off-site hotel. I've got a more effective way of handling things."

There was a cold, viperous tone to her voice that made him pause. "What way is that?"

She flipped her hair over her shoulder. "I'll make a scene. I'll insist that I have a reservation and that they've made an error. If I get bitchy enough, I always get my way."

Another burst of alarm shot through Tom. Oh, Christ—she wasn't above raising a public stink. Kelly no longer looked like a harmless sex kitten. She suddenly looked like a full-grown mountain lion, and he felt uncomfortably like her prey.

She lifted her head imperiously. "I expect you to have dinner with me tonight."

"Kelly, that's impossible."

Her eyes flashed. "If you think I came all the way down here just to sit on the sidelines and watch you waltz around with your wife, you're sorely mistaken."

A chill ran through Tom. This boded ill. Very ill. A whole different side of Kelly was emerging, and it wasn't a pretty sight.

He gave her a tight smile. "We'll talk about it later. Why don't we meet in the hotel gift shop around six?"

"Why not the bar?"

"It's too obvious."

Her forehead puckered in an ugly frown. "I don't like this. I don't like it a bit."

"I don't like it, either." What he really didn't like was the dark, dangerous vibes she was sending out, like a squid shooting ink. He was glad when the line moved forward and it was his turn at the desk. He couldn't wait to get away from her.

*　　*　　*

"What a lovely room!" Susanna crossed to the window of the luxurious hotel room and looked out at the Mississippi River. "And what a beautiful view!"

She presented quite a view herself. The sun shone through the fabric of her casual linen dress, revealing her long, slim legs and shapely bottom. Tom looked away, trying to tamp down the rush of attraction, and watched the bellboy hang their bags in the closet. Peeling several dollar bills off his money clip, he tipped the hotel employee and waited until the hotel room door closed behind him.

"We're alone now, Susanna," he said. "You can quit acting like Suzy Sunshine and tell me what's going on."

Susanna turned and gave him a soft smile. "Suzy Sunshine—that was what you called me when we first married. Remember?"

He did. Unfortunately, he remembered why he'd called her that, too—being around her made him feel warm and relaxed and happy, like a day at the beach. The name stirred fond, tender memories—memories that made him decidedly uneasy, because they made him feel like such a jerk now.

He stared out at the river, watching a freighter navigate the bend. "So what prompted your sudden interest in traveling?"

"I told you. I want to spend some time with you." She turned toward him and stepped close, near enough that he could smell her White Shoulders perfume. Memories, as warm and provocative as the scent, floated through his mind. "I've missed you, Tom. I've missed *us.*"

"I haven't gone anywhere."

"Oh, yeah?" She gave a slow, sexy smile. "Let me see." Before he knew it, she'd put her arms around his neck and pulled him into a kiss.

She tasted sweet and warm, like freshly baked cake—

angel food and devil's food, with passion fruit icing. His body immediately responded.

She reflexively snugged her body against his arousal. "I've missed *this*."

Good Lord—he'd missed it, too. But she was the one who'd created the distance. Just when he'd needed her most, when his heart was breaking, when he needed to give comfort as much he'd needed to receive it, she'd pulled away and isolated herself from him.

Just like his mother had done after his father's death.

The thought made Tom draw back. But Susanna refused to release her hold on him. "Remember the first time we kissed?" she murmured, running her hands through his hair.

As if he could ever forget. He'd never forget any of his firsts with Susanna—the first time he'd laid eyes on her, the first time he'd heard her soft voice, the first time he'd gotten close enough to smell her perfume. She'd looked like a brunette Grace Kelly, sitting in the next aisle of his junior-year statistics class in college. It had taken him a month to get up the nerve to ask her out, and five dates before he'd tried to kiss her. When he had, she'd kissed him back with such passion that it had turned his world upside down. He'd rapidly gone from bewitched to besotted. Within four months, he'd asked her to marry him.

He'd been amazed that she'd said yes. She was the pampered daughter of a wealthy Mobile industrialist, and he was a poor boy from West Texas—poor because his father had died when he was a youth and his mother had chosen to escape loneliness through self-medication.

Susanna had represented all that he admired, all that he aspired to, all that he wanted in life. Respectability. Class. Refinement.

He'd wanted a woman who was the exact opposite of

his mother, and he'd found it in Susanna. She would never publicly humiliate him. He would never have to bail her out of jail or carry her home when she passed out or apologize for her behavior. He'd wanted a woman who would be an asset to him, and Susanna had more than exceeded his wildest dreams. Her social grace, personal warmth, and political acumen had helped him build the strong network of friends and associates that was the cornerstone of his success.

But then Rachel had died, and Susanna had done the one thing that, he now realized, he resented his mother for most of all: she'd emotionally abandoned him just when he'd needed her most.

Susanna nuzzled close now, nipping at his bottom lip with her mouth. He felt the imprint of her breasts against his chest, the press of her pelvis against his. "I want you," she murmured. "I want to make love with you."

He wanted her, too—wanted desperately to fall into bed with her, to pretend, for a just few moments, that the last two years had never happened. But he was torn—torn between the need to get close and the need to keep his distance. Torn by guilt. Torn by a jumble of crazy, topsy-turvy emotions bubbling inside of him like a shaken-up can of soda.

He'd planned to come to New Orleans and cheat on her. How could he just turn around and make love to her now? In some ways, that almost seemed worse— more two-faced, certainly—than actually being unfaithful.

Hell. His thinking didn't make any sense anymore, not even in his own head. Maybe he was losing his mind.

He pulled away and glanced down at his watch. "I, uh, need to go downstairs and see someone."

It was time to meet Kelly. He didn't dare stand her

up. He had find a way to appease her so that she didn't create some kind of scene.

Susanna released him with a reluctant sigh. "All right. How long do you think you'll be?"

"I'm not sure."

"Well, I've made plans for us to dine with the Bennetts tonight. We're going to Commander's Palace."

Tom froze. It would look very odd if he didn't accompany his wife to dinner—especially tonight, when the conference had yet to officially get underway. Especially with the Bennetts. Bob was this year's conference chairman. If the man was free to have dinner with his wife, then Tom most certainly should be there with his own.

"You shouldn't have made plans without talking to me," he said curtly.

Susanna smiled apologetically. "I thought you had more than enough on your mind. If you can't make it, well, I'll just go out with them alone."

Tom sighed. He really didn't have a choice. "What time are the reservations?"

"Seven-thirty. We're leaving the hotel at seven-fifteen."

"I'll meet you back here at seven."

Two mornings later, Susanna checked her wristwatch as she sat in the elegant hotel restaurant. She was supposed to meet seven other wives for breakfast to kick off a day of sight-seeing and shopping, but she was thirty minutes early. Tom had had to get up for a seven-thirty breakfast meeting, and she'd been unable to go back to sleep.

No, that wasn't quite right, she thought dryly, taking a sip of fragrant chicory laced coffee. "Back to sleep" implied that she'd actually slept. For most of the last two nights, she'd lain awake, painfully aware of Tom tossing fitfully beside her. Last night he'd rolled onto his side, his back toward her, and pretended to be asleep as soon as they'd climbed into the king-sized bed together, but she'd known better.

She hadn't made it easy on him. Two could play at this game, she'd decided. Pretending to be asleep herself, she'd curled up against his back and wrapped her arm around him, letting her hand drape strategically across his groin. His body had instantly responded. She'd lain perfectly still, deliberately keeping her breathing deep and regular. After a few torturous minutes, Tom had rolled onto his stomach—a position that couldn't have been comfortable, considering that he was stiff as a kickstand.

Later, when he actually *was* asleep, he'd rolled over and curled up next to her, cradling her against his chest. It had felt so sweet that she'd laid there and wept into her pillow. He'd held her for most of the night, and when the alarm sounded at seven, she'd still been in his arms. She'd pretended to be asleep, and had been gratified to feel him run his hands over her breasts just before he'd arisen.

Susanna took another sip of coffee, but the warmth that spread through her had nothing to do with the hot beverage. Her plan was working. Quietly and noncombatively, she was reasserting herself into Tom's life, reminding him that they shared a common history not only with each other, but with everyone they knew. He couldn't lose her without losing other parts of his life.

Susanna's train of thought was interrupted by the abrupt appearance of Kelly at her table, wearing a short, tight blue suit. Adrenaline flooded her veins, but Susanna forced a calm smile. "Why, good morning, Kelly. Are you enjoying the conference?"

The blonde ignored the question and fixed her with a

hostile glare. "Tom doesn't love you, you know."

Susanna felt as if she'd just taken a sucker punch. She struggled for a reply, but she needn't have bothered, because Kelly wasn't through spewing venom. "He's just staying with you out of pity. He plans to leave you, but he hasn't found a way to tell you yet. It's me that he wants."

Susanna drew a deep calming breath, carefully keeping her features even, grateful for the rigid training in comportment that had been a major part of her upbringing. "How very interesting." She slowly took a sip of coffee, gripping the handle tightly to keep her hand from shaking. "He certainly wasn't acting like a man who wanted you last night. Or this morning, either, for that matter." She carefully put her cup back in the china saucer.

Kelly's eyes narrowed to hateful slits. "I don't believe you."

Susanna raised an amused eyebrow. "Suit yourself, dear."

"I happen to know he hasn't slept with you in over a year."

The words cut right through Susanna's heart. How could Tom confide such an intimate detail to this woman? Pain tore through her, sharp and acute. But then, that was exactly what Kelly wanted to do—to inflict pain. Susanna wouldn't give her the satisfaction of knowing she'd succeeded.

She lifted the corners of her mouth in a dry, worldly smile. "Is that what he told you?"

"Yes."

Susanna shook her head, her eyes pitying. "And you believed him?"

The look on Kelly's face was priceless. Susanna leaned forward and placed her hand over the younger woman's. "Take some advice from a woman who's older and wiser, dear. You can't believe everything a man in the midst of a midlife crisis tells you. Especially about his relationship with his wife."

"He doesn't love you," Kelly repeated coldly.

Susanna lifted her cup again. "Believe what you want, dear. But if I were you, I'd take whatever he says with a grain of salt." She lifted her wrist and waved to her friends, who'd appeared at the door of the restaurant. They headed toward her.

Her glance drifted back to Kelly. "Excuse me, but I have to go." Susanna scooted back her chair and smiled at the younger woman. "And dear, you really should try to get more sleep. You look like a princess who's had too many peas in her mattress."

Kelly's face turned an unflattering shade of fuschia. With a muttered word that was most unladylike, she turned and stormed from the table.

Susanna felt limp and shaken. She longed to flee to her room, to pull the covers over her head and have a good, long cry, but she refused to surrender to the urge.

She refused to surrender to anything. This was war. She'd just had her first direct encounter with the enemy, and she'd walked away victorious.

Tom finished gathering up his papers as the last of the seminar participants filed from the room, then turned around to find his friend Bob Bennett at his side.

The man smiled and shook his hand. "Nice presentation."

"Thanks. Are you going to the luncheon?"

"Yeah. I'll walk that way with you." Bob walked beside him to the door and out into the foyer.

"Susanna said she and Barbara were going on a tour

of the Garden District today with some of the other wives."

Bob nodded. "So I heard. Evidently a group of the gals hit the antique stores on Royal Street yesterday. Barbara bought some Gawd-awful lamp, but from what I hear, Susanna didn't do much damage."

Tom smiled. "I'm surprised. She loves antiques."

Bob glanced at him as they rounded a bend in the foyer. "You know, I was really glad to see you bring Susanna with you on this trip."

"I'm glad she decided to come." And he was; he actually was, he realized with surprise. He'd forgotten what an asset she was to him at events like this, how her charm and warmth made people seek them out, how having her with him made him feel at the center of things.

Bob nodded. "I'd heard some rumors that the Blonde Barracuda had you in her sights. I'm glad to see you're not taking the bait."

Tom nearly stumbled over his own feet. "Blonde Barracuda?"

"You know. Kelly Banyon."

"Ah." Tom's heart pounding guiltily. "We've, uh, worked on a couple of cases together."

Bob nodded. "I figured that was all there was to it. I knew you were too smart to fall for the likes of her." He shook his head. "She's one sick puppy."

"What do you mean?"

"You haven't heard about her?"

"No."

"Oh, sheeze." Bob rolled his eyes. "She's got a trail of wrecked marriages behind her that make Hurricane Georges look like a cakewalk."

"Is that a fact?"

"Oh, yeah. Seems she's got a reverse Oedipus complex or daddy fetish or some such thing going. You know Charlie Young?"

Charlie was an Oklahoma attorney who specialized in civil litigation. "Not well. I know who he is."

"Well, Charlie's one of her casualties. He told me she's a case straight out of a psycho thriller. She's got a thing for getting older men to swear their undying love and dump their wives. Once they do, she leaves them in the dust and heads on to her next victim. Seems her father ignored her as a kid and she was jealous of her mother or some such, and this is her way of getting even." Bob shook his head. "She's a real head case."

Jake had vaguely mentioned that Kelly had some kind of reputation, but Tom had refused to listen. Tom's upper lip broke a sweat. "So . . . there were rumors about me and Kelly?"

Bob lifted his shoulders. "Oh, a few. I never paid them much attention. You know how people talk. Someone saw you out with her a couple of times, that's all."

"We discussed the case over lunch a few times."

"Well, that's all it takes to get tongues wagging. I knew there was nothing to it. I mean, with a gorgeous woman like Susanna at home, why would you bother to look twice at anyone else?"

Because I'm a fool, Tom thought ruefully. *A blind, stupid, self-pitying fool. Hell—I must have taken temporary leave of my senses.*

It all washed over him, the magnitude of what Susanna meant to him, of what he'd nearly thrown away. Jesus Christ, he was an idiot. A woman like his wife was worth a thousand Kellys. A hundred thousand. Hell, a hundred million.

She was one of a kind, a real treasure. She was the best thing that had ever happened to him—the very foundation of his life. Sure, they'd had some rough times—probably the roughest a couple go through. They'd lost a child, their only child, the child they'd created out of their love, the child they'd loved as much as they loved each other.

They'd handled their grief in different ways, and those differences had pushed them apart. It had backed them into cold, painful, lonely corners, into cold, painful, lonely beds.

They'd grown apart. Well, hell—at least that meant they were still capable of growing. If they could still grow, then maybe they could grow back together.

More than anything, that was what Tom wanted.

"Oh, there's Peter Carpenter," Bob said. "I need to speak with him about something."

"Go ahead," Tom said. "I'll see you inside." He turned toward the ballroom, only to hear a familiar voice at his elbow.

"There you are," came a slinky murmur. "I've been looking everywhere for you."

He froze, his chest cold with dread. He didn't have to turn to know who it was. "Hello, Kelly."

"You've been ignoring me, you naughty man."

Tom took a deep breath. He might as well get this over with. "Listen, Kelly—we need to talk."

"We need to do more than that. Want to go my room?"

"No. Look Kelly . . ." He stepped to the side of the ballroom, out of the flow of traffic. He needed to end this now. "Look—I've done you an injustice. I've been confused, and I'm afraid I've misled you about the nature of things between us."

She plucked an imaginary piece of lint off his lapel. Her eyes flashed an X-rated message. "I'd like to put a little more nature between us."

Tom stepped back. "Look, Kelly . . . I really don't

know how to put this. You're a very attractive woman, and I'm extremely flattered at your interest in me, but I'm . . . well, I'm just not in the market for an affair."

Her eyes iced over. "You brought me all the way to New Orleans to give me the brush-off?"

"I didn't bring you anywhere. You brought yourself."

"You haven't even given me a chance!"

"This has nothing to do with you. It has to do with my marriage. I've realized I still love my wife, and I want to make my marriage work."

"No, you don't. You just can't work up the nerve to tell her it's over." Kelly's mouth curved into a smug smile. "Well, you don't have to worry about that anymore. I've taken care of it for you."

Tom froze. "What do you mean, you've taken care of it?"

"I talked to her this morning. I told her you were planning to leave her for me."

Oh, dear God. Tom's stomach sank like a block of cement. "You're kidding."

"I'm not." Her eyes were cold as a reptile's. "But if you don't believe me, ask her."

He wanted to. Immediately. But she was off on an all-day sight-seeing expedition with the other wives. He would have to wait until this evening to talk to her. A lump as hard as a cannonball formed in his throat. "What—what did she say?"

Kelly lifted her shoulders. "Not much. She really didn't seem to care."

Oh, Lord. If Susanna didn't care, then things were in worse shape than he'd imagined. "Did she say *anything?*"

Kelly's mouth curled. "Yeah. She said you were having a mid-life crisis." The woman's fingers slowly played on his arm, doing a two-step up to his shoulder.

"So you see, now there's nothing standing between us."

Tom stepped back, beyond her reach. "Kelly, there is no 'us.' I'm married, and I intend to stay that way. I'm sorry if I've misled you."

"This is a one-time-only offer. Pass it up now, and it's rescinded forever." She toyed with the neck of her blouse, a seductive smile on her face. "You don't know what you're missing."

Oh, yes, I do, Tom thought. *What I'm missing is my wife. And I intend to make up for lost time.*

The poolside reception was in full swing late that afternoon as Tom checked his watch for the fifth time in as many minutes. "I thought our wives were supposed be back by now."

Bob stuffed a dollar bill into the tip jar at the poolside bar and took the beer the bartender handed him, squinting from the late afternoon sun. "They were. Knowing my wife, though, she probably talked the driver into stopping somewhere to shop."

Tom took a drink of his scotch and soda. His stomach was tense and knotted, and it had felt that way ever since his conversation with Kelly. It was eating at his guts, imagining what she might have told Susanna.

If she'd really spoken to her. For all he knew, Kelly was lying, trying to trick him into ruining his marriage himself.

But if she *had* spoken to Susanna . . . The very thought made him feel like he'd eaten a dozen rotten oysters. Susanna would assume that things had gone further than they had. She'd think that he and Kelly had actually done the deed instead of just danced around it.

Hell, he was an idiot—a fool, a moron, a lowlife cad. How could he have been so stupid? He couldn't wait to see Susanna, to talk to her, to make her understand, to beg her forgiveness. He didn't know what he'd say or do, but somehow, he had to make things right.

Bob poked Tom's arm with his elbow. "Hey, man—check out the Barracuda. I told you that gal was a head case." He angled the neck of his beer bottle toward the pool.

Tom looked where Bob indicated, and felt a burst of alarm shoot right through him. Kelly was sitting on a lounge chair, peeling off her shirt to reveal a skimpy red bikini top. She shot him a pointed stare.

"Oh, Christ," Tom muttered, abruptly turning his back on her.

Bob continued to gawk. "Oh, wow—now she's taking off her skirt." Tom felt Bob's elbow dig into his rib cage. "Holy mother of Batman! She's wearing a thong! A thong, can you believe it? I've only seen those things on pinup calendars. Are they even legal? Come on, Tom, you gotta get a load of this."

Tom took a long swig of his drink and refused to turn around.

Bob obviously couldn't pull his eyes away. "Now she's rubbing suntan lotion all over herself."

"Suntan lotion?" Tom said derisively. "It's five in the evening."

"Well, I guess you can't be too careful when you're exposing that much skin. Man, check out her glutes!"

"No, thanks."

"Wow, Tom, she's looking right at you. I think this show is for your benefit." Bob poked him with his elbow again and chortled. "You know what she's saying, don't you? 'This butt's for you!' "

Tom tried to smile, but he couldn't seem to find one. If there was anything he hated, it was a public spectacle. He placed his empty glass on a passing waiter's empty tray. "I'm going up to my room to wait for Susanna.

She'll probably stop there to change clothes or freshen up before coming to the reception."

Without another word, Tom strolled away, never turning back.

"Bob will kill me for the money I spent, but that figurine was just too cute to pass up," Barbara Bennett said as she and the six other wives descended the wide steps to the pool terrace.

"It *is* adorable," Susanna agreed cordially, but her mind was far removed from china trinkets. She scanned the hotel terrace, looking for her husband among the sport-coat clad men milling around the pool.

Barbara abruptly stopped as they reached the bottom of the terrace. "My goodness—would you look at that! That woman barely has a stitch of clothing on. Wouldn't you think that the hotel would close off the pool to swimmers and sunbathers when a group like ours rents out the area for a reception?"

"I'm afraid she's a member of the association," said a diminutive wife of another attorney from Tulsa. "That's Kelly Banyon."

"No!" gasped a wife from Texas. "She's an attorney?"

"I'm afraid so."

"I've heard about her," said another wife. "She's supposed to be a real little home wrecker. Wasn't she the other woman in the Youngs' divorce?"

The stocky brunette wife of an Arkansas attorney craned her neck for a better look. "I heard she collects divorces like wild Apaches collected scalps."

"What does she think she's doing, baring herself like that?" asked another wife.

"Getting every man in the place to look at her, that's what. Imagine showing up for an affair like this in a bikini!"

361

"Well, it *is* a pool party," Susanna said automatically. She immediately regretted it. Why should she stand up for Kelly? It was just her nature to come to the defense of anyone being publicly maligned, and she'd spoken without thinking.

"What kind of woman actually wears a swimsuit to a pool party?" Barbara demanded.

The other wives nodded in agreement. "One who wants to flaunt herself before a bunch of bug-eyed men," said the Texan.

"Look! She's turning over," one of the other wives announced.

"Oh, my heavens." The heavyset woman from Arkansas clutched her chest as if she were having a heart attack. "She's mooning us!"

"No. She's wearing a thong," said the Texan.

"A thong!"

"Somebody needs to put an end to this exhibition," the stout gray-haired matron announced.

"I have an idea," Barbara suggested. "We can go sit at that long table behind her. That way we'll block her from everyone else's view."

"Great idea," said the stout wife. "It'll force our husbands to see us while they try to ogle her."

"Let's go," said the Texan, leading the charge.

Susanna hung back. She didn't want to get within fifty yards of Kelly. What if she tried to resume their conversation about Tom?

"Come on, Susanna," Barbara urged.

She searched for a way to stall. "I'll go get drinks for everybody. What would you like?"

The women gave her their drink preferences, then strode toward Kelly. Susanna watched the women settle themselves behind the blonde, obscuring her from view.

A few minutes later, the thick-necked bartender slid a

tray of white wines and margaritas onto the bar toward Susanna. "Here you go, ma'am."

"Thank you." She dug in her purse for a tip. As she searched for her wallet, her fingers settled around a hard, round tin. She pulled it out.

It was the old, rusty tin of itching powder—the talisman that Annie had given her, the symbol of generations of women determined to hold their families together.

Susanna held the tin in her hand, a deliciously wicked thought forming in her mind. She turned and looked toward the pool. Kelly seemed to know that the women were trying to thwart her exhibition, because she tossed them a snide look as she rose from her chair. She slowly strode to the water's edge and gave a langorous stretch, her hands in the air, her chest and bottom provocatively thrust out. After long moments of flexing and posing, she executed a perfect dive into the water.

Susanna's fingers tightened on the box. Oh, it would serve Kelly right. It would be perfect, poetic justice, and it would be such fun to watch. Too bad she didn't know anyone who had the nerve to actually do such an outrageous thing.

Did she?

Her heart beat fast at the thought. It went against all of her breeding, all of her upbringing, all of the refined behavior she'd been taught to value. It would be unkind, unladylike, and impolite. It would be completely out of character, unlike anything she'd ever done in her entire life.

All the more reason to do it. After all, this was war. Her brow furrowing in determination, Susanna slipped the tin of powder into the pocket of her linen dress.

"Did you need anything else, ma'am?" the bartender asked.

Susanna pulled a bill from her wallet and pushed it into the tip jar, then gave the man a smile. "Could you please tell me where I might be able to find a towel? I'm sure my friend will need one when she gets out of the pool."

Susanna must have gone directly to the reception after all, Tom decided fifteen minutes later. Leaving his hotel room, he took the elevator to the terrace level and strode through the double glass doors just in time to see Susanna hurry from the ladies' changing room toward the pool.

She had a folded towel tucked under her arm, and from the determined expression on her face, she was on some kind of mission. Tom stopped behind a dense row of wide-fronded palm trees and watched her, his heart pounding uneasily in his chest. Through the leaves of the plants, he saw her bend down and speak to someone in the water.

Kelly. Tom's pulse pounded in his temple. *Susanna was bringing a towel to Kelly.* He gingerly moved behind the trees, drawing closer, straining to hear.

"Here," Susanna said. "I'm sure you'll want to cover up when you get out."

Kelly pushed her hair back from her face and sneered. "You'd like that, wouldn't you?"

Susanna placed the towel on a nearby chair. "I'll leave it here. Suit yourself."

"Don't worry," Kelly said, her lip curved in a snide curl. "I always do."

Tom's stomach tightened. From the tone of the exchange, it sounded as if the two had indeed already talked. And yet Susanna didn't appear to be shattered or upset or heartbroken. In fact, she seemed strangely calm and controlled.

364

That worried him. His wife had the composure of someone who'd decided on a course of action.

Oh, God—what if she'd decided to leave him?

Fear, cold and clammy, seized his belly. She couldn't leave! He couldn't live without her. He loved her. With all his heart and soul, he loved her. He'd loved her and only her for his entire adult life, and no one could ever take her place.

Why had it taken him so long to realize it?

He watched Susanna settle in a nearby chaise lounge, her gaze locked on Kelly. The blonde climbed out of the pool, swinging her hips as if she were Bo Derek emerging from the surf in the movie *Ten,* then picked up the towel. With a seductive smile at a group of gawking men, she suggestively ran it over her body.

Tom closed his eyes, then slowly reopened them. Kelly was behaving like a low-class stripper, not a professional at a conference with her peers. How could he ever have been attracted to someone so obvious, so blatant, so lacking in class?

Especially when he was married to a lady like Susanna. Tom looked back at his wife. She seemed strangely riveted by the actions of the blonde, who was now slinking toward the bar.

Guilt, heavy and smothering, made it hard for Tom to breathe. He couldn't just stand here, lurking behind the palms. He needed to set things right, to explain, to try to make amends. He needed to get Susanna alone and tell her that he loved her, that he was sorry, that there would never be any woman in his life but her.

Screwing up his courage, he straightened and crossed the terrace toward her. "Hi, honey," he said, bending down and kissing her cheek.

She looked up in surprise. It had been a long time

since he'd greeted her with a kiss, he realized with cha-grin.

But to his relief, Susanna smiled. "What good timing you have!"

"I do?"

"Yes. Have a seat." She patted a place on the chaise lounge beside her. "The show is about to begin."

He gingerly sat beside her, nonplussed by her cheerful greeting and the odd remark. He was on the conference entertainment committee; aside from the jazz trio that was currently taking a break, no other entertainment was scheduled for this event. "What do you mean, 'the show?'"

"Just watch. Over by the bar."

He turned to see Kelly, leaning on the counter of the bar, slowly rub her arm. The rubbing quickly escalated into scratching—first one arm, then the other, then her neck, then her stomach. A moment later, she was stand-ing on one leg, clawing at her right calf with her left big toe. And then she was flailing at herself as if she were on fire.

"Get them off me!" she shrieked.

The entire party fell so quiet, it could have been a mime convention. All heads swiveled toward her.

"What?" the beefy bartender asked.

"These bugs that are biting me!"

The bartender's forehead scrunched into pleats as he leaned forward and peered at her. "I don't see any bugs."

Kelly jumped up and down, rubbing her arms, swat-ting her neck, hitting at her legs. "I'm itching all over. They're everywhere. What are they?"

The bartender lifted his shoulders. "I don't know, lady. I don't see a thing."

"Well, don't just stand there. *Do* something!" Twitching wildly, she contorted her arms in an attempt to scratch her own back.

The bartender eyed her warily, clearly doubting her sanity. "Okay. I'll, uh, call security."

He picked up the phone and punched in a number, keeping a cautious eye on her the whole time.

Kelly was frantic now, scratching and twitching like a dozen flea-bitten hounds. Her bikini top came loose. She grabbed at it, but not before two pale, rubbery objects plopped out on the flagstone, looking like boneless chicken breasts.

"What are *those?*" Tom gasped. They looked like jellyfish, but it made no sense to him that jellyfish would be in either her swimsuit or the swimming pool.

"Breast enhancers," Susanna murmured, her gaze transfixed. "In our day, they were known as falsies."

Scratching madly, Kelly raced toward the swimming pool and jumped in. Two hotel security officers burst onto the terrace, walkie-talkies squawking, just as Kelly's bikini top floated to the surface of the water.

"What's all the commotion about?" one of the uniformed officers demanded.

A group of attorneys, speechless for what was surely the first time in their lives, pointed to the pool, where Kelly stood clutching her chest.

The taller officer drew an immediate, if inaccurate, conclusion. "Sorry, ma'am—no topless swimming allowed."

"I'm not this way on purpose, you idiot!" she snarled. "I was being eaten alive by a swarm of bugs. I'm going to sue the hell out of this hotel, and if you don't want to be named personally in the lawsuit, you'll hand me my top this instant."

The short, dumpy officer hurried to the side of the pool, leaned in and fished out her bikini top. Kelly held out her hand and reached for it, unwittingly exposing herself.

The officer gaped, open-mouthed, and nearly fell into the pool. In his effort to regain his balance, he flailed his arms, flinging her bikini top into the crowd. It landed on the forehead of an attorney with a self-important air and a goatee, where it rested like a pair of flight goggles.

Someone in the crowd giggled.

"You incompetent moron!" Kelly shouted at the security officer as he scurried to retrieve her top. Her face was purple with rage, her hair hanging in her eyes like sodden straw. "You'll pay for this. I'll sue you down one side and up the other, and by the time I'm through with you and this bug-infested hotel, why . . ."

Kelly continued to spew dire legal threats as she fastened on her top and climbed from the pool. She cursed and cussed as she stormed across the deck, and by the time her thong-exposed backside disappeared into the changing room, the air was practically blue.

The crowd stood in stunned silence for a long moment, then everyone started talking at once.

Tom glanced at Susanna. Her hand was over her mouth, and she appeared to be coughing. He leaned in, concerned. "Are you all right?"

She wasn't coughing. She was laughing! He stared at her in surprise. In all the years he'd known her, she'd never before laughed at another person's distress.

But then, she'd never before been confronted by a woman who was trying to wreck her marriage. Pain tightened around Tom's heart like a boa constrictor. Dear God—what had he almost done? He had to try to set things right.

The jazz trio shrewdly chose that moment to begin another set. The music had a calming effect on the crowd, and the hubbub quickly subsided.

Baby, Oh Baby!

Susanna's laughter subsided, too. He watched her pick an invisible piece of lint off her lap.

Tom hesitantly placed his hand on top of hers. Susanna's hand froze, but she didn't look up.

"Susanna—" His voice broke on her name. He cleared his throat. "Suze, we need to talk."

"Yes." Her voice was low, barely above a whisper, and no trace of laughter remained.

"Let's go find someplace quiet."

"All right."

He tightened his grip on her hand. She let him pull her to her feet, but still refused to meet his gaze.

The elevator bank was full. It would take forever to get to their room. Fueled by a sense of urgency, Tom led Susanna across the terrace to the hotel health club. He pushed the door open, and led her into a large, mirrored gym.

The room was empty except for a lone, sweaty man doing leg presses on a weight machine by the door. Tom led his wife to the far end of the room, where a sign on a wide, wooden door proclaimed SAUNA OUT OF ORDER, Tom opened the door and ushered her inside.

The tiny room was cool and dimly lit, and it smelled of cedar. They sat on a smooth wooden bench.

Tom turned to Susanna. "Suze . . ." His voice sounded as if he'd just gargled with gravel. He swallowed and began again. "Suze, honey, I've made a terrible mistake, and I need to tell you about it."

Susanna looked down at her hand entwined with his. "You don't need to tell me."

"Yes, I do."

"I don't think I want to hear."

"Look—I know Kelly talked to you." The knot in Tom's throat made it hard for him to speak, but he forced himself to say what had to be said. "I don't know what she told you, but she and I . . ."

Susanna put her finger on his lip, her eyes pleading. "Don't."

"I have to. It's not what you think. I mean, we never . . . it never . . ." He swallowed hard. "I never made love to her."

Susanna gazed at him, her eyes searching his, probing for the truth. He could tell when she found it. Her eyes filled with tears. "Oh, Tom. . . ."

"That's not to say things weren't headed in that direction," he admitted. "I'm not guiltless, but that line was never crossed." He lifted both of Susanna's hands—the hands that had made his meals, cradled his child, pleasured his body. His heart ached with the weight of guilt, the heaviness of a love he'd nearly betrayed. "I couldn't. There were opportunities, but, Susanna, I just couldn't."

Tears coursed down her cheeks. She raised her hand to his face, her eyes swimming with warmth.

"I love you, Susanna." His voice came out thick and low. His hand shook as he raised a finger and wiped a tear from her cheek. "I know I haven't shown it lately. I've been a jerk, and I don't even know why. I've been so . . . so *angry*. I don't even think it was you I was angry at."

She closed her eyes, then opened them again. "You were angry that I was depressed."

He nodded heavily. "I'm sorry. I know it's an illness. I don't know why I thought it was your fault."

"I felt so dead inside," she whispered. "So locked up inside myself. It was like I was paralyzed. And the longer it went on, the more paralyzed I became."

"I wasn't understanding. I wasn't patient. I wasn't sympathetic."

"You were hurting, too. You needed me, and I wasn't there," Susanna said softly.

"What hurt was the way you didn't need *me*. You pushed me away. You wouldn't let me comfort you, wouldn't let me even touch you. It was just like when I was ten years old and my father died." His voice cracked, but he made himself continue.

"My mother shut me out then, too. She would lock herself in her room and cry. I was so lost, so scared, so lonely. She was all I had left in the world. I would knock on the door, and she wouldn't answer. Everything would be quiet—completely quiet. I know now that it was because she'd passed out from tranquilizers and booze. But I didn't know that then. I used to think it was quiet because she had died, too."

Susanna looked at him then, her eyes brimming with tears. "Oh, Tom."

"After we lost Rachel . . . Well, it would have comforted *me* to comfort *you*. I needed to feel connected. I needed to be needed."

"I've always needed you," she whispered.

"I needed to know that." He ran his fingers over her palm.

Her gaze roved his face. "Our marriage got worse as I started to get better."

Tom blew out a sigh. "I know, I know! I don't understand it, so I can't really explain it. I just know I felt angry—so very, very angry. Maybe I was angry at the pills. Maybe I was upset that they could help you, but I couldn't. That you'd turn to them instead of me." He looked away as his eyes grew perilously moist. "Just like my mother did."

"Oh, Tom. . . ." Her hand touched his cheek. It was a loving touch, a tender touch, a touch that seemed to soothe his soul. "I'm not turning into your mother. These pills aren't taking me away. They've helped me find my way back."

He gave a slight nod. "It's funny how you can know something in your head, but not in your heart. When you started to get well, it was like all the anger just started bubbling up."

"I told you what my doctor said about anger being a stage of grief."

Tom nodded again. He lifted both of her hands and held them in his. "You know I don't like the idea of shrinks and therapists, but I'll go, if you want me to. I want you back. I want our marriage back. I'll go see a doctor or a marriage counselor or a minister—hell, I'll go see a voodoo queen or a witch doctor, if that's what you want. I'll do anything—anything at all—to win you back."

He shifted closer on the bench and lowered his voice, his eyes searching hers. "I love you. I want to make you happy. I want us to be like we were before. If you need some time away from me, well, I'll even understand that."

Susanna's eyes were luminous and large. "I don't want time away. I've had way too much of that already." She squeezed his hands. Her voice grew low and breathy. "I want you close. Very close."

"Yeah?"

"Yeah. And I don't want to wait another second."

Tom raised his eyebrows. "Want to see if we can heat up this sauna?"

Susanna's lips turned up in a slow, sexy smile. "I don't see why not. No one's likely to come in here with that 'out-of-order' sign on the door."

She would never cease to amaze him, to thrill him. He drew her near, inhaling his wife's scent, feeling her warmth. His mouth fit over hers. It was a perfect fit, a perfect match. They came together like the pieces of a rewoven sail, whole again and stronger for the mending, ready to face the wind together, to maneuver through smooth seas and rough waters alike. She was the other half of his heart, the center of his soul, the human of his being. Together they were more than two, more than the moment, more than this place. Together they transcended and conquered and quelled.

And as they gave themselves to each other on the smooth, cedar-scented planks, they made something older than time and newer than tomorrow. They made love—pure, fresh, timeless, and true.

Chapter Twenty-one

Sawdust, fine as talc, flew into the air and landed on Jake's safety goggles the next week as he guided the electric sander over a rounded piece of wood. The high whine of the tool reverberated off the walls of the barn, and it wasn't until he turned it off that he realized Annie was standing in the doorway.

He pushed the clear goggles up on his forehead. "Have you been there long? I couldn't hear a thing over the sander."

Annie smiled. "Not long." She stepped forward. "You've got company."

Before Jake even had a chance to wonder who it might be, Tom stepped through the wide door behind her. Jake put the piece of wood on the carpenter's table and straightened, immediately wary. "What are you doing here?"

"I, uh, came to talk to you."

"We've got nothing to talk about."

"Yes, we do."

Annie edged back toward the door. "I'll leave you two alone. I need to get back to the house." She shot Jake a look that seemed to beg 'please be nice,' then smiled at Tom. "Be sure to stop back by the house and say good-bye to Madeline before you leave."

"Okay. Will do."

Jake picked up the block of sandpaper and began tackling the piece of wood by hand as Annie disappeared from the doorway. Tom shoved his hands in his pockets and stepped forward. "I want to apologize."

Jake continued to sand in silence. It had been three weeks since he'd walked out of Tom's office. His anger had long since burned itself out, but he still felt somehow betrayed.

Tom cleared his throat. "You were right, and I was wrong."

Jake glanced up. "About what?"

"About everything."

Jake kept sanding, his hand moving in a rhythmic motion.

Tom rested his foot on a bale of hay. "I just got back from New Orleans."

"Is that a fact."

"Yes. It was a good conference. Susanna came."

Jake continued to work the sandpaper back and forth.

"She told me you advised her to," Tom said. "I owe you my thanks for that. Susanna and I . . . Well, we've made a fresh start of things."

"Glad to hear it." The sandpaper rasped on the wood.

Tom cleared his throat. "Look, Jake—things with Kelly never went as far as you probably imagine."

"It's none of my business."

"Well, I want you to know just the same. I was a stupid old goat and my head got turned by her attention, but that was the extent of it. Nothing happened. But, well, you were right about her."

Jake's hand stilled on the wood.

"I told Susanna everything, and she's forgiven me." Jake looked up to see the older man rubbing his chin. "She's one in a million."

Jake slowly nodded. "Glad you realized that."

"I do. I'm a lucky man." Tom shifted his stance again and smiled. "From what I saw of Annie just now, seems like you are, too. She's lovely. And Madeline, well . . ." Tom grinned. "She's a real little honey."

The mention of Madeline cracked through the last of Jake's defenses. He couldn't help but smile back. "She is, isn't she?"

Tom nodded. "A real heartbreaker. Smart, too. She seemed to remember me from that weekend she stayed at our house."

"Is that right?"

"Yeah. She called me Ampa."

Jake grinned again. "Well, then, you're doing better than me. She still calls me Ink."

"Ink?"

"Never mind. It's a long story."

Tom laughed. It seemed to break the awkwardness between the two men. Tom pulled his hands out of his pockets and straightened. "Look, when I said I wanted to apologize for everything, I meant it. I was wrong about Madeline. And Annie."

Tom picked up a piece of unfinished wood laying on the table. "Rachel—well, Rachel is gone. You were a great husband to her. But she's gone." Tom paused. Jake's hand tightened on the sander.

"You promised you'd love her until death did you part, and you more than kept your word. You made her happy." Tom's voice grew rough with emotion. He stared down at the chunk of wood, turning it in his hand. "She'd want you to be happy again. Rachel wouldn't want you to be lonely."

Jake swallowed hard.

"Above all, she'd want you to be a good father to your child." Tom's gaze was direct, his eyes sincere. "I know she would. So I want to tell you . . . well, I know you don't need it and probably don't even want it, but I just wanted to tell you that your marriage to Annie has my blessing. I apologize for any trouble I've caused for the two of you. I've already told Annie as much."

Jake's throat grew tight. "I appreciate that, Tom."

The man's head bobbed in a nod. "There's one more thing. I miss you at the office. I've been thinking about what you suggested, about starting a separate branch for consumer law, and, hell—it's actually a darn good idea. I want you to come back and head it up."

"Tom . . ."

"What I'm trying to say is I want you back in my life, Jake. As my partner. As my friend. As part of the family."

Before Jake knew it, he'd rounded the carpenter's bench and enfolded the older man in a bear hug. The two men held each other for moment, then awkwardly clapped each other on the back. When they stepped away, both men's eyes were suspiciously moist.

"You and Susanna will always be family," Jake said when he could trust himself to speak. "But I don't want to practice law in Tulsa anymore. I'm opening my own practice here in Lucky."

Tom blew out a long breath. He slowly nodded. "I suspected that might be the case."

"There's a friend of Annie's who's just retired from his legal practice, and well, he's convinced me there's a lot of satisfaction in being a small-town attorney. I like the idea of being here with Madeline."

"Well, I can't say that I blame you, son," Tom said. "You've got your priorities right, sticking by your family. Your wife and child should come first."

It was Jake's turn to look at the ground. "I definitely intend to put Madeline first. But as for Annie . . . well, it doesn't look like the marriage is going to pan out."

"No?"

"No. It wasn't a real marriage to start with. It was just a way to simplify Madeline's life. We went into it with an understanding that we'd divorce after a few months. In fact, we've already gotten the divorce papers filed. Our court date is next Wednesday."

Tom's eyes grew somber. "I'm sorry, Jake. I truly am."

"Me, too."

Tom studied him for a long moment. "In that case, you ought to talk to Annie."

Jake shook his head. "She deserves more than I can give."

Tom's eyes were warm. "I won't try to tell you your business, Jake, but I'm pretty sure you've got more to give than you think." He raised his hand and turned to go.

"Don't go yet," Jake called. "Want to stay for dinner? I'm cooking."

Tom shook his head. "Thanks, but I want to get home to Susanna."

Jake nodded. A lonely, hollow space yawned inside him, leaving an emptiness he hadn't felt in a long time. Annie and Madeline had filled the void in his life, he abruptly realized. Now that his marriage was nearly over, the emptiness was back. "Give her my love."

Tom grinned. "Sorry, but I'll be too busy giving her

my own. You'll have to come to Tulsa and do it yourself."

Jake smiled back. "Okay. It's a deal."

The two men shook hands. Tom clapped Jake on the arm and headed to the house, then stopped after several yards and turned back around. "I meant what I said earlier, about Rachel wanting you to be happy."

"I know."

Tom's eyes held an earnest warmth as they locked on Jake's. "Sometimes, Jake, love isn't about holding on. Sometimes it's about letting go."

Jake stood in the barn doorway and watched the silver-haired man lope over the crest of the hill, the older man's words echoing in his mind.

A loud, high-pitched cry woke Annie from a sound sleep late that night. She jerked back the covers and jumped to her feet, her maternal instincts on full alarm. Oh, dear Lord—the sound was coming from Madeline's room!

Annie's heart thrashed in her chest like a fish in a net. It was a horrible, otherworldly wail, desperate and mournful, unlike any sound the baby had ever made before. Like a rocket, Annie shot out of her room and down the hall.

Jake, wild-eyed and rumpled, raced around the corner, arriving at the baby's room a second after Annie entered it.

The ungodly yowl again ripped the night. Jake flipped on the light and Annie raced to the crib. Her first impression was of Madeline, sitting up, a wide smile on her face.

Fine. The baby was fine. A wave of relief washed over her, followed by bewilderment.

"It's the dog. Look." Jake crouched down at the foot of the crib. Annie peered around his shoulder and saw

Hot Dog Junior. The puppy was standing on her hind legs, her head stuck between the slats of the crib.

"Easy, girl." Jake carefully lifted the little dog with one hand, gently adjusting the animal's ears with the other. A second later, the puppy's head slid free.

Jake placed the dog on the floor. Hot Dog promptly shook her head as if she were slinging off water. After two or three shakes, she gave a joyful yelp and ran in a tight, jubilant circle, chasing her tail.

The baby clapped and giggled. Annie lifted Madeline out and held her close against her still-pounding heart.

"Wow. That scared me to half to death," she said.

Jake blew out a loud sigh of relief. "It took a few years off my life, too. I had no idea a dog could sound like that."

Annie patted Madeline's back. "I didn't know *anything* could sound like that. What do you think happened?"

"From the looks of things, I'd guess Hot Dog broke out of the kitchen and tried to crawl into bed with Madeline."

The baby squirmed and grunted, wanting to get on the floor with the puppy. Annie obliged. The dog immediately ran over and covered the child with exuberant kisses, her tail waving like a baton. Madeline squealed with glee.

"Looks like a serious case of puppy love to me," Jake said. Annie laughed, and their eyes met. Electricity arced between them like lightning. She was suddenly aware that Jake was shirtless, and she was wearing nothing but a thigh-length camisole. She folded her arms across her chest, trying to suppress a shiver.

He saw it anyway. He reached an arm around her and rubbed her with a warm hand. "Are you cold?"

"A—a little. I'd better go get my robe. Why don't

you take the baby into the kitchen, and I'll join you for milk and cookies?"

Several cookies, twenty minutes, and three lullabies later, Madeline was again asleep in her crib, and little Hot Dog was once more curled up on her cushion in the corner of the kitchen.

Annie double-checked the baby gate that confined the dog to the kitchen. "There should be no more breakouts tonight," she said, flicking off the light as she and Jake headed into the living room.

Moonlight streamed through the living room window. Annie could see Jake gazing at her, could feel the warmth in his eyes. A rush of heat pulsed through her.

"Oh, you never know," he said. "Maybe you should put a baby rail around your bed just in case."

"In case of what?"

"In case I try to crawl in bed with you." The words were teasing, but his voice was deep and husky, and his eyes held a dark, seductive glitter.

Annie's heart quickened. She knew she should look away, should say something light, should do something, anything to break the escalating tension, but the yearning inside of her was too strong. She stood there and gazed back, her heart hammering in her chest.

Jake took a step toward her and touched her shoulder. The touch was feather-soft, barely there, but she felt the weight of it all the way to the marrow of her bones.

"You've been driving me crazy," he murmured. "I've been lying awake, unable to sleep, thinking about you. Wanting to do this." He lowered his head and kissed her. It was a soft kiss, one that made no demands, that staked no claims. It was soft and giving and wistful and restrained, a plea, a kiss that asked permission.

With a soft moan, Annie granted it. She wound her arms around Jake's neck and kissed him back, kissed him with all the need in her heart, with all the love in her soul.

Jake felt Annie's lips open and flower under his, heard her breathing quicken, and all of his restraint dissolved. He gathered her to him and deepened the kiss. She strained against him, standing on tiptoe, fitting herself intimately against him. When she wound one leg around his hips, he curved his hands under her bottom and lifted her off the ground. With both her legs wrapped around his hips, he carried her to the bedroom and placed her under the Conestoga canopy.

He eased off her robe, then pulled down the straps of her camisole. He trailed kisses down the valley between her breasts, then up each peak, then down her stomach, down, down, down to the indentation of her belly button. She arched toward him, and he moved still lower.

He loved the way she gasped, loved the way she tasted, loved the scent of her excitement. He wanted to bring her to completion, to savor her ecstasy, but she twisted on the bed, reaching down for him, encircling him with her hand. "My turn."

She tugged at his sweatpants, pulling them off, then covered him with kisses. Her mouth played over him, pleasuring him to the point of torture. He buried his hands in her hair and moaned as she drove him right to the edge, then stopped.

More kisses feathered up his belly, up his chest to his neck, then to his mouth. She straddled him, her knees on either side of his waist. "Annie—oh, Annie," he groaned. Slowly, carefully, she slid herself down onto him.

And then he could be patient no more. He grabbed her hips as she rode him, thrusting deep inside her, letting her set the rhythm. He watched her face, watched her eyes close, felt her convulse around him. He felt her deep, rhythmic, secret bliss, felt her implode, and the pleasure of it was almost too intense to endure. He struggled to restrain himself. He wanted to protract the pleasure, to take her on another flight.

"Oh, Jake—I love you," she murmured.

He could hold back no longer. With a moan that seemed to come from the depths of his soul, he gave in, gave up and gave himself over—to the inevitable, to the moment, but most of all, to Annie.

Annie awoke the next morning to the smell of freshly brewed coffee and the sound of Madeline cooing in her crib. She smiled and stretched, a delicious sense of happiness percolating through the lingering fog of sleep, only to have it evaporate when her hand hit something crisp and crinkly. She abruptly opened her eyes.

A note. Jake had left a note on his pillow.

The events of the night before came streaming into her thoughts like the sunshine through the window. She'd made love with Jake. It had been intense and beautiful and emotional—so emotional that she'd told him she loved him.

Oh, dear Lord. A sense of dread clawed at her chest as she sat up and read the hand-scrawled message:

Sorry to leave so abruptly, but I have business to attend to in Tulsa. I'll see you at the courthouse on Wednesday. Give my love to Madeline—xxoo, Jake.

Annie's heart seemed to shrivel and die as she stared at the paper. Hot tears sprang to her eyes. She was a fool—a complete and utter fool. A fool to sleep with Jake again, knowing that she loved him, knowing he didn't return the feeling. A fool to fantasize that they could have a real marriage, when his heart still belonged to another woman.

But worst of all, she'd been a fool to tell him she loved him. Her declaration had sent him running for the hills. He knew she didn't want an unequal relationship, and he probably felt as guilty as sin that he didn't return her feelings. She'd put him in an impossibly awkward position.

And herself as well, she thought miserably. She'd promised herself she'd never end up in another unbalanced romance, yet here she was, in a relationship as lopsided as a teeter-totter with one rider.

"Fool," she whispered fiercely to herself. Last night, she'd actually let herself believe that Jake loved her back. He'd been so tender, so ardent, so giving. But she'd only been deluding herself. Hadn't he told her that he'd never love anyone the way he'd loved Rachel? Why did she think she could change his mind?

"Ma-ma-ma," Madeline called from her room.

Drawing a deep breath, Annie threw back the covers and rose from the bed. The floor was hard and cold under her bare feet, but not as hard and cold as the truth. Annie wanted Jake's whole heart, and he didn't have it to give.

Chapter Twenty-two

The only thing more difficult than getting through the next few days was driving to Tulsa for the divorce hearing on Wednesday morning. Ben and Helen wanted to accompany her, but Annie had refused. She tried to put on a brave front about the divorce, but it was hard, pretending to be fine when her heart was breaking. It was easier just to go alone.

"Well, at least let us keep Madeline for you," Helen said, her brow creased with concern.

"I'd rather have her with me," Annie replied. Having Madeline along would make it easier to deal with Jake, easier to keep her thoughts focused on why she'd married him in the first place, easier to remember that she'd said "I do" to a temporary arrangement, not a life-long love. Somewhere along the line, her heart seemed to have lost sight of that fact.

And now she was paying the price.

The October sky was as gray as Annie's mood as she

pulled the car onto the highway with the baby dozing in her car seat. Annie tried to divert her thoughts by listening to the radio, but the songs about unrequited love and broken hearts only made her feel worse. She'd done the very thing she'd vowed she'd never do; she'd fallen hopelessly in love with a man who didn't love her back. Why, oh, why couldn't she have done a better job of guarding her heart?

She switched the music off and occupied herself by reading highway signs, hoping for an encouraging message from her grandfather. He'd been uncharacteristically silent lately. Just her luck, she thought glumly. Not only had her common sense deserted her, but her grandfather had as well.

A pair of billboards caught her eye as she neared her exit in Tulsa, but her grandfather's voice didn't accompany them. One sign simply said, "Listen to your heart," and the other said, "Just say 'yes!' " It was a clever advertising strategy, Annie mused, making people guess what product the signs were promoting. It was probably something health-oriented, like a low-fat ice cream or a cardiac screening program. A billboard further down the highway no doubt revealed the answer, Annie thought, slowing for her exit off the interstate.

The sky cleared as she neared the courthouse. By the time she'd parked and unfastened Madeline from her car seat, a dazzling Indian summer day had unfolded. Instead of cheering her, the brilliant sunshine only accentuated the rainy-midnight feeling in Annie's soul.

Her heart was heavy as she carried Madeline to the designated courtroom and presented her papers to the uniformed officer at the door. The bailiff read her document, then looked up. "I'm sorry, ma'am, but your hearing has been changed to Judge Arnold's docket. He'll hear your case in his chambers on the third floor."

Oh, great. The divorce was going to be performed by the same judge in the same room where she and Jake had been married. Just what she needed, Annie thought morosely—another kick in the pants by Lady Luck.

Annie's spirits dragged as she herded Madeline into the elevator, up to the third floor and down a long corridor. As she turned into the hallway, she was surprised to see a familiar figure standing outside the judge's office.

"Susanna!"

"Hello, Annie." The older woman was wearing an elegant cream-colored suit and a warm smile. Madeline ran to her. Susanna embraced the child, then turned and gave Annie a warm hug as well.

Annie hugged her back. "What are you doing here?"

"Tom and I thought we could watch Madeline while you and Jake are in the chambers."

"Tom's here, too?" Susanna had visited the ranch after her trip to New Orleans and told Annie everything about her reunion with Tom.

Susanna nodded. "He stopped to talk to another attorney. He'll be here in a minute."

Annie's throat grew thick. "This is very kind of you."

Susanna squeezed her hands. "You were so supportive of me when Tom and I were having troubles. You gave me hope, and I want to do the same for you."

Tears gathered in Annie's eyes. "I'm afraid there's no hope for Jake and me."

Susanna gave a soft smile. "You never know. It's too bad you can't read tea leaves for yourself."

"It's probably just as well." The sound of approaching footsteps echoed behind her. Annie turned, expecting to see Tom. Her eyes widened as she spotted two other people with him. "Ben—and Helen! What on earth are you two doing here?"

Helen grinned sheepishly. "I know you didn't want us to come, but we thought you could use the support."

Annie's heart swelled with emotion. "That's very sweet."

Madeline reached out her arms for Tom. He took the baby from Susanna, who gazed at him fondly.

Annie drew a deep, steadying breath. "Well, it looks like everyone's here except Jake."

"Oh, he's here," Tom said. "He's already in the judge's chambers, waiting for you."

Annie's heart pounded erratically.

"You'd better go on in," Helen said. "We'll wait out here with Madeline."

Annie drew a rocky breath and nodded. She reached out and stroked Madeline's hair, smoothed her own short red dress, and opened the heavy door.

The wooden window shades were pulled, and the room was darker than Annie remembered. Despite the dim lighting, she saw Jake immediately, standing by the bookcase, wearing a dark suit. Why, oh, why did he have to be so heartbreakingly handsome? It was hard to breathe as he stepped toward her.

His gaze moved over her appreciatively. "You look great."

Annie tried to smile, but her lips felt frozen. "Thanks." Oh, mercy, this was killing her, seeing Jake after telling him she loved him. He probably felt guilty for making love to her again. Maybe he even felt sorry for her. She longed to just get this over with and get as far away from him as possible.

She looked around the empty room. "Where's the judge?"

"He'll be here in a little while. I asked him to give us a few minutes in private to talk."

Despair filled Annie's chest. The last thing she wanted

to do was to talk! There was no point in rehashing the situation, and she didn't want to lose her last shred of dignity by breaking down and bawling like a baby. She was dangerously close to doing that now. She turned toward the desk and feigned a deep interest in the judge's nameplate. "There's nothing to talk about."

"Oh, yes, there is." Jake saw Annie's spine straighten, the way it always did when she was nervous or feeling cornered. He took a step toward her. "In fact, I've got quite a bit to say."

She shot him a quick, gauging glance, then skittishly looked away.

"I've been doing a lot of thinking, and I realized I owe some apologies. I owe some to you and to Madeline"—Jake paused and drew a deep breath—"and to Rachel."

Annie looked up, her eyes full of pain. "Don't say you're sorry we made love, Jake. I can't stand it if you say you're sorry."

Jake's heart turned over. He stepped closer. "Oh, Annie, that's not what I'm trying to say. Not at all." He lifted a lock of her flaming hair, and it seemed to burn right to his soul. He stepped closer, close enough to smell the soft scent of her shampoo. "The other night, honey, when you said you loved me . . ."

Annie sucked in a deep breath. Her eyes were huge, and they held a gut-wrenching combination of fear and hope and wariness. Jake hurried to say what was in his heart. "It made me realize how much you mean to me. And I realized that I had a big misconception about love. I thought it was a limited commodity—a one-per-customer, once-in-a-lifetime offer. I thought I'd somehow be diminishing what I'd felt for Rachel if I admitted what I felt for you."

389

He placed his hands on her arms. She trembled under his fingers. He tightened his hold on her. "Tom helped me see how wrong my thinking was. He said Rachel would have wanted me to be happy, that she would have wanted me to love again. And you know what? He's right. He's absolutely right. She wouldn't have wanted me to hold anything back, either, out of some kind of misguided sense of loyalty to her."

"Oh, Jake . . ." Annie breathed.

He slid his hands up her sleeves. "I had another bone-headed notion about love, as well. I thought a good relationship was only possible between people who were similar. I didn't realize that opposites could not only attract, but bring out the best in each other." He drew even nearer. "Annie, I like who I am when I'm with you. When I'm with you, I'm my best self."

The love in Annie's eyes made Jake's voice waver with emotion. "I remembered what you'd said about needing to be loved completely and fully, with no reservations, so I . . ." He swallowed around a huge lump. "Well, I knew I needed to get rid of all my old baggage. So I went to my house, and I boxed up all the photos and all of Rachel's personal effects, and I took them to Tom and Susanna's."

He'd shown up on their doorstep at seven in the evening. The three of them had talked and hugged, and Susanna had cried. Then Tom and Jake had taken all the boxes up to the attic.

"The next day, I went to the cemetery where Rachel was buried, and I told her a last good-bye. And, Annie— a real feeling of peace came over me, a feeling of closure."

His fingers slid down her arms. He lifted both of her hands. "So here I am. My heart is free and clear and unencumbered, and I want to tell you what's in it."

He gazed into her eyes, into her soft, luminous blue eyes, and gently squeezed her hands. "*You* are. I love you. I love you with my whole heart and soul. I love you just as much, just as completely as I ever loved Rachel." He paused, then swallowed. "Maybe even more. Maybe loving her stretched out my heart, making it bigger and roomier than it was before."

"Oh, Jake." Annie's eyes swam with tears.

Jake tipped up her chin with his hand. "I love you, Annie, and I want to spend the rest of my life with you. And if you'll agree to be my wife, I promise I'll love you with my whole heart, for my whole life."

Tears spilled down her cheeks. "Jake—Oh, Jake!"

Jake's heart felt as if it, too, were about to overflow. He swept the tears from her cheek with his thumb, then gently kissed her mouth. It was wet and salty with tears, but it tasted even sweeter than he remembered.

At length she pulled back and looked up at him, her expression quizzical. "If you want to stay married, why did you have me come here?"

"Because I want to say our wedding vows again, with you knowing I mean every word. I want to marry you all over again." He tightened his hold on her. "So what do you say, Annie? Will you marry me for real?"

Her eyes were bright as heaven, and just as blue. "Yes."

He reclaimed her lips, and it was several minutes before he came up for air. "Annie, sweetie—I know it's traditional for the groom to give the bride a ring, but since you already have one . . . well, in this case, I thought maybe we should switch things around."

"How?"

He reached in his pocket. "I went to the jeweler who

made your ring and bought a matching one for myself. I'd like for you to put it on me during the ceremony."

Annie gazed at him, her heart bounding with joy. He loved her—he truly loved her! He loved her enough to wear her ring, to let the world know that he'd given her his heart. Annie's smile came from the depths of her soul. "This ceremony—it's going to happen right here, today?"

Jake nodded. "If that's all right with you. The judge has agreed to remarry us. Tom and Susanna and Ben and Helen—and Madeline, of course—are all here as witnesses."

"So they were all in on this?"

Jake nodded.

"You conspired with them behind my back?"

"Afraid so."

Annie shook her head reprovingly, but she couldn't keep from grinning. "Gee, Jake—I'm not sure I should marry a man who's so devious."

He ran his hand down her back, down to the curve of her bottom. "If you won't give in, I'll just have to find other devious means to convince you."

She smiled up at him, about to lean in for another kiss, when a fresh thought struck her. "Speaking of devious—were you behind those billboards on the highway?"

"What billboards?" The innocent tone of his voice convinced her he was anything but.

She gave him a playful push. "You know very well what billboards. The ones that said, 'Listen to your heart' and 'Just say yes.' "

Jake shrugged sheepishly. "I figured it couldn't hurt to have Grandpa on my side."

"Well, Grandpa didn't speak up, but that's all right." She stepped forward and cupped the back of Jake's head with both her hands. "I guess he knew it was your turn."

Jake's hands wound around her back. "I wasn't leaving anything to chance. In fact, I took out another billboard as a backup plan."

"*Another* one?"

"Yep. In case the others were too subtle." He strode across the room to the window and yanked the cord on the wooden blinds. They rose with a clatter to reveal a giant billboard across the street, facing the courthouse.

Annie's jaw dropped. She was staring at a photo of her grandfather—one of several family photos that usually sat on the entry hall table of her home. In large, black letters under her grandfather's face was printed the message:

FOR HEAVEN'S SAKE, MARRY JAKE!

Annie convulsed in laughter.

"If that hadn't worked, I have a tea-leaf reader on standby," Jake informed her. "I wasn't about to take any chances."

Annie gazed up at him adoringly. "Oh, Jake—don't you know there are no chances when you're dealing with a sure thing?"

The kiss that followed was long and tender. Then Jake's lips blazed a delicious path to her ear. "I've memorized a special love song for you," he murmured. "Want to hear it?"

"Sure."

He held her close, rocking her in a slow dance, and softly sang in her ear:

"Baby, oh, baby; Baby, oh, baby; Baby, oh, baby—
oh! Baby, I love you; Baby, I love you; Baby, I
love you so."

The first time through, he sang it alone. The second
time, they sang it together.

FRANKLY, MY DEAR...
SANDRA HILL

By the Bestselling Author of *The Tarnished Lady*

Selene has three great passions: men, food, and *Gone with the Wind*. But the glamorous model always found herself starving—for both nourishment and affection. Weary of the petty world of high fashion, she heads to New Orleans for one last job before she begins a new life. Then a voodoo spell sends her back to the days of opulent balls and vixenish belles like Scarlet O'Hara.

Charmed by the Old South, Selene can't get her fill of gumbo, crayfish, beignets—or an alarmingly handsome planter. Dark and brooding, James Baptiste does not share Rhett Butler's cavalier spirit, and his bayou plantation is no Tara. But fiddle-dee-dee, Selene doesn't need her mammy to tell her the virile Creole is the only lover she ever gave a damn about. And with God as her witness, she vows never to go hungry or without the man she desires again.

_4042-5 $6.99 US/$8.99 CAN

ROBIN WELLS
OOH, LA LA!

Kate Matthews is the pre-eminent expert on New Orleans's red-light district. It makes sense that she'd be the historical consultant for the new picture being shot on location there. So why is its director being so difficult? His last flick flopped, and he is counting on this one to resurrect his career. Maybe it is because he is so handsome. He's probably used to getting women to do as he wishes. And now he wants her to loosen up. But Kate knows that accuracy is crucial to the story Zack Jackson is filming—and finding love in the Big Easy is anything but. No, there will be no lights, no cameras and certainly no action until he proves her wrong. Then it'll be a blockbuster of a show.

Hot Number

SHERIDON SMYTHE

Jackpot! No one needs to win the lottery more than Ashley Kavanagh, and she plans to enjoy every penny of her unexpected windfall—starting with a seven-day cruise to the Caribbean. But it isn't until a ship mix-up pairs her with her ex-husband that things really start to heat up.

Michael Kavanagh hopes this cruise will help him relax, but when he walks in on his nearly naked ex-wife, everything suddenly becomes uncomfortably tight. Sharing a cabin with Ashley certainly isn't smooth sailing—but deep in his heart Michael knows love will be their lifesaver.

Sleepless in Savannah

Rita Herron

Sophie Lane puts her heart on the line and convinces Lance Summers to appear on the matchmaking episode of her talk show—as a contestant. With a little behind-the-scenes maneuvering, she and the sexy developer will end up together. Then Lance pulls a fast one on her, and Sophie vows not to lose any more sleep over him.

Lance's attraction to Sophie threatens his treasured bachelorhood, so he performs a little bait and switch of his own. Now he is free, but Sophie is on a date with someone else! Tortured by images of her with another man, Lance developes a terrible case of insomnia—one only a lifetime of nights tangling with the talk show hostess will cure.

Aphrodite's Secret

JULIE KENNER

Jason Murphy can talk to creatures of the sea. He also has other superpowers like all Protectors, but none of them really help his situation. The love of his life doesn't trust him anymore. Sure, she has her reasons: When she needed him most, he was focusing on his super-career. But that is all over. He vows to reel her back in.

It won't be easy. His outcast father is still plotting world domination, and Jason's other Protector friends fear his commitment to justice. And though Lane still loves him, how to win her hand in marriage seems the best-kept secret ever. Soon Jason will swear that beating up the bad guys is easy. It is this relationship stuff that takes a true superman!
